W9-BYA-563

OUR LADY
OF BABYLON

ALSO BY JOHN RECHY

NOVELS

City of Night
Numbers
This Day's Death
The Vampires
The Fourth Angel
Rushes
Bodies and Souls
Marilyn's Daughter
The Miraculous Day of Amalia Gómez

NONFICTION

The Sexual Outlaw: A Documentary

PLAYS

Rushes
Tigers Wild
Momma as She Became—but Not As She Was (one-act)

OUR LADY OF BABYLON

𝒜 NOVEL

JOHN RECHY

ARCADE PUBLISHING • NEW YORK

FIRST EDITION

Library of Congress Cataloging-in-Publication Data

Rechy, John.
  Our Lady of Babylon / John Rechy. —1st ed.
    p.   cm.
  ISBN 1-55970-335-0
  1. Man-woman relationships—History—Fiction. 2. Women—Sexual behavior—History—Fiction. 3. Women—Crimes against—History—Fiction. 4. Sex role—History—Fiction.   I. Title.
PS3568.E28093 1996
813'.54—dc20   95–53076

Published in the United States by Arcade Publishing, Inc., New York

Distributed by Little, Brown and Company

10 9 8 7 6 5 4 3 2 1

Designed by API

BP

PRINTED IN THE UNITED STATES OF AMERICA

For the Memory of My Mother

and of Olga

and of Beverle Houston

And for Michael Earl Snyder

"And the woman was arrayed in purple and scarlet color, and decked with gold and precious stones and pearls, having a golden cup in her hand ... And upon her forehead was a name written, MYSTERY, BABYLON ... MOTHER OF HARLOTS AND ABOMINATIONS OF THE EARTH."

—St. John the Divine, *Revelation*, 17:4–5

~

"The most absurd thing is to be conscious of the fact that human existence is unbearable, that the human condition is unbearable—intolerable—and nevertheless cling to it."

—Eugene Ionesco, *Memoirs*

~

"What is truth? What is a lie?"

—Eva Adams, *Pensées*

OUR LADY
OF BABYLON

I

SHALL I BEGIN IN THE BEGINNING?

Yes.

There was a flower that bloomed only in Eden, a flower so glorious it did not need the decoration of leaves. Its color is long gone from the world because it was exiled with me and my beloved.

When he saw me for the first time, as I lay within the verdure of Eden, my Adam plucked a blossom from the leafless stem. He knelt, and with its petals grazed my body.

I sprang to life on a bed of orchids.

Standing facing him, I saw myself through his eyes, and he saw himself through mine, two perfect naked bodies luminous in the light of the first day. Oh, yes, we knew that we were naked.

He placed the blossom in my hair, and he moved back, studying me in wonder, as I studied him. Approaching me, he extended his hand toward me, and I extended mine toward his. We longed to touch —

What first?

Our lips longed to connect with —

What first?

He felt his mouth. With moistened fingers he traced my lips, slowly. To share the exquisite sensation aroused, I sketched his lips just as slowly. We parted, only slightly and for an instant, to separate the moment of our first touching from all other moments still to come. Our hands clasped, raised before us. He brought his mouth to my fingers as I brought mine to his. Our hands slipped down, and our lips connected, the first kiss.

Moving back, he lifted the strands of my hair that looped over my breasts. His lips warmed my nipples. I kissed his chest, so lightly furred. Exulting in each awakening, he explored his body and I explored mine. Then eagerly we located on the other the same pleasurable places we had discovered on ourselves.

Easing me back onto the bed of orchids, he bent over me and kissed me from my forehead to my breasts, across my extended arms, back to my breasts, around my nipples, then down, kneeling at my feet, and up again along my legs, between them, lingering at the exquisite opening there. The moisture of his mouth mingled with my own moisture, arousing a warmth that was growing into —

What?

There was no word yet.

My lips followed on his body the same path he had traced on mine, down, across his chest, down again, between his legs to his own straining longing.

I raised myself on him. Our lips met again, our bodies pressed together, our arms outstretched, our hands linked.

Did I realize then, or only much later, that our lips had drawn on each other a sign of the cross?

What did we feel? What was it, this yearning? Sparks of love — the word was born at that moment! — and desire — our unspoken vocabulary grew! — love and desire, which, in the beginning, were the same. But what was this powerful demand that love and desire were inciting? Fulfilled how?

He located the straining place between his legs as I located the liquid craving between mine. To unite an urgent excitement, our bodies connected the sources of our longing. In amazement, he entered me. In awe, I felt his flushed flesh in me. I clasped it tightly between my legs.

We became one, asserting that startling fact with each movement of our bodies, separating, but not entirely and only to thrust forth and reunite, again, again, each time deeper. Desire spilled, met each other's, spilled again, and then again, spilled even more, again, and then it intermingled and became more love, and spilled again.

Joyous at our astonishing discovery, we held hands and knelt in gratitude for this miracle. We faced each other and vowed our union.

"Adam and Eve," I said.

"Eve and Adam," he echoed.

Was it as we lay soon after in each other's arms that I felt the beginning of a strange stirring, a hint of a long journey beginning? — at the same moment that I saw that there was a shadow in Eden, only one, a shadow created by a tree, its branches contorted, twisted, a tree that had not been there earlier, that had sprouted — I realized this only then — at the moment of our fusion.

No, I cannot begin there, not in the beginning, the first beginning. I should not move too quickly toward intimations of exile. Shall I set another tone for my roaming over time, be immediately defiant in my resurrected challenge?

I did not set out to become the greatest whore of all time!

My lament is too deep for that tone.

Still, shall I begin with St. John the Divine, who branded me that — the Great Whore of Babylon! — in his book of curses and blessings, his raging Book of Revelation?

I loved him from the moment I first saw him, preaching on a street in the City, that intensely sensual holy man, his taut body barely covered with a swath of hair cloth. I was fifteen, alone, surviving on the streets by stealing. I did not have a name.

After he had finished preaching, John found me in a darkened street. He claimed he was "choosing" me to be a part of his "holy mission." I did not ask what that meant, did not even wonder.

I longed for him to cleanse me with his sanctity.

Instead, in a rancid alley, as evening darkened, he bartered with merchants eager to finally taste my body. While strangers ground into me on the dirt, John's somber presence looked on. Afterwards, he took me with a ferocity I called desire because I knew nothing else.

But I was sure he loved me because, every night while we slept in a squashed room we occupied in one of the City's many ruins, he held me tenderly.

The pattern recurred: In the daytime he preached. At night he sold my body — but I gazed only at him — and then he would take me roughly. One such time with him I clenched dirt and found an ebony stone. Later I sewed the stone onto a headband. On a special occasion I would wear it to please him.

I accepted his contradictions just as I accepted, without understanding them, the riddles he spoke about his "holy mission," especially after he had drunk the wine — sprinkled with dried white powder from crushed mushrooms — that he used to invite visions.

Was it madness or despair I saw in his eyes? Once, after he was leading me into the sordid alleys of bodies for sale, he stopped to stare at impoverished wanderers that littered the streets. He uttered in disgust, "To choose to live is to accept decay."

3

He was exiled to the Isle of Patmos by the Emperor, whom he had taunted for "the gross fornications of a dynasty of lust." I gladly shared John's exile to the island at the edge of the Aegean Sea.

On a patch of grass that a clutch of palm trees had kept cool, we removed our clothes and sat on a shawl I had worn, a shawl of ocher and indigo. I held a glass of the powdered wine — I only pretended to sip from it — that John had brought with him, to "celebrate," he boasted, his exile "from the tyrant emperor." The glass caught splinters of light from the burnished sunset. I tied the decorated band across my forehead and tilted my head so that, for him, the stone would glint silver and dark in the sun's stare.

Startled, John gazed at the stone, so intently that he seemed to want to penetrate beyond it.

"It's time," he said, and turned away harshly.

Staring at the red dusk as if it had summoned him, he stood, straining to listen as if to an invisible commanding voice, turning his head at first as if to reject what he heard, then slowly nodding in acceptance. I heard only the agitated murmuring of the sea.

Kneeling, John touched the pendant on my forehead. He whispered one word:

"Mystery."

"What mystery do you see, John?" I was afraid, as I had never been before with him. His eyes had turned black.

"The most profound mystery," he extended his riddle. Every sinew of his body strained to form the words he breathed:

The Mystery of the Whore! . . . Whore!

"You forced me to become that!" I challenged the word he hurled at me. "Why?"

He spat more mysterious words:

"Whore, arrayed in purple and scarlet, decked with gold and precious stones, a golden cup in your hand full of the abominations of your fornications!" He spoke in an astonished voice, as if he did not recognize it as his own.

I tried to embrace him, to soothe his trembling.

He pushed me back and thrust my legs open, holding them that way until I ached and screamed. I tore the band from my forehead and buried it in sand with the stone. He held me like that, a sacrifice, until, with brutal stabs, he forced himself into me over and over, with each stab adding more damnation that seemed commanded beyond the night itself:

"Mother of whores and of all the abominations of the earth!"

4

His strange words exploded, pieces of his curse scattering like maddened birds about me.

With one swift motion of my hand, I attempted angrily to thrust them away.

Was it then, protesting, that I felt a stirring at once terrifying, at once exciting?

Shall I begin in Troy?

I stood on a bastion of the City with Paris and Cassandra, his sister — yes, Cassandra was Paris's sister. Earlier, he had insisted I wear only a diaphanous covering to match his own so that when the breeze of that night kissed our bodies, we would appear, in his words, "even more gloriously naked and look the part for these moments that legend will glorify."

Now he asserted proudly to his sister: "It's love — *our* love — and passion" — he touched my arm — "that brought all this heroism about. And it was worth it."

Cassandra smiled wryly as she looked down at what Paris had indicated, what we stood watching from the highest rampart of the City, the soldiers spilling, almost gracefully, out of the wooden horse.

I knew, of course, that Paris loved — no, desired — only himself. We always made love before a mirror, and I knew on whom his eyes were fixed — not me. Still, that made him a good lover; he carefully prepared his positions.

"Lovely Paris —" Cassandra began.

"I've told you not to call me 'lovely,' " Paris said. "That's a word for a woman."

"Oh, then, *manly* Paris" — Cassandra's head barely tilted — "your affair with Helen is an excuse."

Paris had stopped listening to her. He rearranged himself to bask in the light of a flaring torch below, its flame flirting with the contours of his face.

Cassandra turned to me. "Beautiful Helen, have you realized yet how predictable destiny is?"

I shook my head, not understanding, not then.

She said, "Your beauty —"

"And mine —" Paris had heard that.

Cassandra spoke her words softly, as she always spoke: "Your beauty, Helen, will be blamed for this." She pointed to the bleeding bodies below us.

"My beauty, blamed for *this?* But the reason it all began —"

5

"Helen!" Paris stopped me.

"I've known the real reason all along, dear brother," Cassandra said.

"How could *you* know?" Paris challenged her.

Cassandra laughed at the question she was used to hearing.

Paris turned away from his sister's smile.

It had all begun with the secret he had made me promise to keep after we first made love in Sparta and then sailed on to Troy. That frivolous journey — we were young, aroused by our partnership in beauty — had caused hostile letters between our countries. Words became harsher, accusations grew, reasons for the conflict multiplied and blurred. I had not intended to stay in Troy, nor had I wanted to return to Sparta, to my husband, Menelaus. Just as Paris saw me only as an embellishment to his manly beauty, the King of Sparta had seen me only as a manifestation of his power. In daydreams, I had imagined myself floating . . . where? Anywhere. Away.

"Then I *will* be held culpab —" I began to accept as we stood on the wall of Troy.

Cassandra put a finger to my mouth. "You mustn't encourage destiny," she said.

"Stop that!" Paris reproved his sister's gesture on my lips. "What if someone saw you and deduced that you and Helen are . . . ?"

"It would confound things terribly, wouldn't it?" Cassandra still smiled.

I pulled my eyes away from the field of slaughter. I looked beyond the open gate, beyond blood spilling. Smoke of the now burning city rose in whorls of black clouds. Through thickening ashes — as I looked back down at the carnage — a dying soldier stared up at me and shouted:

"Whore!"

Was it then that I felt myself spinning in waves of dislocated memories? Memories that came from —

Where?

Or shall I begin when, as Salome, I watched from a stairway as Herod's guards brought John the Baptist in chains to kneel before my mother, Herodias?

For nights, from a palace window, I had heard the Baptist hurling his judgments at her from the desert, damning her and the House of Herod as she listened, transfixed, at another window, arousing herself with eager fingers. I saw only his solitary shadow against the blue of night. I tried to imagine to whom such a forceful voice might belong.

My imagination could not have envisioned the awesome presence of the man I now saw being led into the palace, his body stripped in an attempt to humiliate him further. He transformed nudity into defiance.

As he passed the corridor where I waited, I stood within light. A swirl of pastel veils sculpted my body, revealing the slenderness of a girl, the fullness of a woman. The Baptist stared at me. Between his chained legs his craving tensed. He turned away, conquering desire.

Soon, I would dance before him and Herod, my flesh licked by the glow of flames twisting violently from a hundred torches that failed to light the gnarled corridors of Herod's palace.

Was it then — no, soon after, when Herod's rancid voice commanded, "Arouse me with your dance, Salome! Virgin whore!" — that I felt within me an insistent stirring — beginning — striving to connect . . .

With whom, to what?

Or shall I begin as Medea?

Challenging the storms that pursued us, I sailed with Jason on the Hellespont. We made love on the Golden Fleece. His hips strained as he pushed against me to enter me still deeper. My legs locked him in me, as he made me vow to remain a barbarian and make him a barbarian. The dark sea heard his demand and my promise.

Was it then that my soul prepared to protest what was to come?

Or shall I begin when, as Magdalene, I knelt with Mary before the crucified figure of Jesus? He looked down at us with anxious love, then gazed at the man who hung from a barren tree on another hill. The stripped bodies of Jesus and Judas twisted toward each other, as they had once before in joy, not pain.

I turned away from my double loss. I had loved them both.

Out of the storming darkness that smothered Calvary, I heard an accusing voice shaped by the wind and — was it possible? — aimed at me. No, at another. Whom!

Was it then that I looked about the site of this atrocity, attempting to locate other presences? Only ghosts? — ghosts stirred from other places, other times?

Ghosts —
Whose?

Or shall I begin in Heaven, *before* the beginning? — before the rebellious flight of angels beyond the boundaries of Heaven, before the War in Heaven spilled into the first garden, into my life as Eve, when the Angel Lucifer and his sister, Cassandra — yes, she was also Lucifer's sister — descended there to decipher God's design?

Or shall I begin when I was Jezebel?
Or when I was —
There are so many lives I've lived, so many women I have been, turbulent lives within which — only now — I discover that undefined stirring that recurs in each.
Or is it a demand? — a longing to return to the present, in order to redeem —
What!

It should begin *now*, in the *present* present, when I am in seclusion in my quarters in the country, within the château of my beloved husband, the handsome Count du Muir, murdered in the Grand Cathedral by his twin brother, Alix, in collusion with their sister, Irena, and perhaps — yes! — the Pope himself.
Before I proceed, I shall assert this: The subject of my many lives will soon become entirely clear; I am committed to the truth; and I am not — repeat, am *not* — a mystic.
I remain in the country for reasons first explained to me by Madame Bernice. She lives down the road, in the château nearest mine. She is, of course, a countess. The source of her enormous wealth is a plantation, located in another country. You shall meet Madame, as I have come to address her; and you shall meet her presently. Trust me. I keep my promises.
How is all that I have claimed possible?
It is.
Can I prove it?
Yes.
I shall provide evidence, reveal details that only truth can yield, of the blossom that grew only in Eden — how else would I know of its existence? — and the exact place where I buried the ebony stone in Patmos. Yes, and I shall allow you to know the secret reason for the Trojan War.

8

You shall learn the truth about the seventh veil in my dance before Herod, and of the crucial moment during which the life of John the Baptist would be saved or destroyed. With Jason, we shall ride waves of violence that will recede to expose lies. When we travel to Calvary, I shall describe the intersecting shafts of light within which Jesus died. I shall lead you through the battlefields of the War in Heaven during the eternal moments when the sun was stricken with death and there was darkness — except for one single star.

But *now* —

Now I shall enlighten you as to the *present* present, my travails as the threatened widow of the noble Count du Muir.

I take you back to the Grand Cathedral.

Embraced by glowing candles, I knelt with my beloved at the foot of the altar where we were to be wed. In hypocritical attitudes of reverence, Alix and Irena bowed their heads in the front pew; the brothers would have been identical, except that my beloved was dark and noble, his brother fair and evil. Several pews behind them sat a presence of elegance, the Contessa, the Count's mother. Even to these nuptials, she had worn her black *mantilla* over a dark ivory comb, in perpetual mourning — I had heard gossip — for her lost love, a passionate gypsy from her country.

The nuptials were being officiated by His Holiness himself — a first time — for reasons known only to me and him, and soon to you; I use that undeserved title, "Holiness," only because it is the accepted form of address for the Pope, not because I think well of him.

In the Cathedral, hymns of exaltation sung by a hundred choir-boys hinted — only hinted — of the bliss the Count and I shared at the prospect of our union. More handsome than ever, just as I was even more beautiful than ever, for him, the Count reached for my hand to place on my finger the ring of our bond.

Irena hissed at Alix: "Kill the whore now!"

The word "whore" swirled in terrified echoes — and then in triumph — within the Cathedral. I learned only later, from Madame Bernice, why that occurred.

In the Grand Cathedral, Alix stood, a dark object in his hand.

Dropping the chalice, the Pope scurried away. Young acolytes flung themselves like sacrificial pigeons before the altar.

The burst of Alix's gun shattered into frightened screams. Over it all, I heard the Contessa's plaintive protest: "*No!* Don't murder love!"

My beloved Count thrust me away, to allow his own body to intercept the fatal missile. It did, and he fell, his spilling blood forming a deadly rose about him. He breathed, "I do," and raised his hand to slip onto my finger the ring I now wear, this amber-tinted diamond.

As I held my dying love, I was swept by such despair that I did not see nor feel the smoking gun Irena had forced into my hand, did not even hear — though I retained it like a brand — her accusation hurled into the pandemonium in the Cathedral:

"The *whore* murdered my brother! See! The *whore* is holding the gun!"

In my arms, my beloved gasped his last words:

"Save yourself! Flee —" His voice trailed off: "I made preparations —"

I pressed my body against his more tightly, refusing.

"It's the only way I can live now, through you. Stay, and we both die. Flee, and we both live." Those were his last words.

"Redeem true love, my dear!" It was the Contessa, crying out to me as she stood proudly in her pew and echoed her son's demand to live through me.

To keep him forever alive — and as the Contessa blessed me with her black-teared rosary — I fled the Cathedral, the Pope's words trailing after me:

"Damn the wily whore!"

II

SUSPECTING TREACHERY, my beloved Count du Muir had prepared for his most loyal coachman to await us — now only me — outside the Grand Cathedral. A carriage pulled by fleet horses brought me here to the country, where my beloved and I had, in the spring of our meeting, made love and slept and woke only to make love again, but not as reported luridly in what purports to be a "True Account," a despicable installment of which appeared immediately after the murder and is now in wide circulation in the City.

I learned of the existence of the scurrilous "Account" one dusky afternoon — all days had turned dusky for me — when I wandered in sorrow about the vast rooms of this once-cherished château, rooms now haunted with memories of happiness turned to sorrow. I encountered one of the maids, a pert little thing with insolent breasts, attempting to hide what appeared to be a pamphlet — *pretending* to hide it and thus calling attention to it. I detected a faint smile as, on my demand, she surrendered it to me. I read its title: "*The True and Just Account of the Abominable Seduction into Holy Matrimony in the Grand Cathedral and of the Murder of the Most Royal Count by the Whore*: The First Installment."

My heart shattered again at the evil accusation. I did not send the maid away because I suspected collusion, and I must discover its shape, if so. She may be in contact with Alix and Irena . . . and the duplicitous Pope! Without his countenance, the murder would not have been possible in the Cathedral.

Here in my quarters, I shall read again from the vilifying "First Installment" of the malicious "Account." By facing its lies, unflinching, I shall defuse their intent to assault:

In recording this *True Account,* the Writer begins by asserting that he has set down this Chronicle in all its foul spectacle, only in response to his duty to denounce immorality. However powerfully his natural modesty shall surely cause him to blush and hesitate, the Writer vows to evoke that duty, and thus be able to proceed to recount (in necessary detail) the most debased activities of the villainess Whore, who managed, through connivance and debauch, to seduce the righteous Count into holy nuptials (the Writer cannot here restrain a gasp) in the Grand Cathedral.

Some boundlessly generous souls might insist that the Whore was beautiful — "quite ravishing," in the words of one misguided being who had surely surrendered to her array of perversions. Such wayward souls swore her eyes were hypnotic in their splendor (if so, the astute Reader will rightfully infer, they were not hypnotizing *any*one onto a Righteous Path), eyes outlined by dark eyelashes that added to the impression (some swore this was true) that they changed color, the palest shade of green or blue — or brown or even black. Others saw in her a vulgar flashiness that tended (for moments only) to bedazzle. Those who admired her, or fell under her spell (some attributed unholy powers to her, the Writer must note and, doing so, sends a shielding blessing to the Reader) described her body as perfect, a waist whose smallness exaggerated the fullness of her momentous breasts, the sinuous flare of her hips, the flowing taper of her legs, a body, nonetheless, whose every orifice had been penetrated by uncountable numbers of men, including her Pimp.

Among those who frequented a back street which at night became the site of basest orgies, her Pimp (often drugged and known by the sacrilegious title of "Reverend") was notorious for being able to secure, at a price, anything depraved, a word that most aptly describes the Whore.

As the "Reverend Pimp" offered the Whore to passersby, he would utter foul propositions mixed with Gospel to further excite those wayward souls with blasphemy and to coax the Whore into even more debauch. Even at this early point in his *True Account,* the Writer, must, wincing, pause again (as he will be forced to do throughout) in order to brace his courage to continue with the necessary task of exposing degradation. Thus girded, he renews his promise to fulfill the obligation that morality imposes so heavily upon him, and continues, as he must:

Her breasts exposed, her lips spewing the vilest of words, her skirts raised over her thighs, her hungry fingers probing between her moist legs (by which some of the victims of her lustful allure were enticed so powerfully as to describe them as luscious), she would locate herself under a streetlamp. Whenever a lured customer approached, she would spread her juicy thighs (a designation the Writer employs only to emphasize the excess of her appetites) to hasten the act, and so to ready herself for yet another man brought to her by her Pimp.

From the streets, and with the help of the crazed Reverend Pimp, the Whore worked her way (on her back) into the most vile of houses. Men were lured by her specialties, some of which will be described in all their perversity later, a sad, daunting task for the Writer, who is left to feel grateful that this *True Account* cannot be long enough to document them all.

How could two such corrupted creatures succeed in trapping the Noble Count into an unholy union that would defile even the sacred vows of matrimony? This is how it occurred:

Once the Whore and her partner in dishonor had chosen the object of their conspiracy, the Reverend Pimp scouted for the exact moment to lock the trap they had devised. By prolonged scrutiny, he discovered that the Noble Count attended the gala opening of each new opera. Afterwards, his Coachman was instructed to drive, out of the logical direct path to the Count's mansion, through the most lurid part of the City. Now the Reader may well ask: Why would so noble a Count search out such a route? Only because that allowed him, in his beneficence, to give money to any worthy beggars (not all beggars are worthy) who might have stumbled unknowingly into the maze of those streets of corruption.

On such a night —

I cannot go on, not now. I'm overwhelmed anew by these lies. I lean for support against the window of my balcony and hope for a cooling breeze. I gain courage from the fact that from here I can see Madame's château across my grounds, now dark, night.

Let me take you back a few days to my first meeting with Madame Bernice.

In the isolation of my exile, I began to be haunted by disturbing dreams so real that, when I woke, it was as if I had only then begun to dream. Attempting to find a modicum of peace, I decided to venture out into the green countryside, fields of trees and wild flowers sent into confused bloom by an early spring. On any other day I would have noticed with delight ubiquitous jacaranda trees. I would have paused to admire their graceful white limbs sprouting lavender buds about to open, about to become the blossoms whose petals, loosed by the softest breeze, weave a mantle of lavender lace on the ground. Today my sorrow allowed me to perceive only more sorrow. As I walked along, I saw now familiar desultory figures push themselves invisibly into hiding within the density of trees. Every day there are more of those impoverished sad wanderers fleeing the growing hardships of the City.

Not even the sprawl of greenery surrounding me could dissipate the lingering effect of the disturbing dreams that had sent me out on this walk, an effect I can only describe as one of being haunted, though not by the memory of my beloved Count; he was too alive still in my mind.

In my dour mood I did not realize that I had wandered onto the grounds of the neighboring château, and that I was sitting on a bench of elaborate grillwork. I did not realize that until I saw a spectacular peacock strolling by among beds of flowers whose various colors matched the pattern of his feathers.

Yet the moment I saw him, I was not at all certain that his astounding presence had indeed caused my first awareness of where I sat. No, it was as if that awareness had been aroused moments earlier, when I had felt — and then looked back to detect — a presence standing behind me a short distance away on the incline of a velvety lawn. Squinting — yes, this had surely occurred before the glorious peacock strolled by — I discerned the vague figure of a woman, her outline rendered luminous by the sun so that she seemed to have just separated from the sky; and I felt a certainty — no, a suspicion — that from her vantage on her lawn, she had been not only watching me intently for some time but *watching over me*, this perfect stranger now hurrying toward me out of the blur of distance and into full clarity as she stood before me addressing me in a crisp voice:

"Lady! Why are you, a woman who obviously has everything the world cherishes — extravagant beauty, abundant wealth, distinct culture, unique elegance — why are *you* crying, Lady?"

Beside her the glorious peacock inclined his head as if pondering the very same question.

Madame Bernice is a dark, ample woman, with a cascade of lush black hair, whose sheen creates a glorious corona that frames her handsome face. She may be fifty. Some might describe her colorful clothes and abundant jewelry as extravagant, but she is too tasteful for that description to be apt; she clearly has a knowledge of the choreography of colors.

14

That afternoon — I learned all this soon after — she had been strolling with her peacock about the grounds of her château, which she endearingly calls her "mansion." When she saw me sitting on her favorite bench, she paused at a distance — she told me this later, too — in order to infer, she said, my "spirit," a word that gave me a wince, since I am not — I find the need to remind you — am *not* a mystic. Then she had hastened, as swiftly as her stolid form allowed, to where I sat.

"Why are you weeping, Lady," she asserted her question, "on a day when the sky is as clear and azure as that of —"

"Eden." As astonished as I was by the word I had spoken, I was even more surprised that Madame merely nodded. She sat next to me; it was, remember, her bench.

The openness of her face, the tenderness hidden in her steady gaze, allowed me to answer: "I'm crying because I've lost my beloved, the Count du Muir."

"She lost her beloved." Did she lean down to inform her peacock what I had just conveyed? Or was she repeating it to herself? The peacock lowered his head — sadly? — for a moment or two.

How easily I accepted Madame Bernice's presence, as easily as if I had been waiting for her on her bench, waiting to tell her all I did, about the violence at the altar of the Grand Cathedral, the foiled attempt on me by Irena and Alix — and their blaming me for the murder they committed upon their own brother, upon my beloved Count. "Enormous danger surrounds me. I'm at the center of turbulence among powerful factions that may include the Pope." I could not yet bring myself to tell her about the salacious lies being printed in installments.

Unsurprised by all I had narrated, Madame waited in acknowledgment of my enormous loss and grave danger. She added more moments to her respectful silence before she said, "Still, as sorrowful and grave as all that is, I suspect there's more."

The troubled dreams! As I spoke, I tried to pretend I was not stunned by her knowledge of so private a matter: "I have been disturbed by a series of baffling dreams."

She closed her eyes, three fingers at her forehead. She wears a precious stone on every finger, a possible excess I'm willing to grant her, though I myself, since the death of my beloved Count, prefer the simplicity of one single amber-hued diamond, the ring of our enduring bond. During this interval of pondering whatever she was pondering, the peacock had located himself next to Madame and within a pool of

15

warm sun. The light there added such brilliance to his feathers that I considered he might have chosen that advantageous site quite carefully.

"Describe your dreams to me." Madame *can* be peremptory.

"I dream that I am Eve, naked with my Adam —" I spoke that aloud!

In a firm tone, Madame asked: "Are you in or out of the first garden?"

"In it at first. With my beloved."

"And then?" Madame prompted, as if nothing extraordinary had been said.

"I dream that I'm a girl, happy away from Babylon with St. John the Divine. We're on the Greek Isle of Patmos, where he has been exiled by the Emperor. We're lying unclothed on my shawl. Then —"

"Lady —"

"Madame? We *are* unclothed." I had begun to detect that she was greeting my vivid descriptions with a slight frown at certain points.

"Hmmm . . . But you anticipated, Lady. I was going to point out that, although I would be the last to question your dreams —"

I had the uncanny feeling that she was doing just that.

"— at the time of St. John's exile — I believe, correct me if I'm wrong — Babylon was no longer —"

"— was long gone. But that is how St. John referred to Rome — 'to connect all that was evil,' he said." My staunch certainty and exact words came — From where? I had not dreamt *that*. Yet I was so sure of it that I could have recited John's further words: "Babylon — a name for all the transgressions of centuries . . ." I marveled at the knowledgeability contained in my dreams — and at Madame's familiarity with times past.

"And *that* became St. John's Babylon!" Madame's inflection added significance to my just-remembered words. "For reasons we must discover." I had the impression that she had consulted her peacock — she had tilted her head toward his and he had tilted his toward hers . . . "And *then*, Lady?"

Reasons we must discover? As we proceeded with what? She was so eager to hear the rest of my dreams that I did not pause to ask. "Then he gazes darkly at me and utters the word 'Mystery.' When I ask him what mystery he sees, he only adds to the riddle — 'The most profound mystery —' "

"Ah!" This time clearly Madame leaned down toward her peacock — as if to emphasize for him the words she repeated:

16

" 'Mystery! — the most profound mystery'! . . . St. John spoke those very words! Imagine!"

What was exciting her so? "— the mystery of —" I attempted to continue John's strange utterance, but I could not speak the word, although it resounded in my mind.

Madame flinched, as if she had managed to hear the unspoken word — had my lips shaped it? — although she now clearly waited for me to utter it.

I lowered my head. I whispered, "I cannot bring myself to say the word, your Grace."

"Lady," Madame Bernice interjected into my silence, "I readily confess a fondness for amenities, but, considering what you and I shall be involved in —"

What could she mean?

"— I suggest that a certain informality of address between us may hasten important matters we must discuss. So please, dear Lady, please, just address me as 'Madame,' though I do ask that you pronounce it correctly — 'mah-*dahm.*' "

"How else?" I felt a tiny annoyance at her assumption that I would have done otherwise.

"And may I simply call you 'Lady'?"

"You have, since we met," I reminded.

"So I have." I would discover that at times she has a direct manner, which in a person of less refinement might be called curt. She folded her hands on her lap. I noticed more precious stones than I had been able to identify earlier on her fingers — an amethyst, a sapphire. "Now, Lady," she said, "say the word you must. The word John called you in Patmos."

"Whore!" I spat it out. " 'Mother of whores and of all the abominations of the earth.' "

Madame inhaled and closed her eyes. "All the abominations of the earth! Imagine! Imagine!" She shook her head at the enormity of John's accusation.

"And that one dream recurs, as persistently as my dream of Eden." I realized this then, and I spoke it aloud in amazement: "In my recollection of them now, my dreams are even more vivid than when I dream them."

Madame did not even pause to marvel at that. "When St. John utters the word 'whore,' what happens *immediately after?*" She was clearly in pursuit, but I did not know of what.

"Then that word echoes and re-echoes into *all* my dreams, and it

17

resonates finally back into the Cathedral when Irena thrust it at me, and the Pope cursed me with it — and the despised word keeps repeating itself there as if trying to locate another place, another time, far, far away — someone else —"

I am still not certain — it was a fleeting impression — whether Madame Bernice brushed a pesky strand of her luxuriant black hair away from her forehead, or whether she made the faintest sign of the cross. After moments, she pronounced my own words slowly: "Another place, another time, far, far away . . . Someone else." She was quiet then, as if repeating the same words to herself now, considering them gravely.

Then she announced: "It has to be the Whore of Babylon."

Although I believed that she did not expect me to understand, at least not now, her astonishing words, but that she had, instead, spoken aloud her extended thoughts — or was she directing them at her peacock, who had become especially alert, or was he trying to sniff a sudden flower-scented breeze? — I thought it best to assert then: "Madame, I am *not* a mystic."

"Proceed, Lady."

Had she even heard me? Her surprising words, echoing in my mind, seemed especially incongruous on a day full of sunshine as we sat on a bench in the sprawling grounds of her grand château. "And the very next moment," I thought best simply to continue, "I dream again that I am Eve."

"But now expelled from the Garden." Madame spoke her words with assurance, as if at last she was receiving an exact answer, long awaited, to a difficult question, long pondered.

"Yes, expelled, and it is all so clear that I am able to look back at the Garden" — I inhaled because again the dream swept over me — "to look back and see, for the last time, a flower that bloomed only in Eden, a flower so glorious it did not need the decoration of leaves . . ." My voice slowed, to ascertain my new conviction: "It's a flower I've seen nowhere else, except in that dream, except in Eden."

Madame's brown eyes — at times they seem amber, at other times gold — fixed on a distance beyond the horizon, where the mysterious veil of mist that at evening creeps up from the far countryside was beginning to gather. How could I help but remember that in my dreams John, too, stared at something dark beyond his vision? I resumed quickly, "And I dream that I am Helen."

"Of Troy."

"Of course."

"And do you dream you're Salome?"

"Yes!" I was no longer amazed by her knowledge.

"Who else?"

I lowered my voice. "I dream that I am Mary Magdalene."

"Oh?" Frowning, she shared some perplexity with her peacock, who, however, seemed not at all confused. He is an entirely confident bird.

"I dream I stand before the crucified figure," I asserted.

Bowing her head in reverence, Madame said softly, "Let me hear some more about her, about Magdalene."

"In one dream, as children, we — Jesus and Judas and myself — roam happily — naked" — I ignored what might have been a cough or a sneeze from Madame — "near the River Jordan." I remembered that with joy.

"Who can doubt that they, too, were playful children, once?" Though she smiled, there was sadness in her voice.

I did not want to dwell now on the sad events of my dreams of Calvary. "And I dream that I'm Delilah, naked in the arms of Samson, who wears only shiny wristbands —"

"Lady —"

"— that glitter as he lifts me to prove his strength —"

"Lady."

"— his long hair flailing on my bared breasts —"

"Lady!"

My lucid recollection of that dream had refused Madame's attempted interruptions, but now her demand for my attention had become insistent. "Madame?"

"Why must *every*one be naked?"

"Because they *were!*" I bristled. Was it possible that this woman, whose sophistication was as evident as her elaborate jewelry — was it possible that she was . . . a prude? She had folded her arms over her ample bosom. I wanted this matter settled: "Just as I informed you earlier that I am not a mystic, I inform you now, Madame, that I am not a prude."

She winced at the word.

I seized my advantage: "I shall hide *nothing!*"

Her folded arms relaxed, only somewhat.

I had the disconcerting impression that I had convinced the peacock of my point more strongly than I had Madame — he seemed to be looking questioningly at her, an impression enhanced by the fact that — I noticed this only now — one feather on his comb twisted just slightly, like a question mark. "That one feather —" I began.

Madame shushed me urgently. With affection that made me suspect they had been together long, she coaxed his attention momentarily away by pointing to a beautiful butterfly — "Such a unique pattern on its wings — look!" — that was hovering over a rose near the veranda. When the peacock went to explore the butterfly's unique pattern, Madame whispered quickly to me: "One must never embarrass a peacock."

I thought of Paris, dear Paris. "I wouldn't dream of it, Madame."

"He must never know he has what he might consider an imperfection in his comb. I myself believe it adds to his unique charm — like his name — don't you?"

"Of course. And his name is —?"

"Ermenegildo."

"Of course."

Madame's voice assumed its natural tone when Ermenegildo returned to follow our discussion. "Now, Lady, who else are you . . . in your dreams?" Eyes closed — she has incredibly long dark, full eyelashes — she placed her fingertips on her forehead, to encourage even greater concentration.

I felt a piercing chill as the next dream pushed away haughty Samson. "I dream that I am Medea —"

Madame's eyes shot open, she bit her lip. "Who?"

"Medea."

"Are you sure?"

"Yes."

Madame Bernice studied her rings, readjusted two, shifted another — the pearl — returned it to the same finger. She looked about to locate her peacock, who was at her side. She rearranged the folds of her beautiful silk skirt, tugged at the slenderest thread loosed from a filigree of its gold brocade. She cleared her throat, twice. "Are you *absolutely* sure?"

"Absolutely." Oh, I was sure, so sure that it was as if I had slipped into that brutal dream. I closed my eyes, and saw . . . red, only red, liquid red, blackened red.

Madame cleared her throat a third time. "I suggest that in regard to Medea —"

My solemn look stopped her words.

"Let's just move on," she said.

20

I was glad to.

"Tell me more details about each dream."

I trusted her so entirely — although I didn't know exactly about *what* it was I trusted her — that I did not feel tested — about what? I knew instinctively that she needed more information for . . . whatever her reason. So I supplied the details, easily, just as I remembered them from my most recent dreams.

She listened raptly, occasionally bending to touch Ermenegildo while repeating aloud — to herself? to him? — what I had just narrated: "There was already one shadow, a distorted one, in the perfect garden." . . . "John the Divine seemed to be listening to another voice when he claimed to be in the presence of 'the most profound mystery' and when he uttered his cursing accusation." . . . "Cassandra would of course know Paris's secret — of course, of course — whatever it was." . . . "Herod's vile words commanded that the dance begin."

After I had given her the details that fleshed my dreams, I thought it necessary to inform her, "But what I dream, Madame, is different from —"

"— from what others have insisted happened," Madame spoke the exact words I had been about to form. She spoke them . . . triumphantly!

"Yes. And that is true of all the other women I dream of, and there are many more. Jezebel, Hagar —"

"— and Marina? The Indian princess?"

I dredged my dreams. "No."

"Hmmm. That's odd." Madame seemed deeply perplexed that such an Indian princess had not appeared in my dreams. But then, of course, my dreams *were* continuing; perhaps she was ahead of me even in that. "Some of the women appear in brief dreams, others only in a fragment — all as if they're trying to connect to —" I shook my head in bafflement. To what?

Madame Bernice permitted the afternoon's silence to settle over us, a silence enhanced by the many quiet sounds it contained, the rustle of a leaf, its fall to the ground, the flutter of a butterfly. Into that waiting silence, she pronounced her questions, which sounded more like declarations: "All the women you dream of, Lady, all are fallen?"

"Yes."

"All implicated as whores?"

"Yes."

"And harshly blamed for enormous catastrophes?"

"Yes! All! Blamed!" I spat out the word I knew then I had always

21

detested. "Blamed!" I tested its power to arouse my rage. I felt a shiver that did not come from the glorious day. I was aware of a subtle change in me, a stirring that was exulting and weeping at the same time. I looked at Madame, who sat beside me on the elaborate garden bench, her formidable shoulders squared, her proud chin thrust forth, so that, in a flashing moment, I considered whether she, too, had felt the lash of unjust blame.

"Except Magdalene —" I realized and interjected. "She's fallen, but not blamed, and she's most prominent in my dreams."

Madame frowned at the matter she had clearly been pondering since I had first mentioned Magdalene. "We must add that to the questions we shall have to deal with." She held my hands. Her voice was that of a firm but caring teacher. "There's a great mystery we must solve, Lady — 'the most profound mystery.' Its answer lies in Eden. And in Babylon — and Patmos. And it may lie elsewhere, even farther beyond."

The glorious afternoon that had earlier mocked my sorrow faded, lingered for me now only as a faint glow in the sky. I knew that dusk would have no silver haze.

Madame's next words were clearly intended to be gentle and precise; she held them on her lips for seconds before she uttered them. I had the sudden impression that I had been waiting for them for a long, long time, centuries — and that she had been waiting just as long to state them — as she said:

"Yours are not, dreams, Lady. They are memories."

III

I THOUGHT I HEARD the odd cawing of a bird lost in a sudden gathering dusk. It was a sound that was as forlorn as it was terrified. In the next second, I thought perhaps I had heard only my sigh and the beginning of a gasp. There began to seep into me a sadness beyond my sorrow at the death of my beloved Count, a sadness I knew I had felt before that, from a long time back, but whose object I had not even wondered about.

I knew then that Madame Bernice was right. I *had* lived all those lives. I had not been dreaming. Memories of all those various existences fused for me out of the chaos of what I had thought were fragments of disturbed dreams. I remembered! My Adam rubbed his eyes when he saw me standing on a bed of orchids, as if he were asserting that I did not exist only within his vision. Still, now in another garden, Madame Bernice's garden, I forcefully attempted to pull back from this enormity. "But in the present . . . ?"

Madame looked down again into her hands — they are large, sturdy hands for such a genteel woman. Again, she changed rings from one finger to another, the pearl in place of a ruby, the amethyst where a diamond had been. Her face beamed with a gracious smile. "Why, Lady, obviously in the present you're the great Lady in hiding in the country because of dangers surrounding the murder of the Count du Muir. You're the beautiful Lady whose company I share" — she stood, one hand extended graciously — "and whom I now invite to tea."

I took her hand, easily. Ermenegildo led us along the impeccable lawn toward her château.

As we walked, I exulted in the luxuriance of her garden. "Oh, Madame, the beauty of your garden."

"And it *is* all mine," Madame proclaimed her territory with a stout swirl of her hand. Ermenegildo seemed to bristle. The askew feather on his comb shook. "It is all *ours,*" she revised. "But — since we are egalitarians —" She touched Ermenegildo's comb, avoiding the odd feather — as if for agreement, which I suspected he had given, because she continued: "— since we are egalitarians, we shall share it with whoever loves beauty." She said all that with disarming genuineness.

"Well then, it has been waiting for *me!*" I felt almost dizzy, as if I were spinning, whirling — No, it was — I'm striving for exactitude to convey this powerful, strange sensation — it was as if a memory were trying to locate *me*. A memory of what? I wondered, as I felt surrounded by this bliss of colors and sweet scents in Madame's garden. Careful designs of cultivated flowers wound through carpets of wild blooms so that the garden assumed a spectacular order all its own. Hyacinths! Hibiscus! Violets! Roses of every tint and color! Azaleas, freesias, daffodils, poppies, lilies, chrysanthemums, peonies! Orchids, tinted purple, others white and edged with gold! Acacias, hydrangeas! And willows, birches, elms, oak trees, eucalyptuses! A pepper tree! All melded into a profusion of leaves and shades of green, blue, silver.

And overlooking it all — but from a distance, at the periphery of the garden, where it slopes into the road that connects her château to mine — loomed palm trees.

On Madame's grand veranda, which we had reached, the balusters were draped by various vines that formed a tapestry of leaves and blossoms, mostly rivulets of bougainvillea.

We sat at a sculpted table on which an impeccable tea setting awaited us. In a splendid vase one single blue rose exhibited itself. Madame must have signaled for the tea to be arranged while we had been conversing on the bench. She has the invisible manners that come only from breeding, manners exhibited even as she showed Ermenegildo, as if for his approval, the tiny cups into which she was about to serve our tea. A grand selection of tea cakes were the reason, Madame explained, why she was taking her tea later than usual: One of her cooks had intended to delight her with those cakes, which require added preparation. Shaped like puffy stars, they evaporated the moment they touched one's lips.

"A breath of Heaven, aren't they?" Madame complimented them after we were seated and she had poured our tea — and had taken one of the pastries — all with impeccable grace. "I could become addicted to them; so I must have only one more." She popped it into her mouth. "You, Lady, have no problem with your weight, whereas I —"

"— have none either," I pleased her by saying and thus unintentionally encouraged her to take yet another of the heavenly puffs.

We sipped silently, allowing the new setting to adjust to our conversation, and we to it.

It was then that I noticed, on the table, a pair of exquisite opera glasses, adorned with miniature pearls. They seemed ready to be used, not forgotten from another time. It would have been rude to notice them further, and I would have looked away, had not Madame reached for them — they must have been already focused — and fixed her gaze on —

"The mansion next to mine," Madame said, "has been only recently taken by a new tenant — perhaps just for the season." The marked casualness in her voice extended. "I believe I first observed him soon after, or just about the same time, perhaps just before I saw *your* carriage, Lady, dashing by to your own mansion."

I was certain Madame Bernice had determined that I attach significance to this matter. She still peered through her opera glasses. "The new tenant stands before his mansion often," she said. "I've never really had a clear view of him because he locates himself under the eaves of his balcony. I'm more familiar with his shadow than with him! Oh, he's there now."

A wave of fear was stilled by the mere fact that I was with Madame. I felt *protected*. But I had remembered this: During my flight here from the Grand Cathedral, I had noted that one of the châteaus down the road — surely the "mansion" Madame referred to — was just then being occupied. Trunks were being carried in from a coach. The new tenant, a tall presence — I remembered him vividly now; no, I, too, had seen only his elongated shadow — had waited on the outside stairs. Madame put down her glasses. She announced peremptorily: "On to important matters we've kept pending and which I shall now explain entirely. Your essence —"

I received the word with a frown. Hadn't she heard me earlier? "I am not a mystic."

She continued as if I had not spoken. "Your essence has been roaming for centuries from the past into the present."

I was sure I would grasp all this eventually. Now I only listened — to her, yes, but to other voices, traces of whispers out of my dreams.

"It is the essence of all those women you thought you were

dreaming about that has moved into the beautiful body you now possess." Madame sniffed at her tea, a special import sent to her by messenger weekly from the City. "In the Cathedral, when Irena shouted the word 'whore' —"

"— the word swirled in terrified echoes within the Cathedral." I was now certain of it.

"Yes," Madame accepted. "It was then that your essence was aroused to manifest itself into this time, this life. To bring you *here*, for us to meet." She spoke those last words quietly, and then went on: "You are now both present body and timeless essence. That essence is on its journey of redemption, to redeem with the truth the unjust blame on all those women. You are involved in nothing less than correcting the undeserved judgments of history."

I was taken aback by the breadth of the matter. I did not know until I heard her answer that I had spoken my thoughts aloud, without accepting what she had said. "But why me?"

Madame cocked her head. "Because it *is* you." She fed some crumbs from her delectable tea cakes to Ermenegildo — she's clearly *extremely* fond of him. He had demanded her attention by holding for the longest time imaginable an ostentatious display of feathers.

I was catching up with Madame's deductions now, but not accepting them, of course. "And that is why I know — yes, even this — yes! — I know about the War in Heaven, and about —"

"That is enough."

The harsh words jarred me. I protested any possibility that they had been intended to contradict: "I am committed to the truth."

"Who knows that better than I?" Madame reminded me, and explained: "I stopped you only because we must begin immediately to plan for the announcement of these stunning revelations."

"Announcement?"

Madame Bernice looked at me as if my question baffled her, as if she assumed that if a thought entered her mind, it had managed to enter that of her listener. "Yes, to those to whom you must tell your story and who will spread it until everybody knows it. We must rehearse!"

"Rehearse!"

"For interviews."

"Interviews!"

As if realizing only now that her thoughts had *not* entered mine,

Madame touched my hand briefly. "Lady, yours is not an ordinary story. It must be presented carefully."

"Nothing about me is ordinary." Was a part of me still struggling to thwart the words that would define my long journey?

Madame held up a finger for attention. An emerald embraced it. "It must be presented carefully" — she sighed, leaning over as if addressing Ermenegildo — "must be presented carefully and at last."

Surely he had not echoed her sigh? Had I?

"Interviewers will be skeptical," Madame moved on, "they'll even attempt to deride your truths. There are several questions we ourselves must answer *before* we can proceed to present our cause. You must rehearse, rehearse, rehearse, rehearse." She paused to allow me to catch up with her racing mind.

I could not.

She tried to make her voice sound casual, but that only drew even more attention to her astounding words: "There may well be forceful — and dangerous — attempts to thwart our interviews." She had reached absently for her opera glasses. Her words resumed their previous authority: "In deference to your repeated assertion —"

Was she going to indicate that she *had* heard my repeated interjection that I am not a mystic? Yes.

"— I shall say only that from the moment I glimpsed you earlier sitting on my bench and weeping, and soon after when you told me — so touchingly, Lady — the details of what you believed were dreams, I knew the time had come."

"The time has come," I uttered solemnly.

Madame's hand extended across the table toward mine. "I shall devote myself to ensure that you achieve your wondrous goal."

"My goal?"

Her words came with a passion I had not detected earlier: "To redirect blame where it belongs" — she held her breath, and touched her heart — "and to purge the word . . ."

She waited again for me to supply it.

"*Whore!*"

Never in the City — I suppose because of its hectic social pace and the increasing duties required of the genteel within a crumbling society — had I noticed, that I recall, that there are moments when time pauses, when a moment is exposed, yes, naked, as if to be seen from every single vantage in order for its full meaning to be understood. Such a moment occurred after Madame had, with what now

27

seemed to me to have been a wounded sigh, uttered — no, after *I* had uttered — I was no longer sure who had finally spoken it — the word, "whore," a moment that allowed such close scrutiny that I noticed that the leaves on a tree whose branches hovered over the veranda had changed color, become the slightest tint darker. An indiscernible breeze, contained in the same second, must have breathed on the leaves because their original hue returned immediately, just as Ermenegildo looked up, as if he, too, had noted the transformation.

The moment passed. That is, it flowed into the remainder of the afternoon.

"By redefining that word," and now it was definitely Madame who was speaking, "we shall defuse it, so that whoever says 'whore' hereafter shall evoke — redeemed! — all unjustly blamed women from the beginning of time."

My eyes filled with tears.

"Tears will add conviction."

I reared back from her startling insensitivity. "There is no need for forced tears. There have been too many real ones."

"Excellently stated!" Madame congratulated. "I was preparing you for the skepticism you will face."

I was relieved that I had misinterpreted her words, that I had not given my trust easily. Was I catching her excitement? The next thought was like an ambush, though I didn't know by what exactly: "But, Madame, surely in the interviews that you suggest" — I had chosen the word carefully so she would not infer agreement — "I would be asked how Eve connects with Helen —"

"The question of connections will come up," she accepted easily. "That's why rehearsals are essential. For now, let's just observe that Eve is the first woman." She popped another of the puffy stars into her mouth for punctuation.

I *had* begun to catch her excitement. "And so Medea, too —" The dark memory demanded to be included.

"Medea!"

I would have interpreted the sudden wave of Madame's hand as outraged rejection had I not noticed in relief that the gesture had slipped — though carefully — into a pushing away of a strand of her hair that was arguing with a breeze. She smiled, erasing — I had begun to read her signals — any hint of dissent between us, at least for now. She sipped her tea. "I do believe I shall reorder this blend, it's *good*." Was she still trying to move me away from that deeply haunting, haunted life? She touched Ermenegildo's comb, smoothed its crooked feather, which instantly recovered its curve. She leaned back, carefully positioning herself for greatest comfort in her chair. "Now, Lady, tell me how it *all* began, the creation of the world."

I remembered it exactly, and I said:

IV

DARKNESS EXPLODED, turned into itself, entered itself, and thrust itself out in a huge burst that rent the void and erupted once again, hurtling pulsing spurts of itself into orbit, spurts that arced, turned liquid, almost solidified as they spun in space and time. That is how God created Himself.

"Might you underplay the orgasmic imagery?" Madame Bernice suggested.

She *was* a prude! "That is how it happened, exactly as Adam told it to me. I cannot convey a falsehood, and I will not indulge in euphemisms." I decided to face the matter squarely: "Are you, Madame, a prude?"

She pulled her head back. "Of *course* I am not a prude!" Her uplifted chin, and a dazzle of rings as her hand carved a protecting arc before her, doubly rejected my gentle but firm accusation. "I'm speaking only from the point of view of interviewers. You must keep in mind that people are very strange about God and sex."

It occurred to me that she was paying undue attention to her teacup. "I'm glad you're not a prude," I commended, "because my memories contain matters that cannot be camouflaged nor modified."

"If I were a prude, Lady," she continued in a brittle tone, "and you were other than you are, I would have cautioned early in our talks when you were detailing what you thought were dreams — be truthful, but not vulgar —"

"Vulgar!" I drenched the word in indignation.

"You did not let me finish, Lady," Madame said. "I clearly emphasized, 'If you were other than you are.' But you *are* no other than you are" — her words attempted to thaw a growing chill between us — "and what you are is the beautiful, elegant, tasteful woman I see before me, committed entirely to truth. Others — not, of course, you — might even resort to harsh words for the act of lovemaking, use crude words for private body parts —"

"— which I will find occasion to employ when I relate the words of others," I affirmed. I was thinking of the printed installment of the "Account" circulating scandal in the City. Eventually Madame must know all it contained.

Madame extended fastidious concentration to her tea. "Understand this, Lady — I speak only in preparation for interviews. I myself am not affected by crudeness."

"Crudeness!" I added outrage to my indignation.

"You didn't let me finish." She transferred her attention to the folds of her silk skirt; a vagrant strand had caught on one of her rings. "Let me explain. I know what's coming, intimate stories that have never before been told correctly. I know your accounts will contain private details that no one else can know. Still, during interviews, we must guard against anything that tends to distract. People are often distracted when the subject of sex occurs. Now on to *important* matters —"

"Sex *is* an important matter," I reminded, "especially within my memories of blame." My commitment to absolute truth had to be affirmed.

"Excellently said; you must remember that verbatim when interviews begin."

We were both relieved to note that evening had begun to settle on the countryside. "Shall we continue tomorrow at tea?" Madame suggested.

She and Ermenegildo accompanied me down the few steps of the veranda. At dusk, red blossoms on vines looked like blotches of blood. A chill was permeating the approaching evening. I covered myself with the purple cowl I carried with me for just such a possibility. We walked on the lawn. How quickly a bond had been asserted between us — among us; I suspected the peacock had become instantly fond of me.

As I started to move away along the paths of the garden and toward the road, Madame said, "Knowing now that what you thought were dreams are memories, you must, tonight, Lady, invite more memories, willing yourself" — her words became soft, softer, blending with twilight — "back into the primal garden, the edge of Patmos. Remember . . ."

I hardly heard the word, though I repeated it: "Remember."

I had no sooner stepped onto the road than it seemed that I had already begun to dream — to remember — thoughts, memories suffused now with new meaning. The mesmerized evening — dark dusk waiting — augmented that sense.

To my astonishment, I realized that I had headed in the wrong direction and was now facing the château Madame Bernice had been peering at earlier through her opera glasses, the château of the new tenant, whom I had glimpsed on the day I fled the Grand Cathedral.

Only sprinkles of candlelight dotted the windows of the château. It seemed deliberately darkened. I saw a shadow cross a window, then cross another in the same vast room, cross back again. It was he, the tall man, pacing restlessly. I hid behind the heavy foliage of oleanders that enclosed the property. I observed his movements. His pacing increased, slowed, stopped, resumed faster. Plotting what? If he was a spy, how quickly hostile presences in the City acted to have me watched.

I turned away. I lit the candle in the lantern I had learned to carry, should my walks extend beyond twilight. I hurried back to my château. I did not fear the rustling nor the scraping I heard within the brush. I know those muffled sounds now, the sounds of the secretive existence of the pitiful derelicts longing for respite in the country.

At my gate, I stopped. Something had been left there. I held my lantern up. A bouquet of flowers had been placed — shoved — against the grillwork, strange flowers, shaped somewhat like roses but of a dark, disturbing color, the color of long-dried blood. Their scent was heavy; they possessed a — what word? — a *sated* perfume. I flung them away.

By the time I reached my chambers, I dismissed any significance to my discovery, not a bouquet at all but flowers gathered and discarded aimlessly, finding their accidental way against my gates.

In my quarters, the evil "Account" that assaults my life with my beloved Count du Muir draws me to it, where I placed it on a marble table. I open it to where I left off earlier:

> On such a night — when the Count had taken a circuitous route to his mansion after having enjoyed a particularly exhilarating performance at the opera, an exhilaration which had aroused his desire to aid any unfortunate derelicts (not all derelicts are unfortunate) who might have unwittingly wandered into the depraved sector of the City — the Whore, coached by her Pimp,

thrust herself into the night in the torn guise of a Lady (some deluded souls even claimed she played the role quite well; indeed? the Reader rightly questions) in order to intercept the Count's coach while she screamed for his protection: "A man is pursuing me with a knife, your Lordship!"

At the same time, she allowed her tattered dress to faint at her feet in the cold night and thus reveal her full nudity, which to anyone other than the Noble Count, responding only to her supposed need for shelter, might have seemed resplendent, since the favorable light, in conspiracy with the Whore and the Reverend Pimp's intent, cast sinuous shadows that luridly accentuated the whiteness of her flesh, especially the velvety mound that her soft thighs seemed lasciviously to strain to kiss (she had trained them to do that) — all devised for full display (*sordid* display, the Reader justly clarifies). And who was the man in pursuit? — *pretended* pursuit. The Reverend Pimp, who else?

Hastily, the Noble Count opened the door of his coach, not even waiting for the Coachman to perform his just duties, although he, too, had rushed in response to the spectacular display. (How other than "spectacular" to describe accurately such an unexpected sight? the Reader understands.) Ever vigilant to the preservation of morality, the Count was, with swiftness, attempting selflessly to shield others on the street from the assaulting sight of the Whore by bringing her into the cover of his coach immediately. Claiming a fever from the chase, the Whore refused what the Noble Count instantly offered her — his opera cape.

In his innocence (although, along with his Twin Brother, he was the most desirable man in the City, the Count was pure of heart — and body), the Noble Count mistook for sorrow the look in the Whore's extravagantly lashed eyes, a look which was in reality one of satiety, lust, and wantonness.

Once in his coach, the Whore pulled the Count to her. "Protect me, please, your Lordship." She pretended to tremble, thus assuring that her nudity would gleam each time the coach passed lanterns along the avenues. It can only be imagined by the justifiably outraged Reader with what urgency the Count turned away from this vilely opulent offering of naked breasts and quivering thighs (they did not quiver with fear, as he assumed). "Please, your Lordship, hold me close, please!" the Whore pretended to plead.

No matter how affronted by it, the Writer must endure this weighty task and proceed to document —

33

Enough! I shall now, as I lie in bed, invite, just as Madame exhorted, fuller details of my *true* lives.

In the morning — not at all tired today after having roamed continents and centuries — from Eden to Patmos, to the River Jordan and the Black Sea — I was eager to join Madame Bernice again at tea.

As I neared her château, I noticed again, with a flush of warmth, an immediate sense of protection. Ermenegildo waited for me at the edge of Madame's grounds. I followed him up the path, pausing only for a moment while he sniffed a spectacular carnation, mottled pink and peach.

On the veranda, tea was set. The vase on the table displayed a gathering of exquisite violets. Madame was trying out another brew of tea, although she withheld the fact from me, studying my reaction to gauge my approval of her new choice as I sipped it. I did not tell her that yesterday's tea was better. She seemed — I had seen a slight twitch at her nose when she tested its scent — to have reached the same conclusion. Today, she wore a small coronet, with one emerald. She is not ostentatious, but she loves to dress for tea.

She was eager to resume where we had left off yesterday:

"Now I know, Lady, that you learned from Adam what you told me yesterday, in your brilliant and necessarily orgasmic description, about how God created Himself. But how did Adam know such details, since *he* was not created yet? Did God confide in him?"

"Oh, surely you're testing me?" I had gained new authority.

She shook her head, but waited for my answer.

"When Adam was born, he, being the first man, would of course inherit some of God's memories."

"But of course!" Madame immediately grasped the logic. "A sort of collective unconscious," she addressed Ermenegildo, who seemed not at all baffled. "It's quite clear."

"I shall explain it just as clearly during interviews to come."

And with that exchange, so simply spoken with no drama other than its own, I accepted that Madame Bernice and I were embarked on the journey of redemption she had clarified for me — and that during interviews — I welcomed this, too — I would speak my truths with the full authority that only absolute knowledgeability can provide.

I demurred on another cup of tea, an offering made much too hastily for me not to interpret it as a risky test on the new brew. "Later I shall be delighted to have another cup," I tried to assuage Madame's look of concern as I continued my narration from last night:

"The restless Spirit that had created Himself prowled infinite space, verifying His authority. And so —"

"— He created Adam!" Madame anticipated. "After Heaven and Heaven's angels and the Garden were in place?" At the last, she had turned her statement into a question as if she had located a contradiction.

She had not. "Of course they were in place. Keep in mind, Madame, that time had not yet assumed the demarcations we assign to it. Events I shall describe later were all occurring simultaneously in Heaven."

"I would never have thought otherwise," Madame was fully satisfied. "Oh, Lady, how beautiful was Eden?" For a woman of sophistication, Madame is capable of pure exuberance.

"Beyond belief," I told her. "God *did* have extravagant powers and so —"

There were flowers shaped like stars, some that burst open only to reveal more petals, blossoms of every color and hue — yes, and the flower so glorious it did not need the decoration of leaves. As if the air itself had been sprinkled with silver dew, everything glimmered in the first garden.

I was back in the dream — the memory of Eden. It had all returned to me last night when I deliberately summoned it, discovering details that had blurred during the time when I confused memories with dreams. Now I could tell it all to Madame.

"The sky was of the purest azure."

Under it, Adam woke.

He stood, resplendent.

Watching closely, God delighted in the spectacle of Adam's naked body, stretching.

Adam felt joy sweep his every limb, every sinew — and then he was overwhelmed by a wave of loss. How was loss possible when everything was new, just born? Still, it was there, a sadness. No, a yearning. Where? He attempted to find its origin. He touched an arm, the other. He raised his head, felt it carefully from his neck up. Was this longing in his mind? Yes. No. *Something* was there, a fragment of what he felt, but not all. He touched his chest, his ribs. He detected a steady beating. It was there! There! — a longing in his heart.

To assert that, his hand moved away, down along his stomach, to his legs, between them, cupping the warmth there; and that augmented — he thrilled to this — the longing he had located in his heart.

35

Within shadows He had not yet created, God frowned. He had not intended to imbue Adam with such yearning. With shock, He realized that when He had thrust Himself out of the void, spurts of His own craving to exist had whirled into space. One drop, suspended until now, had fallen on the grass of the new garden, exactly where Adam had just assumed his form.

God's eyes glowered.

Adam's hand had returned to his heart. Yes, it was there that his yearning lodged.

It's in his ribs! God was certain. Reckless with anxiety, He plucked out the rib He determined was the offending one.

Out of that opening, Adam's longing was released and —

"— my body sprang to life on a bed of orchids!" I spoke the cherished words to Madame Bernice.

"That was when you and Adam first —"

"— discovered love and desire, yes."

When we wakened in Eden the second day, my Adam and I made love again. Then we wandered to a vine glistening with blue buds, out of which Adam formed a necklace and looped it between my breasts. We roamed to a brook and discovered our reflections. Adam knelt and dipped his fingers into the coolness. In the moisture he had just discovered, we soaked leaves from a tree nearby, and we bathed each other, lingering.

I had dismissed as only a perception of last night the presence of a twisted tree. But after we made love again and fell asleep in each other's arms, I awoke. The pure light of the day confirmed existence of the tree. To its branches had been added clusters of succulent fruit. Seeing it, I felt a coolness that made me press against him. When I heard him sighing in my arms, I detected another sound, a distant summoning murmuring within the quietude of night.

"Eve, Eve!"

I looked at Adam, to determine his reaction to the Voice. He had not heard it. I stood. Adam woke briefly, extending his hand up to me, hugging my hips, urging me to make love again. I longed to, yes, to be within each other again, yes, but I eased away. I had to discover the purpose of the summoning Voice. I leaned over to kiss my beloved, then slipped away, following the Voice to the new tree.

I stood in awe before it. It had grown even fuller, laden with glorious berries, tinted red, sweet red, and purple, all glazed by nectar that glistened silver under — what? — the moon. The branches of the tree — would there have been room for even one more berry? — created a dark shadow even at night.

The luscious berries aroused a longing I hadn't yet experienced. Yes, I was hungry. I marveled at the beneficence of this bounty that would feed us so sweetly. Why else would that tree have been planted there, to grow constantly fuller? Gratefully, I reached out for a gathering of the fruit.

"This is the tree of knowledge," came a Voice out of the darkness. "Its fruit is succulent and it would allay your hunger." The hidden Voice was excited in a terrible way. "But you're forbidden to eat of it."

"Why?"

"It is My will."

I did not marvel at the Voice that had spoken so peremptorily. Everything was being experienced for the first time. I did not yet understand that I had reason to fear.

The Voice continued: "This is the tree whose fruit contains knowledge of good and evil. If you eat from it, you'll die."

Good? Evil? Die? I was baffled by the words' illogic. How could I understand them since I hadn't tasted of the tree that would have given me knowledge to comprehend what the Voice was saying?

"The succulent berries entice you, don't they, Eve?" the Voice taunted.

"Yes." I would share their sweetness, a present, with my Adam. "But you forbade it. Why tempt me with it?"

"To test your woman's spirit!" the Voice asserted. "And Adam's love for you. If you eat, shall Adam reprove you? His loyalty is to *Me*." The Voice was harshly confident. "Find out how much he loves you, Eve. Test his devotion to you. What are you, really, to him? A passing desire? A momentary need? — once met, now over. Do you dare defy Me to prove your love — and his?"

I plucked the lushest cluster of red berries. I brought them to my mouth. "I *will* eat the fruit!"

"You disobey!"

"Your odd admonition?"

"You said that to God, Lady?" Madame seemed not truly surprised.

"I did, Madame. It *was* an odd admonition."

I bit into the berries. The lush nectar filled my mouth with a glorious sweetness.

Adam stood beside me, roused by my voice. I saw him now even

37

more clearly, more beautiful than ever. I loved him even more, desired him even more. The Garden, which I realized only now had been too still — beautiful, yes, but with an imposed beauty, not its own — breathed, as if released from a binding spell. Every flower, every leaf assumed individual life, growing, freed.

"Adam!" The Voice was exultant. "Eve has disobeyed my command. She is doomed! If you eat of the fruit she ate, you will be doomed, too!"

Doom? I understood the word now, and I shuddered.

Adam reached for the rich cluster still in my hand. I pulled it away. "No!" I shouted. "It will doom *you*."

"*You* tasted it."

"But you must not," I pled.

Adam embraced me.

"Adam" — the Voice was soft — "*you* have not disobeyed. You shall never disobey." The Voice grew more certain, firm. "Only she. Renounce her! I will banish her, and you will retain this perfect garden, I will make another woman for you, an obedient one, who shall never disobey us."

"Without Eve, it would not be a perfect garden," Adam said. He kissed me. His lips forced mine to open, his tongue probed into my mouth, seeking pieces of the fruit I had eaten, drawing them into his own mouth, eating them. "If this dooms her, I will gladly share her doom."

God's Voice lowered to a barely audible hiss and whispered in my ear for only me to hear:

"Eve! Woman! — who let evil into the world. Eve! Mother of Mankind! For this, I will multiply your sorrows. In pain you will bring forth children — and be blamed forever." His Voice howled but still whispered: "Eve will be blamed forever for all the pain and sadness that will follow."

"Oh, why such terrifying rage?" Madame Bernice questioned centuries later in her garden. Her long sigh sought to contain all her bafflement of the enormity of what I had remembered. "Lady, we must find that answer, finally — why, truly, was God so enraged at you?"

I could only shake my head, and remember that —

His curse resounded beyond the Garden, into Heaven — where a spirit of rebellion had erupted.

Fascinated by the vastness of the universe, a bold band of angels led by Lucifer and Cassandra had soared in wild exhilaration through the infinity of space. Having tasted the delectable recklessness of freedom, they confronted God.

"Lady, forgive the interruption; earlier you assigned Cassandra to Troy," Madame reminded, "now here she is again in Heaven —"

"She was Paris's sister, yes, but, much earlier, Madame, she was an angel *and* Lucifer's sister. Cassandra's powers of what *you* might call foreseeing came in part from the fact that she could place herself in several worlds." I spoke with an ease that surprised me. "Besides, surely, you, a mystic —"

"*I* don't question your memories — and certainly never Cassandra in anything," Madame Bernice asserted, at the same time that she was clearly trying to convince herself that her new tea was a success, sipping it, tasting it on her tongue, waiting before taking another sip.

In Heaven, there was war —

"Lady, you will deal now with —?"

"The War in Heaven? No, not yet. Later, yes, and fully. Here, I'm condensing certain matters necessary to illuminate the events in the Garden."

"A sound approach, Lady. Our rehearsals are proceeding splendidly, splendidly." She consulted Ermenegildo. "Splendidly."

For an outrageous moment I thought that he had echoed her, but, of course, she herself had merely added even more emphasis to her enthusiasm.

During a lull in the War in Heaven — was it possible that it was really over? — Cassandra stood on a hill and pointed out to Lucifer a beautiful creature in a glorious garden just created. The man had been shaped to look exactly like him, like Lucifer, his face, his perfect naked body —

"Lucifer was naked, too, in Heaven, Lady?" Madame stirred her tea vigorously, although she takes it without sugar.

"Of course, Madame. Angels would certainly not be attired. Neither Adam nor I had discovered clothes. So how could they —?"

"An excellent point," Madame muttered. With grave consternation, she discovered she *had* put sugar in her tea.

I was not sure she was convinced. I said, "Beautiful nudity is like an unadorned gem." I made a gesture toward her simple pendant, an emerald. "The lives I speak of, the women I've been, the men I've known — those who claim to have captured them in history, stories, art — in the very records we've set out to correct" — I gave each word necessary emphasis — "have insisted on clothing them, sometimes even in their baths! But when they're naked, we see them, fully, as they were, as they lived; and that is how I shall portray them — as *we* were — because, remember, Madame, *I* was there." Had I convinced her?

She smoothed out the folds of her skirt, touching the gold brocade that wound through it like a vine. "This was woven by nuns in a silent convent in the interior," she informed me.

I allowed that to stand.

"Still, while acknowledging what you say, Lady, it does seem to me that Cassandra might have worn —"

"*She* wore a cape. Cassandra was always aware of her dramatic presence, and to augment that she wore a cape."

"But of *course* she would." Madame Bernice beamed.

In Heaven, Cassandra wrapped her cape about herself, leaving one shoulder exposed. The cape embraced her slender body and fell just above her feet. Why had God created Adam during this sudden hush in the War in Heaven? she wondered. To arouse jealousy in his favorite angel, Lucifer — who stood now beside her as the smoke of the terrible war diminished — and so to quell further resistance? Oh, and now there was a woman in the Garden. What did God intend for them? Sniffing at the clearing air, Cassandra detected . . . a bitter scent of destiny.

"The two beautiful creatures in the Garden are in danger," she told her brother. She sniffed more deeply. "They, too, have defied him. Now God is plotting —" A gust of wind fanned dimming fires, and smoke clouded her vision. "We must help them." She always tried to keep from sounding urgent. "Urgency excites fate," she would say. "We have to uncover what God intends with them."

And the two angels glided into Eden.

After God's wrathful curse, the Garden had been stilled, tensely intact, as if it had been frozen by the night, which came suddenly with only one cold star. All the life I had detected in the flowers and the leaves of trees — after I had eaten of the berries — seemed to have drained away from them. All that could happen to them now was to die, and they were now waiting to die, I realized, now that I knew the meaning of the fatal word.

In the blue light of the single star, Cassandra and Lucifer were dazzling in the Garden. She had delicate features, and she was pretty, yes, very pretty. Her eyes were beautiful, smiling strangely, sadly bemused. Her body was —

40

"— wrapped in her spectacular cape," Madame asserted.

— wrapped in a filmy, spectacular cloak, which revealed that she was petite, with slender, lovely curves. The Angel Lucifer was as handsome — almost as handsome, I quickly revised — as my Adam, and his body was as imposing — almost as imposing. What at first had looked to me like wings on both the brother and his sister was instead a luminous aura that further lit the night and revealed that Lucifer resembled Adam enough to be his twin, except for their different coloring.

Cassandra — oh, she clearly knew she was enormously grand despite her delicacy — slung her cloak from one shoulder to the other. She smiled a sad smile I would come to love, a smile I would often attempt to find words to describe.

"I'm Cassandra, and this is my brother, Lucifer," she introduced — she was courteous through the centuries. She took our hands, Adam's and mine, and linked them with Lucifer's, asserting our mutual allegiance, which we accepted easily.

"God intended to separate you, Adam, and you resisted." Lucifer said what Cassandra had informed him of during their flight. "Now He's plotting to move next against you. My sister will determine how."

Cassandra shook her head and explained, "My brother's always direct." Even within her light chastisement of him, it was clear how deeply she loved him.

"Not excessively so, of course," Madame inserted.

"It would be impossible to separate us," Adam told the angel. They studied each other, Adam and Lucifer, like reflections in a mirror. To emphasize his assertion, Adam drew me closer to him.

"Impossible," I echoed him.

Lucifer reached for a flower, which opened like a star. "God is capable of extravagant beauty." He held the flower up as an example. Then he laid it gently back on the verdure, adding: "And He's capable of equal cruelty."

Cassandra touched my hair, lightly. "So very pretty," she said. Her cloak slipped down from her shoulders, exposing one lovely breast. Adam gazed at it, astonished that what he had discovered to be so beautiful in me could have a reflection on another.

Cassandra's strange eyes located the new tree in Eden, its delectable fruit glinting in the moon.

"Was that tree there, when you first sprang to life, my dear?" Cassandra touched the berries, which left a film of nectar on her fingertips. She breathed the scent of the nectar. "It *is* delicious." She held it out to her brother to inhale.

"No, that tree wasn't there at first," I answered.

She seemed to be only announcing what she had already known: "He plotted His blame after you appeared."

In another garden, hers, Madame interjected: "We must keep that in mind, Lady. I'm sure Cassandra emphasized it."

"So He plotted His blame after you appeared," Cassandra emphasized, adding even more emphasis by flinging her cloak high across her neck so that now she was covered from her shoulders to her feet.

Lucifer gathered his wings sadly. That's what I thought for a moment, that he had gathered his wings, but he had sighed and raised his broad shoulders, scattering about him the blue cast of night. "Is it too late to change His revenge on them?"

Cassandra looked ahead, beyond the Garden, east of Eden. "For some of His plan, yes, it's too late. But —" She stared ahead.

Lucifer urged her: "What exactly *do* you perceive, sister?"

"More of fate already shaped, some of fate still shaping." She studied the tense Garden. "He will destroy Eden."

"No!" Adam protested.

"Can He be stopped?" I asked, knowing that Adam could still disbelieve because he had not heard God's cruel whispered words to me, promising sorrow, pain.

"No," Cassandra said, "it cannot be stopped. That part of fate is too near its goal. But there's much more which He hasn't determined yet, not yet set on its course — perhaps the worst part of His design." I believe that it was only then that I saw her wry smile disappear, and only for a second.

"And so we can change *that!*" Lucifer asserted, smiling reassurance at me and Adam. "My beloved sister has determined how," he told us proudly.

Madame's words brought me back to the veranda of her château: "That will become clear, Lady, the matter of changing destiny?" She held her cup of tea midway to her lips, to punctuate the importance of her question, or perhaps because she was about to determine what I already knew, that this tea had been a mistake.

"Yes, Madame, it shall all be clear when I narrate in full the truth about the War in Heaven. That's where Cassandra refined her notion about changing fate. That's when it first was tested."

Madame was excited: "Changing fate . . . ! I think I begin to understand . . . Lady!" Her excitement grew.

"Madame?"

"Oh, don't you see? Changing fate — *that's* what we, you and I, must do at interviews, change the course that centuries have been conspiring to assure — even more unjust blame!"

"Yes!" I now shared her excitement.

"I'm certain that Cassandra's method will guide us, coach us exactly on how it can be done — when, of course, we discuss it during your account of the War in Heaven — none of which is to say —" She became instantly shy even as she uttered her confident words; to Ermenegildo? She bent over toward where he rested at her side. "— that I, myself, attuned as I am to Cassandra, may not come up with the same deduction."

Ermenegildo stretched his neck toward her in assurance.

"I'm sure of it, Madame," I said. I would have to rehearse exactly how Cassandra had explained it all.

In Eden, Adam informed the angels: "Whatever God intends now, there's nothing to fear. Eve and I together possess a strength more powerful than each of us."

Cassandra gathered her cape even higher on her neck, a long, sensual neck, which she stroked. "So you must nurture all the strength that your love can give you —"

"— and the strength that your desire can give you," Lucifer reminded.

Cassandra whispered to herself: "The Garden is so still, so beautiful, as if it longs to be remembered before it disappears."

"I shall never forget it," I said. My eyes located the flower so glorious that it did not need the decoration of leaves, the flower with which Adam had touched me when I sprang to life on the bed of orchids on which we made love and which my eyes now sought.

"Could He be so cruel? Create, then destroy —?" Adam still wanted to disbelieve, but he, too, had desperately searched out the flowers of our first encounter.

Cassandra held out her hands. "Come with us now so you won't see your paradise ravaged." Again she spoke as if to herself, perhaps to her brother: "We must travel east of Eden to the end of this new unshaped world — and quickly."

"Where you can perceive further ahead more clearly into fate?" Lucifer understood.

"Closer to its origin, closer to Him, to grasp the worst of His design."

Was it possible she could anticipate God's plans? I would learn that answer later.

A storm lashed at the Garden, cold winds colliding with heated currents, uprooting trees and flowers, tearing at them, scattering petals, their colors fading, leaves ripped away, yellowing, turning brittle, ashen, twigs breaking, dry, bunching into tumbleweeds that whirled madly about us, scratching, carving bloody streaks on our bared flesh. A torrent of dust pummeled us, blinding us, withdrawing suddenly to reveal that —

The Garden had been annihilated.

Except for the single flower that grew only in Eden!

I would run back, retrieve it!

Adam restrained me, pulling me away from warring currents of wind. He held me tenderly, urging me to follow Lucifer and Cassandra away from our devastated paradise.

I looked back, one more time.

The blossom that was so beautiful it did not need the decoration of leaves was *still* alive! Then, instantly, it was dead. It had been left only long enough for me to see it wither and die, its color vanishing as if it had never existed — and it would not exist again, except in my memories and Adam's. I turned away.

Adam touched my eyes. I detected the first frown on his face. With one finger he traced a line down my cheeks. He looked startled at his finger. He touched my eyes again, my cheeks again, more urgently. "My beloved, what is this?"

I kissed his fingertips.

"They're tears," I said. "It's the beginning of our weeping."

V

MADAME BERNICE DID NOT SPEAK FOR A LONG TIME. She understood that I could not continue, must hold the rest for later. She placed a warming hand on mine; the memory of exile had chilled it. Remembered first tears had brought new tears. The afternoon drifted into early graying light as if the sky had begun to die.

After a respectful interval that further honored the events in Eden, Madame eased away the silence with her typical graciousness: "Sad as that is, Lady, we must keep our joyous goal in mind, and that shall allow us to move on."

"As I am prepared to do now," I agreed, although my heart lingered within the moment in Eden when I had looked back and had seen the glorious flower die.

"From time to time," Madame announced, "we must discuss preparations for interviews, anticipate all possibilities. Some interviewers may try to trip you up with trivialities." She assumed the tone of a pretentious interviewer: "Who was the emperor who banished St. John the Divine to Patmos?"

"I believe it was the Emperor Domitian." I had not been political.

"Domitian?" That was Madame's real voice. "I thought it was Nero." She considered the matter. "Let's just call him the Emperor. You must not sound as if you're dropping names."

"Dropping . . . ?"

When Madame explained the odd expression to me — she must have picked it up from one of the servants who goes into the City for provisions — I expressed astonishment that anyone would want to assume grandeur by claiming an undeserved close association with

45

another's life. Besides, she knows I've roamed with kings and princes, the Pope, and God.

"I *meant* exotic names."

"Oh . . . At interviews —" I prompted. How totally committed I was to the interviews now!

Madame was eager: "There will be many persons demanding to be in attendance. I shall select them as carefully as we shall determine when the right time for announcement has arrived. Everything must be exact, from attire to —"

"My attire is always perfect," I would not allow the tinge of a negative observation on my attention to style.

"You didn't let me finish, Lady. I meant that, for interviews, it isn't only *style* —"

She had read my mind!

"— which you have in abundance — that must be considered, but the unique effect of everything — setting, even lighting — that emphasizes the grandeur of our goal." She sighed wistfully. "It's been said that my own attire is perhaps a trifle on the gaudy side." She adjusted her coronet so that the emerald on it would not be so aggressive.

I interrupted, "You have a flair, a unique flair, a beautiful flair."

Madame gave me one of her endearing smiles, almost but not quite shy, a treasure.

She again offered me another cup of the new tea. I rejected it, absently placing a finger on the rim of my cup.

"I shall not order this blend again!" Madame snapped. "Of course, I've inferred your disappointment in it."

I thought it best not to deny it. I ate a pastry, displaying my pleasure in it.

Madame was not mollified. She pushed her own cup away, a signal that Ermenegildo, idling within a lacy filigree of sun, must have taken as an indication that we had finished our tea, at which time he would feast on some crumbs remaining on the silver plate. Madame would not disappoint him. She crumbled a cake, fed it to him, and touched his comb, quite subtly smoothing the feather that immediately twisted away again from the others.

Then she poured herself another stubborn cup of tea. "This brew is really not *that* bad." She refolded her napkin on her lap, fussing with its swirls of embroidered initials. "I suggest that here and there, during the narration of your many lives, you hint at what's to come, keep

46

some matters in abeyance, always, of course, assuring that all will be revealed eventually."

"I understand exactly."

"An example?" She had already prepared one. "When you narrate the truth of your dance of the seven veils —"

"Six."

"Seven."

"Six."

Madame almost dropped her cup. "*Everyone* knows there were *seven*."

"Six. Madame, I was there!"

"Perhaps at times we should adhere —"

"— to lies? Because they've been" — I chose her own word — "entrenched? We're involved in *correcting* lies."

Madame made an airy gesture with her hands — dazzling; every move of her ringed hands is dazzling. "It just seems to me, considering our formidable task, that at times we shouldn't dwell on certain matters that are minor but too well established."

"The matter is *not* minor, Madame, and I'm surprised to have to remind you that truth lies in exact details."

"Well said." She smiled, but at the same time she made a sound I hesitate to call a grunt — perhaps only signaling the beginning of a backache, from which she suffers occasionally; she had straightened up and placed her hand firmly on her back. Ermenegildo stiffened his own back, as if to share her pain.

"I shall say this to any skeptical interviewer — 'I know you believe, like everyone else, that there were seven veils in my dance. There were six. Soon, through my dreams —' "

"Memories."

" '— memories; soon you shall see me remove each veil, and then you shall view me draped only in the sixth as I set into motion my strategy to save John the Baptist.' "

"To save John the Baptist!" Madame relished the prospect of finally correcting a gross untruth.

I considered this a harmonious time to end our evening. When he saw me rise, Ermenegildo rushed to the foot of the veranda, preparing to escort me. Madame walked me there. In the softened voice she had used before when we were about to part, she said:

"When you return to your quarters, continue to rehearse. Pretend a few select people are with you, helping you prepare, the way I do.

47

Soon you'll find that the imagined audience will begin to speak, even to express doubts, questions — and they'll have many. Roam through every single detail for exactitude."

"Madame!" I heard myself pronounce the word in fear.

"Lady?"

I thought the day sighed as it dimmed. "Clarify for me again. My essence —?"

Soothing my unexpected urgency, Madame reminded in what was now a near whisper: "Your essence has roamed throughout time in the various bodies of women outrageously and unfairly blamed."

"In the present, now, I am both body —"

"— and essence."

"My dreams are —?"

"— memories."

"My dreams are memories," I repeated.

I was still repeating those words when I returned to my quarters, to evoke, as Madame had instructed, an invisible chorus of listeners to my rehearsals. How easily done!

I hear them!

Oh, can you believe it? She's trying to convince us that she was all those women, and that —

— that I will finally redeem them, yes! . . . Strange, that one must convince that truth is true. Tomorrow, I must tell Madame that in the suggested rehearsals, I much too quickly encountered hostility.

I informed her of that, at tea the next day.

Madame dismissed the matter with a wave of her hand. "To be expected. It will change."

I realized why she was nervous. Either through sheer doggedness or by mistake — I preferred to think the latter — she was serving yesterday's unsuccessful tea again. She said testily, "It is *not* bad."

Under Ermenegildo's glare, I sipped the tea, knowing that nothing secures order more surely than that ritual of civility, sharing tea. Still, I found it too bitter for a second sip.

"You don't have to pretend. I know you don't like it," Madame snapped.

Well, I would try to pacify her continuing discomfort over her mistake. "Oh, Madame, at times everyone is unsure about one thing or another. Even Mary —"

Madame's dark brows soared, then crashed above her nose. "The Holy Mother was unsure?"

"Yes."

"You must stay away from the subject of the Holy Mother and insecurity," she interrupted.

"But, Madame, Mary *was* unsure, during a poignant moment when —"

"There are certain subjects that —"

"— certain subjects that I shall not — I repeat, Madame, shall *not* — avoid, and the subject of Mary, exactly as I knew her, is a foremost one. Without that, I cannot tell the true story of the Crucifixion." I plunged ahead: "And I shall deal with that, *and* her pain — *and* her sorrowful guilt!"

"Guilt! The Holy Mother felt guilty!" Madame Bernice reared back as if she had been charged. "I may consider that it might become necessary to deal with a certain amount of insecurity on the Holy Mother's part — *during a poignant moment* — but *guilt!*"

I've become accustomed to Madame's occasional silences accompanied by the crossing of her arms before her chest, and by the lifting of her stubborn chin. I remind myself then that although it is she who has clarified the matters we are now about, even she, now and then, must be convinced, not of our goal, nor of our means of achieving it, nor of the justice of our journey, nor, certainly not, of the truth of my memories; no, she must be convinced that we must deal with certain ingrained lies she herself has come to cherish and so tends to want to retain unchanged. Today I decided to ease her out of her staunch silence: "I came to love Mary, to understand her, to believe, yes, that she was . . . holy."

Madame's arms remained crossed.

I folded mine, and we both sat back in our chairs.

Madame uncrossed her arms. "Well, they *are* your memories," she acquiesced.

As she does when she feels that her position may have been compromised — now, because she had unfolded her arms first and had tacitly conceded that we might have to deal with the subject of Mary's poignant uncertainty — Madame proceeded in her most brittle tone: "During interviews, watch that you don't ramble."

"Ramble!"

"Yes."

"Madame, if anyone rambles —"

"You interrupt too quickly, Lady. Have you observed that, that you interrupt too quickly — before I've finished? I didn't *say* you rambled, I said, watch that you don't."

49

I sat in determined silence. My delight in the silver florets the sun was creating on the tea setting helped me to keep my temper.

A shot rent the still countryside!

Madame's hand on mine stilled the fear aroused by the memory of the murder in the Cathedral. Quickly, she reached for her opera glasses, always on the table.

Fixed on the man in the château nearby?

Madame's glasses scanned the territory, from the château of the new tenant to the thicket of trees beyond the road that connects our châteaus, a mixture of trees possible only here. What allows elms to grow alongside oaks, eucalyptus, weeping willows, and the palms that loom along the road is that here in the country we experience a vicissitude of sudden climatic changes, sudden seasons. It is not rare for a sunny day to turn without transition cold and gloomy, a transition that often, I've noticed, reflects my moods. At those times, fog veils the countryside in false dusk. I'm certain all this is an atmospheric matter for which there's a scientific explanation. These moody changes in the afternoon — one was occurring now — always confuse the sad derelicts from the City into believing that sheltering night is about to descend. That emboldens them to straggle out of their hiding places to find more comfort in the night. Even without the aid of Madame's glasses, I could see their outlines. I can now recognize them from the slow movements of their shadows.

"Recently" — Madame still peered through her glasses — "I heard the clap of horses' hooves. One of my servants claims officials from the City are being sent in to pursue —"

"— those sad souls?" I protested, in shock.

Madame Bernice shook her head in outrage. "There's so much cruelty in the world. Who better than you knows that, Lady?"

The countryside was still again. Madame tried to brighten: "It was only a hunter — at times they're reckless in the country." I noted that she had shifted her opera glasses. "The new tenant in the mansion down the road — he's there now, on his veranda."

Ermenegildo fixed his attention in the same direction, his head tilted suspiciously.

Had the new tenant fired the shot at someone who had wandered onto his property? People in the City had begun to do that. Or had he fired — if he had — as a signal to us of his presence? I looked through the glasses Madame had just replaced on the table. I saw him, again no more than a silhouette. He stood on his veranda, very still, looking — if this was an impression, it was a strong one — at me.

I put down the glasses, and told Madame Bernice about the dark flowers I had found at my gate last night. My first interpretation had returned, that it was a bouquet left there deliberately. "Might *he* have left them there? A warning of his presence — like the shot?"

Madame said thoughtfully, "I've heard from one of my servants that he's a man of bizarre activities."

"Perhaps he's a spy, employed by Irena and Alix. Or by the Pope. Or all three."

"*If* their alliance holds," Madame introduced the possibility of further conspiracy.

We both stared in the direction of the dark château. It seemed to darken earlier than any of the others. Of course, that was easily explained by the fact that it was built on a slight elevation, heavily treed.

"Don't be concerned, Lady," Madame assured me. "I shall see that nothing threatens our endeavors. Nor you. Count on me."

I assumed she was referring at least in part to her mystic qualities. So I did not remark. I told myself she was right earlier, that the shot had come from one of the careless hunters drawn to the woods each season. The strange bouquet again became flowers randomly thrust against my gate by the wind, which I now remembered rising as I neared my château last night.

"Do you suppose, Lady, that this might be the time for you to tell me what His Holiness holds against you, and how you managed to get him to officiate at your nuptials in the Cathedral? After all, he *is* the Holy Father."

From the way she paused in apparent awe before and after the title, I assumed she would not greet my story without protest. I considered toning it down, but I am committed to the truth. What I must tell her was simply this:

I had discovered — from a friend of the Count's, a nun of the highest order and true morality — that as the Pope went about his palace — its floors polished to a mirror gloss — he would surround himself with choirboys in their smocks. He would also welcome throngs of visiting little girls in their ruffled dresses.

While seeming to be profusely blessing the little children over whom he leaned, he would delight at what his shiny floors reflected, underpants, or an occasional lack thereof, and if the latter, he would squeal with pleasure, a fact that made the mothers of the children vaunt his love of "little ones" and bring him more. To get a better look, he would "accidentally" drop his miter. That provided him with a bonus. A boy or girl — both at the same time would send him into shivers of joy — would bend to retrieve the holy staff and expose more than a mere reflection.

It was *that* which I must find words to tell Madame Bernice, an even more intimidating prospect now that she had bowed her head and was holding her hands, piously, one on the other, on her lap. I started — stuttered: "I had learned that the Pope — I mean, His Holiness — had certain predilections for —" I would gasp out the truth. I inhaled. "— certain predilections for — for —"

"— for the pink bottoms of little boys and girls!" Throwing her head back, Madame issued a sound I might have described as a guffaw except that she is much too refined for that. Still, it *was* very loud, and her abundant body shook with glee.

"You *know?*"

"And that he allows his miter to fall so they'll bend to pick it up —" She slapped her thighs. Her laughter might have been a roar if produced by someone less genteel. "— and then, bottoms up!" She folded over, unable to contain her laughter, one guffaw producing another, and still another after a subdued pause.

I stared at her, astonished. "Madame?" Of course her breeding does allow her an occasional display of exuberance.

She forced a sober face — which held for only seconds before another burst of laughter erupted from her, and she shook and shook and shook until Ermenegildo pecked at her hand. With grand composure, she said, "Proceed please, Lady."

Draped in subdued veils, I went to the Pope's palace at the time of the day he walked among his subjects, eagerly wending his way toward those with children. He took me for a supplicant and held out his hand cursorily for me to kiss — an ugly fat hand cluttered with garish jewelry. I pretended to bend to kiss it while whispering, "I know about the polished floors." He granted me an audience at the edge of the giant hall.

"What exactly do you know?" he hissed.

I told him.

"Lies."

At that very moment a group of children appeared, including some young acolytes in their loose frocks, a few girls in their dainty smocks. Instinctively, the Pope dropped his miter. The adorable children bent to retrieve it. The Pope's eyes strained to catch each glimpse allowed him.

When the garish interlude was over, I faced him.

"What do you want for your silence?" the Pontiff asked me.

"That you officiate at my nuptials, that you sanctify my marriage to the Count du Muir." This would give to our controversial marriage — his sister and twin brother were already conspiring against me, spreading filthy lies — what others would see as an unassailable acceptance by the Holy Church.

He acquiesced. Should I have considered that he had done so too quickly? I was too elated to weigh that then, looking ahead to my life with the Count, long seasons in the country, a hint of the bliss I had already experienced with him in the château I would later occupy without him. Yes, and we would raise our children away from turbulence.

"I can readily see why he would proceed to officiate in your marriage, Lady, but why do you suspect he was involved in the murder in the Cathedral?"

"In the Cathedral, I saw him dodge *before* the bullet intended for me at the altar was fired," I explained. "Alix and Irena have strong connections to the Church, and there's great wealth they must believe I care about." I touched my nuptial band; it was treasure enough, the diamond I wore like a tear on my finger. "Now, in the vile versions of our love and courtship that are being hastily printed in installments — and there's already one —" I wanted to insinuate this slowly, knowing that eventually I would have to expose her to it.

"Oh, yes, I've heard."

Madame's words surprised me, only at first. Naturally she would know of the existence of the libelous "Account." Even in the country, who could avoid knowledge of anything so outrageous? Surely one of her servants would have heard of it, whispered about it. "In it, they're claiming I seduced him in devious ways —" I wanted to prepare her for its contents.

"We must deal with it all, since it's bound to come up at interviews," she accepted easily, "and it affirms our need to proceed as quickly as possible, without any compromise to the thoroughness of our presentation." She used her most serious tone as she followed her own advice to proceed: "At interviews, we must never seem to be only substituting other conclusions. Motivation is what has most often been altered to entrench the blame we seek to correct. True motives reveal true culprits."

The true culprits revealed! I tasted the delicious words silently.

"So, now, Lady, let's return to Herod's palace — and the dance of sev —"

I waited, readying a frown.

To erase the moment that had almost occurred, she poured herself more tea, but her cup was full and it spilled, a fact she would have ignored had Ermenegildo not brought her a towel with his beak.

Through all that, Madame retained her dignity.

Restored last night with submerged details revealed, my memories returned easily to Herod's palace:

Guards led the naked enchained Baptist to the despicable rulers. Herodias, my mother, and Herod, her husband, sat like decorated puppets on their throne, which was draped with heavy, opulent fabrics embedded with garish stones, a throne propped on golden predatory claws. The palace, all marble and garish-colored glass, rose out of the desert like a cheaply ostentatious diamond. It was beautiful only on clear nights when it inhaled the subtle shades of evening.

It was on such a night that I first learned of the raging preacher. A distant cursing voice had wakened me. I could not hear words, but heard, beyond his anger, a resonant voice that sang passionately. Clothed only in the humid moisture of that hot night, I looked out my window. I saw him, alone in the desert, his exposed body bathed in the glow of a blue moon. The tilt of his head indicated he was gazing above me. At what? At whom? I ran silently up the steps, to locate the object of his attention. Herodias leaned against a window. As she listened to the Baptist's curses denouncing her and Herod for their depravity, their despotism toward their subjects, Herodias's hands probed under her robe, arousing herself to the rhythm of the Saint's curses, her hands rubbing between her thighs in frenzied movements. Groaning, her eyes scorched with lust, she pushed her fingers into —

"Lady —"

— herself; exploring herself in circles, sudden jabs, her robe now raised over her bared thighs, the perspiration of her desire glistening in the blue moonlight —

"Lady!"

"Madame?"

"We were exploring motivations."

"I am." My memories glided past her interruption.

Herodias demanded that Herod arrest the wandering preacher: "The Baptist must be silenced. He's a madman, spawning a generation of messianic egalitarians who will bring us down unless he's arrested — and brought to us."

"If it amuses you," Herod yawned.

I knew it was not her fury at his curses but her lust that Herodias longed to satisfy.

I had come to know my monstrous mother well during long lessons when she coached me in seductiveness, lessons performed only in pantomime so I would remain a virgin — a tool she would use. I knew her lust for the Baptist was aroused not only by his beauty but what defined it for her: his virginity. Deprived of his saintly purity, he would be just another of the discarded objects of her lust. I knew, too, that her unique desire for him was too powerful for her to want to part with it. She would seek to possess him and his purity, forever. How? There was only one way: by being the first — and only one — to have him. To assure that, she would have him slain after her seduction of him. But did she truly believe that she — beautiful though she was — could entice the holy man into breaking his powerful vows of chastity? And how would she coax Herod, a superstitious man, to allow the killing of a man purported to be a saint?

I, too, had fallen under the Baptist's spell! I, too, longed for him. But I longed to save him, his life — *and* his passionate purity — to assure he would always remain what he was, and alive. I had to learn exactly how Herodias intended her deadly violation.

On the day the Baptist was to be captured, Herodias announced to me: "Today you will perform the dance I've taught you, the dance of seven veils — and be barefoot; wear only *this* on one toe." She located a ruby ring on my tiny foot. Together, the veils slashed my body with colors. Certainly all this was part of her cunning.

For long, she had used me to tantalize Herod, who was impotent. She would assure that, at certain times, I would be within his sight, so that a brief breeze lured by the curve of my hips would whip about me, hugging my body. I — and Herodias — could hear Herod's moans of frustrated passion, as he poked at his wasted groin. With a smile etched by evil, Herodias recorded each rancid glance. By increasing the enticement, she connived to control him.

Herodias located me carefully at the mouth of a corridor, where shadows would play on me as the Baptist was dragged past. When he saw me, he stopped, the clanging of his chains proclaiming his daring action, his awe at the sight of me. His intense eyes grazed my body — yes, with desire. I detected the assertive flush of it in his groin. He turned away, his eyes closing — tightly — a shield to temptation.

Herodias had captured the interlude she had arranged. She would use me to possess the Baptist, but how? I must discover that. My longing for him and my longing to save him became one.

55

His struggling body bright with sweat that was feverishly licked by tongues of fire from the torches in the palace, the Baptist stood before Herodias. Away from me, he could allow his eyes to open. They did, in challenge to his captors. Herodias's purple lips received a lush grape that a naked boy fed her, one of several young men she recruited when she roamed the poorest sections of the kingdom. As she stared at John, her lips remained opened, her eyes hollowed by lust. She dismissed the boy beside her.

She said to Herod: "I propose a performance such as you've never imagined, a performance capable of arousing" — she held the promise, allowing it to resonate — "even you." Her eyes gazed, hypnotized at the dormant power between the Baptist's thighs.

"Lady —"

"Yes?"

I had of course noticed that during my recollection of the intrigue in the palace of Herod, Madame had begun to study the gems on her fingers. That often signaled that she would apply even closer scrutiny to a portion of my memories: "How do you account for the fact that in telling the truth about Salome, you're turning Herodias into a blamed woman?"

"Because she *was* to blame, she *and* Herod." I spoke with a firm voice. "I don't speak for women *justly* blamed; I speak only for the *unjustly* blamed, not those who *were* to blame. Keep this in mind, Madame — and I shall emphasize it at interviews — it is *unjustly* blamed women who are remembered and excoriated, and called 'whores.'" Despite my inclination toward restraint, I had allowed a wave of fervor into my declamation.

"Lady," Madame said, "may I congratulate you?"

"Yes." I continued: "Time was narrowing. I must discover how to save John within my dance of —"

"— *seven* veils," Madame startled me by interjecting.

"Six."

"Seven. You yourself just said it earlier, that there would be seven veils. I let that pass without comment at the time, simply accepting your correction. But now that you've gone back to —"

"There were *six*, Madame!"

"Lady, everyone knows —"

"Madame! I shall not continue against such intransigence!"

"Then go to" — she drank her tea, most daintily — "go to wherever you want your memories to travel next. Go ahead."

"I shall travel to —" How was it possible I had not noticed the heavy gathering of clouds that now swept away the light, so that for disoriented moments I thought it was night? "I shall travel to the Black Sea," I said.

"Where?"

"To the Black Sea. When I fled with Jason."

"Medea?" Madame placed one palm flatly on the table. "You insist, then, that your memories include *her?*"

"I must tell the story of the killing of my children," I said firmly.

Madame rearranged our teacups. She took a cake when there was already one on her plate. She dropped her napkin and replaced it by her side. She flattened her hand on the table again. She pulled so hard at one of her earrings — diamonds surrounding a ruby — that she winced but then pulled on the other. She burrowed her lowered head into her chest. She touched her necklace, studied its pendant, an opal, released it. She held her breath for moments, as if deliberating whether or not ever to release it. She opened her mouth.

What was coming?

Ermenegildo sat up, perplexed.

Madame coughed. She mumbled — sounds.

"What is disturbing you?"

She sat forward in her chair. "Just this," she said. "We must make sure we end up in corrected history and not pursued by the Enquirer."

VI

"THE WHAT?"

"The Enquirer."

"Who, Madame, is the Enquirer?" A terrible Inquisitor, rounding up souls to face brutal interrogators, an Inquisition raging in the City to stifle the growing unrest among the violated, some of whom are now spilling into the country?

Biting on the by now desolate tea cake that she had finally allowed to remain on her plate, Madame Bernice said: "Forgive me, Lady. I forget you're not attuned to certain matters you call mystic, and others call visions, but which I shall simply call terrifying hints of possibilities — Cassandra would readily understand this. Sometimes such matters insinuate themselves into my nightmares."

I had always imagined her sleeping soundly. "You're not making sense, Madame." Ermenegildo shook his head in agreement. "First you were talking about an — *the* — Enquirer, and now you're talking about nightmares."

"The same thing," Madame asserted, and went on: "In one such nightmare — last night? — I foresaw . . . I'm sorry the word has caused you to frown, Lady, but I can think of no other. I foresaw —" Madame's shudder caused her to stop.

"— a terrifying Inquisitor pursuing me, because of conspiracies involving the murder in the Grand Cathedral?" I finished for her.

"Exactly — and then there's that . . . other woman you insist on . . . that woman, that —"

"Medea." I understood instantly.

"Surely you'll admit, Lady, that she does produce a strong response in many — even an aversion?"

I was aware of a forlorn, soundless cry . . . I would say nothing that would entrench Madame's assertion. "Perhaps what you . . . perceived" — I had chosen that word with care — "was the possibility that Irena or Alix or the Pope may have hired a spy, a professional Inquisitor?"

"Yes! Religious, political inquisitors are easily hired . . . I didn't mean to alarm you with the full implications of such a pursuit. That's why I floundered."

It was the exalted title and the way she had pronounced it with such terror — *the* Enquirer — and in connection with my life as Medea — that had taken me aback. Now I understood: She had become unsettled by the prospect of too much controversy should news of our interviews leak out. She might even have introduced the matter as a ploy to keep in abeyance the life that disturbed her. I inhaled to add force to my assertion, but my words came out quietly: "I *was* Medea, I know her essence well, and I *will* tell that life."

That occurred during our fourth meeting for tea. Yes, our fourth. The matter of an Inquisitor in pursuit of us, and Madame's overt resistance to my life as Medea, had been introduced yesterday.

It's difficult to believe Madame and I had met only four times for tea. Sometimes it seems we have met much more often. At those times, I even wonder how long I've been in the country. Days — a week, weeks? Longer! Yet I fled the City immediately after the murder of the Count.

There's this to consider in accounting for the occasional inexactitude of my perceptions: Each meeting with Madame has been intense, and we've roamed through centuries together. Our discussions have assumed a continuity of their own, the subject of them lingering in my mind, extending into my quarters, where, later, I invite memories; and, then, time surrenders its boundaries — the time of day, night, dusk, dawn, even the season. Still, it seems I have been in isolation so much longer. Until, of course, I met Madame Bernice.

Only three teas ago?

There are moments when I feel that I have known her all my life, through all my lives; that she has always been guiding me.

At the beginning of our dissent yesterday, she and I agreed to end our tea and meet earlier today than on previous days, since we have so much to rehearse before interviews.

Heavy fog had thickened the darkness as I walked back to my château. My lantern cast only a pale glow as the candle dimmed. Night erased my hooded shadow within a darkness that followed me past my gates, into my château echoing with loss, and up into my quarters, this time to sleep, only to sleep. I did not invite the invisible audience I previously welcomed into my quarters to rehearse with, as Madame continued to encourage. No, tonight I slept, deep sleep without memories.

Morning!

The day had glimmered like Madame Bernice's jewelry. From my window, I thrilled to the spectacle of newly blooming silk-floss trees, dark green leaves parted by lavender-pink flowers that burst open into yellow stars.

But now, at tea, our discussion about my life as Medea — a subject I made sure to continue immediately — threatened to compromise the bright mood of the day.

"We'll be in trouble," Madame said, "if you claim that your essence knew *her* essence!"

"I remember the blood at my feet, I —"

"*That* was a dream!"

I looked at her, darkly. "Then you've lied to me," I said. "You choose what is memory and what are dreams. You lied."

Madame Bernice faced me. Within the silence that followed, I held my accusation by staring unblinking at her. As she retained her gaze just as steadily on me, I felt a sense of terror, yes, terror, as if I were suddenly adrift in — what? — adrift in *nothing*. I heard my voice — in total control, wasn't it? — speaking words I wanted to withdraw the moment they formed: "Madame, *have* you been lying to me?"

Why didn't she answer me!

Although during her long silence, which was still extending, I longed to withdraw my question, I was not frantic. *I was not frantic!* I said calmly: "When we met and you saw me crying —"

I'm not sure whether I spoke more words then, or, if I did not, what I had intended to say, because I was startled by the fact — was it possible? — that it was night. How had it come so quickly? — so quickly that it seemed to have originated in my mind. Had I dozed, was I now dreaming?

"Oh, Lady, how could you distrust me?" Madame's emphatic words asserted that I *was* awake. "It was that very question that I was asking myself during my long silence: How could you doubt me?"

How *could* I have doubted her? Had I? No, this moment revised all the ones that had preceded it. Of course it was not night. The sky was blue, and it was afternoon. My memories had become so real that past skies had become present skies. I was now sure that during a momentary disorientation I had been remembering the sky over the Black Sea.

"Lady, I only wish that I *had* disbelieved you, because the task in which I immediately joined you is daunting. What I said to you from the memorable moment that we met is so. What reason would I have to lie to you? I'm committed to our mutual goal — may I say that it has become mutual by now?"

I was only too glad to nod.

"Of course, your essence knew Medea — and just as vividly as you remember. You're right that truth becomes a lie by editing and selection. Now let's drink our tea. It's the brew we both enjoyed so the first time, remember? I asked my cook to prepare these heavenly delights again."

Brightened by the release of the earlier tension, Ermenegildo strained to peer into the silver platter, as if selecting his pastry; Madame discreetly set it aside for him.

"Still," Madame continued, very carefully, "might we compromise and say that your eternal essence as a blamed woman only *peered* into Medea's soul —?"

Oh, she was relentless!

"— and for a moment, only a moment, lingered — and then fled just at the point when she —?"

"I *lived* through the depth of her despair," I said — and those words opened the wound that was carved by love and desire from the very beginning, and deepened —

— on the waters of the Hellespont when I sailed with Jason, laughing with him, loving him. I was beautiful the way only a woman of tragic destiny is beautiful, with despair. My eyes were savage — like daggers, they said, like green daggers cutting across a swarthy complexion, dark gold in the sun, dark brown in moonlight. Jason and I made love on the Golden Fleece that he had searched for in my country, where the precious hide hung in a sacred grove guarded fiercely. I made the treasure his — ours! — through cruel, bloody sacrifices.

To Jason and to the violence of the sea, I bared my breasts, dark lush fruit. His hands clasped them, and I lowered them to his starved mouth. He licked them until they gleamed with his saliva. "I desire you, my savage beautiful Medea, I love you, my barbarian wife, promise you'll stay as you are, always, promise!" The sea whirled about us and heard my oath: "I vow it, forever!"

"And I'll desire and love you, forever, Medea, forever," Jason breathed.

Waves of night grappled with the sea and thrust his words back in a roar.

Under tossing sails of his triumphant ship, my dark body under his fair body, his fair body under my dark body, I taught him to be a barbarian. He probed and entered every orifice in me, and I explored his. No part of my naked body was left untouched by his tongue, nor any part of his by mine. His mouth between my legs sought eagerly to locate the exact origin of my moist desire, and found it, as my lips embraced his arousal, which I buried into my throat.

I taught him to remain in me for a length of time he had not dreamt possible. I opened my legs, coaxing his naked hips higher. I spread my thighs wider so he could enter me deeper. Still, I ground against him, demanding even deeper probing. I clasped my legs about him, locking him in me, unmoving, keeping him at that height, within that deepest depth. Fused, we rode waves of sensation, reached what was the highest until I unclasped my legs for only a moment so that we rose on another crest, just as another overtook it and peaked, surpassed itself, and still there was another.

I flung my head back to the night, and pulled away from him, only so that the moist tip of his arousal kissed the opening at my legs, and then I slid down, back to the deepest depth we had located, and he filled me and I filled him, joined so close that it was as if *his* body was brown, mine fair, his fair, mine brown, both glowing with the mutual sweat of our passion as we reached crest after crest, mine meeting his, challenging his to rise higher, his meeting my challenge, which I challenged again, and we spilled bursts of love and desire as turbulent waves of the sea swept over our bodies and I shouted his vow that was now mine, that was now ours:

"Forever!"

I must have been speaking some of these memories aloud, at tea with Madame Bernice, because I had begun to notice her trying to get my attention by emitting a few, at first delicate, coughs, coughs that increased aggressively. Until then, I had taken her subdued sounds to be a reaction to a chill in the air during this seasonless season.

"Madame?"

"Lady. I didn't mean to interrupt your vivid, indeed *graphic*, recollections —"

She had, of course.

"— I simply remembered something I wanted to be sure not to

forget — and might if I became even slightly more overwhelmed by your *very graphic* memories." She paused — Madame Bernice is very attentive to the pauses necessary to effectively shift a subject. "Now!" Her peremptory word brought back the afternoon entirely. "We must assume that our vast undertaking and our intention to reveal everything at interviews will become increasingly known to hostile elements. I have a strong feeling that there is already afoot a powerful attempt to keep interviews from occurring."

"What form do you fore —" I rejected that word. "What form do you suppose that ambush might take?"

To my distress, Madame closed her eyes, pressed her hands at her temples as if preparing deepest concentration. When I reared back from the possibility that she might, before my very eyes, proceed to fall into a mystic trance, she laughed aloud. "That isn't how it's done, Lady, except by charlatans."

I'm becoming very fond of Madame's humor and surprises.

She leaned toward me, as if even her whispered words might be overheard. "I'm not sure how. We must be constantly alert to any development. There are enormous stakes involved, powerful forces and factions — and they *are* powerful —"

"— the Count du Muir's brother, their sister Irena, the Pope, a spy, perhaps even the man in the château on the hill —" I reiterated, feeling a compulsion to lessen the gravity of Madame's admonition by donating identities to it and omitting the ominous Enquirer, the possible hired Inquisitor.

"We must keep in mind how strongly our revelations threaten certain parties, a threat to centuries of unjust blame. Once we question those, other entrenched lies may be exposed. A whole structure of deceit may be revealed." Madame stopped to add gravity. "It's possible that whatever is being planned as ambush may occur when we're not together; so we must be in constant touch. I've devised a plan. Now listen closely, Lady:

"Since the largest window in your chambers faces mine across the way, if anything untoward occurs at night, stand there with a candle and move it up and down and I'll respond. I shall do the same. In the daytime, when we're not together at tea, we'll use reflections on mirrors and on windowpanes." She went on to fashion an ingenious alphabet of messages, short and long flashes, slow and fast, up, down, across.

Did she know more than she was telling me? Did she have knowledge of definite developments of danger? Was that the real reason why the matter of the enquiring Inquisitor had come up? Was she shielding me, not wanting to alarm me during this crucial period of rehearsals? Her determination that we must be in touch at all times made me even more aware of her commitment to our goal — and of the import and dangers of our journey — but I was not afraid.

With typical aplomb, she shifted our discussion — away from impending peril, away from my life as Medea: "Now have your tea and tell me, Lady, please — I've waited quite long — the truth about the War in Heaven." Her eyes closed, to visualize it all.

Was I up to describing robed priests, plagues, fires, hailstorms, shooting stars, more plagues? No. But how could I refuse her? Her eyes had remained closed. I began: "God adored the angel Lucifer, the most beautiful angel, but He merely tolerated Cassandra."

"Oh, but of *course* she would annoy Him," Madame greeted that with a fond chuckle.

"Lucifer had loved God. But after he and Cassandra and the other rebellious angels soared into spheres and whorls of blue skies beyond God's Heaven —" My voice grew weary.

Madame detected that. "I needed only a hint of it all," she said. "Let's roam another day through the battlefields of Heaven."

I finished my tea. Madame summoned Ermenegildo for the pastry she had reserved for him, mumbling something to him — this is not a judgment, Madame *does* sometimes mumble.

When we part, Madame and I, we are true to our breeding. We exchange formal pleasantries, but we know our ordinary words are asserting our steadfast closeness and trust. We are, after all, conspirators against history.

As I walked onto the road, I shielded my face with my cowl. I do not like the sting of night's coldness on my face. Unbreathing, the candle in my lantern seemed hypnotized by the night. I encountered a cluster of sad wanderers from the City. They must be newly arrived in the country, since they fled from me, unlike the others who now recognize me and most often only retreat into shadows. These wanderers are not violent, only defeated. Even if one of them were prone to attempt an outrage, he would be subdued by the others.

As I neared my château, I saw what I thought was a figure moving toward me out of the darkness, as if a piece of the night itself had been severed, had moved, and now stood there for moments. I held my lantern up, undaunted, like a shield. The dark presence was not there. It had been an impression created by the shadows.

But this was not:

A piece of paper was attached to the grillwork of my gate. I held my lantern to it. I read, written in bold red letters that dripped like blood down the jagged paper:

"Whore! Stop your lies!"

VII

I'M IN MY CHAMBERS. It's night. I stand at the window, facing Madame's château. Should I initiate communication with her now about the warning posted on my gate or shall I wait until tomorrow's tea?

I can see Madame in her quarters. Her head is bowed. Is she praying? I have long inferred that she is, in her own way, a religious woman. She kneels. Is she holding a rosary? I've entertained the notion that at some time in her life she may have taken holy vows. She straightens up now, lifts her head. In exaltation? She's rising. Oh, she was looking for one of her rings, which she had dropped and just found. I see her put it on her finger.

I hold my lantern up, its candle lit. With one hand, I cover its light, uncover it — three flashes. I wait, repeat the sequence. The signal is returned! Madame is alert to the testing of our system of communication. The proof that it works does not relax me. I listen to silence. Oh, I have heard it. It contains unscreamed screams, protests, pleading whispers. I cover my ears.

Still, I hear it, like the insistent wail of a hurt child. Night is so vast. I feel its magnitude. I close my eyes to it and replace that darkly glowering sky with the pure sky of Eden under which I first saw Adam. Oh, Adam, Adam, you're always with me, the first, the most beloved, my lover through eternity. Our love is made even greater by the subsequent lovers I was destined to encounter in each succeeding life in my journey of redemption. As my essence embarks on its newly discovered journey, it is locked to you from the beginning of time, forever.

Within my quarters, populated only by my memories of past lives, sounds assume a *presence*. I hear — or do I *feel*? — footsteps within that void of sound. They stop. I have had today's meals, always left outside by my most trusted servant. I keep the doors of my quarters locked, of course. They will be triumphantly opened when Madame Bernice agrees that we have reached the exact time to grant interviews. A muffled, quick movement outside my door.

I have a gun, the gun Irena planted in my hand. The gun is always near me in my chambers. When I sit on a chair, I place it next to me. When I lie in bed, I locate it beside me. When I walk about the room, I keep relocating it. I will use it if necessary.

Has whoever left the messages at the gate of my château bribed the suspicious maid to let him in and is he — or she — they! — now leaving further warnings outside my quarters? Earlier, there was a clanging at the gates.

There it is again!

I get my gun, I listen closely at the door.

Nothing.

I breathe in relief. I secure the lock, the key always in place should I have to escape — From — To — Within the thick silence, I hear the lock click as loudly as the clanging gates of a prison. I return the gun to its place.

I must — I must — I must —

A scream!

It invades my rooms!

I wait for its echo. None. Did it occur? I realize this with relief: I had closed my eyes, and in that moment I dreamt — yes, that had been a dream — I dreamt that a woman screamed. Her scream has rendered me fully awake, auguring a sleepless night.

I shall follow Madame's instructions and continue to rehearse with you, those I have allowed into my quarters in preparation for interviews, when I shall replace lies with truth, and redefine the word "whore," and reveal that in me lodges the essence of every fallen woman unjustly blamed, whom I shall redeem —

I hear your sounds of cynicism. Why are you, whom I've graciously invited in, so skeptical, so immediately? I shall disarm you more slowly.

There was a flower that grew only in Eden, a flower so glorious it did not need the decoration of leaves —

I do not have to rehearse that memory. It's firm in my mind. But that was a start. I hope that you may become my ally, at least some of you, in my journey of redemption.

I shall convince you of my commitment to truth by withholding nothing, no matter how painful. How shall I do so immediately? Yes! In an even voice, I shall read aloud more of the gross lies that attempt to taint my love for the Count du Muir, and his for me. I reach for the sullying sheets of the "First Installment" of this outrage:

The Writer of this *True Account* — aware that the Reader (confronted with this Chronicle of assaults on everything deemed honorable) may have chosen a respite before embarking further on this necessary exposure of corruption — here reminds that the Whore had intercepted the Noble Count's carriage (on its way from a gala at the opera) by pretending that she was a lady pursued by an attacker with a knife, actually her conspirator, the Reverend Pimp.

When the Count opened the door, he was overwhelmed by pity for the woman sobbing out a litany of false abuse at the hands of men. A kind soul, as kind as he was handsome, as handsome as he was rich, the Count attempted to soothe her, continuing to cover her nudity with his cape while she slyly persisted in causing it to slip off her salacious flesh, exposed for his uninitiated eyes. (The interior of coaches was not foreign to her; she had often sold her services in the same setting.)

Looking out the window to ascertain that the "man with the knife" was not still in pursuit and having assured that he was not, the noble Count thoughtfully drew the curtains of the coach, taking into consideration that co-conspirators might peer in.

As if to assuage her (pretended) fright, the Whore clutched the Count's hand and quickly transferred it onto her naked lap. Taking advantage of his kindly pat (intended to reassure her that she was safe — he was not aware where his hand had been moved), the Whore opened her legs so that his hand (according to the rules of gravity rather than to those of morality) fell lower, locating a moisture he could not identify. He sought to find its origin. Was it the distraught woman's tears? (Remember he was a virgin.)

The opportunistic Whore added her own delving finger to his while with her other hand she held one of her delicious breasts (that is how some, who must have tasted them, saw them) to her own mouth, licked the nipple, and presented the corrupt offering to the Noble Count, who responded touchingly to memories of his happy childhood and of his little lips nurturing on his wet nurse's plenitude.

A sharp jerk of the coach toppled him to his knees before the wily Whore, who seized *that* opportunity to entrap his face there, clenching her thighs, rendering him helpless for so long that his mouth grew dry and he had to wet his lips urgently with his tongue, which she maneuvered expertly into her desire-moistened parting.

Pretending to faint, the Whore swayed her head over the Count's lap, her mouth availing itself of yet another opportunity, which confounded the Count into believing that the distressed woman was so desperately gasping for air that she had swallowed him into her mouth. By forcing his hands to clasp her breasts, she further confused him by again hatefully arousing (she knew no limits) the sweet memory of his nurturing wet nurse.

Not yet comprehending her cunning (the Writer must here inform the Reader that in his youth the Count had prepared for Holy Vows), the mortified Count eased her up, to breathe her back to consciousness. Encouraged by the fact that she had strength enough to grope at him as if for support, he allowed her onto his lap.

At that moment, the coach entered the route the Whore had dictated, having maintained that it would lead her to the safety of her quarters. The cobbled street caused the coach and its occupants to move up and down, up and down. That, and the fact that the Whore continued to clutch him in her hand, which was lubricated with her odious juices, resulted, for the Count, in a biological inevitability, a stiffening, no matter how powerfully resisted.

The shrewd Whore knew this street well; she had walked it often. In seconds the coach would pass an especially prominent hump on the street. At that exact moment, she spread her thighs over the Count's lap and enlisted the sudden upward thrust of the coach as her noxious ally in forcing the hapless Count into her — as the coach rolled up and down, up and down over the cobblestones.

Do you believe now that I shall withhold nothing? I've exposed lies to reveal the truth, which is this: On that night travestied in these pages a madman was in pursuit of me with a knife. He had come close enough to slash my clothes. The Count du Muir ordered his coach to stop and he opened its doors to me. He covered my trembling body with his cape, which I accepted. In his mansion later, he sheltered me as I wept, and our love began.

That innocently?

So you've joined fully in rehearsals. Must your tone be harsh, sarcastic? I shall discuss with Madame how to deal with hostility and rudeness.

But I would do that later, I decided as Madame and I sipped our tea that afternoon. Madame had just informed me that today's brew had arrived this morning "from the islands; we need not fear disappointment."

We sat on her veranda — the opposite side from the one we usually occupy because, earlier today, workmen had repaired a portion of the marble design affected by a recent temblor I was fortunate enough to have missed. Madame is terrified of such temblors. The slightest quivering, of whatever origin, will cause her to freeze for moments, her hands grasping whatever is firm and nearest her. At such moments, Ermenegildo rushes over to her. I have not yet determined whether he, too, is terrified of the earth's shifts or whether he wants to lend her his support. Today, Madame had let the workers leave early, in deference to the private nature of our conversation.

Ermenegildo was peering at our tea setting, as if to anticipate his treat of today's starry cakes on the silver plate. His endearing comb feather was teased by a breeze as he moved away, to rest in expectation of sweet delights to come.

I told Madame immediately about the note left on my gate.

It was as if my startling news had not surprised her. Because she expected the unexpected? Was she trying to restrain her reactions, not to alarm me unduly? Oh, she had been considering the matter. "You must not be unnerved, Lady. Expect more, even harsher."

This was the appropriate moment I had been waiting for: I brought out from within the folds of my cowl what I had carried with me today: the "First Installment" of the accusatory "Account" Madame had indicated having only heard about. She must know exactly what we're pitted against. To my astonishment, she was not at all surprised to see the pages. She glanced at the title, and then she laid the "Installment" on the table, *as if she had expected it!* I still have difficulty accepting Madame's uncanny intuitions. Or is it possible that she's already read these pages? Her next words dispelled — did they? — that notion: "I shall read it tonight," she said, and continued as if there had been no such intervening interlude:

"If only we had an ally in the City, to discover exactly what's planned —"

"We have an ally!" It occurred to me only then. "The Contessa, the Count's mother." Just the memory of the gentlewoman soothed me.

"Ah, yes, the lady in mourning at the Cathedral, who blessed you after the murder in the Grand Cathedral."

I told Madame about my first meeting with the Contessa: "Soon

70

after my affair with the Count du Muir commenced, she drove her coach to my apartment in the City."

Ordinarily I would not have granted the odd audience. A coachman had come to my quarters to solicit a meeting, in her carriage; he told me the Contessa felt it necessary not to be recognized. "I am not used to being received in darkened coaches!" I reacted. With noted courtesy he assured me that there was no insult in this proposal. I accepted what I anticipated would be a confrontation about her son, my beloved.

I entered the darkened coach.

"My dear, I am here to tell you," the Contessa said quickly, "that the whole City knows of your affair with . . ." It was at this moment that from the splendid comb crowning her head she removed her shawl — she called it a *mantilla,* in the Spanish style — and revealed herself to be a handsome woman of angular features. Forming a perfect peak above her forehead, her long dark hair was pulled back to display her aristocratic cheekbones. ". . . that the whole City knows of your affair with my beloved son, and of your impending marriage," she finished.

I bristled: "Your Ladyship, I believe you mean they know of our *love.*"

She touched me with her gloved hand, an assuring gesture. "Every effort is being made to thwart your marriage, lies are being spread about you. A very high prelate may be involved in the conspiracy against you." She sustained those dangerous words on a long sad sigh. She went on to tell me that, through a source close to her — one who might be in touch with me subsequently — she had learned that a "high prelate" had a predilection for viewing the reflected bottoms of children. "Of course, I'm pained to confess that I speak about the Pope." She made a sign of the cross with the black rosary she always carried about her neck. She kissed the silver crucifix.

I could tell she had become instantly fond of me. "That information might become useful in warding off danger to you during your approaching wedding to my son. Danger from the Pope and" — her pain was visible even in the muted light within her coach — "from the woman I hesitate to call my daughter, Irena. She may already have poisoned Alix against you, as she has against me."

I did not feel it appropriate to tell her that Alix was already poisoned against me. I had spurned his rude advances at some social function or other when my beloved was briefly occupied with a visiting ambassador. "But my brother and I are identical, except for our coloring," Alix had protested drunkenly in the salon. "And except for your souls," I had dispatched him.

In her carriage, the Contessa continued: "I have a weak heart, my dear, and so I cannot stay longer. I have come to warn you because once I was —" She faltered.

"— in love with a man whom you were thwarted from marrying." I announced what her grieved expression told me.

She nodded, adjusting her *mantilla*. "He was forced into exile for a year, but our love would not die. He returned, although" — she stifled a gasp — "although the ultimate closeness of that last time was thwarted." She reached into the folds of her skirt and kissed a dried rose, crushed within the pages of her missal. "He gave me this, the man I shall always love." She said what I had already inferred.

She drew the *mantilla* over her face, ending our close interlude. I stepped out of the coach. I touched my lips to her hand, in gratitude for her allegiance.

She reached out urgently to me, apparently having decided only then to tell me more. In a rushed whisper she spoke these strange words: "Irena is dangerous because she believes she knows about the tulips —"

"The tulips?"

"Yes!"

"Tulips?" Madame Bernice queried now in her garden.

"Yes, Madame," I assured her, "that is what the Contessa said to me, that evening in her coach, and then —"

Before I could question her further, her coach disappeared along the street and into the mist of night.

It was the information from the gracious Contessa about the Pope — information confirmed by a gracious nun, a friend of the Count's — that allowed me to "coax" the Pope to perform my nuptials. How better to keep the duplicitous prelate in sight than to force him to preside over our wedding in the Cathedral? Too, his presence near us would render him vulnerable to whatever Irena and Alix might attempt at the altar. He would be forced to caution any rash act. I had no way of knowing that the seating plan, which I had myself devised, had been intercepted by a disloyal page and that Alix and Irena were assigned a place in the first pew, making a closer range possible, which would allow the Pope to squirm away at the murderous time.

"An ally, indeed," Madame greeted the Contessa. "Tell me, Lady, if you know, was her lover —?"

"Murdered, too, like mine," I said. Oh, I had read it in the gracious lady's voice that night.

Madame Bernice lowered her head in reverence to the Contessa's loss, and mine. "There's a curious riddle there —"

"— about . . . tulips." The mystery deepened on being spoken.

Carriage wheels ground harshly on the road. I stood. Madame reached for her opera glasses. "A black coach!" she cried. Aware of the intrusive noise, Ermenegildo raised his head in the direction of the road. Then he aimed his beak assertively toward my château.

The coach was dashing there. I said urgently, "I must go back immediately, to catch whoever placed those mangled flowers and that warning on my gate!" I was sure that carriage would yield the answer.

"No!" Madame tried to restrain me. "It's dangerous for you to go alone!" I could tell by the rustling of her taffeta skirt that she was rushing after me, to accompany me, but as agile as she is, she had to slow her pace. I heard her harsh breathing. "Lady! Lady!" she called.

I ran across the lawn, past the avenues of Madame's garden, onto the road, along it, faster, faster, past trees that seemed themselves to be moving while I, in my urgency, stood still, carried along, faster, faster, by sheer determination. I knew that I was running because I could see my cowl trailing behind me. I carried it in my hands — not having had the time to cloak myself with it although evening was encroaching with a chilly sigh.

I reached my gate.

A carriage waited there, facing me, like a hearse. Its black horses were motionless. Against the faint light, the coachman was a dark blotch. I walked toward the carriage. There was an eternal moment during which I was sure someone was about to emerge from the darkened coach.

The crack of a whip!

The horses spun about, and the carriage sped back along the road it had traveled. I was able to see only smears against the back window. A passenger. Two?

After the sound of the wheels had faded, I waved toward Madame's château. I knew she would be straining to keep me in sight with her glasses. She would know that the carriage had fled, since it would have to pass her château. Seeing me waving at her, she would know that I was out of danger. I waited until she had signaled back.

I faced my gate. Had I been too late, had something been left there? Another mysterious message? No, nothing. I breathed again. I opened the gate. Something interfered. A basket. I approached it.

On a red blanket within the basket, a cat fed two tiny creatures she had just given birth to, one white, the other dark. She looked up at me. I leaned closer:

Her two children were dead. What I had thought was a red blanket was their blood.

I rushed into my quarters.

How much time has passed? Within the foggy night, I detect the forlorn mewling of the abandoned cat, mourning the death of her children —

Forgive me if I choose now to lie down, I'm tired, forgive me if I close my eyes, I'm tired, I'm drifting, I'm tired, I'm drifting . . . not into sleep . . . into my memories . . . drifting to Corinth, with Jason —

No, no, not now. No!

— drifting to Greece, with Jason . . . no, no . . . away . . . drifting —

— onto the shore of the River Jordan.

VIII

THE SUN FLOATED MESMERIZED over the horizon, illumining the desert in yellow fog. Along the bank of the River and on hills nearby, a throng gathered to be baptized by John the Baptist.

He was much younger than I had anticipated, a young man of imposing presence. Surely he knew it was not only his commanding words but his almost naked body — he wore only a brief hair shirt softened by age — that was luring the crowds to the River.

I, Magdalene, fifteen years old, had wandered amid urgent crowds making their way to the baptisms. I heard awed murmurs about miracles attributed to the blessings of the holy man at the River. The sadness in my life urged me to follow the crowd. Already, I conceived only of a future of despondency on the streets. I remembered no father, no mother. I tried to steal before I sold my body, but often I did not succeed.

"Separate yourselves from the generation of vipers, repent through baptism, receive the blessings of the Lord, whom I shall serve and soon identify," the Baptist shouted.

The blue-veiled silhouette of a woman, so beautiful that sighs and gasps pursued her, appeared on the rim of the palm-thatched hill. She seemed encased in crystal, separated invisibly from everyone else. Firmly, she held the hand of a young man with her. That was Mary with her son, Jesus.

He was sixteen, a year older than I. He was so glorious that it seemed the sun provided a special light to display the perfect highlights of his sculpted face, the lines of his slender muscular body. He possessed a reckless beauty he seemed unaware of as he walked with the woman toward the River, at times still in the awkward gait of a boy. A strand of his hair, which touched his wide shoulders, insisted on falling over one eye. He would abandon it there for moments, then reject it with a toss of his head. His tunic, in collusion with the moisture of his body on this hot day, displayed the outline of his loincloth, white, in contrast with his sun-bronzed flesh that gleamed through in smears.

As he and the woman descended, I saw another young man, determinedly alone, the same age as the young man with the glorious woman. Handsome, with a moody sensuality astonishing for his age — yes, that was Judas — he was ignoring the frenzied crowd by creating, on the side of a hill, an elaborate sculpture out of sand and some water he carried in a pouch. He looked up at the same time that Jesus saw him. Judas tilted his head at Jesus, who answered back. Each had detected in the other, in that brief exchange a signal of . . . I would discover that later.

Jesus pulled away from his mother's tight grip, to join Judas in his sculpting — and to flee from the dramatic ceremony at the edge of the River. Mary's hand restrained him. They marched forward toward the Baptist.

Blessing the water into which he submerged those who came kneeling to him in supplication, John the Baptist would then command them to rise. They gathered at the shoreline to watch others and chant, howl, tremble, moan.

"Lady, I suggest that at interviews you pause to remind that John the Baptist is not the same man with you at Patmos, St. John the Divine," Madame interjected when I told her at tea the next day what I had rehearsed in my chambers last night, the sweet memories that began the journey to sorrow.

When I had arrived, I had been eager for her reaction to the accusations in the "First Installment" of the notorious "Account" I had left with her. She had mentioned nothing. I trust her entirely. She will react at the exact time.

"Since this *is* the same John the Baptist whom you were about to devote yourself to saving from Herodias when you were narrating your life as Salome," Madame had continued, "someone will certainly ask how you were both Magdalene *and* Salome, at the same time. I, of course, know exactly."

I was glad to note that Madame was increasingly composed when she questioned me in preparation for interviews, certain that I would provide unassailable answers. After all, it was she who first gave me the confidence to assert my memories. I was her apt pupil. That did not mean — I hasten to add — that I was becoming a mystic. I said: "I shall make it clear that my essence as blamed woman permits simultaneous lives."

"Splendid."

I listened in terror as the Baptist by the River proclaimed the coming of "the Lord who shall baptize with the Holy Ghost and with fire."

Fire? Why should the Lord whose coming he promised add terrible wrath? I viewed the people surrounding him. Surely misery — they were ragged, hurt, gaunt — had brought them here. *I* had known enough wrath on the streets. I would not linger long.

The Baptist's hand had been about to rise before a kneeling supplicant; it froze. He had seen the glorious woman leading Jesus to him.

With the barest touch, Mary surrendered her son to the Baptist, as if Jesus was a divine offering.

Judas stood and stared toward the River.

Jesus smiled at the Baptist, the smile of a young man still a child, playing a game for adults, although John was hardly older. It was only then that I noticed that a bearded man had accompanied Mary and Jesus. He waited a few feet away from the water, staring forlornly at the young man and his mother. Yes, the bearded man was Joseph, the husband of Mary, the man who wanted to believe he was the father of Jesus.

Mary said to John the Baptist: "This is my beloved son. His name is Jesus. Surely you recognize him."

John studied the radiant youth.

I could not hear Mary's next words clearly, only fragments — ". . . the angel . . . conceived . . . announced . . . Son of . . ." — words spoken only to the young Baptist, who listened, waited — and then he nodded, solemnly.

Nearby, Joseph bowed his head, not in reverence but in sorrow.

The Baptist spoke to Jesus: "Yes, it is you. I have need to be baptized by *you*."

Jesus laughed joyfully. "I'm here for your baptism, preacher."

"I believe, Lady," Madame again interrupted my recollections, "that you have reassigned some words. It was God's voice out of the clouds that introduced the child as 'My beloved son.' I believe it was St. John the Baptist who said to Jesus —"

"I know what others have claimed, Madame," I tried to be patient. "Those events, too, have been changed." I faced that, from time to time, it would be necessary to reiterate my strongest evidence: "I was there. I know the truth."

"Indeed."

Why was John in such awe before Jesus? I wondered that day by the River. What had Mary whispered to him?

The Baptist stripped Jesus to his loincloth — the boy's body was even more beautiful than I had imagined — and he held him in his arms, then submerged him in water. Standing, Jesus bowed his head, but I saw a conspirator's smile on his face. Mary's solemnity — and a sharp tug at his hand — attempted to subdue him.

The Baptist and Jesus emerged from the River, their flesh glistening with water and perspiration. Mary stood before the two, asserting the bond established in those moments. As he tossed his head to dry his hair, Jesus glanced sideways toward Judas, still before the sculpture he had created out of sand. My admiring gaze shifted between the two.

The Baptist had reached over Jesus' head, as if to run his fingers through the careless hair. He stopped his gesture, a spell broken, aware again of the crowds surging into the River for his blessings.

Mary moved away with her child. Joseph followed them, a vague ghost.

Lingering behind as if he had stumbled on a stone, Jesus waved secretly at Judas. I had moved swiftly toward Judas and his sandy sculpture, so both he and Jesus would see me at the same time. Jesus extended his secret wave to me, his hand beckoning at his side. His smile — he lowered his head and looked up briefly — directed Judas to look at me.

He did and smiled, too, he and Jesus sharing their awareness of me. I knew I was desirable — yes, beautiful. My breasts were already fuller than those of most of the women I saw in the marketplace. At night alone — after I had made enough money to sustain me through another day — I would lie naked under a watchful moon that courted every curve of my hips, the dewy —

"Lady," Madame interjected after a series of assertive coughs, "I must make an observation. It does begin to seem to me that you're describing *everyone* as being very, very sensual —"

"I do so *only* when they — we — were, Madame." My tone matched my firm words.

Madame had continued to mumble: "— everyone, *everyone* is very sensual — *and* very beautiful in addition" — she inhaled as if to pronounce her words with greatest emphasis — "and either in a partial state of undress — or quite nude." She rushed on as if that might ease the look of outrage on my face. "I want to make a strong point about the matter. It's possible that interviewers might begin to remark on that, perhaps even become somewhat offended or even" — she sneezed into her embroidered handkerchief — "even aroused."

"And why *not*, Madame!" That's all I said, and I looked quite coolly at her before I resumed my narration of the fateful afternoon by the River Jordan:

The conspiracy of glances and smiles between Jesus and Judas invited me to join them on the hill where Judas had remained.

Jesus broke away from Mary, who called out to him, but he had already rushed past me. "Come on!" We both ran toward Judas. Mary stared after her son until we had disappeared.

Along the glistening bank, Jesus and Judas and I ran laughing. Then Judas fell and Jesus stumbled over him, and I almost stumbled over them. I suspected Judas had only pretended to fall. A lone child like me, he was wily, and this was a trick to invite the closeness of our bodies. The two wrestled on the sand, their bodies tossing and turning so that at times I couldn't tell them apart — except that one was fair, the other dark. They beckoned me to join them, their almost naked bodies glowing from the exuberant exertion of their game.

"Yes, Madame?"

I waited for her to speak after she had called attention to herself with a series of unnatural sounds made on the tea service. "I don't think you'll misunderstand" — she soothed her throat with tiny sips of tea — "what I'm about to suggest. Might you just say that, like the children you were, you merely ran up the hill to play? That is such a charming image, three beautiful healthy children playing by the side of the hill — and fully clothed — while a watchful, caring mother waits for her son and in the near distance a holy man continues to baptize his flock under a clear blue sky."

I was sorry to have to be sharp with Madame Bernice. "Madame, the details are essential to prepare for what is to come."

"What do you mean, what is to come!"

Ermenegildo peered at the table as Madame's tea spilled.

That afternoon on the hill, I watched Jesus and Judas wrestling playfully. I delighted in their beauty, to which I would add mine. I slipped out of my dress, exhibiting myself.

"Lady —"

I enjoyed their stares, Judas's much more knowing, Jesus' surprised, excited. Judas tossed his clothes off carelessly. Slowly, Jesus tentatively began to undo — then fastened, then undid — his loin-cloth, keeping it for seconds before him, finally allowing it to fall. "You're both beautiful," I told Jesus and Judas, and they were, oh, they were. "No!" Jesus protested, and shook his head to affirm his protest — I saw his hair whip across his forehead. "It's *you* who are beautiful," he said, "you and Judas." "No, you and Magdalene," Judas asserted. With delight and excitement, we studied each other's nudity.

Ermenegildo winced when Madame's cup fell from her hand and shattered on the marble.

Jesus and Judas and I embraced like gentle lovers — no, like children not realizing they've embraced like lovers. We lay on the warm sand under sheltering palms, holding on to each other, cherishing and extending this new excitement, the beginning of our love. Judas knelt over me and kissed me on the lips. Jesus closed his eyes, waiting for, accepting, and returning Judas's kiss — and then he passed it back to me.

"How beautiful, Lady, yes, yes, how beautiful," Madame Bernice said too eagerly. "Three children kissing, only kissing, nothing more, just kissing, even if they had removed some of their clothes in the heat of the day —"

"We had removed *all* our clothes, Madame," I emphasized my strictest commitment to truth.

Madame fanned herself, in response, no doubt, to my having evoked the heat of that distant evening, since *this* evening was growing somewhat cool on her veranda. "And that was all that happened, a kiss, a —"

I said quietly, remembering, oh, yes, remembering, "That was all that occurred then, Madame, a playful kiss of children."

On that hill by the River Jordan, I did not know how fervently I would wish later that we could have retained those moments forever, that time when as children we embraced, not knowing that we were protecting each other from destinies whirling and shaping about us, leading us all to that bloody mountain.

A shadow fell upon us.

It was Mary's, a blue apparition when I looked up.

Jesus stood, covering himself. "Mother —"

We all dressed hurriedly. Mary looked only at her son. She touched his shoulders with firm gentleness. "Have you forgotten you have a mission to fulfill?"

"Must I?" he asked.

"Nothing will interfere with it," Mary said.

I heard solemn firmness in her voice, even as she smiled.

Sadly, Jesus looked at me, then at Judas, who sat with me on the sand. Now Mary scrutinized me and Judas, our somewhat disheveled appearance. I tried to conceal the rips in my clothes from an earlier encounter when a man had grabbed at me out of a darkened doorway. I could not have imagined then that Mary and I would become close and that I would come to understand her, and love her.

"Come." She extended her hand to her son. He took it. He looked back once and smiled before they began to walk away.

Then Mary turned to face me and Judas, who was playing, suddenly moody, with some sticks. She said:

"My son has a mission to fulfill." Her words were assertive, no longer whispered. "Today, the Baptist confirmed it."

The whispering with John the Baptist by the River . . .

Judas and I sat silent until the sky grew dark and a field of stars appeared. We tried to banish Mary's strange words by not remarking on them. Then Jesus was back.

I ran to embrace him. Judas tried to conceal his joy — by kneeling in playful awe before him.

"No," Jesus protested seriously, pulling Judas up. Judas drowned his own laughter. Jesus gathered us in his arms. His hands —

"Lady —"

That was all. We fell asleep on the hilltop under the embrace of palms.

I was wakened by the howl of an animal in the desert. Only Judas lay beside me, asleep. I saw Jesus sitting alone on a rock, pondering . . . what?

Adhering to the unspoken contract made that first day between the Baptist and Mary, John traveled beyond the Valley proclaiming the coming of "the Lord." I knew — but neither Judas nor I gave the knowledge words — that the Baptist meant the boy, our friend, whom the beautiful blue lady had brought to the River.

" 'The beautiful blue lady' — that is how Judas and I came to think of Mary," I explained to Madame Bernice that day at tea.

Madame said, "I like that for Mary, a gentleness, a touch of rue, yes, I like that image of the Holy Mother — the beautiful blue lady." She tested the description on Ermenegildo, who responded in apparent approval by resting his head briefly on Madame's lap.

Years passed. I became a woman, and Jesus and Judas were men. The powerful love among us grew. We slept together in the fields, in rooms they occupied, and that I shared but left at night, returning. Oh, there was intense desire among us, a common current in which we all swam. We were aware of it, of course. At times, our hands, as if with a life of their own, would touch, then withdraw. Both Judas and I would have fulfilled that growing desire; but if we had done so only with each other, we would feel we had betrayed Jesus. It was Jesus, troubled, who kept desire in check. Mary was the invisible admonishing presence between us, reminding Jesus of his mission, thwarting any divergence.

By then, we were wandering among idealistic revolutionaries. Jesus and Judas were the most fervently — and youthfully — committed to "overthrowing emperors and tyrants." Oh, how ardently we discussed it all, and zealously plotted to bring it about.

I was too proud to tell them I had no home, that the body I knew they desired, as I desired theirs, with love, I sold to others, often with rage.

A rich merchant refused to pay me. When his wife discovered my presence in his shop, the merchant accused me of being a robber, infiltrating his room, stealing from his wife. They pushed me into the street. "Whore!" they screamed.

"*Whore!*" The word echoed along the streets and alleys.

I stood defiantly before them.

A crowd was upon me. The rabid mob hurled stones at me.

Jesus and Judas, who had been looking for me, had heard the shouts, had followed the encircling mob. "Stop!" I heard Judas command. Another stone hurtled toward me. I crouched, quickly standing, to challenge the jeering crowd. A stone hit my arm. I heard Judas's startling words as he pointed to Jesus beside him: "This is the Prophet whose coming the Baptist has been proclaiming." The crowd only laughed, picked up more stones. "Crush the whore to death!" the cry went up. "Crush the whore, crush the whore!" Soon stones would rain on me, smashing my life.

Jesus stepped forward. Although I recognized him, I was startled. His face was as beautiful, his body as lithe — everything was the same, except for this: There was a new aura about him, a commanding radiance.

The crowd backed away.

"He who has not sinned," Jesus said, and his voice now matched his powerful presence, "hurl your stone." I heard stones dropping to the ground, one by one. Jesus moved next to me and said, "Woman of Magdala, you're saved, sin no more!" Then he whispered in my ear, in the voice I had known and loved from that first encounter, when he and Judas and I had romped on the hill near the river: "Hurry, Magdalene, before they find out what we're up to."

I ran to a sheltered ruin in the City, where I often slept. Jesus and Judas caught up with me, soothing me as I wept in their arms. I was not hurt, only bruised, bruises they tended to with leaves. "Magdalene," Jesus said, "why did you keep this from us? You'll live with us." Soon, we were all three laughing at the ruse they had used to save me from the hungry mob.

"It's all they would understand, it's all we could use to arouse their fear of judgment," Jesus said. "It was Judas's performance that convinced them." He was generous, always generous. "No, it was *yours*," Judas insisted, "you looked . . . so Godly." Yet again that night, Jesus separated himself from me and Judas. He sat alone in the dark.

Our performances, begun that day when the mob had attempted to stone me, continued. We roamed the mean streets of the City, helping those similarly accosted in those violent times. While Jesus played "the Holy Prophet proclaimed by John the Baptist," Judas and I pretended to be strangers supporting his claims. Once I mimed being possessed by "demons."

"I might have been a great actress," I told Madame. The afternoon was waning. The blossoms of jacaranda trees were preparing to glow at twilight.

"Indeed you might have been a very great actress!" Madame agreed. Then she coughed delicately, and added, somewhat wistfully: "But, Lady, beautiful as they are, those trees don't bloom here, in our environs."

I did not realize till then that I had spoken aloud my admiration of the lavender-blossomed trees. "Perhaps the magic of pre-dusk light created the impression?"

Madame stared ahead at gracefully limbed trees beyond her garden. "Why, yes, I believe it does; I, too, might have mistaken them."

"Or perhaps my memories of them in the lost paradise — where they were bountiful, where *all* flowers blossomed — are so vivid that they've infiltrated my waking days' reality?"

Madame brought her opera glasses to her eyes. Ermenegildo stared ahead — and nodded? "Why, Lady, I believe you're right," Madame agreed. "They might indeed be jacarandas — a new addition to our lush countryside."

"Precisely." I resumed:

At times Judas would play a madman, whom Jesus cured "miraculously." We delighted in the eagerness with which the crowds accepted our games, even the chancy time when Judas pretended to be dead, brought to life by Jesus.

Then, without Judas's participation nor mine, Jesus exhorted a crippled old man to walk — and the man did. "He just needed to believe," Jesus answered my amazement.

I was becoming increasingly aware of his power to convince. When he played messianic prophet, his beauty was a magnet and his words grasped the crowd.

There was tension about the City. Unrest, discontent, oppression, poverty, intolerable conditions. With even greater fervor, we joined the City's radicals.

"Only a revolution can save us," Judas said.

Jesus agreed: "God will be on our side because He's just." There was passion in his voice: "Suffering is evil, poverty is evil, absolute power allows both. Freedom is holy."

Gathering larger and larger groups, he began to deliver, at first slowly, then with growing conviction and passion, his first "sermons." Judas and I listened and watched in loving marvel as our beloved mesmerized with his simple messages of justice and freedom — ordinary matters that became extraordinary when he spoke them.

I saw Mary moving toward me through the crowd listening to her son. "Do you and he and Judas —?" Even this close, she sustained the impression I had first had of her from a distance, of a blue apparition. She had deliberately not finished her question.

"We love each other, yes."

"But to court — whatever you're courting! — with a man who has a holy mission, Magdalene? — a destined mission." Mary had kept her voice so subdued in response to my deliberately vague declaration of our love, so subdued that her words were even more startling.

"What is his mission, Mary?" I chose a large pomegranate from a passing vendor. Did this beautiful woman hate desire? Why?

"A holy mission announced to me . . . by an angel. No one must attempt to thwart it." She smiled, a glorious smile.

In the heat, I felt cold as Mary moved away, followed by the gasps and sighs that her startling presence always aroused.

Joseph had remained by a wall. Wanting to speak to me? Had he overheard us? I nodded in greeting. He smiled, a wearied smile. There was so much I wanted to say, to ask. But exactly what? All I could think to say was: "Your son, Jesus —"

Joseph shook his head, no. Mary waited for him, and he joined her.

Had he meant Jesus was not his son? Or had he meant to convey that he didn't want to speak to me about what he had overheard? I recalled that ambiguous moment often.

In the desert soon after, Jesus, Judas, and I came upon a field of lush bushes with tiny buds sputtering like flames. I knew of them, knew of the magic of these buds.

We — Jesus and I and Judas — he, too, knew of their magic — ate the mushrooms.

In moments the bush we ate from flared alive in flames of fire!

"The flaming bush of Moses." Jesus reacted in wonder to the magic of the mushrooms.

We held each other, discovering each other's tearful joy, joyful tears — Jesus outlined them on my cheeks, then on Judas's, then on his own, fusing them into our tears. Laughing, we coated ourselves and each other — suddenly we were naked — with sand and grass, petals of yellow flowers, which became yellow stars.

As if it had summoned us, we witnessed the bursting miracle of a sunset: Paling shades of red erupted into crimson in the same moment. And we discovered within the lucidity of the mushrooms the hidden universe as it had been shaped long before our time. We saw a star spin, fall, shatter, soar back into the sky.

We embraced, all three of us. Desire swelled. Would our aroused longing for each other manifest itself now? We remained like that, only like that, for a cherished eternity, one precious moment. I understood then, within the lucidity of the mushrooms, that Judas loved Jesus in a special way, the way he loved no one else, and that Jesus loved Judas in the very same way — and that both loved me, in yet another way; and with that knowledge came a sudden conviction that between the two men there was an added dimension to their love, the suspicion of interlocked doom that had begun its course the moment they had glimpsed each other as children by the River.

As if commanded by a voice that only he heard, Jesus broke away from us. Mary's voice echoing — admonishing? Judas and I remained lying on soft sand. The magic of the mushrooms was withdrawing, abandoning us on a desolate shore.

Jesus stood alone on the edge of a hill overlooking the Valley. Afraid, I stood up to join him. I heard him shout to someone neither Judas nor I saw:

"Leave me! Move away from me!"

Much later — hours, minutes, seconds — he returned silently to us from his strange outpost. We saw deep pain on his face, new fear. "Satan offered me the golden kingdoms of the world — they appeared as broken jewels before me," he said. "I rejected him."

Judas laughed. "It was only the magic of the mushrooms."

"He tempted me," Jesus asserted. "I rejected him."

"That was all unreal," Judas said. "But *this* is real." He embraced me and Jesus.

I wanted to weep when I saw Jesus move away from Judas and run down the hill. Judas and I followed.

Jesus was with Mary when we caught up with him in the City. On the street, he was gasping out his strange visions to her.

Mary took his hand. Radiating with triumph, her eyes swept from Jesus to us. Her stare remained on us as she spoke to him:

"Jesus, my beloved son, you've been tempted, and you've re-sisted, you've been offered kingdoms of gold, and you've resisted, you've been exposed to the power of sensuality, and you've resisted. In the burst of colors you describe, you've been given a vision of the Creation, and now you must accept why." Then Mary whispered to her son, only to him.

I grasped Judas's frozen hand, to warm it, but mine was just as cold.

Mary spoke aloud to Jesus: "Now you know whose son you truly are."

Jesus' eyes — terrified — sought Judas's, then mine.

Nearby, Joseph turned away.

Jesus slipped down, kneeling before Mary. He grasped her body urgently. "I'm afraid!" he said.

She caressed his beautiful long hair, just as I had, just as Judas had. I knew Judas was remembering that, too.

Joseph moved away, surrendering Jesus to Mary.

From the clouds of evening a sudden wind attacked the leaves of a tree, tearing at it until all its limbs were bare. The barren branches thrust upon the ground the shadow of a cross.

IX

WHEN I FINISHED NARRATING to Madame Bernice those once joyful interludes that were beginning to twist and turn into the terrifying events we both knew I would eventually reveal, she was silent and solemn. She removed several of her rings, as if to strip herself of decoration in deference to what she had heard. Her pondering extended so long that I felt it necessary to occupy myself with another distraction.

I observed the intricate motions of a butterfly. After having noted the stunning symmetry of colors on its wings, gold, azure, purple, I watched how carefully it chose the exact flower to alight on. Was it being selective of the color, the shape, the scent? It floated over one blossom, considering it, its wings barely fluttering. Now it rose, veered away, so motionless that it seemed to be carried aloft on a sigh — perhaps my own — and then it descended — no, it drifted down, almost but not yet touching, the center of another blossom before —

"We're back to that — the Holy Mother Mary is about to be pronounced guilty." Madame's tone was untypically flat, as if something crushing had landed on her. She took off another ring, an onyx, turned it upside down, and mumbled — she *does* mumble: "Well, we're in deep water again."

I was beginning to infer, without exactly understanding them, what Madame's unique expressions mean; it is her inflection that reveals what they convey.

"Because of my view of Mary?"

"You were her, too, the Holy Mother?"

I did not like her tone, but I addressed her consternation: "Mary was a complex woman, Madame. For purposes of dramatic presentation — honed, I might add, under your expert tutelage — I'm describing her as I saw her at each stage, not as I came to see her. Who knows what we will discover in the maze of betrayals we must roam through?"

"A sturdy point. Still —"

I've come to know Madame's responses so well that her single last word alerted me to prepare a look of reproval.

"It seems to me that Judas is emerging somewhat sym —"

I issued the look I had readied. "The story is not finished," I sought to mollify her.

That did not appease her — I read dissatisfaction in her fussy actions: She dabbed meticulously at her lips with a napkin embroidered with her initials — I assume all her embroidery is done by nuns in the silent convent she supports. She restored all the rings to her fingers and extended her hand to Ermenegildo as if to have him choose his favorite. He chose an emerald, which matched the green of his tail. Then he raised his beak, and she leaned over as if — yes — to listen to his opinion on the subject pending between us. Of course, that was only an impression, I was sure, even when, immediately after, Madame broke her silence and suggested:

"Shall we leave, for another tea, further matters pertaining to the Holy Mother and to Judas? Perhaps move on to rehearse —"

"— another life?" I readily accepted her offer. Which life? — resume with the time when —

. . . the voyage with Jason ended. The vortex of the ocean released us. I walked proudly with him in Greece, flaunting the darkness of my skin . . . I saw Princess Creusa make a motion to draw his eyes to her. In response, his gaze sliced across me . . . When I felt the stirring of his children, I resisted pain . . . but later he would feel it, multiplied . . .

Madame was not ready for that. So we ended that day's tea.

As I neared my château, I hesitated. What would I find at my gate? Nothing. I breathed in relief. Brief relief, because tossed onto my lawn and wrapped with a coarse piece of string were sheets of paper I recognized even before I read the malignant words: *The True and Just Account of the Abominable Seduction into Holy Matrimony in the Grand Cathedral and of the Murder of the Most Royal Count by the Whore: The Second Installment.*

Read from it to us!

Oh, how quickly you've asserted your presence as audience in my quarters. You're eager to begin rehearsals. You want to learn what new lurid lies are contained in the new installment. I shall not keep you waiting. I read aloud:

> To allow the Reader to perceive the enormous corruption of what was soon to follow involving the Whore, the Writer of this sad *True Account* will here provide background to the saga of depravity he bravely proceeds to explore, while asking the Angel of Modesty, since such there is, to blush for him:
>
> The Count's Mother, of Spanish origin and lasciviously passionate blood — and to flaunt that fact she insisted on being known as "Contessa" — had, at an early age, attempted to thwart a wise marriage arranged by her family to a Nobleman of great wealth and aristocracy, a fair man, whom she proceeded immediately to malign for reasons known only to her erratic mind, claiming (falsely, the indignant Reader will anticipate by now) that the stalwart Nobleman had somehow betrayed his first wife (who had early — alas, too early — gone to her reward in God's Glorious Heaven and could therefore not defend, as she surely would have, staunchly, the reputation of the upright man) in a scandal that involved their grown son (who, also all too early, alas, shared his mother's Heavenly Reward). With cunning, this "Contessa" left her imputations vague, to arouse infamous conjectures, as gossip always does in those of impure minds.
>
> The truth of her rebellion and the reason for her defamation of the Nobleman came out, as Truth must always when it grapples with lies: The "Contessa" proclaimed defiantly her love for a swarthy, crude gypsy. Her rightfully concerned family encouraged the Gypsy Rogue to leave the Country, extending certain less attractive (but just) suggestions if he did not follow their encouragement. Thus, under the devout guidance of a Pious Nun solicited by the wise family, the Contessa would be ushered back to her senses.
>
> A year passed, during which, the wise Reader will deduce, the Contessa must have awaited the return of the Gypsy Rogue. Her dutiful family saw to it that that did not occur. The marriage to the fine Nobleman took place. But the Contessa would not allow its consummation. The Nobleman believed her claims — substantiated by the Pious Nun, whom he continued to retain as the Contessa's Advisor on the worthiness of a spiritual life — that, especially in the evenings, the Contessa suffered from severe bouts of petit mal, which rendered her incapable of satisfying her wifely duties.

A man of trust — and of equally strong loyalties to his Class, his Country, and God's Church — the upright Husband and Nobleman strolled one restless evening through his grounds in order to be pacified by the moonlit beauty of his many fountains and flowers. He delighted in his roses, vines of bougainvillea, and especially his favorite blooms, tulips, which he had himself directed to be planted with great care and abundance to create intricate but symmetrical patterns throughout his garden. He was pleased to encounter the Pious Nun in serene meditation as she sat on one of many gracious benches strewn about the lawns. On seeing him, she began reciting her rosary in a sonorous voice, pitched higher and higher, in a gracious attempt, the Noble Husband understood, to extend her blessings to him.

Loud as her *Aves* were, the Noble Husband heard gasps and moans emanating from shadows nearby. He assumed that an animal, perhaps a deer (the kind man imagined the hurt eyes) had been helplessly entangled in one of the vines. He followed the sounds toward a fountain guarded by a statue of a soaring angel.

Double blasphemy! Under the angel's spread wings, he found the Gypsy Rogue straddling his Wife lying on the ground. The lurid Gypsy's engorged quivering organ was so monstrous that for moments the concerned Husband thought his Wife was being assaulted with a terrifying weapon. The moon revealed otherwise. The Gypsy Rogue was about to enter the Contessa to spill his huge villainy into her welcoming thighs (hugged lewdly by the brightness of that night). The year-long separation had added to the ferocity of their renewed concupiscence. The Contessa's Husband acted just in time. He pulled the Gypsy Rogue off his Wife at the very moment that the lustful fluid erupted and spattered on her wanton nude body and among the violated flowers, which, in her belated but still surprising shame, the Contessa clutched hurriedly, to cover her most intimate part. A fearful coward, the Gypsy Rogue disappeared. Forever.

The once again defiant Contessa walked back (without so much as a stitch) to the Noble Husband's mansion, so brazen in her resurrected insolence — after the few moments of unexpected modesty on the ground — that she even winked at the Pious Nun, who, finally realizing to her horror what the night and her own loud orisons had concealed, knelt praying in the garden with such passion that her body shook as if convulsed.

The very night that she had been rightly severed from profane intercourse with her Gypsy Rogue, the Contessa swore she would never bear the children of her righteous Husband.

The Reader will surely applaud the justice of the Good and Noble Husband's action. He drew a rigorous document that stated that his wife would continue to enjoy the protection of his wealth only if (within a designated period) she fulfilled her obligation to him as a wife and provided him with heirs. If that did not occur, or should he die childless, the perverse Wife would be cast into the streets, a pauper. A most generous punishment, the Reader will surely agree.

And *still,* the usurious Contessa refused to fulfill the wifely duty assigned to her by the laws of her Maker! — that is, until, with the impetuous suddenness of her hot blood, she announced to her Noble Husband that — under sage instructions from her holy counselor (the Pious Nun) — she had determined where her sacred duty lay: with him in her.

She gave birth to twins, one fair, the other dark, children no less robust for being somewhat premature, a tribute to the Noble Husband's stout fertility.

For reasons found only in her convoluted mind, the Contessa favored the Dark Twin, although she would claim that it was the Fair Twin who rejected her. The Fair Twin, naturally, turned to his loving Father. After a Daughter of startling intelligence, wisdom, and acute discernment was born, the Noble Father died, surely claiming his just place among those who serve their Maker with beneficent donations to His cause on this orbit we call Earth.

Years passed, the Sons and Daughter grew, as is the wont of sons and daughters launched on their journey to fulfill the Holy's needs. Increasingly the Daughter sensed injustice in that mansion of secrets, as only a brilliant, perceptive, agile mind is able to. In addition, she overheard whispers between the Mother and the Dark Twin, whispers at times interrupted with laughter at some shared intimacy, gasps of false and imprudent indignation at some past imagined scandal involving the Noble Dead Father.

The Daughter naturally sought the advice of His Holiness the Pope. His Holiness graciously extended it, just as he had so often to her generous Father. From the Holy Prelate, the Daughter learned that her beneficent Father had added to his will a codicil, executed with perfect authority by the best legal minds that donate their intelligence to moral causes. Said codicil — whose existence was made clearly known to the Contessa — assured that the offspring of the Nobleman's male heirs, the offspring of the Twins, would eventually inherit the vast bulk of the family wealth. This was the Noble Husband's way of ascertaining that his fortune would remain among those of his own blood into perpetuity, and never be grasped by the Contessa — ever!

With great sorrow, the Holy Pontiff informed the gravely concerned Daughter that her notorious Mother, the Contessa, had once, in her Confession to him, revealed "a transgression so vast" that he "often wished his Maker would allow him a special dispensation of his vows of confidence" so he might "divulge it to someone pious who might right the outrage." After that interlude (he sadly informed the alert, wise Daughter) the Contessa had never again sought the surcease of Confession, nor had she continued the generous indulgences to the Holy Church long established by her late Husband.

"Her scandalous confession involved matters that might determine who eventually inherits the vast wealth involved." The Pontiff surprised himself by speaking aloud, so moved was he by the rightfully concerned, supremely intelligent Daughter.

"Please, Holiness," the sagacious Daughter exhorted, "please, just a clue more."

"Tulips."

"Again the tulips!" Madame Bernice contemplated when she reached that point in the "Second Installment."

I had brought the new installment of the growing "Account" to tea with me this afternoon. Again, Madame's casualness had surprised me earlier — shall I get used to it? I suppose it has to do with her mystic orientation, that she moves into exceptional matters without introduction: "I read the 'First Installment,' " she had announced, and left the matter at that, at least for now — she does often return, with passion, to subjects she has only earlier seemed to glide by. Indignant at what the "Account" contained, Ermenegildo shook his head, his twisted feather furiously astir. That caused Madame to shake her own head. While I waited — trying to compose myself, knowing what she would be exposed to at each turn of the page — Madame read from the "Second Installment." Ermenegildo peered occasionally over it and then at me, his head tilted sadly. Surely his responses were based only on subtle signals he had learned to perceive from Madame? Since all the lies in the "Account" were fresh in my mind, I knew exactly what passages Madame was reading:

The committed Daughter informed her two Brothers that their Mother had once, in her Confession, revealed to His Holiness the Pope "a transgression so vast" that he "often wished his Maker

92

would allow him a special dispensation of his vows of confidence" so he might "divulge it to someone pious who might right the outrage." (The Daughter had a startling, retentive mind that allowed her to use the Pontiff's exact words.) Always an innocent, and always, always beloved by the Fair Twin and their Sister (despite everything), the Dark Son, later to be referred to as the Count, refused to believe any such outrage existed. "My mother," he kept insisting, "always tells me the truth." With vast illogic (not to say gross injustice), he accused his own loyal Sister and his equally faithful Twin Brother of "plotting something against Mother."

The Writer might be led to suspect that the Dark Twin knew more than he admitted and so *refused* to uncover the harsh duplicities of the Mother, but that supposition is much too grievous a conclusion to be drawn upon the morality of so noble a man as the Count.

Such an innocent, pure man should surely be encouraged into the Sacred life, his concerned, loving Fair Brother and their perspicacious Sister determined during private hours. They again enlisted the help of His Holiness the Pope, who bountifully gave it, agreeing personally to sponsor, and strongly persuade, the Dark Twin to join a chosen order of most sacred character. His Holiness revealed only then, in a fond moment that clouded his eyes with the warmth of its memory, that, indeed, when the Dark Twin had been but a child he had been a favorite of his, to the point that the Holy Father had given particular attention to the boy's officiating in the Cathedral; and had, on his own, even then, begun to prepare him for a holy life.

Responding finally to what he had been correctly convinced was his duty to the Holy Mother Church — through sustained, thoughtful encouragement from his Brother and their Sister — the Dark Twin announced that he would receive holy vows.

"Madame," I interrupted her reading to explain, "my beloved Count du Muir told me the truth of that distortion. For reasons of their own, Alix and Irena wanted him out of the way, and so they coerced him by threatening vile allegations about the Contessa. He pretended to agree to their 'suggestions' in order to outfox whatever they were plotting."

"And *still* are plotting," Madame underscored.

Only then did their Mother, the sinful Contessa, purport to reveal, through horrifying words interrupted by false gasps of sorrow, that in the lineage of their Father's family, in each succeeding generation, twin boys were born. One was always incapable of producing an heir, always spilling his seed before a fruitful union was achieved. The "seedless" son was always —

"— the fair one," the wise Daughter anticipated.

"Yes, how did you guess?" The Contessa tried to resume her tears. "If my Dark Son accepts the monastic life, the family name shall die, and who knows what will happen to the family wealth?"

"Then the family name shall not die." The Dark Son tried to disguise his disappointment by pretending to be overjoyed, hugging the spiteful Contessa, and whirling her about.

The Reader will not be surprised to learn that the keen Daughter and her Fair Brother disbelieved their Mother. Her "revelation" was obvious subterfuge to shift the wealth of the estate to the Son she assumed would protect her, the one who would retain control by bearing offspring. How most dramatically to reveal her lie than to test it?

The Fair Son tried, over and over (by special dispensation of the Pope), to disprove the Contessa's allegations. Attempt after attempt, with the most enticing of women, failed, only at the crucial moment, even though he dutifully persisted to the point of exhaustion. The Contessa's false revelation had been so powerful and cunning that it had succeeded in its intention, to paralyze him at the decisive stroke.

That was the atmosphere of the troubled household on the night when, riding through the depraved part of the City to give some surcease to the deserving indigent (not all the indigent are deserving), the Count, a pure man who had been denied his choice of a holy life because of his Mother's stratagems, met the Whore pretending to be a Lady pursued by a madman, actually the Reverend Pimp.

If there exist "minor blessings," the Writer of this *True Account* does not deem this to be one; he deems it a *major* blessing, that, having already chronicled the profanities the Whore invited in the carriage with the Noble Count, he does not have to roam through that carnage of lust here, though there are other incursions into that tainted territory that he must take as he continues (begging the Mightiest of Mighties for courage to be able to do so) in this dutiful pilgrimage.

Madame Bernice put the sheets down firmly. "Vile!"
Ermenegildo had turned his head away earlier, in clear disgust.

"There's no question these pages have been dictated — some of them written — by Irena herself." I stated to Madame Bernice what I had deduced last night: "I detect her schemes and craftiness. Alix has contributed, too. I detect his lasciviousness throughout. And the Pope's hand is clearly here — I detect his lecheries and hypocrisies. They all take grains of truth and cultivate them into monstrous lies to destroy me —"

"— *attempt* to destroy you, Lady. They shall not succeed. Yes, their clear purpose is to harm you, slander you, blame you — but I begin to infer other purposes — and mysteries that seem to baffle the writers themselves, especially the mystery of —"

"— the tulips." It still amazes me, the harmony of thought between me and Madame Bernice. My mind had been spinning with questions, which I now shared with her: Why did the "Account" dwell in such detail on the Contessa's interrupted encounter with the Gypsy among the tulips? The Contessa had herself warned me that Irena might become "dangerous" through a knowledge of . . . tulips. What was the "vast transgression" the Pope claimed the Count's refined mother had confessed to him? "The proud courageous woman *I* knew, Madame, did *not* consider her love a transgression. She would have made a point of *narrating* the event, proudly, boldly, to the Pope."

To allow Madame time to consider these matters, I sipped my tea. When I arrived earlier, she had met me at the edge of her garden, to show me her new roses. Ermenegildo had pointed out two that needed special attention and she had lingered to give it to them. So our tea was cool. I did not remark on that, since Ermenegildo seemed to be cautioning me. Surely by now he must know I would never offend Madame?

She was too deep in thought to notice the condition of the tea.

"I'm certain of this much, Lady — these grotesque assertions contain many clues that we can use." Madame moved briskly to lift my cloudy mood.

And so, in search of clues, we roamed over my true life with my beloved Count du Muir:

Our love grew, sparked from the very moment I entered his coach that night. We carried our happiness with us everywhere, to the opera, on long carriage rides in the City's streets. We were lovers for the whole world to see, to gasp at in admiration as we passed. The Count was wildly handsome. His dark hair, dipping in waves, kissed, yes, kissed, the nape of his neck. His smile, tilted just slightly more to one side than the other, dazzling girls and women — and as many boys

95

and men — who barely glimpsed him in his coach. Tailors battled to fashion his clothes, knowing all fine materials would court his body.

Yet he would insist: "It's only *you* they're staring at, your beauty." In truth — I am committed to it — I, too, received an equal share of admiration.

From bruiting in the City, I knew that there were conflicts in the du Muir household, a tight and hostile allegiance between the Count's Twin, the fair one, and their sister, Irena. Whether the Count was not himself aware of the full extent of those conflicts or was trying to shelter me from them, I did not know.

As I wandered in the market one day in search of the best berries in season — I always considered the color, not just their texture — for a compote with which I intended to surprise the Count at dinner, I heard the word "whore" whispered by various voices. I had the acute sensation that at any moment stones would rain on me, and so I rushed away.

It was soon after that the kind Contessa informed me of the plot to thwart our marriage. Well, I would be thrilled to defy all threats and to marry the Count, and to do so with the blessings of the Contessa, who remained with me in my mind from that interlude in her coach.

From my trusted coachman, I learned that, to recall lost happiness, the Contessa often went to a secluded place sheltered by trees along the River. I would never intentionally intrude on such cherished reverie. But riding along the bank myself, I recognized her coach. I saw her standing outside, alone, at the River's edge, her watery, mournful reflection like an extension of her tears. I did not see her coachman, and so I was concerned.

Instructing my driver to leave me a short distance away, I approached the solitary figure, slowly, so that I would not break her reverie, nor startle her. She turned her sad eyes to me, as if she had expected me. She said, with moving simplicity: "My lover was murdered on orders from my husband after he interrupted our lovemaking under the statue of an angel near a fountain." She touched my arm. "My dear, do everything you must to thwart a similar fate . . . Irena has been following you. No ruse is beyond her. She's been inquiring about you, trying to gain the confidence of your attendants, claiming she's your devoted sister seeking you on behalf of your father —"

"My sister!" I was more appalled by the association than by the spying. I recovered quickly: "Inquiring about —?"

"Your past."

The Contessa's voice gained urgency. "There are things I can tell only you. When, in the tulip garden, I and my —"

At that moment, another carriage stopped abruptly over the bank of the River, and waited.

"It's Irena!" the Contessa said. "She follows me, too! She mustn't suspect we've ever spoken!"

I pretended to be sauntering along the River.

"Lady —" Madame seemed unduly casual. She sipped her tea three times, selected a pastry, rejected it, substituted another. "Irena was inquiring about . . . your past?"

I had the unsettling sensation that she, too, was inquiring. "Who knows that better than you, Madame? My essence has traveled —"

"We both understand *that*, Lady." She sipped again from her tea, munched on a pastry. "But in your *present* life, your past, which Irena was investigating —?"

"My present past, Madame? . . . It was ruled by a cruel father." I punctuated the finality of my declaration by meeting her gaze over my own cup of tea.

"Ah, but of course," she said.

An odd heaviness had clouded our tea. So I chose to narrate to Madame a precious tidbit from that "recent past":

"The Count was so marvelously close to his mother, Madame, that, often, preparing to make love, he would stand naked before me, grasping his imposing groin — that act required both hands — and he would say, '*Now* I feel like the son of a gypsy that I am! — not of that ugly old codger my mother had to marry.' "

"Son of a gypsy?" Madame grasped at that so eagerly she did not notice the Count's imposing nudity.

"That was just an expression of closeness with the man his mother truly loved."

Madame considered, considered. "Of course he could *not* be the son of the Gypsy. The Contessa and her lover had been separated for a year —"

"— yes, and the consummation of the renewal of their love was interrupted; she told me that herself."

"And all of it occurred in the tulip garden," Madame said. "Hmmm."

My recollections of that day with my beloved Count du Muir, when he had proclaimed himself the "proud son of a gypsy," had led me into darker moments, which I narrated to Madame: "My beloved Count detested his father — whom he referred to only as 'the ugly old

97

codger my mother was forced to marry,' a ruthless man who justified any barbarity to assert his power — that's how the Count described him, always with rage, Madame. 'The old codger' had betrayed his first wife constantly, and when their grown son and a close friend were charged with treason against the Crown — 'so mysteriously,' my beloved Count told me — the old man had refused to intercede, and the son and his friend were assaulted by a mob. My beloved, whose compassion embraced all the violated, Madame, could only gasp at the horror of those deaths."

Madame extended her contemplation so long, and so sadly — and the evoked violence was so harsh — I had imagined the frenzied mob as vividly as if it, too, belonged to my memories — that I forced my attention away, to the silk floss trees blooming in profusion and already spinning their gauzy veils, which draped their trunks gracefully. The blossoms had assumed a deeper shade, their former pink closer to red, even purple. The burst of yellow in their centers seemed paler, and so even more startling. I noticed that the leaves, darker green than —

"There are so many secrets. What the old man did to his first wife, how he was involved in his first son's horrifying death . . . Has it occurred to you, Lady" — Madame had leaned toward me, but I had not become aware of that until she had begun to speak — "that the object of murder in the Grand Cathedral was truly the Count? — not you. I believe we must consider that."

The Count's murder as part of an extended plot in which I have become the central object? For me at this moment, that altered nothing; all that had been aroused by Madame's words was the memory of his death in my arms . . . I touched the amber diamond on my finger, the ring the Count had placed there as his last gesture of eternal union, to assure that we would be forever husband and wife. *They* had been too late to stop that!

"Oh, and by the way, Lady —"

It would not be a casual observation.

"— the man in that 'Account' of lies, the man referred to as 'Reverend' —

She was being careful; I would dissuade her caution: "He's referred to as the Reverend Pimp, Madame."

"Yes, him. Of course, the 'Account' distorts everything, relying on its effect by using only kernels of truth —"

"You want to know — don't you, Madame? — whether that man has an antecedent in . . . reality?" What an odd ring that word has. Reality . . . I closed my eyes and heard words spoken by my voice: "For years, Madame, I didn't know that what I called my life was . . . drift, just drift. Within that drift, a man convinced me to stay afloat, just afloat, to believe that I was swimming while I continued to drown. I confused all that with love, even his cruelty —"

"— the man pursuing you with a knife during the night's events distorted in this 'Account'?" How gently Madame was able to speak those harsh words!

"Yes, a man turned cruel in the most terrifying way" — I touched my stomach — "a man I left forever. That was when I met my beloved —"

"— the Count du Muir."

"Yes — who shared everything with me, exquisite love, and even the pain of the past that I had fled but which had left open wounds he tried to cauterize with love."

"And the other man —?"

"The allegiance this 'Account' asserts no longer exists. The writers assign him a prolonged role for only one reason — to remind me of a bitter past, where he belongs — and he belongs only there now."

"I understand entirely."

X

I MANAGED TO SLEEP A PART OF THE NIGHT.

I did not realize how fitfully until now, when I see evidence of my restless tossings on the tangled covers. Dawn finds me standing naked by my window. I part the drapes to invite some warmth to dry last night's tears; I just saw the moisture on my pillows . . . Even before I draw the drapes — they must be changed as soon as my period of meditation is over; I noticed a mote of dust free itself into the air — I know it will be a drear day, a day in seasonless limbo, without even the full drama of a storm.

I slip into my robe. The pages of the despised "Account" rest on a table marbled with intricate dark veins; I've placed the noxious pages next to my gun. I shall take the pages with me every afternoon to tea, to proceed at appropriate times to deal with their relevance to our journey.

How desolate gray light turns even this lush landscape when it drapes it in gloom — but especially so the huge patch of barren land beyond the road, acres stripped by a fire that raged a year or so ago and in seconds devoured everything on the hills. Slowly, new life is claiming the seared acres. I notice swatches of purple heather among weedy bracken that has managed to produce tiny desperate flowers. Near gnarled branches of dead oaks, soft plumes of foxtail ferns attempt to disguise patches of scorched earth. Laurel shrubs dot the area with green and yellow. The blackened trunk of a palm tree has succeeded in yielding new green fronds that open, triumphantly, above the ashes.

How persistent life is!

Look beyond at the destitute figures emerging from their hiding places exposed by twilight, preparing for yet another day of . . . what? Nothing. I see a group of them piling their pitiful belongings into their carts to be carried . . . where? Nowhere.

As soon as interviews are over, I shall open the gates of my estate to these poor creatures and divide my wealth among them. I believe that I have become, under Madame Bernice's expert tutelage, an egalitarian. She has told me she eventually shall share her fortune similarly, retaining a few of her cherished jewels. She will, of course, make sure that she and Ermenegildo have ample comfort; she shall deprive him of nothing. Madame is already such an "egalitarian" — her marvelous word — that she dismisses the servants immediately after everything has been set — correctly, of course — for tea.

As it was, set perfectly, when I arrived at her château this afternoon.

"I admire your eagerness to share your wealth, but that must wait," Madame asserted. The way she had poured our tea — elaborately sniffing at it — inhaling it — made me suspect what I would soon affirm: She was trying out a new brew. I longed to love it.

I did not. I took three quick, but tiny, sips to disguise the fact that it was much too spicy.

That apparently satisfied Madame, who continued briskly: "Interviews must occur in a setting as opulent as your many lives. For interviewers — imagine, that this should be so! — such a setting will donate plausibility *before* interviews begin." Under the hazy sun, her complexion was a chocolate color, beautiful in contrast to the exquisite whiteness of her teeth.

Yesterday, after we had roamed through some of my memories trampled upon by that defiling "Account," the subject of the setting for interviews had come up, but we had left it pending for today.

"If we were one of those poor lost souls roaming beyond our gates, no one would listen," Madame said. "Life is so cruel." She grew deeply pensive. "Oh, I do wish that —" A sustained sigh stopped her words.

Oh, I do wish that — What particular longing, what retained pain, had stabbed her memory so keenly to have elicited such unexpected words? I was startled anew to realize that this wonderful soul, my cherished friend and ally in truth, must have known grave sorrow to understand it so intimately in others; that this extravagant presence living in one of the most beautiful châteaus in the country and surrounded by always green lawns, among which her gorgeous peacock saunters, that this same Madame Bernice must carry unhealed

101

wounds, one of which had opened unexpectedly now — prodded by what memory? When she looked up, I saw a confirmation of particular pain; her eyes had turned the color of smoky cataracts — misted by contained tears?

"Madame, what grave sorrow are you remembering?" I held her hand, in mutual trust. I waited for this singular moment — so simply allowed — to open like a fan to reveal her life.

"What are you talking about, Lady?" she startled me by asking.

"The way you looked down, the way you said, 'Oh, I wish that —' " I floundered.

"Yes, I wish that I had *not* decided so quickly to purchase this new opal." She indicated it on her finger. "I'm not sure it was worth the price."

How quickly she tried to mask her pain, her huge compassion! I allowed her her camouflage. I accepted another cup of tea because Ermenegildo was eyeing me in an unfriendly manner, sensing, I knew, my displeasure with the new brew.

"Now!" Madame said. "I'm sure interviewers will expect some evidence of social consciousness, an element that most effectively purges unjust blame in certain of your lives. In such lives, your essence very probably lodged for only one redemptive moment, a significant one, like when you were — so recently — Madame du Barry."

I couldn't recall my life as the famous paramour, though I knew of her.

"When at court she — you — protested the King's excesses?" Madame prodded.

Like a magic key, her words opened the brief interlude into an exact memory. It was its brevity that had allowed me, not to forget it, no, but merely to put it behind so many other lives lived much more fully. Now it pushed assertively forward:

As he sat squashed in his flamboyant throne attempting to enjoy — he was so jaded he enjoyed nothing — a dance he would soon lead with me, the drunken King, wearing his most preposterous robe, a sunburst of gold on white fur, was told by his Minister of State of the growing restiveness in the country. Earlier a group of peasants had stoned the carriage of a despotic nobleman.

"The people are too weak to be feared," the King's slurred words addressed the corrupt court. Nearby, the crafty Madame Pompadour, his earlier mistress, reduced now to a painted manikin, led applause among the pampered courtiers. Feeling her harsh smile on me — she knew that recently I had traveled across the City, and I had seen pain

102

and poverty everywhere — I warned the King, "But, after you — and soon — will come a deluge that will sweep away our children and your subjects."

He shrugged.

To emphasize my commitment to my warning, I removed all my clothes and jewels. Surrounded by gasps, I stood gloriously naked, my arms outstretched to emphasize that I had retained nothing, nothing. "I shall contribute all my possessions to the welfare of my country and its violated citizens."

Pompadour, seeing an opportunity to regain her squandered power, strode to me. "You're finished, du Barry," she said. "The King thrives on lavishness. There will be no revolution." She turned to the leering court for approbation and agreement.

"Betraying whore!" a voice accused me — and the words were echoed throughout the opulent hall.

Now, in Madame's garden, I grieved anew for the violated, the armies of the destitute displaced, homeless, hungry; the sad breed that daily I encounter on my way to Madame's château.

Apparently Madame, too, was thinking of them. She fixed her look where I had directed mine, beyond the trees, where lost figures huddled among their carts full of tattered possessions, hiding until night sheltered them more fully.

Madame put down her glasses now and waited.

For me to wander through more lives to be redeemed, of course. Jezebel's? Reveal the truth about my life with Ahab, who loved me despite my alien color; and of General Jehu who, longing for me, had him murdered and made me violate my mourning, forcing me to paint my face in grotesque colors and decorate my nude body with cheap jewels, and then raped me and thrust me into the street for dogs to tear at while the people screamed at me, "Harlot! Idolatress! Betrayer! Whore!" . . . I did not feel up to returning now to snarling dogs.

Pandora? The myriad evils unleashed on the world and blamed on me . . . on my curiosity that forced me to open the forbidden jar. And my release of hope for man, hope contained in that same jar? An accident, unintended? No! *That* was why I opened the fateful box! . . .

"Why are you taking so damn long to continue?"

"Madame!" Her tone disoriented me.

"Yes?"

"You were being a hostile interviewer, weren't you?" I hurried to clarify.

She brushed some crumbs from her lap. "Well, you *were* taking too long and I was trying to assert a certain pace during the narration of those briefer interludes."

How expertly — and now with variations — she played adversary, I marveled as, heeding Ermenegildo's unwavering stare — he was uncannily able to seem to be frowning — I allowed my cup to reach my lips instead of, as I had intended, setting it down and having no more of this brew.

"The perfect blend, isn't it?" Madame said exuberantly. "Apparently you agree?"

"Yes, indeed, this is the best of all." I am committed to the truth, but a gentle camouflage to protect those one loves is a duty, not a lie. Besides, Ermenegildo's stare was unnerving; had Madame fussed exceptionally about her new brand before I arrived today?

"I shall order only it from now on," Madame said.

"Well —" I wished I could have yanked my single word away.

Madame pushed her tea away. "It's much too spicy! You think I didn't see through your reaction?"

"Madame —" That I would hurt her, even in so minor a matter, pained me, as did Ermenegildo's glower.

"Oh, Lady, let's go on. We haven't time to waste. We must succeed at interviews *this* time, because if we don't —"

"If we don't succeed —?" I could not believe I was repeating those startling words, that they had been spoken.

"Yes, Lady, if we do not succeed this time, your essence — of course undaunted — will continue its journey."

How casually she had spoken that. Yet nothing I might have imagined could have aroused the terrifying impact of her words, that we might fail, this time, that this journey of redemption might have to extend, that there would be others blamed, others to redeem. The forlorn woman whose scream I had heard in a dream . . . Had I myself, without recognizing it except in that dream, considered such a possibility, the woman's scream a warning to me to succeed *this* time?

"We shall *not* fail!" I said, and saw my hand turn into a fist that struck the table. "The interviews we're now rehearsing will clarify it all and there will be no more unjustly blamed women, no more branded with the word 'whore' except as we shall redefine it."

Ermenegildo winced when my fist crashed on the table, and then he turned his full grave attention on Madame.

"Of *course* we shall not fail!" Madame held my hand in double reassurance that wiped away all the implications that had terrified me.

Of course! She had been testing my determination to triumph!

"Well, did I pass your test?" I was delighted to ask, knowing the answer.

"Yes, Lady," she said earnestly, "you passed." Then, smiling broadly and charmingly, she leaned toward me across the vase of today's flowers, daisies startling in their simplicity, and whispered: "I'm just dying to hear how Salome intended to save the Baptist's life and purity — and whether she succeeded."

And so rehearsals for interviews resumed!

In the palace as he stood captive before Herodias and Herod, John the Baptist's body was almost translucent, like a pearl against bright light.

Herod, decked in a monstrous cloak of peacock feathers —

"There, there, it's all right." Madame was trying to soothe Ermenegildo.

"*Imitation* peacock feathers," I adjusted.

Ermenegildo was not pacified, so disturbed that he did not notice a beautiful butterfly, white with wings gilded blue and gold, that was dancing over today's vase of flowers. His unique feather continued to quiver.

So I added: "Herod was garish, he liked dyed things. He wore only *false* feathers."

Herodias said to Herod: "We shall torture the Baptist."

Herod leaned back, bored, in his throne. "You promised me a performance such as I've never seen," he sneered. "Torture doesn't amuse me any more." He yawned drunkenly. His jaded hand was planted on his groin, forever hoping to find a stirring.

Herodias waved her jeweled fan impatiently. "This shall not be just another torture." I read in the slant of her eyes her determination to consummate her evil. I added to my own determination to save the Baptist's life and the purity that was the source of his magnetic power. I would also join him in his ministry. Perhaps, eventually, he would come to love me.

The Baptist had remained unbowed in all his naked splendor. Each time he tensed against his restraints, my body wrenched with love, Herodias's with lust.

"And how" — Herod perceived in Herodias's fevered eyes the possibility of an enormous barter — "will the Baptist's torture satisfy *me*?"

Herodias advanced her tantalizing riddle. "Salome shall perform a dance that will thrill *you* — *and* torture the Baptist."

Herod strained his nearsighted eyes to locate me. His hand

squeezed his feeble groin. "Only a dance?" He pretended disdain. He waved his fleshy hand toward the beautiful naked men and women who had failed to excite him with a dance of copulations moments earlier.

Herodias brushed away the robe draped over her, exposing her lavish body as if to underscore her promise of sensual opulence. "You shall be aroused," she said.

"By you?" Herod yanked his hand from his groin. "You never —"

"*Nothing* ever aroused you." Herodias froze her words.

I must stop feasting on John's luminous nudity, I must take action. My mother's cunning was already in swift motion. I was being forced to move within her current without yet knowing its direction.

In that hall of sated lust, Herodias spoke to the vile Emperor: "Salome will dance a dance I've taught her, a dance to be danced only once, only for you — and for the Baptist."

"The Baptist! Why him?"

"To torture him. He will be chained, unable to move, while Salome's dance entices —"

"But he'll close his eyes. He has already. Look!" Herod lamented.

The Baptist *had* closed his eyes, to contain the longing that the sight of me would stir. Herodias had known that.

She leaned forward, her garish face propped like a death mask on her clasped fists. "That's part of the entertainment, that he won't dare see what he craves to see. His precious purity will be taunted, his imagination yearning for the fulfillment that he must deny."

There was more. I detected it in her voice, exacerbated by her urge to convince.

Herod applauded. "Torture indeed for the prophet! Well done, Herodias!"

Herodias's purple lips smiled. "Afterwards, Sire, I shall ask the granting of a wish."

"*Only* if the dance succeeds —" His hand coaxed his desire.

She would ask for the Baptist's death, to possess him forever that way. Well, my dance would succeed so expertly that I would propose a barter of my own.

I had grasped more pieces of Herodias's elaborate contrivance to seduce the Baptist. It had to be elaborate to overcome his saintly resolve, strengthened by years of imposed deprivation, isolation, vows. I did not have to wait long for another piece of my mother's cunning to fall into place:

Herod had ordered his guards to secure the Baptist against a farther column.

"No! That one!" Herodias insisted on the one nearest her, a few feet away. "I want to watch his torture." A snap of her fingers brought forth two of the disposed objects of her recent appetite, two nude guards whose oiled muscles gleamed orange under the light of the torches they carried. They bound the Baptist to the column Herodias had chosen, and they flanked him.

I suspected, almost knew, Herodias's plan! I would willingly dance the dance she had long prepared me for, the dance of seven veils.

"Lady! You insist there were *six*" — Madame was vastly irked — "and just now you —"

"There *were* six, Madame." I did not want to dwell on the matter now.

Herodias had taught me well, the lessons begun soon after the Baptist's curses rang nightly, arousing her. She would coax me: "Hold this veil to your breasts for a moment, seem about to remove it, let the edge of it touch only one of your nipples, but don't expose it — there, that's it, just the very tip — and then whirl around, glide, barely curve your leg, exhibit only a flash of your thigh, then let that veil fall, only to reveal another. Astonish with each one! Then astonish again! — and even more the next time. Astonish! And at the seventh —" Herself aroused, she ran her hands down my body.

This day, Herodias had painted my face herself, carefully adding highlights with her saliva-moistened fingers. She had leaned back to admire her creation. "Yes!" She held a hand mirror before me. I had seen a startling face: the face of an innocent child and the face of a corrupt woman, the face she had painted on me so deliberately.

"I await the dance!" Herod's sated eyes clasped me to him. I felt contaminated even by his voice, rancid with festering desire.

Pulling her robe behind her, Herodias walked imperturbably down the steps of the throne. She commanded me: "Dance the dance exactly as I taught it to you, or you, too, shall . . . suffer . . . my beloved daughter." She whispered feverishly: "And dance it near the Baptist's closed eyes. Let the perfume of each falling veil waft the air about him. He must hear, or imagine he hears, each slide of your flesh, each twist and turn, each sensual moan I've taught you — *withhold nothing!* — and let him know that each veil has fallen, one by one —"

To keep him in a state of agitation she would then manipulate.

What she intended would occur in one moment, which I must thwart. I understood more of her secret plan now. "I shall dance the dance you taught me, Mother." Yes, and I would surprise her.

She lingered before the Baptist, whose eyes remained closed. With one finger of her decorated hands — nails painted a blackened red — she outlined, carefully, slowly, without touching him, his exposed virginity. Then she brushed her own thighs with that same hand. Confident, she returned to her throne.

Under her watchful stare, I walked toward the Baptist, my legs parting my veils, my flesh glowing silver as I passed shadows, golden when I entered the embrace of torches. As I neared the holy man — his eyes resolutely closed — my veils sighed, a sensual sigh that he heard.

I drank in his beauty as I stood before him, to shield him from Herodias's gaze, and to be able to say this undetected:

"You must open your eyes only when I tell you to!"

He shook his head, turning away, asserting his vows of chastity.

"It's all that can save you from Herodias's lust — and your death. I swear it! Please believe me!" Even then, I longed to draw his body to me, into me. The thought of risking death for that dashed into my mind like lightning. I looked away from his beautiful face and limbs. I was here to save him, not to lose my virginity to a saint. "Promise me. Trust me! Swear!"

"I shall. I swear!"

My devotion had convinced him. "Your eyes must remain closed until the exact moment," I emphasized — and the moment *must* be exact, I warned myself.

In affirmation of his vow to trust me, his eyes locked shut.

His voice! — just those few words: "I shall, I swear" — the voice I had heard distantly for nights, like the sound of the ocean after it crashes on the shore and then turns gentle on the sand.

I allowed my lips to brush his ear, ending my whispering.

"Don't touch him!" Herodias cried out. She tried to explain to Herod: "That will increase the torture, Sire."

I located myself before the vile rulers — and so near the Baptist that I continued to hear his breathing. I arranged my hair so that it framed my face in a shiny dark corona, I smoothed the veils that adored my body. I must look beautiful beyond belief, and I did.

"Lady."

"Madame?"

"May we pause for a moment? Thank you. Listen to the words you just spoke — 'I must look beautiful beyond belief, and I did.'"

"It's true. I must and did."

"I don't doubt that. I'm referring to your own designation of your own breathtaking beauty. Having you say it sounds —"

I warned her with my silence.

"Let's look at it this way, Lady," she said. "Those who will be listening at interviews may bristle at such self-description, no matter how true. People are peculiar about admiring oneself too much, however deserved that admiration may be." She poised her cup of tea before her lips — "I'm getting used to its spiciness" — to indicate the care she was giving her next consideration: "I suggest that at certain points in the telling of your many lives, you might use the more familiar *name* of the person you were at the time. Like this — 'Salome was beautiful beyond belief.' "

"But it was *I!*" I seldom lose my patience so totally with Madame. "It would be odd to refer to myself as 'her.' " I considered adding emphasis to my position by ending that day's tea. The afternoon was waning early.

Madame pondered what I had said. "A good point indeed. A *very* good point, Lady." She smiled her most conciliatory smile. "It would seem odd if suddenly you began speaking about yourself as 'she,' 'her.' " She made a motion that, if she had been standing, might have been a slight bow.

"Thank you." I returned to Herod's palace.

Herod raised his huge goblet to me, his lips puckered lasciviously within the heavy folds of his flesh. He shouted at me:

"Arouse me with your dance, virgin whore!"

Whore!

I began my dance.

109

XI

IN THE SILENCE OF MY QUARTERS, I listen fascinated to the sounds of my existence — footsteps stifled by my carpets as I walk to the windows; a smothered whoosh when I decide against opening the drapes — they had swayed, allowing only a slice of night's light into the room. I move away, very slowly, to soften my footsteps even more, studying my dark shadow as it follows me. I reach out to the marble table to touch my gun. I create the slightest sound as I smooth my fingers over the cold iron. I move it slightly, determined that that motion shall make no sound. It does — although I strain not to listen — the sound of surfaces barely separated, reconnected. I hear my breathing. Shall I stop? Create absolute silence? I continue breathing *as if it is demanded!* I hear the pulsing of my heart.

I exist!

Chirping! A bird's urgent chirping outside my window!

I draw the drapes. On my balcony I peer into the night. I have an uncanny ability to see clearly into darkness. A bird trapped within branches! No, the bird is building a nest on the tree. She peers at me. I retreat behind my drapes. I want her to continue her task, twig by twig, creating the place where she will give birth to her children.

I interpreted it wrong. I see now that the bird has already laid her eggs, tiny birds have emerged; it's their chirping I heard.

Before I can turn away in horror, I see the bird pecking fiercely at her children! They're screaming! Their wings are matted with blood! She's killing her own children! The nest is drenched in their blood!

I was wrong. Darkness had altered my perception into a violent one, no doubt affected by the bloody offering left at my gates an earlier night. Wind had grasped the leaves of trees and tangled them so that I thought I saw what I thought I saw. Looking again, the wind stilled, I realized that the bird was lying peacefully with her children.

Dawn confirms that.

I will bring this up without introduction: Last night when I returned from Madame's château and rehearsed with you what she and I had roamed over during afternoon tea, I detected your doubting, recurrent whispers: *What she claims occurred in Herod's palace is not what we've been told!*

Precisely!

And why did she stop just as she began to tell us about the dance she claims she performed to save the Baptist's purity and life? To concoct more lies?

I note you're eager this morning to reassert your accusations. I stopped my recounting last night at the same point where Madame Bernice and I had terminated that day's tea, and only because I had become too drenched in the weariness of remembrance to continue then. I shall stop your conjecturing about my motivations by continuing this instant to narrate the truth of my dance before Herod and Herodias to save the Saint.

Quivering tambourines, muted drums, heralded my dance as the sweet sound of a single innocent flute strove to insinuate itself into the pulsing rhythms.

I stood for moments illuminated by the flames of torches held by naked slaves. Fiery reflections coiled about my body draped in veils.

Swiftly I swept into my dance, veils swirling, clinging to my body. I stopped and stood with one arm up. The fingers of my other hand touched the top of the first sheer veil, azure silk, the color of the holy man's eyes. Slowly my hand encouraged the first veil to fall, but only from one shoulder.

I exulted in this: The Baptist was blocking the image of desire, of me, from his sight. He must continue to do so, even as I must heat his darkened vision with the sounds of my dance — moans, gyrations of flesh, the whispers of falling veils, perfumed scents that would float into the air with each movement I made. The tensing of the Baptist's glorious body straining not to respond, twisting away from me, told me that I was succeeding in agitating his desire, Herodias's goal, and, now, mine for another purpose.

I whirled. The first veil, weightless, lifted on its own, and fell, as quietly as a sigh of innocence sensing its passing. The veil kissed my bare feet, the ruby on one toe. The flute lamented innocence, while insistent tambourines and drums demanded its corruption.

111

I heard the Baptist sigh.

I let the second veil fall, a breath of pale-lime chiffon, allowed to be discarded, to astonish expectations of another slow removal and arouse anticipations that another veil would follow instantly, but it would not.

The flute wept, drums pulsated for more. Herod's face brimmed with sweaty lust. Longing for the moment when she would secure her unholy prize — I knew exactly how now — Herodias did not remove her eyes from the Baptist. He wrenched against chains as if to thrust his body and his imagination away from the desire I must keep festering, only festering.

I let the third veil — a yellow smear of gauze — drift down, to rest of its own will upon my breasts. My slow inhaling lowered the filmy veil farther, held now only by the tips of my nipples. For how long? Only until I exhaled, and it fell to my hands, which tossed it away, up. The veil remained suspended for moments in the air before it alighted on me again, again veiling my body, even more fully because it had been briefly exposed.

Herod grasped his groin, demanding that it grant him his despicable victory.

I danced, twisting one leg before another, dropping to my knees, my hands tantalizing my thighs, not touching them, tantalizing my breasts, not touching them. I lay on the floor, my gleaming body extended, curving one leg over the other, the next veil pulled downward by those motions, now gathering between my legs. I stood, and the fourth veil, a blush of the most delicate pink lace, faded off my body.

Oh, how I longed to stop this necessary cruelty toward the Baptist, to drape my body in a shawl and lead him away, to end the struggle I must continue to stir, keep simmering, only simmering — in order to save him.

I faced the throne like a bewildered child exposed. Then with a moistened finger I outlined my eyes, then my lips, displaying the blatant woman's sexuality Herodias had stamped upon my child's face. Beyond her expectations, I would manage Herod's lust.

Sordid sweat dripped down his garish clothes and gathered on his costly beads. Her stare scorching the Baptist, Herodias bit her lip with such fierce desire that it bled. She left the smeared blood like decoration on her mouth.

The Baptist's eyes — I asserted with triumph — remained closed.

112

Within his darkened imagination he must control desire. And he was succeeding! And I was succeeding.

I curved my body into sensual shapes, shifting from one form to another. My hands boldly caressed my breasts, the curve of my hips, returned to my breasts, which I held forth like an offering, then withdrew them, toward me, kissing them, wetting them so that they gleamed under the next veil.

I spun, allowing the fifth veil to unwrap, quickly spun again in the opposite direction. The veil now caressed me more tightly than before, saffron marquisette that, for only one moment — as I stood unmoving — I allowed to sketch my nipples and the triangle between my legs. The flute surrendered its last sigh, which drowned in the delirium of tambourines, the growl of drums as I spun and the fifth veil glided to my feet, became a cloud on which I stood, now draped in the sixth veil, a mist of gossamer, the last veil — but the one Herodias was certain would reveal still one more, the merest tissue.

"I begin to see —" Madame Bernice greeted enthusiastically when I reached that crucial point, having resumed, this afternoon at tea, where we had left off yesterday. Beside her, Ermenegildo glanced at her in surprise, as if, all along, he had made the assumption that had eluded her.

Seduced, the flute now added its own sensuality to the drums and tambourines in Herod's palace.

The ovals of my breasts, their nipples, the puff between my legs — all were drawn on the veil, which, with each breath I took, alternately strained to reveal all that was left and then quickly to hide it. As I allowed the veil to roam lower, lower, it clung to me, a tiny portion of it squeezing into the glistening parting at my legs, as if this veil demanded to be the only one to possess me, must be torn, forced away.

Herod's fingers plucked deliriously at the insignificant lump that had sprouted at his groin. Herodias's hands tensed on the sides of her throne as she prepared to consummate her plan when the next veil fell, the one she *thought* would be the seventh.

"Of course, of course," Madame seemed thrilled. She leaned over to Ermenegildo. "You see, Herodias expected *seven* veils, but there were only *six*." Ermenegildo eyed her coolly.

Herodias's guards flanked the Baptist even more closely, their flaring torches prepared to execute her final orders in the plot I had deduced correctly: When what she thought would be the seventh veil fell and I stood entirely revealed, the guards would force the Baptist's eyes open by flashing the lit torches before his vision. Desire — gathering throughout my dance and kept at the very edge of control by the protective darkness of his closed eyes — would require only that sudden exposure to the one sight capable of arousing his virginal passion — my naked body. In that moment Herodias would thrust herself into his arousal prepared by me —

She would not succeed!

I danced, moving with each perfect contraction of my body until I stood directly before the enchained Baptist.

Herodias rose in anticipation of the falling of the seventh veil.

"Open your eyes!" I shouted the crucial words at the Baptist, and I ripped the sixth veil away, and stood naked before him, my arms outstretched.

His eyes devoured my naked body, beautiful as a girl's, beautiful as a woman's, more beautiful than both, luminous in the moon, which stared spellbound through the glassed dome of the palace and bathed me in silver.

Desire engorged the Baptist's groin.

Herod moaned, releasing himself at the sight of me.

Understanding that I was about to trick her, Herodias shouted, "No!" just as —

I thrust my body at the Baptist's full erection and he came — "Lady!"

My memories could not slide past Madame's sharp interjections. "Madame?"

She was extremely agitated. "I don't for the life of me see how you saved the Saint's powerful purity if he entered —"

"Madame —"

"*Please,* Lady, I must be heard on this point. Interviewers will have to understand exactly how on earth it was possible for the Saint to retain his own virginity while you sacrificed yours to him, even if you did deprive Herodias of her cunning and lustful intent. The effect is the same, whether he lost his virginity to you or to her. It was nonetheless *lost!*"

"He did *not* lose his virginity to me, and I did not lose mine, Madame," I said. "You have not allowed me to finish."

"Oh? Really? Well, I anticipate an enormous problem that must be dealt with because there is no way that —" Not even Ermenegildo, sensing her state and sidling up to her, could calm her. She touched him absently. Her testiness grew. "And I may as well deal with this now — rather than saying that you 'thrust' your body at his — his —"

"— his full erection."

"— yes, that; might you simply say you *eased* your body into his arousal? After all the man *was* chained. But — whatever! — that *still* leaves us with the matter of how you saved his virginity and preserved yours yet thrust your body at his arousal — or eased it — and he — he —"

"— came," I finished for her.

"Whatever, whatever, whatever! But if —" Forgetting she did not have a fan and that a breeze had cooled the afternoon that day on her veranda, she nevertheless "fanned" herself, her fingers splayed awkwardly — and Madame is *not* an awkward woman. "For the life of me, I just can't see how —"

"If you will let me proceed, Madame, you shall understand, I promise."

"Well, promise all you like, but how in the world —?"

I determined not to say another word until she controlled herself.

In a further attempt to calm her, Ermenegildo jumped onto a white marble bench on the veranda, remained there for a second against splays of peonies, then spread his tail with a *swoosh!* and turned slowly in an arc, each feather courting splendid light.

To my surprise and his horror, Madame did not notice. When he returned to her side, he seemed about to peck angrily at her hand, but restrained himself, perhaps because Madame was now attempting, not quite successfully, to compose herself. "All I'm trying to do, Lady, is to give you an opportunity to go back and adjust —"

Oh, I could not keep silent at *that!* "Adjust the truth? With lies?" I was aghast. I was resolute in my announcement, which I made with unequivocal firmness: "I choose now to keep the matter of the Saint's saved virginity in abeyance, Madame Bernice. I refuse to speak my truths to such resistance — before they're heard."

"Fine, just fine! Absolutely fine! If you won't listen to reason," Madame Bernice extended her intransigence, "let's spend our time more profitably by exploring another life. Anything! I just don't see how in the world —"

I welcomed being able to push away the sorrow that would follow in Herod's palace. I grasped for the memory of another life, when I was —

— Magdalene, and I saw Mary for the first time. From the way she led Jesus to the Baptist performing his rituals in the River Jordan — she walked erect, proud, directly to him — I was certain of her iron will.

Madame almost gasped when I had barely begun to move away from the enchained Baptist to Mary.

"*Now* you're referring to the Holy Mother again in an unsuitable manner. You're walking on eggshells, Lady."

"Mary did have an iron will." I was terse. And truthful.

"Well, well, well." Madame's disquietude was growing. "I'm sure you realize — don't you? — that you've just reintroduced John the Baptist by the River Jordan and he was only moments earlier enchained to a column in Herod's palace and with — with —" She was flailing.

"— with an erection, yes," I finished calmly. I explained the obvious: "My memories just now took me to a former time, *before* his capture ordered by Herodias."

I knew what was distressing her, the impasse she had created when I had reached the crucial moments in Herod's palace. She wanted me to continue, to clarify the matter of how John's virginity was saved, but she was trapped by her own obstinacy. I could see her battling with herself to ask me to return to Herod's palace. She would put her hand on her cheek, one finger touching the edge of her lips; then she would remove the finger, then the hand, and try again. She bowed her head, to conceal flickerings of indecision on her face — and I noticed only then a remarkable hairpin on which there was an amethyst. Her chin jutting defiantly, her lips clasped, she raised her head.

"Very well, then, let's return to Eden," she said.

She had decided to remain obstinate.

Well, I would last her out. I would *not* return to Herod's palace until she herself asked for clarification!

Already, time had whirled me about, spinning me back to the unwinding of the beginning, when the first wind howled, destroying the beautiful Garden, destroying Eden, exiling me and Adam.

Cassandra's cloak thrashed in the wind as she urged us to follow her and her brother to the edge of the world.

Then squads of other rebel angels joined Lucifer and Cassandra and blew trumpets against the wind to celebrate our defiant love, honoring yet another challenge to the servitude imposed by God as the fierce storm thrust us farther away from the Garden.

Snow fell. Unaccustomed to the coldness, the rebel angels who had just joined us clustered against each other. Then they wearied, needed to rest, snow flecking their bodies like beads. Only Lucifer and Cassandra continued with us through the icy storm that howled. To protect us, Cassandra extended her robe over us like wings.

My body wrenched.

I touched the place of sudden pain, between my legs. I saw blood. God had split me deeply where Adam had entered me. Adam grasped some roses the snow had not yet buried. He crushed them in his hands, and with their petals he covered the opening between my legs.

"You're not bleeding," he tried to soothe me, and himself. "See? Only crushed roses."

His finger bled! God had added thorns to the roses.

Adam bent before me. With his bleeding finger, he touched me where I bled. Then he licked his finger and kissed me, joining our blood.

We spent the night in a cove draped with dying flowers. Adam wrapped my long hair about my body, and warmed me with his breath. Lucifer and Cassandra huddled in the silver darkness outside, speaking in muted tones.

Cold morning came. We journeyed farther east of Eden until we reached the edge of a stark, barren precipice.

Cassandra glanced ahead. "Of course."

"There's more you hadn't perceived?" Lucifer asked anxiously.

"Yes, more is in place."

Lucifer held her by the shoulders and stared into her eyes, into the reflection of her own vision. Then he passed his hand before her face, guiding her gaze away.

Adam stepped forward. "What is already there?"

"Tell him!" Lucifer said urgently to his sister.

Cassandra touched Adam's eyes gently. "I perceived . . . the lineage of Adam and Eve."

"The lineage —?" Adam understood only vaguely.

"Your children," Cassandra said.

"Children?" Adam wondered.

Lucifer explained: "Out of your love and desire, when you fused, out of that, there'll come extensions of you — in your image."

Adam smiled joyously. He held me to him. I rested my head on his shoulder, rejecting sorrow. "We, together, our love, together, our desire, together, shall produce . . . ? You did see that correctly, Cassandra, the children of Adam and Eve?" he asked eagerly.

"Exactly that," Cassandra said.

I turned away from Adam, so that my tears would not dampen his joy.

As Adam held me, Cassandra addressed me in her softest voice: "Bless you, dear Eve. Blamed forever."

Adam looked, bewildered, at her. "What possible blame, when out of all this will come our children?"

Lucifer urged his sister: "Is there no way to —?"

"— foil His new plan?" Cassandra nodded. "Only one."

I clutched my Adam's hand. He was still smiling, had stopped listening to their words, still exulting in the prospect of extending our love to other lives.

To keep him from following Cassandra's and Lucifer's stare into darkness, I kissed Adam's eyes shut, extending the time of joy before he would discover what I realized then that Cassandra understood.

XII

"LADY!"

Madame was standing next to me, an urgent look on her face. "Didn't you hear me calling?"

"Now?"

"Yes. You were sobbing with your eyes closed."

I touched the ancient tears from Eden, augmented through centuries. "Madame . . . I'm so very sad —"

"— because?"

"— of life, everything." As we sat cooled by the shade of bougainvillea, I noticed that when they face the sun, their blossoms are scarlet, and when the sun glances away, they turn fuchsia.

"I understand, Lady. But think of this — soon, we will right so much wrong."

That's how our tea ended, that afternoon.

I have suggested to Madame, and she agrees, that from time to time we rehearse further the precise wording of certain crucial matters to be brought up at interviews. Now in my quarters — no new mysterious threat was left at my gates — I shall restate to you the goal of my journey — our journey, Madame's and mine — as clarified and refined up to now. We shall redeem with the truth the lives of women unjustly blamed and called "whore," a word we shall defuse so that it shall evoke those thus redeemed. Since Madame has surely not felt the sting of the word herself, I account for her passion like this: Being a mystic, she is able to absorb the feelings of the wronged.

Oh, am I incorrect in concluding that some of you are less hostile, do I dare suspect one or another of you may become . . . my ally?

I have fortified myself with a piece of fruit, a pear, until tea with

Madame tomorrow. Hunger sharpens my memories. I *feed* on them. I eat nothing else.

She's hallucinating from hunger.

I'm glad I did not anticipate allegiance from all of you. I ask *you:* Why must one fight for credulity?

I have begun to consider — I shall discuss this with Madame — organizing my more casual thoughts into a volume of *Pensées,* observations of a more general nature, accounts of brief encounters in my many lives. I shall make all entries clear, while leaving room for intelligent interpretation, always guarding against inviting rampant impositions, as all artists and dreamers must. The great Dramatist told me that. Shall I enter something from that encounter now, begin my *Pensées?* Yes.

I met the famous Dramatist in a salon done in shades of mauve. He was in a sour mood because he was aware of the clumsy attacks by noisy "critics" dismissing as "vile" his writings illuminating the darkest chambers of the human heart. Our hostess, who was fond of reckless pronouncements, had just predicted, in a false whisper, that he and his work would disappear "with coffee . . . fads which will pass" — a remark that aroused derisive laughter about the salon. My eyes met the Dramatist's across the room —

Not beyond using a cliché!

That is how it happened, and I am committed to the truth. Our eyes did meet across the room.

"What do you think of them, dear sir?" I used my beauty as passport to approach him boldly after dinner — the Great Dramatist enjoyed only the breast of chicken, poached, with a sprig of tarragon, especially in winter. "Those 'critics' who create nothing yet dare to scorn a great artist like you."

"Critics? Why, beautiful lady — and you *are* beautiful, indeed," he noticed, "they end up in history as derided footnotes." With splendid laughter, he aimed his next words at two of the most notorious of that breed, Alfred Chester and Richard Gilman, who at dinner had quibbled breathlessly about whether or not a writer I had known quite well "truly existed": "Why, Lady, those two are like gnats believing their buzzing is arousing interest rather than mere irritation. The dream — the art — my dear, needs only the dreamer — the artist — to exist."

Into my *Pensées* that goes: " 'The dream needs only the dreamer to exist,' said the great Dramatist in a mauve salon."

I saw him again when I attended the opening of his most controversial drama, which would soon be mauled by immoral "moralists" determined to drive him from the theater. I had chosen to appear at the theater alone, an act of daring received with ugly whispers. Amid them, the great Dramatist knelt before me and kissed my hand. "I recognize your elegantly defiant act of solitude — I know you well. I know your essence."

"That is my word," Madame said at tea when I told her about that encounter remembered in my quarters. A strange, hot wind was rising. I heard the rustle of distant palms, their dried fronds falling, scratching at the ground.

"Oh, Madame, you cannot be competitive," I laughed goldenly. "That was a literary man —"

"*I* explained it first to you, your essence." Madame did not change her tone.

"But of *course* you did, Madame, and no one else shall get credit for that —"

"I don't want credit. I simply call your attention to the fact that I said it *first*," Madame upheld.

"Madame, he used the word differently, certainly not with the new meaning you've given it, that you've explained to me, the central meaning that brings all my lives together." I said all that with passionate conviction. "Surely, you know that's yours, only yours, Madame. And now, mine — ours." I placed my hand on hers, noticing a new gem, a marquise, she was wearing. I made a note in my mind to comment on it at the appropriate time, which was not now. "The gentleman used the word cursorily, although in other ways he was most precise."

"I understand now," Madame said. "Thank you."

The dream . . . the dreamer . . . In my chambers, I reread the Dramatist's words entered into my *Pensées*.

I *feel* my solitude — and I add to my *Pensées* these sudden thoughts: Who first named the sensation we call feeling? We say it so easily — I feel love, I feel hatred, I feel desire, I feel . . . pain . . . fear. Feel! A wondrous word, coupled with others quite as startling: love, hatred, desire, pain, fear! *Feel!* Composed of what? — invisible molecules, smaller than that, atoms, much larger, as large as multiple universes, as vast as space and all its spinning stars, still shining although dead, or so they claim, but who can tell?

When I verbalized those thoughts for Madame Bernice's consideration, she took an inordinately long time to nibble on an extravagant bounty of creamy petit fours on a platter before us. She sipped her tea, prolonging even that simple act. She was in an odd mood today, perhaps related to the flare-up of an allergy.

"Imagine, Madame" — I expressed my sudden concern — "the first person who ever felt yearning — and gave it words — and said, 'I yearn —' "

"As long as you're at it, imagine the first person who ever sneezed!"

There was no ignoring her sarcasm.

"I can explain why I've had those thoughts." I assured her of my seriousness: "This morning when I woke, Madame, I wished . . . I wished that I could die." Not wanting her to see my tears, I pretended to drop my napkin, which Ermenegildo — he continues to astonish me — picked up with his beak and extended subtly back to me.

"Lady" — despite my attempt, Madame had discovered my tears — "why are you speaking like that?"

"Oh, Madame," I dismissed the matter, "surely you know I was talking only metaphorically about wanting to die, just an expression. After all, my essence is eternal . . . even though the body dies."

Madame Bernice's gentle voice soothed me immediately: "Let's rehearse the love affair between Helen and Paris, shall we, Lady?"

The dry wind abated, leaving a carpet of burst blossoms on the lawn.

"Surely there were some lovely times?" Madame coaxed.

"Oh, yes." My memories returned me to Troy, to a mild spring day when I encountered Cassandra as I was on my way to meet Paris at the seashore.

She walked along with me, looking very pretty in the reflected light of the calm sea. I spotted her brother ahead. He lingered at the edge of the water, gazing at his own reflection, beguiled by his own seductive form, aware that along the sandy bank admiring eyes gazed, as always, upon him.

"Troy will soon fall," Cassandra said. It amazed me, with what casualness she announced terrible events. I did not believe that the bickering that was going on between the two countries over my Trojan escapade with Paris would lead to war. How could she deduce this?

"What is more certain than doom?" She had answered my silent question.

I was no longer surprised by her quickness. "As simple as that, dear Cassandra? — all your prophecies?" I tried to match her casualness.

"Deductions," she corrected me.

"Oh, Lady, Cassandra was *so* very wise, wasn't she?" Madame would not permit my reference to pass without paying homage to the woman she so admires.

"As fond as I was of her then, I did not understand her as well as I have come to now, through your expert guidance, Madame, centuries later when you've explained my lives to me, here on this very lawn on which we sit having tea . . . Oh, and what a lovely marquise." I admired her new ring.

Madame responded with silent pride on all compliments, her understanding of Cassandra, her explanation of my many lives, and my comment on her ring. Then she urged me on: "I assume we're now rehearsing the real reason for the Trojan War?"

Did I detect the slightest bit of impatience? I quickly deduced the reason: Earlier she had, with great subtlety, attempted to bring up the matter left pending from an earlier tea, the matter of how I had saved John the Baptist's virginity. She had said, "Oh, I should have worn a *veil* today, the sun is brazen," and later, "Look how beautifully the bougainvillea *veils* that wall, in sev —" She stopped herself. "— in several *layers*." When, still later, she passed a puffy cake to me, she had said, "This is a beautiful *silver platter*, isn't it?" As much as I adore her, I was resolute in my determination not to return to the pending matter until she asked me directly to clarify the event she had claimed, with such assertive agitation, was not possible.

So I went on, quickly gaining her full attention to my memories of Troy.

Cassandra continued as we slowed our walk, enjoying each other's company: "Trojan and Greek blood will spill, all because of my brother Paris's little secret."

"You know?" I refused to believe that even she could have discovered the intimate secret Paris had confided only to me.

"Of course." She waved at her brother.

"Cassandra! Helen!" He waved back, knowing he looked startling against the azure of the Hellespont, his torso bared to reveal his broad shoulders and to exhibit the tight ridges on his stomach, his tunic lowered in a slant on his hips to display a glimpse of golden hairs.

Cassandra sniffed the clear air of the day. "It will all be so romanticized, dear Helen, that your glorious face will be said to have launched a thousand warships."

I laughed at such a gross exaggeration, although it was true that I was beautiful.

123

The day was much too clear, much too splendid to portend such horrors as those she had implied. After all, even Cassandra might be capable — mightn't she? — of being playful. Nor could I take offense at her dismissing my affair with Paris as trivial.

When Paris had first arrived in Greece from Troy — a short time ago — my husband, Menelaus, had received him gladly in our palace. Menelaus was unattractive, much older than I, and he wore me like a jewel to enhance his image. In bed, his goal was penetration. I was fifteen, longing for adventure and romance. Paris had a magnificent physique, a manly beautiful face with perfect cheekbones, shiny eyes adorned with long lashes; often he chose the glow of candles that would elongate them even more.

He had heard of my own legendary beauty. Certainly to uphold his reputation as the most beautiful of men he must conquer the most beautiful of women. I would be his defining conquest. His reputation for romance was such that women often astonished their husbands by admitting — no, announcing proudly in the company of others, at dinner — that they had been intimate with the greatest lover. Indeed, those men, feeling that their wives' returning to them reflected on their own prowess, did not object nor refute. "My reputation enhances theirs," Paris once told me, "and it will increase Menelaus's, I promise you."

Perhaps I loved him, perhaps I was infatuated. He might have loved me similarly. In truth, I believe he cared most for reflections of himself, and for his admirers. Once, he held my hair tightly against my face, and kissed me. I suspected he had seen me as a reversed image of himself. Still, he was sweet, with a boyish charm. He ran like a colt along the Greek beach, always dressed only in a brief tunic, which extended noticeably long between his legs. Often, when he rested in his jogging, he would let his hand slide slowly from his waist until it rested at his tunic's lowest point, an impressive length. He flirted outrageously with everyone, men, women, girls, boys.

Menelaus was fascinated by him. I could see him stealing secret looks at him at banquets. Paris was an expert at locating admiration, and that gave him permission to court me openly. Once when he detected Menelaus hiding in a corridor to watch him pass by with me, Paris coaxed me into pretending that the strap of my white dress had fallen, without my help, revealing one delicious breast, which he kissed briefly but loudly.

"Think of it, Helen," he said, "they're all hiding behind the

124

columns, watching us, the most beautiful woman in the world —
you! — and the most beautiful man in the world — me! Perhaps
they're even masturbating," he predicted.

A prediction affirmed when I heard Menelaus's familiar puny
moan.

Yet Paris made no move to seduce me. I was too young to think
anything about that — and too repelled by Menelaus's fumblings,
which I defined as sex. One night, I sat with Paris on some steps of the
palace. The moon silhouetted us in silver. "Do you ever, Helen, feel the
weight of your beauty?" His words astonished me; they contained a
note of honest rue. I agreed that I, too, felt the burden of beauty at
times. He held my hand and kissed it. He walked me to the rooms he
occupied as Menelaus's guest in the palace.

Feeling free, warmly sleepy, I let my tunic slide easily off my body.
I lay on a satin bed. My skin was smooth and fair after a bath of goat's
milk. I stretched naked, curling one leg over the other so that wisps of
the puff between my legs glistened like sequins in the moonlight. Paris
lay beside me, contrasting my fairness with his bronzed body, covered
only with a golden tunic, which dipped amply between his legs.

He kissed me. The warmth between his legs connected to the
warmth between mine. He stood up.

"Paris?"

"I'm not large!" he gasped.

"What?"

"I'm not large, here," he said, and pointed to the huge bulge
under his loincloth.

"But it's —"

"— stuffed," he said.

I laughed.

"Please!"

My laughter was not in ridicule. It was simply that the matter
seemed unimportant, did not affect me. I told him that. "And certainly
none of the hundreds of women you've seduced have cared," I reminded.

"They make it up, in order not to be the one I haven't been with. I
uphold their stories. And the matter *isn't* unimportant." He was a
pleading child: "Don't you see? I'm the symbol of male beauty, and
yet —"

"You've kept this to yourself, entirely?" I was moved by this
stunning man.

"Yes. I'm a virgin." He faced away from me. "You're the only one I've ever told, because you're beautiful and will understand what that demands."

"Oh, I understand," I said.

"And it really doesn't matter?"

"Not at all," I said.

He removed the loincloth.

"How small *was* he, Lady?" Madame blurted, in an untypical manner.

"Madame!"

I tried not to look between his legs, that time together, but I thought it best for him if I did. It was true he wasn't large, but he wasn't terribly small. He was . . . average. "You have no reason to be embarrassed," I told him.

Deliriously, he thrust himself on me.

We made love, very good love, Paris and I, so different from how it was with Menelaus, who would push himself into me and then topple over, and so in a sense it was a first time for me, too. I came five times, and he came three, and he was thrilled.

Afterwards, he said, "Now we'll have to be a couple, and you'll tell everyone that I'm —" He parted his hands, measuring at least a foot's length.

I not only agreed, but I extended my hands slightly wider.

"Well, it has to be within reason," Paris cautioned thoughtfully. "Now promise."

I did.

I saw no danger in this new situation. I knew that Menelaus would bask in Paris's borrowed glow, perhaps be excited to think he was entering the same place Paris had entered, brag to others that I had chosen him over the manliest of beautiful men.

The adventure proceeded. I sailed with Paris to Troy, always intending to return to dull Menelaus, although I longed to escape to a life of my own. Then, as Cassandra would say later, a series of accidents conspired, and Paris and I became the center of the storm threatening both countries. Menelaus, not knowing that I intended to return to him with his reputation enhanced, thought his manliness was being assaulted, especially on hearing my "confirmation" of Paris's prowess, confirmation Paris encouraged and I contributed only to please him. So the conflict between Greece and Troy grew.

For the last few seconds of my narrating the encounter with Paris, Madame had been covering her mouth, looking down, turning sideways. I had noticed all this but had chosen not to remark on it, until now, when her body — Surely her body was not shaking?

"What is the matter with you, Madame?" I said.

Her hand fell from her mouth and she emitted a loud guffaw — I have to call it what it was. Her body shook with raucous laughter. Between attempts to restrain herself, she managed to gasp, "Now *that's* a good one! The Trojan War fought because Paris wasn't hung!"

"Madame?"

"A figure of speech, just a figure of speech I heard from —" Madame again lost control, gales of laughter emanating from her. Ermenegildo raised his head in surprise. She would stop, resume, stop, become sober, and then a roar would erupt once again, and her body would quake. "Well, that's one for the books!" She even slapped her thighs.

"For Paris it was a serious matter, Madame," I told her, with loyalty.

Wiping tears from her eyes, she controlled herself, after some unsuccessful attempts. Then she said soberly, "Lady, do remember that out of *that* a war was fought and you were blamed."

I nodded yes.

When the wooden horse was pushed forward past the gates, and raiding troops spilled out, materializing Cassandra's perceptions — when the City was sacked, and blood mixed with fire and smoke, I saw Cassandra wandering like a ghost through the rampage, and I understood the profound despair her smile always tried to veil.

It was then, as I stood with Paris on the bastions of Troy where we had remained, that a soldier — Greek or Trojan — pierced by a lance, blood spurting out like a melted rose, looked up at me and shouted —

"Say the word, Lady, so it will lose its power!" Madame encouraged.

"Whore!" I supplied the word of blame with which the soldier had cursed me, only me.

The day had shifted without transition into dusk, a time I often cherish, when perception is least definite, when distance and shapes become vague, yet assume another clarity.

"He's there." Madame was aiming her opera glasses at the château on the hill. "The new tenant is there. He's greeting . . . someone who just arrived in a dark carriage."

"Madame! That earlier time when I rushed to intercept the coach hurrying toward my château, I found it waiting there. When it dashed away, I discovered a basket left inside my gates. In it was a cat! — with two kittens, slaughtered!" I blurted out the incident that had filled me with terror.

Madame put down her glasses. "We must waste no time in preparing for interviews," she said.

XIII

HAVING SEDUCED HIM IN HIS OWN CARRIAGE, the wily Whore, in collusion with her Pimp, set out to ensnare the honorable Count ever more deeply within their web of corruption so that he would be kept in their control for what they ultimately planned: a forced marriage.

There are those who claim the Whore and the Reverend Pimp drugged the Count; others echoed the suspicions that the Whore had the "dark powers" of a sorceress. (The Writer performs a slow sign of the cross and extends it to the Reader.) Still others, much more knowledgeable and sagacious — *and the Writer exhorts the Reader to consider this* — attributed the Count's succumbing to the Whore to the fact that *she connived to arouse his pity with a falsified version of an act so harrowing that the Writer pulls back from it here.*

As I read those words aloud to you in my quarters, they open myriad wounds with their violent insinuations. I try to erase them by continuing to others perhaps less cruel — perhaps not, but right now my heart demands the risk:

Now the Writer proceeds to document other profanities to which they exposed the virtuous Count to assure their nefarious ends: a series of sexual charades, often an affront not only to morality but to — the Writer inhales — patriotism.

Pretending to be the Queen, the Whore connived to reduce the staunch Count to play her loyal Subject summoned from a long voyage in order to be reprimanded, for some breach or other, committed on the high seas. Remember that the Count was an innocent enticed by experts in vice. So he proudly wore the clothes they brought him, clothes which signified a devotion to country: a jacket fitted perfectly in the military mode, with gold-fringed epaulets, a holster to attach proudly to his belt, a cap resplendent with authority, and shiny boots. But where was the rest of this illustrious uniform? There was no more.

In such a state, the Count was now compelled to kneel before the Whore as Queen, the Whore having cleverly evoked his patriotic fervor, as, an earlier time, she had stirred memories of his gentle, loving nurse in order to coax him to nestle within the lavishness of her breasts.

Arrayed with cheap stones, the Whore-Queen sat on her "throne" while drinking wine out of a tawdry brass goblet. Her bountiful breasts were luridly exposed over a golden belt, which reduced her waist and made her already opulent breasts seem, if possible, even more formidable. (The Writer returns recurrently to the subject of the Whore's endowments only to emphasize his thorough dedication to his *True Account*, here reflecting the description offered by those — and there were many! — who knew of the bounteous endowments.) A cape of garish red and tawdry purple flung cursorily over her bare shoulders parted to reveal the eager entrance to her sated body.

Thus abominably propped, the scheming Whore-Queen demanded an expression of her "Subject's" loyalty. The Count-Subject, already on his knees, was urged to kiss her hand, which the Whore had shrewdly placed on her lap. When the Count-Subject was about to do as she had bade him — lulled by memories of aristocratic fealties he had inherited from his noble family — the lustful Whore removed her hand, causing the Count's face to fall forward and sink down. No justifiably shocked Reader will fail to imagine — though certainly not to the fullest extent that the abomination provoked in the entrapped man — the confused horror with which the hapless Count discovered what his lips, aimed at her hand, had kissed instead.

Having thus exhausted the Count's fortitude through a shrewd disorientation of his senses, the conniving Whore, in a moment of pretended compassion, encouraged the Count to rest upon her throne. To shelter his groin, still confounded by the events that had occurred during his coach ride with the Whore an earlier time, the Count placed his hand sturdily on his lap, a virtuous attempt the

Whore foiled with her searching tongue — with such avid determination that the unfortunate Count clasped her head in a futile attempt to control her sordid delving.

As wearily as Pilgrims undertake their righteous journeys, sustained by the knowledge that their trying goal is an honorable one, and that their reward, if no other, shall be the symbolic Grail of Truth, the Writer must proceed with his *True Account:* Further to secure their wicked purposes, the Whore and her Pimp devised even grosser acts.

The poor Count was manipulated into pretending he was an Arabian Captain being given his "just reward" for triumph in a recent battle. As part of this debased charade, the lecherous Whore had brushed her profane body with honey so that it glowed amber. The Count as Captain was coerced to bathe away the sweet glaze with his tongue. How was he coaxed? The righteous mind cries out for an answer. How else? By then the Whore and her Pimp had starved the Count, and he longed — perhaps now in a delirium — for sustenance, any sustenance to calm his ravenous hunger.

The Whore writhed on the floor, exploring herself, screaming obscenities as the Count devoured the honey that, by the nature of the Whore's lush dips and curves, gathered in special abundance between and on her breasts and at the entrance at her thighs. The Count added urgency to his performance in order to end this most loathsome of all banquets, and, exhausted, fell upon the Whore, who writhed under him and once again managed what she and the Reverend Pimp needed to assure for their eventual ends, the spilling impalement of the hapless Count.

Between my beloved Count du Muir and me, love augmented passion, passion augmented love. It is that profusion — oh, and so much more! — that this record of calumny attempts to sully, transforming the joyful spectrum of our sexual desire into lust, only crude lust, the Count's eager passion into forced compliance, the spontaneity and delight of our lovemaking into crass manipulation. I shall provide you with an example of such coarse conversion:

On the day that my wedding gown was to be tried on me for the first time, assuring that every one of its hundreds of tiny pearls was in place, my devoted seamstress was so delighted with the result that she coaxed her handsome husband, a tailor for the most noble gentlemen in the City, to come over from his shop next door to witness her creation. Other seamstresses, a few customers, and the tailor's helpers were so overwhelmed by exhilaration at my approaching marriage that they joined in what became an impromptu "rehearsal" of the wedding to occur within days in the Grand Cathedral. They pretended to be "bridesmaids" and "attendants" lavishing praise on my beauty and my gown, admiring me from every angle.

The Count du Muir would often suddenly yearn for me and appear unexpectedly wherever I happened to be. That occurred that day in the bridal shop. He rushed in — yes, like a boy, an exuberant boy delighted to be in love; and he lifted me in his arms, spun me around. My veils swept about us, enveloping our love and kisses while the others in the shop applauded.

That lovely incident, a spilling out of our abundant joy in each other, is exploited in the salacious "Account," like this:

> The dastardly Whore was often called upon by her Pimp to satisfy the most depraved and blasphemous fantasies, recurrent assaults on all established values, including — the Writer puts down his pen for a saddened moment and bows his head in heavy grief — holy nuptials. Once she pretended to be a pure bride, surprised by her betrothed during the fitting of her gown. The young Lieutenant — for so they assigned the role — was played by a sturdy, tow-headed Lad from the country with strong loins and thighs developed from honest Christian work and in healthy display because he wore snug pants he had almost outgrown, to the point that one seam, at his back, had begun to separate. Only the Devil knows what deception was perpetrated to coerce such an untried Lad into participation in this gross charade.
>
> The Whore-Bride wore the travesty of a wedding gown, including veils, which she often used to entice, because they clung to her exaggerated, wanton body that some persisted in describing as "overflowing with sensuality," a phrase the Reader will detect as not the Writer's. The Reader can surely surmise who in that company played the officiating Holy at this mockery of a wedding. Who other than the Reverend Pimp?
>
> As she walked toward the Lieutenant-Lad, the Reverend Pimp's friends, men and women, plucked at the blasphemous Whore's nuptial adornments, until, when she stood before the robust Lieutenant-Lad (who was quivering so from fright that the weakened seam, at the back of his snug pants, split), she was "clothed" only with the bridal veil, which she raised over him, engulfing him under it for practices that the Writer must — the Writer must — the Writer must — Yes, engulfing him under it —

for practices so lewd — engulfing him — vile, oh, vile, and lewd, yes, yes, lewd, it was vile, and — oh —

The dutiful Writer, having, at this point, pushed himself to the verge of exhaustion in recording these lecheries, must leave the Reader for a moment. He shall resume this *True Account* when, through rest and pious thoughts, he regains the necessary strength.

Madame Bernice shook her head after she had read that passage during that afternoon's tea. Along with my cowl and my lantern in preparation for cool nights, I carried the base "Account" with me, to explore its lies for clues. "Alix's contribution is clear — his festering desire for you, Lady." Madame announced what I well knew. "And we detect the Pope's predilections, don't we? And Irena's sharpened malevolence is obvious throughout. But we cannot attribute only malice to all this. There are added purposes in this 'Account,' disguised questions . . . We must expose its lies and the lies of history."

"We shall!" I asserted our resolve, and proceeded to tell her what had occurred at the bridal shop after my beloved had left and the fitting resumed.

I looked out the window and saw a slight, plain woman, pallidly fair, peering in. With her was another woman, a stolid matron, older, heavy, indeed cumbersome in her awkward bearing, staid to the point of drabness, with only one partridge feather in her hat as intended but unsuccessful decoration. I assumed they were poor souls who would never know the joy of love and so paused to spy wherever they detected it. What harm? When a coach stopped on the street near them, the two rushed on.

The Contessa emerged out of the carriage and swept into the bridal shop. I dismissed all those attending to me, knowing she would have an urgent message.

She did: "My dear," she rushed her words, "your every step to the altar must be watched — even at the altar. Those two people peering in; one was Irena —"

"I thought I recognized her," I realized only then. "But the matron —"

"— was the Pope."

As the Contessa departed in her coach, I looked out and saw that with her was a nun.

"The nun originally employed as her guardian," Madame

connected. "But most important, Lady, the only other witness to the interlude in the garden under the shadow of the angel."

"Witness?" I did not know what significance she was adding to that. She had gone into deep concentration.

"You described Irena as fair?"

"Yes. What an odd question, Madame."

"She's not beautiful?"

If the first question had been odd, this was startling coming from Madame, the same who had objected to my dwelling on descriptions of beauty. "No, she is *not,* and the thought of *her* naked —" I shivered.

Madame said something under her breath, something that clearly amused her privately — she smiled behind her hand. I heard only a fragment: ". . . the only one not . . ." Seriousness returned to her face as she leafed through the pages of the "Account" that was the scandal of the City. She located a certain part. "The Contessa's husband was fair, too! It says so here!" She jabbed the page with her finger.

I glanced at it. " '. . . a Nobleman of great wealth and aristocracy, a fair man,' " I read. "Madame, that means the writers want it to be believed that he was an equitable man, although of course we know he was a tyrant."

"That's not what 'fair' means here." Madame's odd excitement escalated. "Note how others are described as fair or dark throughout, meaning coloring." She was unaccountably exultant. "You do remember — dón't you, Lady? — that your beloved husband referred to the Contessa's husband —"

"— who was his father —"

"— as an old codger, and he referred to himself as acting like 'the son of a gypsy I am' — his words, Lady."

"A figure of speech at an exuberant moment."

"A gypsy who was dark, like the Count, and handsome, like the two brothers." Madame leaned back triumphantly. "I believe we've uncovered, Lady, what Irena wants to believe about the events in the garden between the Contessa and the Gypsy, events she assumes *you* may have gained intimate information about, from the Count and the Contessa."

My head was spinning. Where was she going?

Wherever it was, she was continuing: "The Contessa vowed she'd never have her husband's children, true?"

"Yes, but she did, the twins —"

"No doubt about Irena, an unattractive girl who resembled the Contessa's husband," Madame was mumbling to herself. "Don't you see, Lady? If Irena could prove what she wants to believe, it would be to her vast advantage."

"Madame, what are you saying?"

"That Irena would like to uncover that the Gypsy was the father of the twins!"

The thought was staggering. And impossible. I had to stop this illogical pursuit. Irena was capable of horrors, yes; I didn't have to be convinced of *that*. But she was *not* illogical. The area Madame was delving into was beyond possibility. "The Contessa herself told me that her husband interrupted her last interlude with the Gypsy, who had been in exile for a year. The passage in the novel — a passage clearly directed by Irena — confirms it."

Madame whispered, unnervingly enigmatically: "The life-fluid of gypsies is lavish and mysterious, and there were flowers —"

That did it. "Madame, you're rambling. And what is not a ramble is utterly illogical."

"Illogical? My clearly presented perception of what Irena's conjectures may be? I — illogical? *And* rambling?" Madame Bernice was so furious that Ermenegildo, dozing at her feet — he seldom dozes during our encounters, but Madame had explained to me that he had had a restless night — woke with a start and scurried nervously about. "If you believe that — before I even finish, Lady — then I shall keep the matter to myself until your resistance lessens!" She folded her arms, sternly.

She had become as adamant not to proceed with her account as I had been not to explain how I had saved John the Baptist's virginity, a matter she had greeted — I might have reminded her of *that* but did not — with at least as much skepticism as I now greeted her preposterous suggestions.

The rest of that afternoon's tea, a brief one, occurred in chilly silence — despite a warm sun-sprinkled afternoon and the delight provided by a profusion of new magnolias that had begun to lean over the edges of the veranda. The air was so serene that not even the leaves of weeping willows stirred.

As I returned to Madame's the next day — that night in my quarters I rehearsed what she and I had gone over earlier — my trepidation that our frosty silence of yesterday might extend into today's tea caused me to stroll slowly through the countryside. It was a lilac afternoon, a hint of purple in the sky. A derelict newly arrived from the City was following me; I first became aware of him from the sounds of the rattling cart that contained his meager possessions; that

135

sound is now familiar in the cities, and increasingly in the country. Others like him — they often band into tribes — are used to my astonishing presence as I walk unescorted and unafraid through the countryside — sometimes we nod; but he was seeing me for the first time. I faced him down. He scurried back into invisibility off the road, sliding down one of the scarps created by temblors that often shake this territory.

Impulsively I walked beyond Madame's château, toward the château of the new tenant. From a distance, I gazed at his grounds. No one was about. Deep purple oleanders asserted boundaries. As beautiful as those trees are, their blossoms are said to be poisonous, especially the blood-red ones. The bouquet left at my gate — roses? — or dried oleanders?

When I arrived at Madame's, my trepidation about yesterday's chilliness between us evaporated. She announced peremptorily: "We have no time for sulks. We must begin to consider what we shall do afterwards."

"Afterwards?" The familiar word terrified and baffled me. I thought only of our goal: Redemption!

Even Ermenegildo was caught off-guard by Madame's assertiveness. His twisted feather defied a rising breeze.

"Yes, afterwards — after we announce to the world the fact of your many lives." Madame sipped her tea as if she were saying nothing astonishing.

I was even more terrified. I could repeat only that one word: "Afterwards?"

"A book first. There's always a book," she said.

Oh, she was referring to my *Pensées*. Was she?

"Naturally, that presupposes our success at interviews."

She was reintroducing the possibility of not succeeding!

The growing breeze — the day might turn windy — tossed a palm frond against the marble columns of the veranda. It remained there, scratching desperately, as if it were dying. I stood up and shouted at Madame: "We *must* succeed *this* time! If not, *I* foresee" — where had that word come from? — "a woman ... women ... blamed to the point of madness."

"Lady —"

"No," I protested further words.

She poured me fresh tea, inviting me to sit back down. I did. Her voice lost all its rigid authority: "Even in this ancient crumbling world, Lady, you will be redeemed." She looked up at the clouding sky as if demanding that the sun illuminate this suddenly altered moment. "I shall see to it."

A sheet of light squeezed through gathering clouds.

"Now, Lady, shall we rehearse another life?"

"Yes!" The life Madame would have me deny, a life I will not deny. Medea.

"Magdalene." She chose one of her favorites. "We still have a long journey to take with Magdalene."

Yes — a journey that contains some of the greatest joy, some of the greatest pain. I remembered with sadness: "Without me, Mary would have been alone, that terrifying night of sacrifice. Yes, the crucifixion occurred at night, Madame. There was a purpose for that. Joseph, Mary's husband, was already dead — or he had faded as silently as he had lived, always perplexed by what part an angel had played in his life —"

"The Angel Gabriel," Madame said. She fingered her priceless necklace of rubies and diamonds, an emerald as pendant, as if it were a simple rosary. "The Angel who told the beautiful blue lady —"

"— what she believed with all her heart, Madame."

Madame Bernice poked her temple with one finger. That is a signal I've come to recognize, that she is retaining a certain point firmly in her mind, a central clue in our quest. I trust her so entirely that I seldom question such epiphanies. I discovered only now that instinctively I had begun to tally them. Her storing of what Gabriel told Mary, I added to other matters she has similarly emphasized: the exact sequence of the events in Eden; the assertive choice by my essence of Magdalene, a fallen woman but not blamed; the overwhelming mystery announced in Patmos.

I continued my narration: "When Mary saw Judas, so despondent —"

"— because he had betrayed Jesus, yes!" Madame said harshly.

"Madame, *you* are fixing blame."

"Where it belongs!" Her voice turned ominous: "I must now state forcefully what I've attempted to assert during your earlier accounts of the first interludes among you and Jesus and Judas: I've felt a growing apprehension that you're moving in a certain sympathetic direction concerning that man. I must remind you that *everyone* knows that Judas betrayed Jesus." She raised her chin staunchly in anticipation of whatever I might counter.

"We're exploring just such entrenched lies, Madame, not creating our own restrictions on the truth. Do remember that Adam loved me so much that he chose me in defiance of God's damnation, and he, too, was unfairly blamed."

"Yes. He, too." Madame closed her eyes for moments and bowed her head in honor of my Adam's great love for me. Then she eyed me warily. "But I don't see how that —"

"Perhaps we may discover that Judas, too, was an unjustly blamed man —"

"— or *not!*" Madame's intransigent tone resurged.

"Or not."

That contingency might have placated her. I wasn't sure. But I did not want to continue. Restless gray clouds roamed the sky. Still, it was not yet dark enough to light my lantern, but the cooling wind coaxed me to cover myself with my cowl as I parted from Madame and Ermenegildo, who walked me to the edge of the grounds.

Nothing waited for me at my gates.

Now, in my quarters, sad memories evoked earlier persist. Oh, Judas . . . sad, beloved Judas, and, oh, sweet, beloved, sad Jesus . . . bound together in that terrible way.

Leave me, memories, leave my mind, rush out, grant me peace here in the solitude of my quarters, at least a respite from this litany of memories!

Hush!

I remember —

Hush!

Remember!

No!

I rush to my window, for breath, for air!

There's a nest on my balcony, and in it are feathers matted with blood mixed with the jagged white fragments of broken shells. Then I did see it, what I thought I first saw last night, or was it the night before? — a bird slaughtering her children, turning a nest into a grave. Why did she return to leave this terrible mangled "present" on my balcony?

Or was it she!

With each terrifying signal, are my pursuers coming closer? Onto the grounds of my château!

I see shadows shifting outside!

A light flashes across the grounds. With a candelabra, Madame Bernice is standing by her window facing mine. She lights a second candle. Another. Three!

Our signal of urgency!

I gather my own candles, to signal her back that I'm aware her message is forthcoming.

Madame's candles spark, at the same time that she catches the moon's reflection on her windows. She's employing our most urgent code of communication, flashes from candles, reflections of the moon caught on windowpanes.

The first letter of her message:

B —!

The next letter: *E —!*

BE —

A pause. Be what?

U —! The signal is doubled: *W —!*

A cloud obscures the moon, rendering the next letter vague. Madame reasserts it only with candles, a slower code. I look up into the sky, pleading for the moon. There are three patches within sweeping clouds. In moments, reflections will be possible again. The moon will provide swifter transmission of the urgent message.

BE . . . W —

The moon pierces the smear of clouds. Madame grasps the interlude to add reflections on her window to the flashes of her candles.

H —? BE . . . WH —?

Whore!

Has someone hostile intercepted our code? Gauzy light casts the last letter into ambiguity. An "A," not an "H."

BE . . . WA —

A cloud threatens the moon, which races away for moments.

Madame is emboldened to confirm the message up to now:

B — E — W — A — R . . . !

BEWARE!

A flash, another reflection on the glass panes, a brief covering of the third candle, a shifting of the first, confirm that word and begin another:

D —!

A —!

N —!

Clouds stifle the moon. Madame must again use only candles. I wait. *D — A — N —* Daniel!

BEWARE OF DANIEL!

The sinister man in the château beyond hers? His name is Daniel?

139

A woman? Daniela? A spy of Alix and Irena? The Pope's? Approaching my château? Do I have time to retrieve my gun? I must wait for the full message.

The moon, our ally, parts the clouds to allow Madame to flicker more rushed letters.

G —!

Daniel G. At the opera before the Count's death . . . ? At Mass in the Grand Cathedral . . . ?

E —!

Daniel Ge —

Clouds seize the moon. A sudden drizzle! Madame must withdraw farther back into her room, weakening reflections. She manages two more letters.

E —? N —?

Madame's gone!

No, she's rushed back to get larger candles. She stands in the wind and the rain to signal at least one more decisive letter before even the new candles are stifled.

O —

She adds a quick slice downward.

Not an "O," a "Q"! Question? A certain question is going to be asked, must be rehearsed immediately, so urgent we cannot wait for tea tomorrow?

BEWARE OF DANIEL'S QUESTION?

BEWARE DAN — GE —

DANGER!

E —! N —? The candles are dimming. *I —N —*

Danger in —?

E — N — Q — Those letters are clear now — the rain shifted direction for crucial seconds.

U —! I —! R —! E —!

ENQUIRE! Enquire about —?

Fierce rain lashes at me. I hear the rustle of wings. The desperate mother has returned to pluck the bloody nest away from the rain.

Madame! *Madame!*

The storm hurls me away from my window. I huddle in the darkest corner of my room. Before her last candle is hopelessly extinguished by sheets of rain, Madame has made a convoluted swirl, adding one more letter.

R —!

BEWARE DANGER ENQUIRER!

XIV

THE DAY IS GLORIOUS! Golden light streaming into my quarters sweeps away the events of last night. No . . . not entirely — I'm just waking, huddled in the corner where I fell into protective sleep. I remember . . . Madame's urgent message!

Was it urgent? If it had been and the urgency had persisted, she would have rushed over, an act that would have called attention to her — and we're trying to avoid that — but one that might be resorted to if necessary.

I walk to the window, the drapes left open from last night. I notice that rain abandoned clusters of leaves torn from trees and that the wind bunched them against the corner of the balcony. *That's* what I imagined was the bloodied nest, the mangled birds. *Did* I imagine it? — an image retained from the bloodied blanket left at my gates. Last night's storm created . . . impressions. The day is too benign to permit them to extend.

Look across the way!

Madame is calmly attending to her flowers. She might have been only practicing our code last night, under exceptional circumstances, having sensed the impending storm. She's determined to think of everything. I will of course question her during today's tea.

When I arrived at her château, I detected nothing unusual about her that would suggest the seriousness of last night. We sipped our tea, an exceptional brew that Ermenegildo seemed especially fond of sniffing, Madame holding out her cup periodically for him to do so. On the usual silver platter — it's a different one each day, today's engraved with a single, yet intricate, wreath — a delightful mixture of "breathy sugars," Madame's description of the tiny dainties, awaited our delectation. I accepted one. It was much too sweet; so I let it melt slowly in my mouth. "About last night, Madame —"

"Quite a storm, wasn't it?" Madame said. She looked about, to locate her opera glasses. They were on her lap. Apparently she had just used them. "The weather in the countryside never stops surprising us, does it? Did you hear the thunder?"

"Madame!"

"Lady?"

"Your messages."

"I'm embarrassed about all the fuss I made, Lady. I thought I heard unnatural scurrying on my grounds. I surmised, you know, that, perhaps, there were prowlers who might move onto your grounds."

"But your message warned me of danger from" — I paused before I could speak the forbidding title, not wanting to acknowledge the possibility of such a vastly empowered Inquisitor recruited against me, us — "from the Enquirer."

She sighed. "I have to admit that's where my suspicions led me. The clouds and the moon — and, oh, the storm — were stirring up shadows. I admit I acted rashly, and sent my signals. If there was anyone about, it was probably only one of the wanderers from the City, lost in the storm." She ate the "breathy sugar" she had kept on her napkin to tantalize herself. "A bit too sweet, aren't they?"

I was glad that she was trying to assuage any lingering fear she may have aroused in me, and I was pleased that she had acted "rashly" since it indicated how alert she is to our situation. What continued to disturb me, to the point that I did not bring it up, was that she did consider quite possible the threat of the roaming Inquisitor, evoked an earlier time, investigating us. She wouldn't otherwise have inferred his presence so immediately. Was the dreaded Inquisitor perhaps now firmly in the camp of Irena and Alix and the Pope? Did Madame have reason to suspect new developments? She had previously indicated being privy to information gleaned from one or another of her servants.

Madame cleared her throat. "Now, Lady, on to unfinished business, the further unveiling of the truth in the lives you've lived."

Oh, she was eager to prod me to return to the account of my dance of six veils and St. John's salvaged virginity. I smiled triumphantly, too soon, because when she resumed, she said, "Perhaps more about the Trojan War?"

"Madame," I reminded, "I believe I finished rehearsing the pertinent parts. Perhaps *you'd* like to proceed with —" It was my turn to invite her to resume her impossible interpretation of Irena's conjectures concerning the unfinished copulation between the Gypsy and the Contessa as set down in that monstrous "Account." Yes, I was bartering.

Her arms, firmed across her bosom, indicated that she expected me to go first. Well, I would discuss another life. I would tell of —

Oh, memory, sweep me away from Patmos — sweep me back to Eden, only to the very beginning, when, lying beside my beloved, I redefined paradise as closeness to each other. That memory eludes me now. Memory has its own determination.

"My brief interlude as Delilah," I chose.

"Oh, very well."

She was *assuming* that eventually I would go first in our checkmated narrations. I would pretend not to notice. I said, "Samson was a vain little thing."

Madame roared with laughter in a tone that some might call boisterous. "Samson was even smaller than Paris?" Apparently she found great delight in that.

I did not answer right away, allowing her pleasure to linger before I would correct: "I meant the pejorative 'little' only metaphorically, Madame. *He* was *not* little, not small!"

That did not restrain her. "More like a bull?" she screamed out with delight.

"Madame?"

"Please proceed, Lady." She sipped her tea with emphatic correctness when Ermenegildo shook his head, his twisted feather upset.

Samson was proud of his bulging muscles, his strength. He went about killing lions and foxes, breaking the jawbones of jackasses to use for weapons, always aggressive. He was proud, too, of his long flowing locks, constantly tossing them about as if recklessly but actually quite carefully, to emphasize the breadth of his shoulders, accentuate his every move. He bragged about his sexual prowess. He had many women, two of whom he married, others of whom he used only once, denounced as whores, and discarded —

"— a womanizer." Madame provided an apt designation.

"— and bragged endlessly, endlessly," I told her.

He performed with me as he did with all his other women: Arms decked with shiny wristbands, he held me from the waist — I wore only a scarlet bandanna above my forehead — and he lowered my silky body just onto the tip of his rigid member, then raised me, lowered me again, barely entering me, until, after a dozen repetitions, he would penetrate me fully, and proceed entering and exiting.

With each movement, his hair would flail triumphantly, like a whip. Often he would count aloud its tossings, matching them with his insertions and the contractions of his muscles:

"One! Two! *Three!*"

At other times, he would sit me on his lap. My legs would be about his hips, my breasts would brush his inhaling and exhaling mouth. But he concentrated on this: He would squat while he was in me — and, of course, his locks would toss with each powerful contraction of his thighs, and he would count each movement loudly, proudly:

". . . Four! Five! Six! *Seven!*"

He bragged that his primary purpose in his constant seductions, the repeated movements, was to make his muscles grow.

". . . Eight! Nine! *Ten!*"

And he kept stalking lions.

I would teach him a lesson. While he slept, I took a knife and cut what he was proudest of.

Madame's cup of tea froze on its way to her lips.

"His hair!" I finished. "That is recorded correctly."

Madame's cup reached her lips. But they trembled perceptibly, and some coloring had left her face.

"Madame?"

She shuddered. "It's nothing, Lady. For a moment I had a glimpse of something horrifying that might distract some of the interviewers unduly."

For days, Samson sulked, claiming his strength was gone.

"But he *was* blinded?" Madame continued to insist that we retain the outline of long-accepted versions, even while clarifying with previously unknown details.

"Blinded? Only by his hair and his vanity, and finally only because he hid himself, blamed me for his retirement, and made up fantastic stories to immortalize it — all because, he claimed, without his flailing hair he had lost his strength. Just insecure — he was embarrassed, that was all. After that, my essence moved on."

"Of course. Now about the Holy Mother —?" The abruptness with which Madame Bernice often introduced a subject to be most carefully rehearsed should no longer startle me. But it did. Being a mystic — although an unconventional one, like Cassandra — she assumes that others follow the rapid shifts and turns of her quick mind. She took another of the "breathy sugars" and waited for me to continue with my life as Magdalene:

Mary guided Jesus away from us, me and Judas, that day after we had eaten the mushrooms on the hill and Jesus' mind had exploded with visions of kingdoms and satanic temptations. After that, we saw him less and less often, although we sought him out. Even then, he was quiet, pensive, smiling only when we reminded him of earlier times that evoked our closeness. Alone now when I did not go with him, Judas continued to wander restlessly among the revolutionaries we had joined with Jesus.

Mary sought me out in the marketplace. I had bought a basket of pears, so ripe they were almost red. I sat eating one on the steps when I sensed the awe that Mary's crystalline beauty always aroused. She was a beautiful woman, yes, one of the greatest beauties. You've seen her depicted in paintings. None does her justice.

The day was hot in the market, and so we roamed, Mary and I, to a patch of grass shaded by an embrace of palms. We sat for moments, speaking idly about the especially hot summer that year. "One of hottest in memory, don't you agree, dear Magdalene? Do you suppose we shall all survive it?" she asked me. The beauty of her voice matched the beauty of her presence; an observation as ordinary as that which she had just made assumed a resonant ring that turned everything she spoke profound.

Courteously — "how kind, how thoughtful" — she took the pear I offered her; she had impeccable manners. She ate a tiny bite, another — "your choice sweetened it, dear Magdalene" — before she put it down, having satisfied all the requirements of a gracious acceptance of my offer. She waited a few moments before she said, "Neither you nor Judas must attempt to be with my son — that way — ever."

I knew what she meant by "that way." Though our encounters had become fewer, desire remained, just as powerful as ever, perhaps more powerful than ever. When we met, our eyes sought anew the outlines of our bodies, especially when our flesh was licked by moist desert heat. Then the wind might conspire with us to expose a shoulder or the upper part of a leg, a starkly bare portion of a chest. When we emerged from bathing in a river, the flimsiest of coverings we retained would mold our bodies, flaunting the triangle between our legs, a faint darkening.

145

"Why not, Mary?" I did not want to reveal the specialness — and pain — in our desire. Although my hunger abandoned me, I reached for another pear, something to hold in my hands, which were trembling.

"Jesus is the Messiah, the Son of God, proclaimed by John the Baptist."

I bit into my pear, to do anything to lessen the impact of the words I was hearing. "You believe that, Mary." I had forced myself not to make that a question.

"The Angel Gabriel sent to me by God announced it," Mary said.

Was the Gabriel she spoke of . . . a . . . real . . . angel? Or was he a man? It was known that her marriage to Joseph — a simple, kind, though somewhat dull man, much older then she — had been arranged. Consummated, ever? Had she, before that, been a fanciful girl, dreaming of a handsome young man, her "angel"? I could easily imagine her, her hair long, her lithe body yearning as she ran with open arms across a field of wild flowers to meet him, his strong arms stretching to embrace her.

In Madame's garden, that image of centuries past had become so vivid that I shared this observation: "Perhaps a great love story we shall never know, Madame, is that of Mary and her first and only lover when they were young and she was free of the burden of what she saw as her mission with her son. Can't you see her lying among flowers, strands of her beautiful long hair over her lover's shoulders?"

Apparently, Madame could see that, and didn't want to. She blinked. "I believe it would be enough to leave the subject with her running across the field of wild flowers," she said. "Perhaps holding a bouquet of them in her hands. That is a lovely image."

"But, Madame, surely the Holy Mother sometimes flirted, when she was a beautiful young woman. Surely she laughed. Yet have you ever seen her depicted smiling? Surely she played, and disobeyed, and longed for happiness and loved life until — with what was surely unjustified guilt," I emphasized, "she discovered secretly that she was pregnant —"

"— or was informed of it by the Angel Gabriel." Madame was firm in asserting the familiar account.

That deceptively indolent afternoon when Mary had sought me out in the market and we sat under the shade of palms, the Holy Mother bit one more piece, a tiny one, of the sweet red pear I had given her. "Jesus was divinely conceived — purely — in my womb," she aimed at my doubts.

Looking at her, so composed, so resolute, I knew that, whatever the reality of it was, at that moment she did believe that she had been visited by an angel, who had announced her mission, and her son's.

Despite my reveries of her as a yearning young woman, who was I to say that what she claimed wasn't true? Yet I had to question, that day near the market: "Dear Mary, did you only envision an angel . . . Gabriel . . . someone you once loved and came to remember as an angel?"

So I had asked my question of Mary with all the kindness I put into my voice. I would have touched her hand, except that her crystalline aura made her seem unreachable.

"Gabriel . . ." She sighed the name, and her vision seemed to travel beyond where we sat. Her gaze returned to me, her eyes unflinching on mine. "No, I did not envision an angel," she said, with not a tinge of anger, her face tranquil. "The Angel Gabriel told me that I, also, was conceived purely, in my own mother's womb, in preparation for the birth of the Messiah."

I said to Madame, who had listened with what I detected was more than a touch of apprehension: "I believe we must consider this, Madame. Those were vicious times. A mysterious child would be deigned the child of an adulteress, and she would be stoned —"

"— but not the man," Madame said.

"— only the woman," I continued. "That day with Mary, Madame, I couldn't help thinking of that, and whether that was pertinent to what I was hearing."

On her veranda Madame Bernice sighed at the sad enormity. "What you're saying, Lady — and with admirable taste — is that if the Blessed Mother had not been believed about the virgin birth, she would have been stoned, in the barbaric style of those days." She did not even have to touch her forehead to signal the emphasis she was placing on our words just spoken. She only stared ahead. I thought her eyes might have misted. We had entered a labyrinth of mystery we must eventually search through, but one she would prefer to leave unexplored. Quickly she cautioned: "None of which is to claim that the virgin birth was not announced to her by an angel."

"That is not the intention, Madame," I agreed.

Gray clouds had claimed the sun. The lawn was draped in

mourning for a length of time so extended that I leaned back wearily in my chair. Everything in the garden had stopped, everything was quiet, everything had darkened.

I waited for time to move.

Finally it did. I determined that from the sway of distant palms.

XV

AFTER MY MEMORIES OF MARY and of Mary's memories of an angel named Gabriel, Madame and I agreed to end our tea. We had reached a dramatic moment neither of us wanted to venture beyond, not today.

I began to rise.

"Lady, a word —" She changed her mind.

"Madame?"

"Each time we part after tea, I keep thinking that during rehearsals in your quarters, you'll remember another blamed soul your essence surely located. She was known as —"

"Marina." I remembered that name from an earlier time when her reference to it had baffled me. "An Indian princess?"

"Oh, you *do* remember the woman of Cortés." Madame seemed elated.

"Cortés?"

"Why, if you remember the beautiful Aztec princess branded La Malinche — traitor — you must remember the Spanish conqueror to whom she was given to pacify the brutality of his invasion."

"Oh, I —"

Madame continued: "There was a young lover — you don't remember? — a lover whom the princess-turned-slave must leave."

"Why, yes, Madame, I believe I do!" It was natural that my vast recollection of past lives would sweep over some, leaving them submerged, still to emerge, because as Madame spoke her own vague knowledge of the princess, her lover, and the conqueror — "Those were dangerous times for adventurous souls," she commented, "and the brave princess was suspected of conspiring with her captor, having

149

his child, betraying her people, or so I believe I've heard" — it all sprang into my mind!

"Oh, yes. My essence lodged in hers!" In my future recollections, I must cope with this discovered factor: The memory of a past life is firm, but the names involved may be submerged. Now, here on Madame's veranda, I relived the crucial moments — when, a captive princess, I stood proudly, refusing to bow, before the Conqueror. I would bring *him* to his knees, if only like this: I dropped from my shoulders the only frock I wore. I stood naked. The handsome Conqueror knelt on one knee. "I moved back, demanding *both* knees," I was now speaking my fresh memories aloud to Madame, "and that he strip himself before me, equals —"

"I suspect that, tonight, you will remember even more of your life as Marina, La Malinche." Madame's enthusiasm had grown at the infallibility of my memories.

Although it was only dusk when I left, I noticed small fires pocking the distant landscape among the density of trees, fires already lit because this was as warm as evening would become. Shadows of those fleeing the cities crouch about the flames. They attempt even more to be invisible, Madame informed me, because the harsh roundups by mounted officials have increased. Where are the destitute sent? I had asked Madame. Away, she said, away . . . It occurred to me then that the dreaded Enquirer might be reporting on them in his role as Inquisitor, although it is clear Madame believes that she and I are the main objects of scrutiny. Those hunted, dissolute, displaced souls sometimes greet me now, with a word, a sound. They sense my compassion and they know I am not to blame.

I found no message at my gates. I shall not be lulled into complacency.

That night in my quarters, just as Madame Bernice has continued to exhort, I invited more memories, and they came, of Eden, Patmos, the River Jordan, the Black Sea.

And I dreamt . . . I remembered the exact moment when, as La Malinche, I promised the young Aztec Warrior Xuan that I would return to him.

I was so eager to recall for Madame that evolving memory that I awoke when it was still dark.

I shall use this time to tend to my *Pensées*. Madame thought it "a smart idea." In my journal, I write a question that has been nettling me for some time: "What is truth? What is a lie?"

She's trying to blur the distinction, convince us that her lies are truth.

You spoke with a tinge of triumph. I shall answer you: Nonsense! But I'm delighted to know you continue to be eager to join me in these rehearsals.

You're a liar!

Yes! I am!

But —

I startled you, disarmed you. Exactly as I meant to. Here in the intimacy of my quarters into which I've allowed you to rehearse with me, I wanted you to hear from me what you *want* to hear, and never expected to hear. You wanted to trap me by evasion. I wanted you to wince at the impact of what you dared accuse me of — lying; an accusation I thwarted though it struck like a bolt of cold fire. *Why* must you put truth on trial!

You're nothing but a whore!

You dare —? Even now —? Oh, you anticipate. You're being kind in your harshness. Should I thank you? You want me to rehearse for the time when that accusation occurs, inevitably, in interviews. I shall discuss the matter with Madame.

But I had no time to do so when we met the next day for tea. She had hardly served it into my cup when she said with curious sharpness:

"When your essence lodged in the body of Joan of Arc —"

I stiffened. "Madame, I was never Jeanne d'Arc."

"— and you accompanied the Dauphin at his coronation, triumphant as —"

"Joan of Arc was not a fallen woman, not called a whore," I said the obvious.

Had Madame Bernice been caught in a giant gaffe? She mumbled: "But, Lady, you would be broadening your subject of exploration by including Joan of Arc. After all, she was very badly and unjustly treated."

"That is, of course, true, Madame, and we would find many, *many* such women, used, abused, but I cannot claim my essence lived where it did not." Ermenegildo was aware that she had managed to annoy me; he had become increasingly conscious of my sensitivities, a fact I relish; he doesn't give his loyalty easily. If I did not know better, I would say that at that moment he leaned toward Madame and said, gently, Shhhh.

Whatever — it accomplished its purpose. With a wide smile, Madame leaned toward me and said: "Of course, I know Joan of Arc was not a fallen woman! I was keeping you on your toes, and you are, Lady, you are on your toes."

I decided her good motives overrode my irritation at her testing.

This time she assumed the overtly interrogative voice of an interviewer: "Lady! Where were you born in *this* present reincarnation?"

"I am not involved in reincarnations."

"Excellent!" Madame applauded. Misinterpreting the source of her approval, Ermenegildo, who had at that moment gracefully perched on a small pedestal on the veranda — even when he's playful, he displays unassailable elegance — fanned his tail once, twice, again, a display that caused Madame to extend, now to him, her genteel applause. Then she cleared her throat, to prepare for the firmness with which she addressed me: "The word 'reincarnation' must *not* be allowed. The key word is —"

"— essence," I finished firmly.

"Let's go through that succinctly now, Lady. That is the most complex part." Once again, she was a harsh interviewer. "When did your . . . essence" — she furthered her performance by sniggering — "when did it first most strongly manifest itself to you, in retrospect, of *course,* after the interlude in the Cathedral?"

I answered with dignity: "In Patmos. During a late orange dusk. With St. John the Divine —"

"And that was when he called you a whore, the mother of abominations?" Her own question jostled her to mull her earlier stored considerations. "Why was that girl so vastly blamed? For what catastrophe? What mission did St. John choose her for — you? What 'mystery' did St. John read on your forehead? — a mystery he himself proclaimed the 'most profound'!"

I continued my own rehearsal: "It was then that my essence rushed back to the beginning of time, to Eve."

"At that timeless moment —" Madame rejoined my rehearsal.

"— my essence embraced all fallen women blamed for great catastrophes."

"Perfect word — embraced." Madame applauded my rehearsal.

Again Ermenegildo performed on the pedestal, even more effortlessly this time.

Flush with the prospect of success, we finished our tea. A festive moment, indeed. Flowers promised to bud right before our eyes, new ones bloomed on the vines nearby, others sprouted more petals, tiny flames of blue fire. I love the time in spring when nature makes its promise of summer most aggressive and even an occasional coolness asserts it.

"Now, Lady —"

"Now, Madame?"

"Let's itemize some of the matters we've kept pending —"

Oh, she was at it again. She meant my saving of John the Baptist's virginity. It was still not the direct exhortation my pride demanded. Much as I love Madame Bernice, I was not going to allow her to get her way in this stubborn evasion.

"Perhaps the full story of the War in Heaven," I offered. "I have barely begun it."

"Yes, a very important matter that requires one whole afternoon." It was now midafternoon. "What else?"

"The sad eternal interlude" — my voice lost all its joy — "that occurred at the edge of the world with Cassandra and Lucifer, and my beloved Adam."

"Most certainly that." Madame borrowed my sadness. "That will require a less joyful mood in the day . . . Where else?"

"Calvary."

Madame bowed her head for a length of time saturated with anticipated sorrow. "Much too vast before the afternoon declines. What else?"

"Medea." I knew Madame would turn her head. A grayness cloaked the veranda and spread throughout her grounds. If I had been tempted to convince myself that I had imagined the moment, Ermenegildo would have dissuaded me. He stared into the darkened sky until the sudden cloud that had swept across it released the sun. I moved on: "Guinevere, Lucrezia Borgia —"

"Lucrezia Bor — !" Madame tried unsuccessfully not to stammer. "Poisonings? Incest? Extravagant vices?"

"Madame," I reminded her, "we do not accept the rumors some call history." I shall enter that, rephrased, into my *Pensées*. I knew she would be relieved by my next words, so I uttered them quickly: "Still, my memories of Lucrezia Borgia include only one redemptive incident, when she provided a nurturing love to the beautiful young poet Ariosto, who sat naked —"

"I'm convinced," Madame ended that. "I think perhaps today we might deal with *unfinished* matters that were well on their way toward resolution, coming, so to speak, to a *head*." As if she had not been obvious enough, she touched the silver platter on the table, although,

153

catching herself, she extended her gesture toward the vase next to it, as if to rearrange the breath of lilacs that graced it today.

She *still* would not ask directly that I resume my account of the dance of the six veils to save the Baptist. Intransigence would meet intransigence. "The truth of my life as La Malinche?" I offered my fresh memories, which had extended even further during my walk here, providing details my earlier recollections had omitted.

Only the slightest irritation, quickly dissipated, greeted my substitution. Madame was fully "in the spirit" — an expression she had once used. "Let's rehearse that life."

This is how I, a maiden of fifteen, became the woman of the brutal conqueror of my people.

In the lush jungle, priests announced a time for the sacrifice of a young warrior to the sun. I would be that chosen warrior's last earthly prize before his further reward, the guarantee of a special place in Heaven. I lay naked atop the highest pyramid. My proud breasts were bared to the sun. On each was the flake of a diamond, a glistening reminder of Heaven on each nipple. Sprinkles of splintered gold dusted the parting between my legs, where a white rose had been placed, a further virginal offering.

Priests chanted as the ritual proceeded.

A chorus rose from warriors volunteering to be sacrificed. "I'll die gratefully for the double favor," cried a bronzed youth, his hard organ emphasizing his sincerity.

Another warrior pled, "I shall enter Heaven through the love chamber of the most beauteous maiden." He might have been chosen — one of the priests admired him especially — but, in his frenzy of desire, the young warrior came — and even so, gasped, "Please choose me, I can come again —"

Yet more petitioned.

The Warrior Xuan won because of his beauty, his elegance — and the resplendence of his headdress, feathers of myriad colors. His skin was golden brown, intercepted only by a strip of cloth that attempted to, but could not, conceal his regal member. Under his bare feet, the stones of the pyramid burned. Still, he walked gracefully, step by ascending step, to where I lay for him to take me under the gaze of the thrilled sun. Growing with each step, his arousal struggled with his brief covering, and won, finally disdainfully thrusting the strip of cloth away. It fell to the bottom of the pyramid, where a boy grasped it, praying on his knees for a day when he might be worthy of wearing it.

The Warrior was not afraid. Why should he be? He would enter me and Heaven. He stood before me, knelt over me, began to pluck with his mouth the petals of the rose between my legs, raising his head each time to release each petal, which floated to the base of the pyramid, where beautiful naked maidens scurried to claim one, to cherish forever until it would be given to their lovers as an added token of their gift of virginity.

The Warrior lingered over the last petal. Then he blew away the gold dust, glints sprinkling the pyramid. While priests intensified their chanting that courted the sun, and while they hoarsely approved the spectacle atop the pyramid, the Warrior parted his muscular legs and straddled me. When we would fuse, the sacrifice would be completed by a high priest, who, with his sword, would send the Warrior to his favored place in Heaven. The Warrior Xuan lowered his body to enter me.

I had fallen in love with him, yes, at the apex of the pyramid in those brief moments. My heart protested the imminent separation. "Stop!" I shouted, only to hear my word much more loudly shouted and rendered unheard.

"Stop! She must remain a virgin!" I blessed whoever had demanded that, not knowing it was the Conqueror from another world who had spoken those words, the man who would cause me to be branded forever a betrayer of my people. With him were his companions in exploitation, pale, hollow-eyed friars from his country, and squads of helmeted soldiers mounted on horses and carrying deadly weapons my people could not match.

The elders knelt, believing that this fair conqueror, in his blazing armor, must be the God long foretold.

Soothsayers had prophesied that his coming would be preceded by strange events. On the day he had first been spotted with his men at the edge of the ocean — and the sun had turned him golden — noon became midnight, and yet his hair remained gold, soothsayers quickly claimed; and pale children, specters in tatters, paced outside a nearby village, scattering birds, which turned black in flight as they flew toward a star that burned the edge of the night.

At the site of the pyramid, the Conqueror seized this time of terror and vulnerability. He would demand and be granted whatever he wanted, demands emphasized by his menacing weapons, already spewing out fiery blasts of warning into the sky.

And he chose me as his woman.

Xuan reached out, to hold me back, but I knew now what I must do. "Follow me secretly through the jungle," I whispered to him. "When I signal you by looking back, remain there and wait for me. I'll vindicate our love."

I traveled with the Conqueror to his camp. Unseen, the brave Warrior followed. It was while the Conqueror and the others celebrated that I was able to penetrate into the jungle, to reassert my vows of fealty to the Warrior.

To remind me of our passion, he stripped himself before me. I welcomed his nudity with my own, our bodies darkened a deeper brown by the night and licked gold by the watchful moon. His desire for me had not abated. But nothing more must happen now. I must return before I was missed, I warned, begging him to promise to trust me. And he did, even as he informed me what I already knew: that my people were accusing me of having gone too quickly with the Conqueror; I should have struggled against our own compliant priests, they said. "And they're saying that you'll betray us, become his ally, reveal secrets, that will allow him to defeat our people. They're calling you a wh —"

With a kiss I stopped Xuan from repeating the word that would wound him and me. How quickly I was being blamed.

"Wait here," I told my lover. "I came only to reassure that I shall not betray you nor my people. I'll return to you." I sealed my promise with a kiss. I walked away proudly, knowing what I had to do to save my people.

That same night the Conqueror took me and fell into complaisant sleep.

I returned to Xuan in the jungle. Our bodies fused. I felt his life surge into me — as the Conqueror's had *not*.

As I parted from my young lover, I longed to tell him what I must not: That although they would be *his* children whom I would bear, it must be believed they were the Conqueror's.

"Lady, the Conqueror had already —"

"— yes, Madame, he had, but I had inserted in me a leaf as thin as a tissue to keep his seed from me."

"Ah!"

"It was the seed of the Warrior Xuan that would bring me children. With the Conqueror, I always retained the thin leaf, but not with the young Warrior, whom I continued to see and love. Out of the union with *him*, not the Conqueror Cortés, would come a people who would overthrow the Conqueror . . . Oh, yes, he would have other

156

women, and they would bear his children. But mine and Xuan's would teach *them* to rebel against all tyrants."

Madame was ecstatic. "Of course! I knew that the proud race that came from her emerged from an unbroken heritage. I always suspected something like that. That's why I was sure your essence had existed in Marina —"

"La Malinche, Madame," I insisted. "We shall purge that designation, too; it was meant to have the same sting as 'whore.'"

Madame marveled: "She — you — used a leaf. How extraordinary, that such a tiny bit of nature could become an ally." She sipped her tea, bit on a cake, and added: "And then there are tulips."

Though I did not know exactly how, I did know she was tantalizing me with an evocation of the Contessa in the garden with the Gypsy; her husband had cultivated tulips. It was an odd way to remind of our respective stories kept in abeyance by *her* intransigence. I would not comment, although she was clearly waiting for me to do so.

Ermenegildo rushed down the steps of the veranda, across the lawn, farther, farther, to the very edge of Madame's grounds. He stood there, peering into the thicket of dark red oleander blossoms. He considered himself the keeper of the grounds, and so this must be a serious threat. Would he discover only a poor wanderer from the City? If so, since he undoubtedly shared Madame's attitudes, he would allow the sad soul to rest on the luxuriant grounds. That wasn't what he had found. He was running anxiously back to us. He pulled at Madame's silk skirt. "There's something there?"

He nodded.

"For me?" I was already certain.

He nodded twice.

Before Madame could rise, I dashed down the veranda, to the edge of the grounds, where Ermenegildo had found —

— a sheaf of sheets tied with a coarse ribbon.

I looked through a parting of the dark foliage, to the château on the hill. I saw the new tenant moving up onto his veranda. Another shadow crossed behind him. A woman? The sense that even at that great distance our eyes — the man's and those of whoever else was there — were connected was so intense that I reached out with my hand as if I would be able to touch the two distant presences. I pulled back.

I lifted the sheaf left there and returned to Madame, who stood waiting for me.

I looked at the first page, and I handed the sheaf to Madame to read what I had read: "*The True and Just Account of the Abominable Seduction into Holy Matrimony in the Grand Cathedral and of the Murder of the Most Royal Count by the Whore:* The Third Installment (in Which the Writer Exposes the Appalling Duplicities of a Renegade Nun and Presents Much More Evidence in the Continuing Case Against the Whore)."

"The writers are here emphasizing the nun who may know what occurred in the tulip garden!" Madame grasped at that.

But this had accosted me: "The continuing case —" I repeated those ominous words. I am on trial, as I have been through the ages! "Madame!" I had not intended hysteria to seep into my voice. "To what extremes will they go in their pursuit of me?"

Madame Bernice said, "The stakes are high. They'll resort to anything, everything, even —"

"— even?" I did not want to hear.

"— even to . . . inverting reality."

Inverting reality . . . I put my hands to my ears to indicate most forcefully that I did not want to know what she meant. When her lips did not move, cautiously I uncovered my ears.

"Madame! Another memory — no, no, *that* is a dream — has been recurring, a very disturbing one, a very assertive one, of a woman I don't recognize. I cannot fully grasp the dream because it occurs in fragments. At times I dream I hear the woman's voice — at other times that I hear only her sobs — or a scream — echoing in my quarters when I'm rehearsing. She, too, protests a harsh loss, a harsh verdict, a harsh judgment — but all unnamed — loss so deep, so terrifying that even when I've wakened, the dream seems to persist." I was about to touch my face, to test the uncanny sensation that the tears of the forlorn woman in my dreams might have streaked my face. Rejecting the impossible notion, I reached instead to touch one of the lilacs in Madame's vase.

Madame's voice was so soft I did not hear her words until they returned to me as echoes: "At interviews, shall you consider her, the woman in your dreams?"

Madame's words now seemed not to have occurred at all, and so I felt no need to answer them.

XVI

MEDEA! TELL US ABOUT MEDEA. Whatever Madame Bernice may feel about it, we're ready to know how she was "unjustly blamed" for killing her innocent children! Try to convince us. We're beginning to believe it's you who are avoiding the dark life of the barbarian whore. Why?

You're full players in my rehearsals now. You've become a jury? A chorus? If so, you've found an ugly voice in a group. No, not all of you have joined; others — my allies? — did not speak with you. It's with Madame Bernice that I must first rehearse the life you demand, and *she* is not ready. You — yes, *you* — I do not like the way you smirk, I don't like the way —

When you were Eve, did you have a navel?

I'll resist your taunting. Few of you joined in that crude laughter. Madame Bernice insists I answer all questions, with dignity, even when they're not *asked* with dignity. She has warned of the danger of allowing reckless anger. I evade nothing.

Of course we had navels! If for no other reason than that we, the progenitors of mankind, would have looked odd otherwise, especially in the paintings of the masters, the slight curve of my stomach undotted by the knotted flesh, the subtle separation between the two triangles of fine hair on my Adam's chest and groin erased. You must know that no one has painted me more masterfully than my Adam, nor him more than I. Our longing eyes drew every line on each other.

And navels?

Yes!

As I stand this morning by my window, I notice that Madame is not in her garden at her usual time. I'm not alarmed. She told me yesterday that her cook was preparing "something especially scrumptious" to accompany today's tea. Madame is probably overseeing that.

I shall make use of this interim to rehearse: When I was Camille —

She's a fictional character.

She existed *before* she was written about. I was she! — Violette Lacomme! You didn't know her true name?

When I was Camille, Armand was certain his love was powerful enough to resurrect me even while I lay dying. My hand had fallen, limply, toward the floor, spilling petals from the withering camellias I had held. He kissed my fingers, my arm, weaving a necklace of kisses till he reached my breasts. He tried to resurrect my fading breath by licking my nipples alert. When they hardened, he dredged at hope. All night he remained inside me, giving me his strength, keeping me alive that way, forcing himself to remain erect to the very point of exhaustion, succeeding in extending my life for precious moments.

Still, I died, having been judged a whore.

Her accounts are riddled with inaccuracies.

Were you there?

No. But historians and literary —

Were *they* there? *They* thrive in finding lies in each other's accounts. You believe them? *I* was there.

Read to us from the new installment of that "Account" you detest so much, the one everybody's talking about in the City. We saw you read silently from it last night.

And I was sickened even more by its lies. Still, I accept your challenge.

I shall read aloud a passage that reveals how cunningly the writers attempt to defuse truths they suspect I know and they're afraid I might reveal, including the Pope's secret.

Read about the Renegade Nun.

Notice that there is ample evidence for Madame's contention that the falsifying writers of this "Account" must deal with —

Read about the Nun.

Notice ample evidence that the falsifying writers must deal with the "outline of truth." Into it, they squeeze their lies.

More about the Renegade Nun!

I withhold nothing!

No one who has read the title of this record of corruption, *The True and Just Account of the Abominable Seduction into Holy*

Matrimony in the Grand Cathedral and of the Murder of the Most Noble Count by the Whore, might be blamed for continuing to wonder, during the restless nights this Chronicle necessarily produces in the cleansed of heart, how such a seduction could have been permitted not only to culminate in the rites of holy matrimony in the Grand Cathedral but to be performed by the most worthy High Prelate of the Holy Church. Abhorrent as it is, murder is more readily grasped than the blasphemy of sullied Christian nuptials.

The astute Reader may recall that in an earlier Installment in this *True Account,* reference was made to a Pious Nun. The Writer here publicly confesses, having already confessed in the quietude of his soul and been forgiven by a Mightier Power, that he erred violently in his designation. Subsequent events have proven that his longing for holy allegiances and virtues led him to an incorrect conclusion about the Nun. She was *not* pious.

Why would a Nun sworn to a holy life of meditation and prayer — it was claimed that she was quite pretty, with spicy nipples that did pert battle with her habit — fall into a pit of villainy that only the Unholy One would welcome? It happened like this:

As a young woman, she had been discovered in a terrifying situation with a family friend. The Writer will save himself the need to dwell upon the matter by simply identifying the place of the encounter: a stable in the family estate.

Fearing for her well-being — and they determined that what had occurred had occurred in a moment of rare weakness (which, however, must not be allowed to become less rare) — her virtuous family (whose close allegiance with His Holiness had earned them a special pew in the Grand Cathedral, a pew into which His Holiness, in added appreciation, had commissioned to be carved romping little angels in all their natural splendor) encouraged her to remain in her room, carefully becalmed so that the troubling encounter would not cause her more grief than that which a Righteous God intends to befall transgressors.

During that period, she fell into a state of amnesia. Fortunately her moral family recalled with astute exactitude everything that she forgot: Repentant, she had announced her decision to become a Bride of the Holy Mother Church. She herself did not remember that, until she woke one day (with a sob of gratitude) to find that she had become Sister Celestine, a member of the Holiest of Convents, a silent one, the one she had herself most fervently chosen during her period of lost memory.

161

Sister Celestine was befriended by another Nun, from another country, Sister Monica, who, given another set of less fortunate circumstances, might have become — these were the words of an observer — a "tangy wench with flashing eyes." One can only imagine what the holy habits these women wore concealed — curves and soft partings, softened even more by tiny puffs that nature places there, and which slide and press, press and slide, so warmly, so cozily, against each other — not unlike the way reverential hands are clasped in attitudes of prayer as their possessors sigh their *Aves* during evening meditation.

Within the hallowed corridors silenced by piety, an abrupt burst of giggles emanating from the cell of Sister Celestine — and someone else — resounded like the explosion that must have rocked Heaven when the recalcitrant angels disobeyed the Holiest of Holies. It was through God's guidance that the chastest of holy sisters, Sister Alphonsine, was idling nearby and heard the raucous intrusion. Alarmed by this breach of silence (surely an intruder was involved in this puzzle), she devoted herself to exploring the origin of those unnatural sounds that once again rang, in this temple of silence, as loudly as discordant bells must toll when yet another wayward soul is hurled into Hell's abyss and fires.

Sister Alphonsine had offered the first blink of her eyes — and every blink thereafter — to the Holiest One, a worthy offertory that resulted, in latter years, in the dear Sister's not being able to discern earthly shapes clearly, though she often spoke to angels invisible to others. God in His beneficence had granted her the gift of acute hearing. Armed with that gift, she stationed herself the next night (within comforting shadows that cooled her troubled brow) in such a way as to better overhear any sounds that might emanate from Sister Celestine's cell.

Her eyesight (donated, the Reader will recall with adulation, to her Maker) did not allow her to discern to whom belonged the curvaceous figure that knocked softly on the door of Sister Celestine's room. Sister Alphonsine was aware, however, that the door had opened — it squeaked — and quickly closed. Soon after, she heard words that troubled and baffled her, words that interrupted the giggling, which preceded them: ". . . it tickles . . ." ". . . now you . . ." "No — leave the habit on and raise it . . ." "You, too . . . and bounce."

After more giggles, breathy words, and the sounds of tosses and turns — and, soon, horrifying gasps — subsided, Sister Alphonsine's acute hearing detected the quiet turning of the door-

162

knob of the violated chamber and the squeaky opening of the door. Certain a thief had defiled the sanctity of Sister Celestine's room, and, to disguise his activities, had forced her to utter mysterious words, Sister Alphonsine thrust herself on the figure who emerged.

It was Sister Monica adjusting her habit.

The need was clear: More fervent dedication to her vows must be coaxed out of Sister Celestine. She was assigned to a post that guaranteed close contact with His Holiness the Pope, a wish His Holiness granted her distraught family, and did so (to emphasize his commitment to their mutual goal of leading her back into the holy stream of the devotional life) in a quiet ceremony held in a chapel the devout family had donated to the Cause of Goodness.

Feeling chastised instead of elevated, the treacherous Nun turned against her Holy Benefactor and proceeded to initiate repugnant lies concerning him, the Most Devout Prelate of the Holy Mother Church. Seized by only the Devil knows what, Sister Celestine kept her sacrilegious accusations deliberately vague —

Ha!

— revealing only that they concerned the High Prelate's daily walks about the Cathedral's beautiful gardens and his kind invitations, extended to especially devout mothers and their beguilingly innocent children, to receive his special blessings in the holy palace, whose polished floors gleamed as God's Heaven must have when God hosted his loyal angels to sing their Alleluias.

When a Nobleman most worthy in the eyes of the Holy Pontiff requested that a Nun be appointed to oversee the actions of his rebellious wife (the notorious Contessa, the Reader may by now have surmised), it was Sister Celestine whom the Pope himself assigned. Although he would have preferred to dedicate his own life to steering the wayward Nun onto the virtuous path himself, he nonetheless responded foremost to the Nobleman's great need.

The Reader (at this point familiar with the circle of corruption that this *True Account* wearily but dutifully continues to draw) will not be surprised to learn that it was this same Renegade Nun (that depraved Celestine!) who witnessed, and shrewdly abetted, the atrocity that occurred in the abundant gardens of the great Nobleman, when he pulled the lustful Gypsy Rogue from an intended position over his wife, a position that, if assumed, would have resulted in . . . (The Writer will allow the Reader to remember,

163

from an earlier page in this *True Account,* what was about to occur among the tulips but did not occur, thanks to God's intervention and the quick wits of the Nobleman.)

What, the Reader asks, was the connection of this transgressing Nun to the wayward Contessa so that holy loyalties would be so displaced?

What else?

The swarthy Gypsy Rogue was the *brother* of Sister Monica, who fled the convent and surely became — (The Writer will not judge a scarlet woman.)

Time passed, as time is wont to do in the Calendar that leads us ever closer to Salvation — and, for some, Damnation. The libelous Nun insinuated her poisonous rumors into the ears of the ever-eager Whore, who, with the Reverend Pimp, quickly saw a way to entrap even more deeply the kindly but gullible Count, the Contessa's favorite son — *and confidant.*

They *do* suspect the Contessa confided . . . *what?* . . . to my beloved Count du Muir.

The Writer, unbowed by his heavy moral obligation, now returns to this inevitable malevolence: the extorted agreement by the Count to marry the Whore. The Contessa's wavering morality clearly contributed to this decision, since, infallible witnesses report, there occurred secret meetings between her and the abominable Whore.

It *was* Irena by the River — and outside the bridal shop with the Pope — *and* she followed the Contessa's carriage on the night the gracious lady first came to warn me of danger! Madame is right. The writers of this calumny believe I possess information they want . . . Do I? About what? Information the Contessa gave the Count and that she attempted to give me, information that he *did* give me? What! . . . I shall inspect my memories much more closely when I meet with Madame for tea. Of course, Madame may be ahead of me, since, I suspect, it may all involve the matters she conjectured about so wildly, the interlude in the tulip garden.

I continue to read aloud, without your even having to reiterate your challenge:

Such a marriage, of the devilish Whore and the Count, might easily be annulled, given the nature of the coercions, and the power of his noble family name. So the Whore and her Reverend Pimp set out to gain the greatest imprimatur of legitimacy to secure the unholy union — and the Count's vast fortune: the officiating by the devout High Prelate himself in a wedding to be performed (the Writer ponders, ponders, ponders that which is beyond the grasp of the righteous, the enormity of wicked cunning) . . . in the Grand Cathedral. If not, the Whore threatened to make available to the ever-salacious Press the scurrilous rumors that the pernicious Nun had conveyed to her.

How could the Shepherd of the Righteous allow such an impious mockery of holy sacraments to proceed in the Grand Cathedral? The High Prelate retreated to a monastery of total silence and fasting, there to ponder the matter in holy meditation. He ventured out only in solitude in order to be inspired by the profligate innocence of country lasses (in flouncy aprons which flapped in the wind about their pink unblemished thighs, and sometimes fluttered — just a bit, the slightest, tiny bit — higher) and among equally uninitiated shepherd lads (who romped about the hillsides as insouciant to the immorality of the world as they were to their trousers, too short for their burgeoning loins, as they, those romping lads, herded goats that pretended to be eager to escape the lads' playful poking and prodding).

Not once did the Holy Father consider his own well-being during this period of imposed separation from the world. He knew that not even the most vicious gossip could imperil him. (Since no one would believe it, the Reader adds with due indignation.) Any attempt to defame him would fail. His purity, his devotion to the Holy Mother Church, and, above all, God's Benevolence, would shelter him from all slanders. Still, what of his flock? Daily, he guided those of his vast congregation of souls into the holy life of pilgrims, exhorted them to trust in goodness, to bring their children to him for special blessings. All those congregants would be severely harmed if only by learning that there existed beings so base as to attempt to harm him. He must think of them, only of them.

So the Pontiff returned to the Grand Cathedral, to allow matters to proceed. Who knew better than he that God's mysteries are infinite? Who knew whether during the performance of such a marriage, an Angel from Heaven Itself would be assigned to rip from the debased Whore the mockery of the sacrilegious bridal veil she insisted she would wear? Or perhaps God's mysterious ways would choose an intervening angel (in the form of an upright woman of sturdy intellect and vast wisdom) to become the

165

instrument of the corrupt Whore's downfall, banishing her into silenced contemplation of her evil for the rest of her unworthy life, or even hurrying her entry into the abyss prepared for such as she: an *earlier* judgment *in addition* to that which the Almighty guarantees.

And (the Writer hears the pious Reader marvel — but who among his readers is *not* pious?) all of these sad convolutions stemmed out of the Whore's determination to seize the sizable fortune of the great dynasty involved, a fortune, the Writer emphasizes, *which will surely find its rightful place — and that rightful place is not within the Whore's sullied hands.*

More asserted threats, more gross accusations. Whatever money I shall acquire, in whatever manner, I shall donate to the destitute. Surely that is known.

Exhausted but undaunted by this *True Account* that he is honor-bound to record, the Writer now divulges that, throughout this pilgrimage of devoted exposure, he has been carrying an added weight of outrage: *knowledge of a most harrowing act in the Whore's contaminated past, an act so heinous that —*

Stop! my heart cries out to the pages themselves. I will not turn the page. I wipe away today's tears, and the ancient tears of centuries of blame, tears I was still shedding, or resumed shedding, as I walked to Madame's for tea the following afternoon.

I cannot explain why I continued past her château. I realized, only when I had stopped, that I was once again facing, though still from a distance, the residence of the new tenant. I could not see whether he was there, at what I've come to think of as his "station." There might have been a form there, but perpetual shadows — the château is draped in heavy vines — did not allow further identity. I moved closer, still remaining concealed by brush and trees. He was there! He took a step. Toward me? No. He couldn't have seen me. He took another step. He clutched something before him. He extended it. Certainly not toward me. The fact that he had stepped forward into full sunlight allowed me, even at this distance, to see what it was he was holding.

White orchids dipped in blood!

I ran to Madame's château to discuss this urgent matter with her. But when I saw her beaming face, and the exquisite band that held her hair in a most becoming new manner, a band gilded with the tiniest of gems that I would remark on later, I became certain that the strange offering of orchids dipped in blood was only an impression created by the play of light and shadows, and a sudden flash of red concocted by the sun's reflection on the glass covering of my unlit lantern, a brightness left momentarily impressed on my eyesight.

I handed Madame the "Third Installment" of the loathsome "Account" for her to read. Peering at it, Ermenegildo looked up tensely at me after each page was turned.

I had to distract myself. So I detected a sweet mixture of scents in the air, grass, flowers, leaves. The sun lingered longer these days to enjoy the spectacle it helped create. Now and then the weather reached back to winter, even turned cold, almost as often as it reached out for snatches of the summer to come. Today, the afternoon was so warm that I had considered suggesting we have iced tea, a custom quite accepted in other regions, but I did not risk offending Madame, since today's pastries, half-moons of butter and sugar — the promised "surprise," which I greeted with ample appreciation — were meant to compliment hot tea.

"Note, Lady," Madame observed, putting down the new pages when she had reached the place where I had indicated I had stopped reading — reading to the same place keeps us mutually informed — "that they emphasize their warnings, even underlining them."

"Yes."

She muttered as if to herself but clearly for me to hear: "And once again, we return to the Contessa in the garden . . ." She left her sentence pending.

I waited, hoping that that further reference would prod her to clarify her assertion that there was evidence in these pages that Irena would like to uncover that the Gypsy was the father of Alix and the Count du Muir, a conjecture quite impossible. Irena is everything horrible, but *not* illogical.

Just as once I had kept at bay her expectations that I might resume, on my own, my account of how I saved John the Baptist's virginity, Madame now seemed determined not to resume the matter I had somewhat testily interrupted — unless I asked her to. I would not! To emphasize her own determination, she replaced on the table the "Third Installment" of the "Account." We would read no more of it today, nor discuss it.

We sipped our tea in emphatic silence.

"Lady" — Madame held up an admonitory finger. On it, a ruby

squeezed by tiny diamonds multiplied a single ray of sun into a glittering corona. Today she wore a tiara, of amethysts and more diamonds; she is very fond of diamonds. "Don't be lulled. Keep in mind that interviews will be rigorous. You may be forgetting, because your lives are increasingly familiar to you, that yours is not a conventional story, but quite extravagant."

"Extravagant? The story of my essence populating the bodies of the great fallen women, to redeem them in this life, to allow them, finally, a hearing in the court of revised history, to tell the truth at last — you consider *that* extravagant?" As I compounded my answer, it did occur to me that I was indeed becoming too familiar with my lives.

"Lady, sometimes you slay me!" Madame had added an odd tone to her odd words.

"Madame!"

She spoke in her own voice: "Well, no one will think it all that extravagant if you tell it like you just did, putting that expert quiver in your voice when you said 'to tell the truth at last.' Expertly done, very effective."

"I did not *put* a 'quiver' into my voice. My passion did," I told her coolly.

"Lady, do you sometimes forget that I'm your ally?"

"Never. If I thought otherwise, Madame —" I couldn't find words that would even consider such a terrifying impossibility.

She sat back, dusting sugar from her lap. She readjusted her tiara. "Now! We must discuss a matter we can no longer avoid."

"Medea."

I suppose Madame did not hear me; she continued: "Yes, we must discuss a matter we can no longer avoid: What's in it for me?"

"Madame? That tone —" It had returned from earlier.

"Get used to it. What do I get out of all this?"

This wasn't occurring!

Did even Ermenegildo wince as if he, too, was hearing a different person? I was so disconcerted that I bent down to retrieve a blossom I had held in my hand and had just dropped, a blossom I had plucked from the adornment on the table near the tea setting, a beautiful yellow rose tinted only at its edges with a flush of red. When I began to lift the fallen flower, it crumbled into scattered petals. I gasped and withdrew from it.

"What is *my* purpose in all this?"

I tried not to stammer, not to gasp, not to plead. "Your commitment, like mine — The truth, finally — My essence —"

"You believe that?"

Ermenegildo jerked back his head.

"Yes, I do believe you're as committed as I am." Why was I speaking these words?

"But *they* won't. They'll be looking for ulterior motives. They must not anger you, Lady."

Her voice was back! Madame Bernice's voice was back! Oh, to emphasize the import that this matter will be given by interviewers she had succeeded admirably in coarsening her voice, altering its tone. Perhaps she had done that for a further reason — I was sure of this now — to camouflage how much it hurt her that this matter should have to come up at all. "Oh, Madame, if *you* are questioned, I shall, I'm sorry, be quite angered."

"They may claim" — she was so clearly hesitant even to speak these terrible words of unwarranted suspicion that she forced them into casualness — "that I may be using your revelations for purposes of my own. What would you say to that?"

I wanted to weep at the possibility of such an accusation. "Our purposes have been the same since that memorable day when we met —" I indicated the bench where I had first encountered this remarkable woman and her peacock.

"Are our purposes the same?"

What internal strife she was experiencing to have to discuss such unpleasant matters! That's why she had slipped into the disturbing voice she had used earlier, an unconscious slide perhaps in this most difficult task for her. "What if you're told that I'm exploiting you to get attention for myself, seeking publicity for my mystic powers, inviting the notoriety that would get me money for my own version of —"

"Notoriety? Pub —? Money? Why are you putting yourself through the pain of expressing such outrageous thoughts, Madame? You'll be known as the catalyst for all my revelations." I was trying to indicate to her how well I would handle the matter.

"Oh, will I? You're sure?"

What was happening? What was Madame intending? She had never, this long, sustained the role of interrogator, nor in quite this voice, which Ermenegildo must have continued to detect, since he had cocked one ear carefully toward her. Her voice had become...

169

frightening! I felt a dizziness, no, I felt stable within the whirling landscape, as if all the colors of Madame's garden had been whipped about and I was at the bottom of a vortex. But why was I staring up? Oh, Madame had pointed into the sky, and Ermenegildo was following her gaze.

Directly over us, a hawk — I had seen it earlier, circling the sky all afternoon — was pursuing another bird! The bird dipped toward the ground! The hawk pounced on it! The bird's wings flailed! The hawk attacked it savagely, withdrew, returned to assault it — over and over — until the bird fell to the ground, a bloody pulp! The hawk soared away!

"Madame! Please help me through these moments!" I screamed, at the same time that I saw my hand reach out calmly to my cup of tea as I smiled and brought it to my lips and sipped.

XVII

MADAME DID NOT COMMENT on the terrible spectacle of the hawk attacking the bird, although she was still pointing to it — no, *now* she was pointing out — and Ermenegildo was staring at — a dazzling cloud that had burst like a white blossom streaked silver. I concluded that the latter had allowed Madame to leave unmentioned the pantomime of violence in the sky — and my reaction to it. Had my scream been silent, contained just at the point it would have been uttered? Like Madame, I welcomed pushing the ugly matter away.

Now I needed boldly to clarify and so defuse the distressing words she had been speaking just earlier, questioning her position in our journey that will culminate at interviews. I would do so by indicating to her how well I would handle the disturbing matters she had introduced: "You *do* want what I want, Madame, to revise false judgments — and to solve the Mystery of Babylon and Eden . . . So I forbid you to continue your earlier line of questioning —"

"Then I should stop," Madame said, her eyes pulling away from me, looking down into her hands on her lap. Sadly? She had spoken those words so quietly — and with such moving sincerity — that they were almost stifled by the flutter of a butterfly.

"Yes!" I welcomed.

"Except that there is more —" She looked up, her stare newly challenging, determined to continue, and in the odd, disturbing voice that she had used earlier.

"No, Madame."

"— more that must be discussed in a related vein —"

"No."

"Yes." She affirmed her resolve by assuming a rigid posture in her chair. I told myself that she had done so because her back was troubling her especially today. Her words contradicted my hope: "— and that includes speculation that will be aroused about" — she sipped — "about who you really are."

Who I really am.

How strange, to hear those words as I sat at tea on the lawn of Madame's château. I looked at my shadow on the marble veranda. Who I really am.

Madame proceeded: "Surely you agree that some may deem your stories so extravagant that they will grasp for ordinary — yes, more understandable — deductions?"

"Please clarify." I did not want to speak those words. I do not welcome cruelty, and — whatever the intent might prove to be here — the subject was cruelty. But explored by Madame, it would be done with kindness, I tried to convince myself.

Still, the casual voice resumed: "Oh, I suppose someone may claim" — she leaned over to stroke Ermenegildo's comb; he eased away, closer to me — "that you're a woman who has not lived at all and is conjuring up extremities."

"Not lived at all!" My subdued laughter masked my bitterness at that remote conjecture, and it assured her I could easily dissuade such a vagrant confusion.

"Oh, perhaps not *that*, but someone might indeed conjecture that you are really the woman in —" She glanced at the "Account" of lies on the table with our tea.

"Those are distortions of my lives," I reminded her. I must keep composed. This would soon change.

"And we can't ignore," Madame moved on quickly, her tone unyielding, "that someone will attempt to identity you as a woman — oh, missing — someone in hiding —"

"I am in hiding, Madame."

"We both know that, and why, and from what, according to you. But they may claim you're someone *else* in hiding . . . because of, well, some kind of . . . violence . . . beyond, you know, what occurred in the Cathedral —" What did her unflinching look anticipate?

My voice was calm. "I have known much violence, yes."

"In the extreme, some may even claim that you're in —"

I reached out toward a flower on the vine nearby, but before I could feel its petals, I saw that it was almost dead. I withdrew my hand. I touched my forehead, sheltering my eyes from the sudden return of a terrible white glaring sun. "— in the country, Madame," I finished for her. "That is exactly where I am. In the country! And I — And I — And I —!" Madame's garden was fading, everything was fading into darkness and I was plunging into its depths. I gasped, and struggled to push myself out forcefully.

"Lady!"

Madame stood up, over me. She raised her hand, as if to touch me. She sighed. "Lady —"

"Madame?" The darkness receded in waves.

Madame's hand finished its gesture, a gentle gesture; she touched my hair, stroked it softly. "Oh, Lady, Lady, I'm sorry. I went on too long, far too long! Ermenegildo tried to warn me, did you notice?"

I breathed. Her voice was back, Madame's caring voice was back.

"It was all necessary, Lady. You had to know the wild conjecturing that will occur — but only in the very first minutes, because, once you present your evidence — once you've cast your spell of truth" — she indicated with a snap of her hand how quickly that would happen — "there will be not one solitary interviewer who will doubt a single word you say." She sat back down, but across the table she held my hands, returning blood to them. "It racked me, to put you through that most grueling ordeal, oh, I shared it, I promise you I shared it." Was she dabbing at tears, pretending to be holding the napkin only to her mouth while actually drying tears?

I felt . . . reprieved. Yet a wisp of sadness lingered. "Who I really am," I echoed those strange words.

"Oh, Lady, that was the most difficult part I had to go through. You are the beloved of the Count du Muir, and, most important, you are the essence —"

"— of all fallen women unjustly blamed."

"Who better than I would know that, Lady? It was I who first explained your dreams —"

"— as memories."

"I had to be cruel, Lady. If you could endure the kind of brutal skepticism I put you through — and you did, Lady, you endured it — you will hold the interviewers in your hands."

"And I will!"

It was over, the harshest rehearsal was over, and I had passed. How quickly the sense of trust that bound us was restored. I felt a resurgence of my determination — *our* — determination.

Ermenegildo brushed his head against my lap and then strolled over to Madame and brushed hers, formally announcing that the troubling moments had passed.

"Lady! Let's continue with another life!"

"Yes!" How wonderfully it was all restored. It took restraint for me not to rise and hug Madame.

Now we would resume our rehearsals for interviews!

Roam through the War in Heaven, the fiery plains, plagues, fires, trumpets, shooting stars, and locusts? No.

Could I bear now to face memories of Jesus' and Judas's naked bodies, dead, one on the cross, the other hanging from a barren tree? Could I bear to remember with what franticness I longed to disrobe to the storming night, to share their nudity in death just as I had shared it in life?

Was it that this day's light was about to melt into dusk, so soon — was it that which made me decide? Had the strange interlude with Madame contributed, warning me that I must recoil from nothing? "I believe, Madame, it's time to continue the story of Mary and Jesus —"

Madame touched her forehead solemnly; perhaps she made a sign of the cross.

"— and to see Judas clearly." My eyes demanded that she face me.

She fussed — it is the only word I can think of to describe her series of movements — with her tiara, finally abandoning it at what might otherwise have clearly seemed to her an odd angle. She was preparing to be intransigent, that's how completely the Madame Bernice I had known had been restored after the strange interlude, which had now lost its strangeness entirely. "I do believe that as we proceed into that sacred territory, we should keep in mind that Judas has been powerfully implicated —"

"— as powerfully implicated, yes, as Eve."

Ermenegildo peered — I might even say stared warningly — at her.

She broke one of the delectable pastries into crumbs and extended them to him. He did not take the . . . bribe? "The point I'll make here," she said, "is that we've already had Lucifer in a very unconventional light — which I know is the correct light, since you were there —"

"Precisely."

She had trapped herself. "Oh, let's go on and find what we shall find." She hurried to add: "And that might be what we've accepted for centuries about that man."

My silence allowed her that possibility before I resumed:

Eventually, it lifted — the moodiness that had separated Jesus from us after we had eaten the magic mushrooms, the moodiness that had settled over him after Mary's declaration that in his visions of kingdoms and satanic temptations he had discovered whose son he really was. Even more fervently, Jesus denounced injustice, of rulers, priests, all despots. "Resist oppression!" he demanded simply but powerfully of the people he gathered easily at street corners. Even those bowed by misery were stirred by his challenge.

"— defiance *and* possibility, that's what he offers," Judas said proudly. "*That's* a real miracle, Magdalene, to give hope to those who've lost it, real hope, not false hope." He had spoken loud enough for Jesus to hear as we sat in a tent we often pitched outside the City for a night, a day.

"You could do all that, too, Judas," Jesus extended generously, but Judas shook his head and said, "No, only you."

Jesus lowered his head, trying to conceal his smile at Judas's praise.

"Lady," Madame brought me back into her garden, "did Jesus blush?"

"Yes, Madame."

"Charming, yes, charming, indeed lovely. Might you —?"

Jesus blushed and lowered his head, trying to conceal his smile at Judas's praise.

In the deep of night, Judas and I woke — Judas first, and, sitting up, he startled me — to find Jesus gone. We knew where. Earlier, he had informed us — and we assumed it was Mary who had informed him — that John the Baptist was outside the City. "I must speak to him," Jesus had said. We found him and the Baptist in an improvised thatch hut by the River.

Judas and I remained a distance apart from them, remembering when we had first met on the bank of the River Jordan. The reflections of John and Jesus were dark smears in the water as they talked until dusk cooled the desert and Jesus joined us silently — and then stayed away that day and night.

In the City, at dawn, we walked by Mary's dwelling. Awash in the day's new light, the exquisite blue lady and her bedazzling son stood watching the sun rise.

"No painter ever captured that splendid moment," Madame Bernice rued.

"Alas, no, Madame."

The sun appeared, adding new splendor to the two presences. Mary nodded to us graciously, and Jesus greeted us warmly, holding our hands. In that moment, we recognized our beloved again, unchanged. As we walked away, we heard the soft murmurings of Mary's voice: "The holy Baptist confirmed —?" When she spoke, it was always as if she were praying.

The next day, a hot, sultry afternoon of violent desert winds, Jesus returned to where Judas and I huddled in our tent. He smiled and embraced us. We lay on the sand, holding on to each other, moments that did not calm, only intensified, the sensual currents within which we swam, always deeper. When the wind had settled and the sky was bright with stars, we gathered from a hill the mushrooms we had eaten an earlier time, and we ate them, restoring the bursts of color and sounds we had first experienced, the sight of dipping stars.

After the drugged hallucinations were over and Judas and I lay on the cooled sand, Jesus stood over us. His robe rested only over his shoulders, framing his exposed, feverish body. He trembled in the heat; the moon turned his perspiration into a silver glaze.

"All begins and ends with me, and before me there was nothing."

Judas laughed.

Jesus' look of astonishing seriousness did not relent.

Angered, Judas challenged him: "Are you sacred, then?"

"I am the Son of God."

Judas reached out to touch him.

"No," Jesus said.

I watched unbreathing as the two men I loved gazed at each other.

Judas completed his gesture, his hand on Jesus' shoulder, tentatively; I sensed Judas's fear as his touch firmed. Jesus embraced Judas. Only I saw Jesus' tears. Judas felt them on his bare shoulders. Jesus pulled away.

In the morning, dark clouds roamed undecided in a blue sky when I woke. Judas lay near me. Jesus was gone.

"It was only the mushrooms that made him say that, that's all. Nothing's changed," Judas said anxiously.

For a time, that seemed to be true.

So gradually that at first we did not notice, new words infiltrated Jesus' talks — now sermons — words that soon replaced his exhortations of just defiance; he spoke about "God's reward in Heaven . . . joy in the Kingdom of God . . . comfort only in God's love . . ."

We no longer performed in his "miracles," which we had staged. Now when he came upon the sick and the insane, he tended to them by taming "afflicting demons." And he did allay their pain and fears with his intense, powerful insistence; soothed them for brief moments of dredged faith that were witnessed by increasing crowds that rushed to spread the word of miracles. Some began to call him "Lord," a designation that soon spread. Now men and women knelt before him — and reached out to touch him for his blessing, which he granted "in God's name."

For moments, I, too, was swept away by Jesus' growing power to mesmerize. "*Is* he the Son of God?" I spoke aloud, immediately amazed at my own words.

Judas shook his head. "He's a man."

I told Judas what Mary had claimed, that day in the marketplace, about Jesus' divinity, her own pure conception.

Although I warned him not to, and I ran after him, Judas wouldn't stop, didn't stop even when we encountered Jesus sitting on the edge of a fountain, instructing a smattering of people gathered about him.

Judas and I found Mary weaving a blue shawl in her home. Mary kept her rooms impeccably clean, and she chose to sit in a place where, in the morning, light from a window would sprinkle her presence with azure.

"Tell Jesus the truth of his birth! Whatever it is!" Judas demanded.

Mary glanced up at him, with a vague smile of greeting. "The truth?" She seemed just slightly baffled. She continued her weaving. Nearby, her husband, Joseph, absently crossed two pieces of abandoned wood.

Does she know the truth anymore, whatever it is? I wondered urgently.

"Yes, the truth, Mary!" Judas demanded, and added softly, "Please." He spoke cautiously, with kindness: "Perhaps about what you consider your own sinful transgression — but it wouldn't be, Mary, it wouldn't be sinful," he pled.

Joseph looked up, questioning. Silent, Mary was more distant, more like blue crystal, and more beautiful than I had ever seen her. The aura painters would give to her never compared to that which truly embraced her.

Judas sighed his words to Mary: "Were you taken against your will? Is that why you're claiming —?"

I preferred the image I had had of her on an earlier day, of her lying on a field of flowers and laughing exultantly with her lover.

When she heard Judas's question, Mary stopped her weaving. She inspected the blue shawl, and then she looked up at him. "I am pure,

Judas, and Jesus is the Son of God. The Angel Gabriel announced that to me."

As Judas and I were leaving the impeccably ordered lodging, Mary took me aside. With a gentle touch of her hand — so soft I hardly felt it — she led me to a courtyard, a small garden to which at serene moments she retreated. I noticed that, here, too, the morning light filtered blue on her.

Under an acacia tree, its white blossoms radiant in that light, I sat with her on a bench. Absently, from a luxurious shrub nearby, she plucked a perfect anemone, its center so pale it was almost as white as its outer petals. "Magdalene," she began, "I know how sincerely you and Judas believe that I'm wrong, or even" — she smiled at this as a clear impossibility — "that the Angel Gabriel was wrong." She lowered her head. "You cannot understand certain things because" — she touched me again, to lighten her words — "because, once, you were a . . . prostitute."

I stood, aghast. Her words had scorched me with hurt.

Centuries later, in Madame's garden, I felt a pang of that hurt. "I thought then, Madame, that I would never be able to forgive her; that Mary and I had been separated forever . . .

"Mary and I had been separated forever!"

Madame repeated the same words I had just repeated, words that lingered, echoing, in my mind, now with the hint of a new meaning, the barest hint, like the withdrawn touch of a hand. I saw Madame emphatically add the same words to the essential evidence she was collecting. Her hands pressed her temples for moments longer than usual.

"Oh, Lady," she soothed me, "of course the Holy Mother was wrong to say that to you, that you couldn't understand because once you had been a — I'm sure she meant no harm. She was simply confused by the rush of events she must have seen coming. I'm sure that she —"

My heart was filled with joy that Madame Bernice had hurried to my defense, without abandoning her staunch support of the Holy Mother she so revered. I was happy to tell her what I said next: "I only thought that I would never be able to forgive her, Madame; I was wrong. I did, on the torturous road to Calvary." And, here, too, in Madame's garden — I did not yet tell Madame this — where my words, recounting the sense of separation I had felt with Mary, resonated with a significance I could still not grasp.

When Jesus, Judas, and I were alone again that starless night in the desert, Judas grabbed Jesus by the shoulders, forcing him around, kissing him on the mouth — no longer the kiss of children. Judas withdrew in horror from the cold lips that renounced him.

"Nothing must interfere with my Father's mission," Jesus said. "Especially not" — his eyes shimmered with tears — "our love."

Judas winced. "Your revelations are nothing but hallucinations aroused by the mushrooms!" he shouted. "I've had visions, too; so has Magdalene. Tell him, Magdalene! We've seen the same visions." Turning to me for the affirmation he received, he pled with Jesus: "When we touched, you and I and Magdalene, when we kissed, remember? — remember! — was *that* wrong? Would even more — what we all long for — be wrong?"

I waited, eagerly, to hear Jesus answer. And he did. He shook his head, no.

"Whether as much as has happened was wrong or not, whether more would be wrong or not, my son must remain pure in body and soul now, pure to undertake the holy journey he's been chosen for." Within the azure glow of the sudden dawn, Mary was there speaking those words.

Judas said softly to Jesus, "If she convinces you of your divine conception, she may purify herself of whatever she considers her own sins, but she'll destroy your true spirit — and your life. And mine," he added.

"Your mission will not be interrupted," Mary said to Jesus.

Jesus wiped the gathering tears from his eyes. "It will not be interrupted," he said.

In Madame's garden, I could not continue, not now, not to where my memories must move. Madame understood.

I lit my lamp. I draped my cowl over my head. I nodded to Madame Bernice, and I made my way back to my château.

In my quarters now, I am still drenched in the sorrow of my earlier recollections, the long approach to Calvary. I shall resume the true story of the Crucifixion later. I cannot approach that monumental event without having to pause. Its pain never lessens.

From my window, I see the destitute wanderers from the City, whose numbers — there are more fires glinting within the night — increase nightly. There are so many now, Madame informed me earlier, that they have begun to construct dwellings out of wood and debris within the countryside. From this distance, I join their painful desolation.

Those recurring sounds at my door!

Someone listening, watching, reporting to . . . those determined to silence what I will reveal at interviews.

I touch my gun. I'll defend myself. Interviews *will* take place!

Sounds fade. I glance through unread pages of the "Third Installment," more words of accusation and slander I must eventually roam through. Beyond my will, my hand leafs to the end. I gasp! I read . . . ugly words. No more! Not now!

I must sleep, just sleep, must welcome darkness . . .

Tomorrow — or the next day, or soon — I shall tell Madame that the "Third Installment" in these defamations ends with this:

In the following and Final Installment of this *True Account,* the Writer will fulfill his promise to reveal the most heinous of the Whore's despicable acts — the slaughter of her children.

XVIII

MADAME'S SLY LOOK AT ME the next afternoon alerted me to what I quickly discovered: We were having a new brew of tea. I smiled and nodded in approval.

"It *is* especially fine, don't you think, Lady?" She wanted to hear the obvious.

"Splendid, splendid."

There were very few pastries on the plate when I arrived. I became immediately aware of that because silver-embossed flowers glinted on the almost barren dish. Ermenegildo glanced at the meager remains, a few crumbs — and then aimed a reproving stare at Madame. She explained that she had not had time for lunch — "not a bite, and I had a very light and early breakfast." She then turned quickly serious: "Since those opposed to our intentions are plotting to move soon, to block interviews, or to rush them before we're entirely ready — oh, they are clever —"

I did not ask what new indications led her to that deduction. I assumed she meant the "Third Installment" of the "Account," which, again, she had read only to the point where I had left off last night — before I had begun my leafing and fallen into a churning sea of terrifying sleep.

"— we must take some time to ask: What are the matters we must resolve?" She began counting them on her fingers, which even in the light of a dull afternoon blazed as if they carried their own illumination. "First, the connection between Eve and the girl in Patmos, since it was in Patmos with St. John that your redeeming essence first stirred and rushed to join Eve in Eden —"

"— when he claimed he saw the word 'Mystery' written on my

181

forehead and cursed me as a whore and the mother 'of all abominations of the earth.' " As often as I might pronounce those words, I
never failed to reel at the immensity of the curse.

Madame Bernice continued her itemization. "That's one; and
two is: Why did your essence so forcefully choose the life of
Magdalene? — a 'whore' but not a woman blamed; some would call
her a woman redeemed."

The subject of Mary was coming up; Madame always bows her
head when she introduces matters pertaining to the Holy Mother.
There was a further signal, one that indicated that she was going to
admonish me. She crossed her arms, firmly, over her bosom. Today a
startling emerald lodged there, the pendant of a stunning necklace she
had not worn before. The tiara, I did remember. "We must define the
Holy Mother's full, moving, and *very* touching role in the Crucifixion." She paused for doubled emphasis. "In that respect, Lady, I do
think that the beautiful blue lady" — she caressed her favorite of my
descriptions of Mary — "may be emerging somewhat harshly."

"She is *not* emerging harshly! She is emerging truthfully. I've
made it clear to you that I came to love the beautiful blue lady. *You*
remember, Madame, that it was only I —" And Judas, but I did not
want now to remember him joining us for a short, so very short, time.
"— who accompanied her to Calvary." I recalled with what bitterness
I had searched vainly for the disciples.

Madame said quietly, "I would have accompanied her, too, on
that agonized journey."

Ermenegildo indicated his intention would have been the same;
he thrust his head up proudly.

I had chosen not yet to tell Madame this until it was all clearer:
During rehearsals in my chamber, I have often dredged my recollections about the very questions I know she often ponders concerning
Mary: What did she truly believe? And why? At those times of deep
consideration, submerged memories surface on my mind, like flot-
sam, memories almost drowned within the overwhelming ocean of
despair that swept through Calvary that fatal afternoon. Then, I
remember a powerful accusation uttered on Golgotha. But at whom?
By whom? At me, Magdalene? By me? No. An accusation hurled by
Jesus? Or Judas? No, the words of startling accusation I try to recall
in those moments belong to Mary, spoken by her. Sometimes it all
seems about to become clear, but only for the sliver of a second, as if
a lantern has been lit in a dark room, then snuffed. All that remains is

the image of the Holy Mother staring up at the sky beyond her son on the cross —

"And," Madame continued her tally, "we must explore where, I suspect, many answers lie hidden." I knew what she meant, of course, but I knew she liked to announce, herself, monumental matters: "Where else but in Heaven?" She shrugged.

Into my *Pensées* that shall go, with accreditation: Where else but in Heaven?

Madame inhaled so mightily her bosom seemed to blossom. "After we connect all *that,* everything else will fall into place as evidence." She leaned back in satisfaction at the prospect of soon bringing order out of chaos. Then she seemed to slump at the monumental undertaking. "But that's not for now, it's late, we should resolve lesser pending matters. So now —" She waited.

Waited.

And waited.

Oh, I knew where she was attempting to go without committing herself — to Herod's Palace and the pending subject of St. John the Baptist's salvaged virginity. "Yes, Madame, and now?" I felt no compromise in offering her a gentle prod.

Her lips tightened.

Well, I would wait as if I were not aware of her discomfort, a discomfort created, I reminded myself, by her intransigence. I touched Ermenegildo's comb; he had sidled up to me. His wayward feather has become even more beautiful than the others in his glorious comb — to compensate for its unconventional direction? But then, who's to say that it is not all the *other* feathers that are pointing wrong? That thought will surely find its way into my *Pensées.*

"Oh, for Heaven's sake, tell me how you saved John the Baptist's virginity and preserved your own, while nevertheless thrusting your body against his arousal to the point that he came." Madame threw her hands up in a gesture that sprinkled the air with brilliant pinpoints of light reflected from her gems.

Now that the impasse of several teas had been broken by her, I felt somewhat remorseful — rather than triumphant, as I had anticipated — that my entrenchment had remained longer. Fair was fair. I said, "I shall — and will you, Madame, kindly explain to me how, from that evil 'Account,' you inferred that the wicked Irena would like to uncover that the Gypsy was the father of the du Muir twins, something so —" I was about to say "utterly illogical," but that had been the original accusation that had brought about her silence; so, instead, I finished: "— something so carefully interjected that it requires someone of your formidable acumen to discern?"

Madame said: "I shall — and with even more evidence now —" She indicated the early pages of the "Third Installment" of the "Account."

I allowed her to gloat. After all, it was *she* who had withdrawn her intransigence. "Very well, Madame."

I returned to Herod's palace on that day of love and sex and blood and death. But it had been so long since I had recounted those moments to Madame, that I reoriented her — "Not that I need any reminder, but do go on," she said — right up to the moment where I had left off: "You will remember, Madame, that —"

I was now clothed only in the last veil, the sixth, gossamer just slightly darker than my skin, the veil Herodias counted on to introduce one more.

Herod's hand had readied his groin. In all her brazen nudity, Herodias was preparing to spring. At her order — when I removed the veil she thought would be the seventh — flanking guards would flash their torches before the Baptist's eyes, forcing him to blink. Once he glimpsed the spectacle of my body, his eyes would remain open on the only sight capable of arousing his virginal passion. Herodias would then push against his body chained to a column, and his saintly virginity would spill into her and be destroyed. Then she would have him slaughtered, to remain the only one ever to possess him.

My body would *not* prepare him for her, nor for death.

Whirling, swirling, turning, bending, reaching up, down, I coiled and uncoiled my body in a frenzy, moving steadily toward the Baptist. Before him I stopped. "Open your eyes now!" I ordered.

He did.

Bedazzled, he saw my body as if drawn upon the tissue of cloth, every arch and curve, my nipples darkened dots, the tiny puff between my legs lightly shaded, a tiny portion of the veil penetrating the glistening parting. Instantly, simply by inhaling, I allowed the last veil to fall. I stood naked before the Baptist's gaze and his fully grown desire.

Herodias realized then she had been duped, there was no seventh veil she had awaited. "No!" she screamed.

But I had already flung my body against the Baptist's full erection and he came.

"Well, we're right back where we started from!" I could not

believe Madame had interrupted me again at the exact point as before. "In hot water, with egg on our faces —"

I was not going to allow another impasse. I continued:

Herodias did not know that I had been careful — despite my longing otherwise — to press my body in such a way that the Baptist's arousal would slide up my stomach, but not enter me.

"Ah! Of *course,* Lady, I see, I see!" Madame cried. "How brilliant! No one other than you would have conceived of something that . . . *grand.*"

I withdrew from the Baptist, feeling his abundant moisture on my stomach. I would have left it there forever, a purifying warmth. But I must convince Herodias that his virginity was lost forever within me, lost forever to her. Secretly I rubbed away the saintly moisture from my body.

Moaning, Herod had collapsed against his throne, into a pool of his foul sweat, hardly dotted by his insignificant spurt. I faced my mother's wrath as she approached me.

"You've stolen his virginity!" she screamed.

"Yes," I uttered the necessary lie. "The way *you* sought to."

The Baptist bowed his head in gratitude at my sacrifice.

Herodias glanced at him, then away, discarding him. Draping her cloak over her naked body, she returned to her throne.

Now I would barter with Herod. "In return for what only I can accomplish for you, I ask that you release the Baptist." Without me, Herod would have only this one memory to hoard. The assurance of more would persuade him.

"Let the Baptist go," Herod ordered.

"Salome will follow him!" Herodias plotted new vengeance.

"Will you, Salome?" Herod demanded.

At that moment I glanced at the holy man. Love engulfed me so powerfully I could not lie, could form only one word, the one that would assert our unbreakable allegiance, which I wanted him to hear: "Yes!" Herod's superstitious fear would not allow a prophet's murder. Whatever other fate he would assign him, I would overcome, my love would overcome.

"Give the order to behead him!" Herodias demanded.

"But to kill a holy man, a pure —" Herod clutched his amulets.

"He's no longer pure!" Herodias shouted. "Salome assured that!"

The terrible crucial detail that I had not considered!

"Behead him!" Herod ordered.

The head of John fell at my feet.

I knelt and kissed his lips.

I wrapped myself in the many veils of color I had shed. I would replace them with black for the rest of my brief life, a bride in mourning, blamed, and branded forever a whore . . . blamed.

Madame joined my silent sorrow, that day at tea.

Deceived by today's brief, intense heat that had pretended to be summer's, the buds that had sprouted on the vine next to where we drank our tea shriveled and died. The day unexpectedly threatened to turn harsh. A gray cloud lurking in the distance waited to seize the opportunity to ride on a rising wind, a heated wind. The sun became a fiery light draping Madame's garden. It was in that light that I noticed — and I gasped; how had I missed them on my arrival? — that an extravagant gathering of orchid lilies had blossomed along the veranda and they resembled — like a reminder, a warning? — the flowers of the stunning, leafless blossoms that grew only in Eden, but they resembled them only in their shape. The ones that brushed Madame's veranda were almost white, no, grayish — not the color that disappeared from Eden. In the center of the lush petals of these new flowers, there sprouted several stems on the tips of which were small dots of scarlet, like drops of blood on a bridal veil. Yes, they resembled also the flowers I thought I had imagined — had I? — that the new tenant had held out toward me, on an earlier afternoon when I had wandered close to his château. I welcomed Madame's spirited words that broke the powerful impression:

"Now, Lady, I want to explain to you about the Gypsy and the tulips and what Irena would like to discover —"

"Yes!" I was eager.

After she had reached for the earlier installment of the despicable "Account," she instantly located the relevant passage, poking her finger forcefully at it. "Right here, these pages of lies and buried truths say that when her husband discovered her with the Gypsy, the Contessa covered her most intimate part with flowers she clutched from the lawn."

I was attentive but still skeptical.

"Does it seem logical to you that a woman as brave, as defiant — and hot-blooded — as the Contessa — and remember she was young when she was involved with the handsome gypsy — would become suddenly modest? No! Now note that moments later, she's described as walking defiantly back to the mansion — 'brazen in her resurrected

insolence — after the few moments of modesty on the ground.' "
Madame read the exact words.

She certainly had a point, but where would it lead?

"Remember, Lady, among the flowers in the garden, especially plentiful were —" She waited for me to join in her exploration, although she had apparently already concluded it.

"Tulips," I remembered — and I remembered the puzzling moment in the Contessa's carriage that urgent night of warning when the she had said Irena was dangerous because she "thinks she knows about the tulips." I had been as baffled then as I was now.

"The latest installment of the 'Account' pointedly refers to the incident in the garden as 'what was about to occur among the tulips but did *not* occur.' We know, of course, what that was."

Again Madame had no difficulty locating the exact words in the pages she now reached for. I was sure she had rehearsed this withheld presentation in order to display her investigative acumen.

"To someone not as familiar with these matters as I," she gloated, before adding, graciously, "and you — this passage" — she stabbed at the pages again — "would seem to introduce the flowers, and especially the tulips, only as an element of description. To those more attuned — and to those it wants to address privately — the reference is clearly emphasized, masquerading as refined detailing. Now, I've had reason to observe that gypsies are notorious for their lush ejaculations —"

Oh, her superior tone would soon annoy me, but I refused to reveal that.

"— and the Gypsy and the Contessa were lying on tulips. Tulips, dear Lady, are shaped —" She bunched her fingers in imitation of a tube. She leaned back, like a queen on her throne, about to make an unassailable declaration. "It wasn't to *cover* her most intimate part that the Contessa reached out to clutch flowers, but to place — *into herself* — the fluid that the Gypsy had spattered so copiously into the receptive tulips!"

I was chagrined that it had taken me so long to deduce what now became so obvious. Madame was being so impossibly superior that I considered pretending that I had reached the same conclusion — and asking her how she knew about the lush ejaculations of gypsies; of course, she is a very educated woman. My natural graciousness won out: "How utterly brilliant of you, Madame, to deduce it all so exactly." She looked like a smug detective with a tiara.

"Thank you, Lady." Sharing her triumph — her smugness! — Ermenegildo spread his tail so that it seemed an extension of the resplendent skirt Madame wore that day.

"Then it's only Irena who's the husband's daughter!" The vast implications assaulted me.

"Yes, but Irena only suspects the truth, truth that would make *her* the heir to the du Muir fortune after the Contessa. But to sustain such an enormity, she needs a witness, or someone with knowledge gained from someone knowledgeable. She needs proof, information she's certain the Count possessed. He was his mother's favorite, remember, dark and loving like his real father. Irena suspects the Count gave you that information, and he did, Lady —"

"— when he proudly called himself 'the son of a gypsy,' " I recalled with a wrench of sorrow at that precious moment, gone.

"Irena suspects that the Contessa, too, divulged her secret to you," Madame went on, "and the dear lady was about to, that evening in her coach — and that day by the River, remember, Lady?"

How could I forget the gentle, lovely figure alone by the River? "She had gone there because she had learned that was where her beloved gypsy had been buried," I was now certain.

"Tossed into the River's waters by her evil husband's minions," Madame had arrived at the exact conclusion. "Oh, that despicable husband of hers was capable of that — and more, torturing his first wife, and" — Madame was thoughtful before she proceeded — "perhaps even himself arousing the mob that assaulted his own son from that earlier marriage —"

"— assaulted in that brutal way that had made my beloved Count wince with horror at the memory." I had long considered what Madame had concluded. I even more clearly now envisioned the savagery.

Madame paused for a few respectful, solemn seconds — her hands clasped before her lips in a wordless prayer — before she resumed with her earlier investigation: "And how does Irena hope to draw out from you information she wants about the Contessa and the Gypsy? By arousing your indignation with these distortions" — she poked several times at the pages of the installments on the table — "she hopes to unsettle you, to drive you to protest, make you long to separate your beloved husband from the villainies of the du Muirs, especially hers — and then trap you into stumbling, giving her information she needs, and at the same time — this is most important — ambushing interviews by forcing you to blurt your truths before we're ready . . . Now! Let's continue. Since it's clear from the 'Account' that Alix still believes himself to be Irena's ally and the Nobleman's son, who else other than the Contessa do you suppose knows the truth which still eludes Irena?" she asked, eager to astonish me with her answer.

"The renegade nun, who saw it all."

Madame had apparently not considered that, because she frowned and for a moment almost ceased her gloating. "She, too, of course," she mumbled. "But I meant someone much more important in this tapestry of cunning."

"The Pope," I again irritated her by answering before she could.

Madame glowered at me for a moment. But she is nothing if not grand, and so she continued: "Yes, the one to whom the Contessa confessed —"

"Confessed? Oh, no, not the Contessa; she *told* the truth, with justifiable pride."

"Exactly what I meant," Madame agreed. "So the Pope has been keeping Irena in check for *his* own purposes, by withholding from her what he knows."

"And I'm certain *she* is keeping him in check," I acknowledged Irena's craftiness.

"Ah, I suspect an ultimate confrontation between those two, the creature and the Pope."

"But before that, Madame, I shall become the primary object of their machinations." Although I had known from the beginning of their pursuit of me, these new discoveries added graver, even more reckless, urgency. "They'll have to deal with me."

Ermenegildo's twisted feather trembled.

Madame brushed away our apprehension. "Yes, Lady, but they'll also have to deal with *me!*" she reminded me. "And we're not pushovers!" She squared her shoulders and thrust out her bosom; the emerald bobbed.

"We are *not*, Madame." All the annoyance I had felt at her gloating evaporated.

I was excited, exultant, ecstatic, overwhelmed, flushed with the prospect of certain triumph during interviews!

Then why was I crying?

No, it was someone else I heard, another's cry, not mine. A scream? Not mine. A wailing echo . . . I closed my eyes, to listen —

"Lady, were you dozing?"

"Yes, Madame. So deeply that I even dreamt —"

189

"About the woman whose scream you think you hear on waking?"

"Yes."

Madame Bernice's softened words guided me away from the sad dream: "No need to cry then. You're awake now, Lady, not dreaming. So shall we continue to deal with your memories?"

XIX

"I SHALL TELL YOU ABOUT MEDEA."

"Lady, it's late — The sun —"

"— is still bright enough," I said, although it seemed to me that twilight, beginning at the edge of the horizon, had encouraged my decision.

"Still, I think that if we —

"This cannot be kept in abeyance any longer, Madame."

"But —"

I did not give her further opportunity to object.

It began, that journey toward violence and blood, with the Golden Fleece —

"— which sent fate to find its deadly course," Cassandra told me when I narrated to her in Corinth the events I was again recounting to Madame in her garden. Cassandra had befriended me then — and beyond — the only one to do so during that forlorn eternity in the foreign city Jason and I fled to.

"You will, Lady, of course, clarify — again — that this is the same Cassandra whom we saw in Eden and who was with you in Troy?" Madame Bernice interjected brittlely. "That's clearly a complicated matter that might require more time than this day, and so I suggest leaving it for —"

"No, Madame."

Ermenegildo rested nearby, his tail gathered as modestly as such luxuriance can be. He had located himself halfway between me and Madame. His usual position is closer to her, but periodically he strolls over to allow me to stroke his head; I assumed this meant he was sharing his allegiance and encouraging the telling of the life Madame seemed intent to exclude.

"Besides —" Madame tried to woo him over to her side by crumbling a cake and holding it toward him. He stretched his neck and took the offering, but he did not alter his position. "Besides, do remember that the interlude out of Eden is a matter we would do well to rehearse very, *very* soon — and, also, the truth about the War in Heaven. Perhaps, do you suppose, we might do that now, at least begin, instead of —?"

I was firm: "It's time, Madame. It must be told before interviews begin and the last installment of the 'Account' appears."

She was clearly not listening — so determined to dismiss any reason that supported my resolve: "Do remember that there are many other lives — much more important ones — that we still have to explore. Yes, and there's one — I've been meaning to bring this up — that I'm surprised you haven't even mentioned, the woman whose ghost roams the jungles of —"

She would not dissuade me. Before I resumed with my life as Medea, I would try to assuage the deep frown on her face: "Perhaps we shall find a most unjustly blamed . . . whore." My eyes locked with hers.

"And perhaps not!" She raised her voice to what veered on anger.

I started again with my odyssey of fury:

It all began with the Golden Fleece. Yes, some — though little — of what has been recorded is correct. Of that little, it is true that the Golden Fleece was ransom paid by a mother to secure the safety of her children.

"Oh? By a mother? To secure the safety of her children? I didn't know that." Madame seemed to relax, just somewhat and only for a moment, that day on her lawn under a hazy sky, the air saturated with the scent of the newly born orchid lilies touched with drops of red. I proceeded:

The King of Thessaly had grown tired of his wife, whom he cast out of his palace, although she was the mother of his children, Phrixus and Helle. He replaced his wife with a young, ambitious princess, who quickly gave him another son. Taking advantage of a drought that rendered the land barren and the people hungry, the new wife hired a priest to claim that an oracle demanded the sacrifice of Phrixus. The Prince's death would allow her own son to assume the throne.

When the King agreed to the sacrifice, the abandoned wife was determined to save her children. She bartered with a man reputed to be a magician, a cunning man, who demanded all her jewels in exchange for assuring her children's safety.

"I'll need that much — perhaps more — to buy what is necessary, a dye made of the most precious gold," he told her.

She surrendered all that would have allowed her to survive in exile, if at all, after the new wife would discover she had been foiled, if the sorcerer's plan succeeded.

When the boy Phrixus was bound upon a rock to be slaughtered, the magician, true to his word, released a ram with fleece dyed so golden that in the sun it blinded the executioner and everyone else in attendance, except the mother and her children, who had been prepared for what would follow. The executioner's blade shattered on the rock. The mother strapped her son and daughter to the ram and sent it on its way to safety with her children. Triumphantly, she faced her own dour fate, knowing her children were safe.

"A mother's true devotion," Madame commented, still tense but allowing herself another second of ease.

The girl, romping while the ram rested, fell into the sea that would be named after her, the Hellespont; but the boy Phrixus was carried to the Kingdom of Colchis, east of the Black Sea. Dazzled by the beauty of the ram's fleece, the King of Colchis welcomed the boy. As arranged by the magician, the ram shed its precious skin, which Phrixus gratefully gave to the King. The ransom for the lives of a mother's children was placed in a consecrated grove, guarded by six ferocious lions, to guarantee that one would always be awake. To assure that Phrixus would never long to return to his kingdom with the treasured fleece, the King of Colchis gave him one of his two beautiful daughters in marriage.

In another neighboring kingdom, King Aeson, the father of a handsome youth named Jason — the ruler was also a distant relative of the man whose child had been saved by the golden ram — tired of the chores of governing and surrendered his crown to his brother, Pelias, on one condition: When Jason became eighteen, the crown would pass to him.

Jason roamed the territories of Greece, becoming stronger, preparing for his time as king. With his virile beauty, he also conquered the hearts of women, surrendering his virginity several times — to young girls eager to lose theirs for his, and to older women lured into believing he would restore the memory of theirs.

When Jason was of age to reclaim his place as king — and under Pelias the country had grown weak, poor, dispirited — Pelias agreed to surrender the throne to the proud young man who stood before him in a leopard skin. Even as he conferred with the King, the young man's eyes roamed among the gathered, locating the prettiest women and girls he would choose to lose his virginity to, yet again.

"Look at the country you'll inherit," King Pelias told the handsome youth. "It's lost its spirit. Both can be recovered — and greater pride brought to your father and mother."

"How!" Jason was eager to restore the kingdom of his aging father to its former grandeur.

"Only by the power of a youthful prince — you. There's a Golden Fleece that belongs in our family. It was stolen by the barbarians of Colchis. Recover it, Jason. Gain your throne in triumph," Pelias exhorted. He knew how ferociously the Fleece was guarded in a kingdom whose inhabitants, of a darker skin and violent ways, were considered "barbarians." He was certain Jason would never return from his voyage.

"I'll recover the Fleece," Jason vowed, displaying himself to full advantage to a young woman who had begun to fondle and reveal her breasts to him.

Jason had a vessel built, the *Argo*, larger than any before, to contain fifty daring young men, the most adventurous, who would join his voyage. Among these brawny young men were Hercules, Orpheus, Nestor. The Argonauts set sail to regain the treasure of the Golden Fleece —

"— the ransom a mother had paid for the lives of her children, sacrificing her own life," Madame interjected with a sigh. Then she frowned. "I believe from here the narrative will become somewhat more . . . controversial?"

I preferred to think that she had spoken to herself; and I resumed:

The journey was not without its sorrows. Hylas, the young armor-bearer and lover of Hercules, wandered into the thick forests of an island where the *Argo* docked. Yelling out the boy's name in grief, Hercules hunted for him day and night, with his bare hands ripping the thick limbs of trees, abandoning the journey with Jason to dedicate himself to finding his beloved.

"Really? Hercules loved a boy?" Madame asked. "That muscular symbol of masculinity loved a boy?"

"Yes, Madame. My lives have encountered commitment to love in all its shapes."

"And with what devotion the strong man hunted for his lover!" Madame asserted. "Imagine! Such sensitivity in so massive a hero."

Using all the bold cunning of his now twenty years, Jason and the Argonauts braved all the dangers of the seas to reach their destination. Colchis was clouded in fog, which protected the young adventurers from being seen as they made their way to confront the King, Aetes.

He was waiting for them under the arced entrance to his crude palace of jagged stones. In the years since he had inherited the Golden Fleece, the King had become despotic, hoarding the country's wealth, so that his people split into roaming tribes, hunters. Becoming obsessed with the possibility that Phrixus would attempt to reclaim the precious fleece, he had exiled him and his own daughter.

"I've come to reclaim a treasure that belongs to our family," Jason said to the King of Colchis, and he planted his sturdy legs, firmly, to assert his determination.

"It's been waiting for you," King Aetes agreed easily.

Behind the King had appeared a young woman of fifteen, so beautiful that Jason had not even heard the King's easy words of acquiescence, only their echo. The girl's eyes, black as onyx, were outlined by thick, long lashes that required no paint. Her lush hair was so lustrous that even in the moonless night it created a dark-silver aura about her face. Her lips were as red and liquid as fresh blood. Her skin was the brown color of her people, but of a golden hue. Her breasts had already assumed their voluptuous maturity, challenged in their sensuality by the curves of her slender hips. She wore a dazzle of bracelets the length of her arms, and anklets over her bare feet. Sheathed in an amber tunic so sheer that it revealed the shaded smear between her legs, she appeared naked.

That is how Jason saw me — Medea, Princess of Colchis, daughter of King Aetes.

And this is how I saw him as he stood before my father and affirmed his claim with powerful dignity: fair hair that framed his handsome face and rested on wide shoulders, a slender waist that asserted the muscles of his chest and arms and legs. As I watched him and listened to his voice and heard his words, I felt desire and love, love and desire — I tried to separate them but could not.

"Of course for such a treasure, there must be tests that will make your people proud of your feat before you claim the Fleece at its site," Aetes said to Jason. He noticed Jason's eyes fixed on me. "Surely a young man like yourself would like to prove his prowess, wouldn't he? — especially before our lovely women" — his lustful glance indicated me — "and know, Jason, that our women are renowned for their sensual sorceries, ignited by courage and daring."

My father — a cold, conniving man whom I had never loved and who had never loved me, though I knew he desired me — was challenging this young man into a plotted struggle that could not be overcome, luring him to certain death, and he was offering me as part of his enticement. I had gone often to the grove where the Golden Fleece was guarded by unsleeping lions, had gone there since I was a child, always at night, the only time when the brilliance of the Fleece did not blind. I had made friends not only with the animals that roamed the hills — sheep, deer with their fawns, wolves — but also with the lions that guarded the Fleece. At first the lions would growl at me. Each time, I came closer so that they would learn to know me. Now when I approached, they would scratch out with their paws toward me, as if in greeting. I would touch them in return. I would stand dazzled by the Fleece. Even under the moon it shone gold.

It was not its beauty that lured me to it. It was what I knew about it. That it had sprung into being out of a mother's great love for her children. I longed for a strong man to whom I would give children we would love with a devotion that great, as we would love each other. To whoever listened, I prayed for that at the Grotto of the Golden Fleece under the darkened sky. On nights of the full moon the Fleece became even more radiant. I imagined that spirits of unyielding loyalty and love that had produced the guarded treasure had come to celebrate its origin. Other times I imagined a dark angel of night, her wings extended toward me in approval.

Before my father now, Jason accepted his challenge: "I'll prove my prowess in any way you desire." He had aimed his words at me.

I mimed the words: You shall, beloved . . . Remember, I was only fifteen.

"Lady, why does your essence so often choose that age to stir within unjustly blamed women?" Madame's voice contained more than a tinge of sadness, and her eyes sought mine.

"Because that is the age I was." I met her full stare.

"The age when life makes its greatest promises — isn't it? — or withdraws them. Expectations rise and fall."

"Exactly, Madame."

"I understand."

I resumed:

This was the test proposed by my father as Jason demanded the fleece of his heritage: The young man must yoke to a plow two ferocious bulls. He must then seed the fields with their teeth. I knew that if the young adventurer accomplished that — if the man I continued to stare at while he stared at me survived — a squad of armed men would be ordered by my father to kill him.

That night, mist thickened in Colchis. I waited in my room in that palace of stones, concentrating on the young defiant man I had seen, willing him to come to me; and I sewed a toga for him, for the tests he would undertake tomorrow.

He did come. He stood framed by moonlight. He took my hand. "Will you be the first woman I have ever made love with?"

I could not speak. I nodded: Yes. Then I found words. "I, too, am a virgin, and I've been waiting for you." From the unguarded talk of the proudly passionate women of Colchis, I had heard about the refinements of lovemaking among "barbarians." I stepped out of my amber tunic. I allowed my bracelets to slide from my arms. I left the anklets on my legs.

Jason gasped, desire rejecting his toga. Under a slash of moonlight that penetrated the crags in my room, Jason and I made love — tender, yes, then mounting in desire, then tender again, then in lust, and then in love and passion and lust and desire and love, over and over. For moments only, we would lie as close as two bodies can next to each, and doze, and then wake to make love again.

He said, "You're not only the first woman I've ever made love to, Medea, but you shall be the only one. That would be so if I die tomorrow during Aetes's challenges, but it will be so if I live forever."

Forever. I spoke the word only silently, to the spirits I had detected when I wandered at night to stare at the Golden Fleece under a full moon.

"You won't die tomorrow," I told him.

"The feats the King demands are hard, and I have to perform them, to reclaim my rightful kingdom and to" — he held both my hands in his and brought them to his lips — "and to have you always."

"The animals you'll have to tame are vulnerable."

"Vulnerable to what, Medea?"

"To the color red," I told him the secret only I and my father knew. Tomorrow, I told Jason, he must wear the bright red tunic I then presented to him. "When the bulls charge, remove the tunic and toss it between them. They'll charge at it from opposite directions. Their horns will tangle and they'll fight each other to death."

"My beloved Medea!" Jason embraced me and kissed my breasts in wide circles until he reached my nipples, which he dabbed with his tongue. Smiling up at me, he said, "But if I remove the tunic, I'll be naked before everyone."

"No one will see you because they'll be astonished by the warring bulls," I told him.

I smiled at his disappointment. "You can wear a loincloth underneath the toga."

"Oh, that won't be necessary. I mean, why? — since no one will be looking," he insisted.

We made love again, even more passionately, devouring each other's body, becoming each other.

"After the bulls are vanquished —" He was thoughtful again.

"— Aetes will immediately release a squad of armed men. When that happens, you must throw these before them" — I gathered precious gems I had hoarded for a time when I would flee my cruel father and his growing lust — "and the warriors, who are poor, will fight each other for them."

Again we made love.

"But to get the Fleece —" He pondered tomorrow's events.

"By then it will be dark. You'll follow me to the grove. The lions who guard the Fleece know me. I'll take the Fleece."

"You'll do all that, for me?"

"Yes. All that — and more." I reached for a decanter of a wine fermented only in Colchis. "And this will give you even more strength!" I promised him.

"But just this drop?" He laughed at the insignificant portion I had placed in his goblet, an equal amount in mine.

"It's potent beyond your expectations," I told him. "Just one drop can give you strength" — I turned away from him, not wanting him to detect that with him I could become shy — "and it can augment desire."

"I can use more strength." He laughed. "But I'll never need anything but you to arouse my desire."

The wine was made from berries that grew only in the driest part of the desert, clinging to the stems of velvet cactus blossoms. To the rich nectar were added spices and one bitter root, ground to a powder with the sweet petals of a *malva rosa* bloom. Fiercely scarlet, that root emerged in three stems and only for moments under mossy rocks. The wine from this brew stirred blood into fierce courage — and fierce desire. It must be imbibed in small sips, increased only over a measured time to create a tolerance for more. Taken in a large dose without such gradual initiation, it burned like fire, and it killed.

I had never drunk it, but I would now, with Jason. "You must sip it, only sip it," I warned him. "Like this." The single drop of liquid filled my veins with a warmth that was almost heat, just as I knew it flowed through Jason, who tilted his head and closed his eyes for seconds. When we made love yet again, this time after he had spilled into me, he remained aroused, and we came together again and again without separating, our bodies tightly locked.

We slept. We woke. He knelt before me — and it was only then that I truly realized how young he was, five years older than I, yes, but, at that moment, a boy; and I was a girl in love when he said, "Yes, I'll return to claim my kingdom" — he kissed my hand — "with my beautiful beloved wife, my Medea!"

His wife. My heart inhaled.

He rose, still holding my hand. "We'll marry now! I can't wait! God hears our vows everywhere."

"Yes!"

"Choose the angel to sanctify our union."

"The Angel of the Dark of the Moon, because she'll shelter you from the brilliance of the Fleece," I said. I realized fully only now the wish I had been forming on my night journeys to the grove: At last, the fleece that years ago had made it possible for a mother to save her children would vindicate her again. With Jason, I would find redemption for her violated love by her husband — and I would produce children who would be protected forever by a love that honored hers.

"The Angel Hecate, yes," Jason understood and encouraged.

So we stood outside, Jason and I, naked to the night. My bridal veil was the mist turned silver by the moon. Aloud, we vowed our promises of devotion and love to each other.

"Forever."

"Forever."

Holding hands, we stood under stars and moon and night until dawn brushed the sky with blue light.

As he was ready to leave, Jason turned back and said exultantly, "In my country, you'll be cherished." He ran back to kiss me. "Our love will be so great that our children will be immortal!"

When he was gone — when my husband had left — I echoed our prayer of only one word:

Forever.

Madame Bernice had been so attentive that she had not even reached for her tea as I had recounted my marriage to Jason. "I think I may have begun to feel —" she started. Then she crossed her arms stolidly before her bosom. "Still, there will be no way you can avoid the carnage we all know occurred —"

"And I shall not," I promised her. I saw her trying unsuccessfully not to wince.

As I breathed the subtle scents of late afternoon in Madame's garden, I let my eyes wander to the splendor of some jacaranda trees. Yes, those trees I had first seen in Eden were newly gracing her garden and the countryside. Pink, lavender, a breath of both colors, their buds decorated the sparsely leafed branches; some delicate petals had fallen to the ground, like lavender snow. I avoided the sight of the new orchid lilies. Their perfume, as the afternoon progressed, had become heavy, opulent, not like the delicate scent of the glorious blossoms that wafted through the azure air of Eden.

Aware of my attention to her extravagant garden, Madame Bernice commented: "Have you noticed, Lady" — she indicated one of several graceful inclines on her lawn — "that birds of paradise are now in bloom, too?" She smiled at the irony, birds of paradise.

I smiled back. But sadness draped the world and Madame's garden as I proceeded:

It happened exactly as planned. Jason conquered the bulls, whose horns locked, and he confounded the warriors, who fought each other for the gems. By then it was night. I led him to the Grotto of the Golden Fleece, where the lions roared at him — and he pulled back — until they saw me. I took the Fleece and gave it to my beloved.

We fled on the *Argo*. And we made love —

"— yes, on the Golden Fleece, at night, with the storming sea washing over your bodies. I remember your very detailed account of that, quite well," Madame said.

I was not sure whether or not she was commending my powers of description.

Jason and I sailed to other islands.

Our passion grew, equaling our love, and our love equaled our passion. At times we would sip from the wine of Colchis, a sip or two more each time, but our desire needed no embellishment. Everywhere, people celebrated our contrasting beauty, our bravery. Kings opened their palaces to us, as we extended this time of adventure and love and celebration before Jason would return to claim his kingdom.

In Thessaly, where its journey had begun, Jason and I, silently, at night, placed the Golden Fleece in a Sacred Temple. A mother's love for her children was finally redeemed.

"I'm ready to claim my kingdom," Jason told his uncle, Pelias, who received him before his palace, his two powerful daughters beside him. "And Medea is my queen." I stood boldly next to my husband, feeling the menacing, envious eyes of the daughters. "Where are my father and mother, to share my victory and my happiness?"

"Dead." Pelias had grown feeble with age. He leaned on his daughters. "He killed himself while you were away. Your mother died soon after."

I placed my hand on Jason's arm, to share his disbelief.

In the palace at night, Pelias roamed like a restless ghost, uttering words to himself: ". . . foul death . . . blood . . . my kingdom now . . . and, soon, my daughters'." Pelias's daughters disguised their father's nocturnal ranting: "He's old, he's confused in time."

"He murdered my father and mother," Jason told me what I knew. "I have to avenge them. Help me!" he pled.

"I know how," I told him. "The daughters are fiercely loyal to their father. You can tell by the way they carry his weak body about. I'm sure he's promised them your kingdom, but he's too weak now even to attempt to resist you. The daughters would do anything to restore him to his youth. They hate you and me. I've seen the soldiers, and they're still loyal to Pelias. We're in danger. We'll have to act immediately."

"Anything." Jason was too grieved to plot.

"I'll be gone for a whole night," I told him.

"With someone else?" Jason's grief had led him to speak those impossible words.

"Never anyone else. We swore. Forever," I told him.

"Forever," he echoed. "I'll never question you, just as you never question me."

As I left, he said forlornly, "This will be the first night that we don't make love."

"No," I said, removing my clothes, removing his. We sipped from the powerful wine of Colchis. For moments that turned into an eternity of bliss we made love. That night, I clasped him even more tightly in me, pulling him into the utmost depth of me, as he searched for it with the full extent of his passion.

Then I ventured out into the night. I had placated lions and wild animals in my own country. I could do that here. The stars, the dark heat of the night, had awaited my return like friends. The moon kissed my breasts, making them glow silver, almost as luminous as they became when my husband painted them with his saliva.

A fawn stood before me, its eyes lit red by the moon. I coaxed it to me, humming. Nearby, his mother lingered. The fawn licked my hands as I sang softly to him. Then I released him to his mother. Both waited while I hummed and sang the same song. I marked the place where I had found them. I resumed my search for what I knew I would find within the depths of darkness: the carcass of an old animal, not long dead. I pulled the heavy carcass into some bushes, where I hid it and marked the place.

I returned to Jason. I told him I must venture out again into the night. This time he must follow me, unseen. Before that, we must let it be known to Pelias's daughters through their servants that I had begun to go out alone, in hiding, into the night. "They're convinced we're plotting against them, and they'll suspect anything secret. So they'll follow me. We must make them believe, through careful rumors planted in the palace, that I'm a sorceress."

"You, my beloved Medea, a sorceress?" My husband added: "Yes, I believe you are, to arouse me even when I'm avenging my father's death."

While he followed me into the night, a distance apart, I felt the hostile eyes of Pelias's daughters as, hidden, they pursued me, just as I had known they would. Near the place where I had left the decayed carcass on an earlier night, I made a clearing with a hack I had brought with me. In full view of the daughters, I raised my hands to the darkness, the moon spilling my shadow across the cleared ground. "Hecate!" I wailed out the name of the angel who had witnessed my marriage to Jason. "Angel of Darkness! Give me the power to restore the dead to youthful life."

When the fire lit the night and smoke screened me from view, I dragged forth the carcass I had hidden. I hacked at it. I flung pieces of it into the fire, which devoured the dead flesh.

Then I began to hum the song with which I had earlier enticed the roaming fawn. It appeared; and shaded by the veil of smoke, it came to me. As the flames diminished and smoke cleared, I held the fawn up, triumphantly as if I had lifted it from the fire, the carcass restored into its youth. Then I released it to its mother, who had waited in the dark.

I looked up at the sky, as if in gratitude. "I know now how to restore the dead to their youth," I said for the daughters to hear.

The brush rustled with the sound of feet hurrying away along the soft earth.

Exultant, understanding, Jason carried me back in his arms through darkness.

Pelias's daughters waited for us at the palace. They held their weakened father between them. "We saw your sorcery. Now restore our father's youth, or —" There was no need to speak the threat of death.

I affected reticence. Jason pretended to protest their demand. They motioned to guards armed with spears pointed up toward us from the foot of the steps. I simulated angered surrender to the threats. "But it must all be exactly as you saw." I spoke for only the daughters to hear. "He must die first, like the animal you witnessed." I raised the bloodied hack.

"Give it to us!" Both daughters grabbed for it.

"Use it," I told them, "and then he'll return, young like the fawn you saw in the desert."

The daughters hacked at their father until he lay before them in blackened blood.

"Now build a fire."

They did, their faces streaming with perspiration.

"Fling his flesh into it!"

Flames consumed him. Blood dried into ashes.

More soldiers and others in Thessaly had gathered, watching the daughters in horror.

"Bring him back to life!" one of the daughters demanded.

"Make him young!" the other said.

"I cannot restore life to the man you've murdered, your own father," I said for all to hear.

Soldiers surrounded the daughters, binding them.

I stood with Jason over the charred bones of Pelias.

"Your revenge is done," I told him.

That night, Jason and I made love as we listened to the wails of the grieving daughters.

We fled Thessaly, together, laughing, more in love than ever.

And we went to Corinth —

On the veranda of Madame Bernice's château, I felt her eyes upon me. A lone star had appeared at the edge of the sky.

"The plotting daughters killed their evil father," Madame pronounced her verdict.

"Yes. Justice for evil."

"I see that." Madame spoke very softly.

Now that night was approaching, the orchid lilies with tips of red like drops of blood exuded their heavy perfume even more strongly, a sickening sweetness that made me reel, to the point that only moments later did I realize that Madame Bernice had asked a question, which, turning away from the noxious lilies, I answered: "Yes, that was only the beginning of the horrors to come."

XX

A DARK NIGHT CAME INSTANTLY, snuffing out the single star that dusk had offered. I had stopped my recollection of my life with Jason, but its sorrow extended. I would, of course, continue, perhaps tomorrow. I prepared my lantern for my dark way home.

Usually, when we announce our leave-taking, we part in a quiet ritual of temporary separation. For all our closeness, we adhere to amenities that are disappearing from the world. I had already draped my cowl over my shoulders and was about to proceed down the steps of the veranda when Madame startled me:

"A moment, Lady, to deal with another matter I was able only to mention earlier."

Was she still trying to dissuade, even into tomorrow, my continuation of the life I must roam through?

At the bottom of the steps, Ermenegildo, waiting for me, looked up quizzically at Madame. Wondering what was possibly coming at these late moments? Recently, he had begun to escort me a few steps along the road. Then he would hurry back, concerned at leaving Madame alone for long.

"It's surprised me, Lady, that there's a certain life you haven't mentioned —"

There were enough. In my urgency to be on my way, to invite the return of our usual silent ritual — yes, I was tired — I almost stepped on Ermenegildo's tail, but before his unique feather twisted in protest, I apologized. That caused me to stall and to allow Madame to continue:

"When you leave each time after tea, I keep thinking that during rehearsals in your quarters you'll remember another blamed soul your

205

essence surely located. She was known as" — she spoke each word with exceptional precision — "the Xtabay."

"The X —?"

"Xtabay."

The ghostly woman she had mentioned earlier, roaming jungles? "I don't re —"

"Perhaps not yet."

"Another Indian woman, blamed?" The moment I spoke those words, I remembered . . . something . . .

"You knew!" Madame couldn't restrain her delight at this indication of an emerging new memory. "A woman of great beauty."

"Of course." Another spark of recollection stirred.

Madame proceeded to display her own knowledgeability of my still shaping memories: "A soulful woman of such quiet ways — or so I've heard, and you'll correct me if I'm wrong — that is, *if*, of course, your memories guide you there — a woman of such soulful ways that her jealous husband was incited to suspect her of —"

"— infidelity, of course."

"Ah."

"But the woman was not unfaithful, though she was accused," I knew.

"Why, Lady, your memories *are* taking you to that same distant shore as that of another blamed woman, of the same country, the woman known as —"

"— La Malinche."

"Yes, she! Lady, did the husband of the Xtabay believe malicious gossip instigated by those in her village, gossip that led to violence? Oh, how they must have envied her — and her loving husband, to turn him against her —"

"Yes, they envied us both, and he believed their lies."

"Remarkable, the persistence of memory, even when we think we've forgotten," Madame observed. "Perhaps the life of that blamed woman will return to your memories this very evening. After all, her life did extend into a long, long night, within which she searched vainly to be redeemed. Surely you will remember the truth of it all."

And I did.

As I rehearse with you now in my quarters, it all returns:

Yes, the men and women of the village resented me and my husband, because they perceived our vast love. And his jealousy. I first became aware of their piercing eyes of envy on a warm day as we strolled into the village near which we lived. Until then, I had not been

206

aware of the enmity my hauteur — that was what they named my quiet, shy independence — had aroused.

I was wearing a tunic of white muslin, my brown breasts like ripe fruit, my nipples resisting even the soft press of light cloth, so that if I had breathed more heavily they would have been bared. My dark hair was tied into one thick braid, through which wound a strand of beads my beloved husband had given me, beads that then extended into a necklace whose pendant nuzzled the deep demarcation between my breasts.

Beside me, he swaggered, challenging the admiring stares of others at me even while he invited them, proud to be the sole owner of my beauty, oblivious to his own beauty, his skin just slightly browner than mine, his bare chest and legs darkly furred. A white wrap of the same muslin I wore hugged his slender hips. A woman and her husband selling pottery — I had dismissed the man's advances once without even a look — lured my husband away on a ruse of having acquired "something special" he might want to give his woman as a gift. Others gathered about them.

Remaining at a distance, I heard only whispers. I detected the woman's covert inviting glances, shifting between my husband and someone else unaware of her: another man, also handsome, clearly new in the village, idling nearby, his eyes devouring my beauty. I rejected his stare, and so I did not see the malice that had sparked there, malice already festering in the two potters still whispering to my husband.

Soon after, when we had finished making love — and I retained my husband in me, keeping his desire warm — he shocked me: "How many others have you lured? — along with the potter, who resisted your advances, and the new man in the village who claims he's only the latest?"

"There's been no one but you." I released him. Forever — but he did not know it.

"Liar. Others in the village confirm it."

I was too outraged to deny it.

"You were right not to, Lady," Madame approved the next day. She had been so eager to hear whether I had remembered this life further that she had poured my tea before I had even sat down, a breach that caused Ermenegildo to remain standing quite formally beside me until I was seated. "It was a baseless accusation. Those were terrible times, weren't they? Gossip was capable of inciting a lover, not to say a husband, to extreme violence, joined in by the monstrous people of the village."

"Yes. But I did not give them the opportunity to harm me. I left the village, by myself that very night. I wandered into the jungle. I gathered black orchids, which I held close to my heart, and there, in the jungle, I willed myself to die."

"Lady, I don't think that's —"

"— what you may have heard? Madame, I was there. I'm correcting untruths." I continued:

I willed myself to die, but life thrived in me and I did not succeed.

"Oh, what speculations that must have aroused in the village. Gossip travels fiercely, especially when fueled by inevitable false sorcerers. There are always those in such villages."

Madame was correct.

Incited by the potter's wife, a woman who claimed to be a sorceress roamed frequently now into the village. She, too, envied my beauty and pined for my husband. Subsequent events revealed this:

When she saw him alone in the village one day, she dared to speak to him. "Oh, and where is your wife?"

"She likes to wander into the jungle, alone," my husband told her.

The woman knew I did that; she had followed, hoping to discover secrets she might use against me. "Alone?" she asked him. As if just remembering it, she added, "I believe I saw the handsome new man in the village venturing there, too, earlier." She added more poison: "Perhaps if you go there, you will discover —"

"What?" My husband was enraged with jealousy.

"— whatever you shall find," the Sorceress said.

I had gone alone to a river outside the village. Frequently, I longed for the exquisite solitude of the jungle, exulting in the call of exotic birds, the rhythm of a stream. I would roam naked along bending palms, gather wild flowers, rampant mariposa lilies, and lie on fields of meadow-foam blooms, a misty yellow cloud on the ground, and I would laugh and cry with the joy of existence, and with love for my husband.

He had followed me secretly. Seeing me naked with my arms extended to a deer hidden from his sight, he assumed what the Sorceress intended, that I was meeting a lover. He returned to her.

"Your wife is restless, depraved, an evil woman, a whore. She lures her lovers to the jungle, then drives them to despair. The new man in the village, the man she was seeing, I've learned he's disappeared. You must have seen her with yet another. She'll drive you to the same madness — I see in your eyes that she has already begun to incite it — unless —"

208

"Unless?" My husband wanted to hear other than the fatal words he heard.

"— unless you kill her, for the sake of others she'll entice; most of all, for your sake."

And so — accusing me — he did kill me, with one almost graceful sweep of the machete he used to gather corn —

Ermenegildo nervously lowered his head.

"— murdered me after he had forced himself upon me one more time and shouted, 'Whore!' The last word that I heard."

"Such terrible, terrible injustice!" Madame shared Ermenegildo's outrage. He had uttered a sound of protest. "Such unjustified blame! So horrible it might even cause a ghost to roam the jungle in sorrow —"

My ghost roamed the jungle at night wailing in desolation, a ghost accused beyond death.

My husband, now my murderer, heard my sad crying nightly. One such night he hanged himself, naked. Screaming with frustrated desire, the Sorceress attempted to make love to his dead body, forcing him into her, blood having engorged his groin. She was slain, still impaled on him, by the people of the village for her sorceries . . . And I wandered on, wailing in the night, blamed even for my husband's death.

"I wouldn't be surprised if her wailing — your wailing in that life — gave rise to wild speculations of violent transgressions even after death," Madame voiced what I had been about to convey.

"They claimed I seduced hunters."

"You must have remained as sublimely beautiful as you had been in life."

"I did."

How wondrous, to have a mind like Madame's, to be able to anticipate another's memories when they've just begun to form, poised to be recalled.

And I recall every detail now that I'm back in my quarters rehearsing with you. Yes, our tea this afternoon was short; I had arrived late, so attentive had I become to my new memories evoked in my rooms.

More sex.

What?

More sex.

You're amusing in your interruption. Oh, I see. You want more intimate details to verify that my essence lodged in the body of the Xtabay and extended into her ghost.

209

More sex.

My ghost walked naked in the night, its outline as if brushed with silver. When the moon parted hovering clouds, its light licked my breasts and the mound between my legs. Sweaty with lust, naked hunters waited for night in order to penetrate the jungle and my luminous form. I retreated from them as far as I could, to the very edge of a cliff. Believing me trapped, they attempted to grasp me and push into me, only to find that I had evaporated into the dawn and that they were lunging, aroused, to their deaths.

I have now satisfied your requirement to verify my truth with details only I can know. Now I must move on. Time is narrowing! There are other matters that must be rehearsed, my life as —

I'm battling a terrifying mood. You sense it? You've come to know me that well? Perhaps . . . to care for me? I spoke that slowly because I'm not sure. At times during these rehearsals I feel isolated, alone. No, I am not alone. I am with —

My memories. My memories of —

The Crucifixion.

That memory pulls me deeper into the threatening mood. Senseless death, senseless violence, senseless cruelty always depresses me.

Jesus, you haunt me.

Judas, you haunt me.

Blessed Mary, you haunt me.

Jesus spent even less time with us as his following grew. Often Judas and I would stroll through the City, remembering where this or that had occurred when all three of us were together. We wandered out into the desert, to see the new blooms that summer had brought out: We lingered over a velvet cactus, its yellow blossoms so strangely delicate among piny thorns. Nearby, red godetias flared as if ignited by the heat. Judas pointed to a gathering of trees near a small pool of water, beyond which a mount rose, gray, bare, stark, ominous. "See that tree, Magdalene, the one with that large branch? Jesus and I sat there one afternoon, just sat there quietly —"

"— without me?" I pretended surprise. Was I truly hurt? I had long accepted the special union between them.

Judas adjusted quickly, "You had gone to the market, and we were alone." He said with a seriousness that turned the hot afternoon cold: "If I ever lose Jesus, entirely —" He shook his head, rejecting the thought. "Oh, I can continue to live desiring him, *only* desiring him — and you, Magdalene," he added quickly. "But if I ever lose him entirely —" The thought persisted. He stopped it again. "Our lives —

our love, his and mine — are interlocked. It was so from the moment I saw him, by the River. We sensed in each other — what? — shared doom."

"No!" I rejected.

"I meant shared destiny," he said.

Those stealthy footsteps outside my quarters! You heard them, too, recurring. I must speak softly during these rehearsals, give nothing away to whoever is listening. Madame continues to remind me that sudden circumstances may force interviews to begin sooner than anticipated. Shall I get my gun, go to the door, unlock it, and see who —?

"Under no circumstances will you open that door other than when you're ready to come for tea, Lady, and then you will walk along the path you always take, as if you're out for a stroll, not arousing suspicions of anything else," Madame told me at tea when I informed her that I had been tempted to open the door last night. "If interviews are forced to begin suddenly, I shall choose one of our prepared ways to inform you immediately, and, if urgent, I shall rush over. Even so, don't open the door unless you verify it's me."

It was late in the afternoon when Madame said that. I had told her the rest of my memories of the wailing woman.

Our teas are lengthening. So are the days, now that summer is almost here. The strange orchid lilies in Madame's garden continue to proliferate, daily more aggressive in their distorted reminder of the perfect banished flowers that shared exile with me and my beloved, flowers that remind, too, of a bloodied wedding veil. I had not mentioned them to Madame, because she's proud of her garden. I didn't want to risk saying anything about them that she might interpret as criticism. She had never remarked on them, although they seemed to have grown overnight, and usually, when she plants a new bloom and it begins to bud, she comments on it. She seemed not even to see these.

As my attention had paused on the mesmerizing orchid lilies, Madame had begun discussing "small but important details that must be tended to when interviews begin." She enjoys going over that. She calls such interludes "necessary lighter moments."

"Of course, interviewers will be dazzled immediately by your beauty," she stated. "We must use that to our fullest advantage."

Ermenegildo chose that exact moment to spread his tail especially dramatically. Understanding, Madame lowered her head and whispered to him, "As they shall be dazzled by *yours.*"

To add his own assertion of that fact, Ermenegildo located

himself near a cluster of birds of paradise, those glorious flowers named after the Garden of our exile. His beak assumed the exact tilt of those scandalously gorgeous blossoms, clearly to call attention to the similarity between them and his stance, but more, to his own greater beauty.

Madame had continued: "Of course, Lady, some interviewers will *pretend* not to be impressed, in order to attempt immediately to unnerve you. Some are cynical, and we all know there's something about beauty —"

There's something about beauty! I shall adapt her words into my *Pensées* later, perhaps connect them with Mademoiselle Léonie's observation when she arranged my hair, simply, for my first night at the opera with the Count: "Beauty needs a frame only so it will not spill out into ostentation." If I include that, I shall of course give her full credit.

Madame resumed her discussion of our presentation — she likes to dwell on this at times before we move on to more important matters: "We've agreed, Lady, that you shall choose your own appropriate attire with your usual impeccable taste. And I" — she became charmingly shy, a trait, you may have noticed, that is not usually in evidence in her — "shall choose most carefully what I shall wear."

"Whatever you wear, you shall look resplendent!" I told her.

"Well," she smiled, "we both do know — don't we? — that we must not gild the lily." She composed her taffeta dress. Although it was somewhat heavy for the season, I assumed it was a favorite of hers; her fingers frequently and lovingly located the strip of gold lace that decorated it.

"We shall both look breathtaking," I assured Madame.

"We'll arrange the drapes exactly so, in your quarters," Madame opined excitedly. "Not that *you* need special lighting, the way other great stars do."

"Great stars?"

"A wonderful phrase — don't you think? — for impressive presences?"

"Oh, yes, and I believe I shall borrow it, with your permission."

"Given."

Madame ended our banter with her assertive, "Now, Lady!" and went on: "One matter we mustn't rush, and must rehearse at length — and get to very quickly — *now!* — is the War in Heaven." She did not even pause to acknowledge the immense challenge.

I was ready. "In Heaven, Cassandra abruptly —"

212

"A moment, Lady, please, before we go there."

I braced myself.

"I assume you'll be dealing with tumultuous events?"

"Oh, Madame, hail and fire mingled with blood, and a great mountain was cast into the sea, and burning stars —"

"Precisely my point. In dealing with such events, there's always the risk of melodrama, even in the tone of delivery."

"Melodrama!" I was insulted.

"The risk, Lady, only the risk. I didn't say there *was,* had been, or *would be* melodrama in your account." Realizing that her veiled admonition for restraint had been unnecessary, she moved on:

"Let's proceed to explore events that only *you* are able to reveal." She crossed her arms formidably before her, signaling a major test: "But *how* so, Lady, since *you* were not there?"

Her abrupt shift into a question was meant to underscore a major challenge she anticipated from interviewers. I met it easily: "All was learned, Madame, from intimate versions given to me and to Adam by Cassandra —"

"Ah! Who would doubt her?" Madame greeted.

"— and by Lucifer — who were there — and by events that extended into the lost Garden."

Madame leaned back in emphatic approval of my unassailable answer. "*Now* let's hear the truth about the War in Heaven."

XXI

Abruptly, Cassandra stood within the blue mist of Heaven. She sniffed the morning air. Beside her, Lucifer remained lying on a field of wild grass. He stretched lazily, wondering what had alerted his sister's attention. All he had detected was the breath of a breeze that had flirted with her airy robe, finally embracing her lustrous flesh before whispering away to brush over his naked body.

Cassandra's slightly tilted eyes, so thickly lashed that they appeared outlined in black, followed a bird as it soared beyond. Its white wings were streaked with azure so that it seemed to have sprung from the sky itself. Head lifted, Cassandra waited for the beautiful bird to return, but it did not. She said:

"There are no boundaries in Heaven."

"God says otherwise," Lucifer spoke automatically. He had not really registered his sister's startling words. Searching idly among the daffodils that sparked within the wild grass, he located an iris, purple fading to light lavender, one of its petals tinted with a dash of yellow, a speck of red. He swept the flower along his body and then along his sister's bare feet as she stood next to him.

"Lady, there were daffodils and irises, in Heaven?" Madame Bernice wondered aloud. "And grass?"

"Yes," I assured her, "there were fields of grass and flowers, including —"

Trilliums — wake robins! — white, pink, dark red, yellow, even startling silver green, side by side; and purple nightshades with bright yellow centers like tiny cones; and splendid mariposas, all reddish streaks; ithuriel's spears, so simple in their pearly beauty; and — favorites of Lucifer's — rhododendrons like crinkled roses bursting amid leaves of evergreen shrubs; yes, and masses of gilias shaded not-quite-lavender, not-quite-blue; and penstemons, rosy streaks of violet; and yarrows, each a white bouquet; and magenta redbuds floating over white meadow foam; and — Cassandra's favorites — poppies everywhere, lightening from deep orange to pale yellow, then blushing into red. Cassandra, watching the poppies intently, longed to detect the exact moment when their hue deepened.

Those and myriad other flowers surrounded her and Lucifer on the field where only moments earlier they had lain, looking up at the clouds and daydreaming. Yes, there were clouds in the sky of Heaven.

Still gazing away, Cassandra saw another resplendent bird disappear. She said to her brother, who was tickling her ankle playfully:

"God says that Heaven is enclosed. It isn't. There's a vast universe beyond Him." She stated that easily, as something that had just occurred to her, and it had. She always made a point of denying that she was able to "prophesy."

"She did *not* consider herself a mystic," I explained to Madame Bernice.

Madame waved my last few words away with an indifferent flourish of her bejeweled hand.

Cassandra claimed only to be able to "perceive." Other angels referred to her "special gift." Cassandra was certain God had awarded it to her for His own amusement only, the way He dispensed other unique "gifts" to His angels from time to time. He would always make grand announcements when He granted one, then fashion tests and entertainments involving each — fleetness tested in a race, a glorious voice challenged by a soaring scale, endurance tried in a series of obstacles — all permitted, after long moments of suspense, to end in triumph, to arouse in the angels wonder and gratitude at His beneficence.

Diligently practicing every day, concentrating rigorously, fiercely committed, Cassandra had honed the perceptions given to her so casually by God for His amusement. Each day she strengthened them more, making them her own, increasingly connecting her gaze to God's. Often now, when He caught her scrutinizing Him intensely, He would lean from His throne and say: "Now tell Me, Cassandra, *what* do you see, My dear?"

One such time she quickly described wild grass, daffodils, poppies, a dazzling array of flowers in widening fields. The angels — but not Lucifer — laughed with delighted disbelief at her imagination.

215

Lucifer had seen God's look grow sober. The next day all the flowers were there, in stretching fields.

Cassandra had assumed that God had created them to support her "vision," and so startle her and all the others with His capacity and willingness to grant them their wishes. And indeed, at that day's gathering, He announced to Cassandra, but for all the others to hear: "It was such a charming image your imagination conjured, darling, that of course I had to grant it to you." The angels applauded yet another manifestation of God's beneficence, His startling shifts and turns, His unexpected "entertainments."

As, that morning with her brother, Cassandra continued to stare toward the horizon into which the beautiful birds had soared, Lucifer also stood abruptly, startled, because he had suddenly understood his sister's meaning. He ran his feet over the grass, to feel its thrilling touch on them. "Beyond God, there's more?" he asked.

Other beautiful naked angels, who had been lazing on the fields of Heaven, heard the exchange between Cassandra and her brother. The youthful Sisyphus, his face always expectant; Electra, a pretty girl with enormous black eyes; Narcissus, a dreamy angel; Ishtar, proud of her divine breasts, even aggressive about them; Isis and Osiris, insepa- rable, who often joined Cassandra and Lucifer on warm evenings, competing to see who would spot the first star — Cassandra always won; Iphigenia, a playful, exuberant child with long wonderful legs; Oedipus, fond of gentle riddles; Prometheus, his young muscles begin- ning to assert themselves: Those and other angels all gathered about Cassandra and her brother, and they listened raptly.

"They were all angels?" Madame Bernice asked.

"Of course." I saw no reason to dwell further on that matter.

Apparently Madame did. "Those angels — I believe that to most of us they're known as gods and goddesses. That might create a stumble during interviews." Her voice deepened, into that of an inter- viewer: "Lady! Why are so many of the angels Greek?"

Of course, Madame was simply preparing me. I would pass this test, as I had passed all others. "The names of many of the angels, I agree — but do recall that there were prominent exceptions — correspond to those of Grecian gods and goddesses. It was one of the properties of angels that they would be granted other names, by other people, in other countries, at various times."

Madame was not only satisfied, she was clearly thrilled: "An egalitarian nomenclature!"

At first, the Angel Gabriel, gentle-eyed, somewhat shy, remained a distance apart from the other attentive angels listening to the astounding words Cassandra and Lucifer were speaking; but he inched closer and closer to them, until he was among the congregation.

Only later did the thrilled angels detect that the Angel Michael was scrutinizing them closely from a hill. The handsome Michael always carried a sword with him, in a sheath at his hip. No one had ever seen him draw it. So it was rumored that he wore it only to emphasize his muscular thighs. It was Icarus who commented that Michael looked like "a general."

Excited by Cassandra's easy announcement of unbounded heavens unscouted, Lucifer said to his sister, "If that's true, can we explore them?"

"Yes!"

Lucifer's delighted smile invited the other angels to come with them. He spread his arms, in preparation for a new flight, a new adventure. Cassandra raised hers. The others imitated their motions.

Their luminous naked bodies rivaling the glimmering dew of the bright morning, the angels soared! They flew, laughing and thrilling, twisting and turning on waves of space and wind that tossed and swirled about them and with them and guided them even farther into the deepening blue sky, beyond, until their bodies glowed, illumined red by the disappearing sun, till night shaded them and the moon painted them silver, and still they soared, exhilarated, dipping in and out of space.

"Farther!" Cassandra coaxed.

"Yes, farther!" Lucifer met and surpassed her challenge, offering his own, which she matched and surpassed, until they flew together, side by side, leading the others even deeper into the universe, between stars and constellations, beyond, far, far beyond what they had thought were the boundaries of Heaven, far beyond and into the infinite space out of which God had created Himself, claiming as His own the portion He had carved out, proclaiming there was nothing more.

Within the sphere of stars, Daedalus and Icarus broke away for moments, discovering yet more fields of sky, returning to recruit the others to witness those new plains. Exulting in waves of wind, even Gabriel grew bold and soared ahead of the others, then waited, and they all flew together in a flank of gliding angels.

Below, Michael watched. He raised his arms, as the other angels had done in preparation for their flight. Then he lowered them and touched his sheath.

Their bodies gleaming with the fresh perspiration of their delirious journey, the adventurous angels returned to God's Heaven.

"Father," Lucifer eagerly addressed God, who sat on His throne for His usual early-evening gathering of angels. "The Universe is vaster than Heaven."

"It is not!" God was starkly handsome, with eyes that were fierce under thick eyebrows even when He laughed. He located Himself with posed casualness on His throne, but in such a way that His powerful muscles, though in repose, conveyed His strength. He wore only gold sandals, which wound their straps up the bulging calves of His firmly planted legs. A rainbow-colored scarf curled about His shoulders and came to rest, as if almost carelessly, but actually studiedly, upon His lap. After a dramatic array of gestures that He often displayed, one of His large hands would inevitably come to rest, firmly, upon His formidable groin.

"*My God, Lady!*" Madame Bernice had shot up, almost overturning our tea setting and startling Ermenegildo so that he let out an awful squawk.

"Lady, I —"

"Madame, I —"

We were at a serious impasse.

Madame was sputtering. She bent down as if to gather the tea setting, although it had not spilled. To placate Ermenegildo, who was still rattled by her exaggerated behavior, she crushed a tea cake in her hand and tried to stuff it into his mouth, an untypical development that he resisted with yet another fierce squawk, which sent the twisted feather on his comb into a whirl.

I watched this performance, letting it play itself out.

At last it did. Somewhat. Madame sat down, her face framed by glittering hands, her elbows propped uncharacteristically on the table. "Now, Lady," she said firmly.

"Now, Madame?"

"Surely you're not going to have the Heavenly Lord step down from His throne and then proceed to —"

I didn't know whether she was fanning herself or shooing a butterfly away; she usually loves butterflies, especially the white ones.

"As far as I know, Madame, He remained on His throne," I said to her.

She seemed only somewhat relieved, oddly soothing her neck.

"But keep in mind, Madame Bernice, that my memories *do* continue to evolve," I said, "so I cannot guarantee —"

Before I could finish, she flattened her hand — astonishingly loudly — on the table. "Well, then, Lady, I'm forced to point out that your description of the Heavenly Lord is much, *much* too —"

"— graphic? For prudes perhaps," I measured out my words.

"For *interviewers*," Madame amended quickly, "*only* for interviewers."

"I see. Still, that description will remain, Madame, because it's the exact description of God as conveyed by Lucifer, confirmed by Cassandra and later by my Adam, who was created, without clothing whatsoever, in His image — do remember *that*, Madame."

"I simply will not, will not — *will not!* — be responsible for how interviewers will react to —" Her voice tangled into mumbles.

This might assuage her concern: "Besides, Madame, there was no sex in Heaven, just desire, just longing —"

"God? Was *He* a prude?" Realizing that she had spoken her question almost eagerly and in a tone that might lead me to infer that she was trying to find in God an ally for her own attitude, she repeated the same words, this time with shifted emphasis: "God! Was *He* a prude!"

"Whether or not He was," I clarified, "withholding His desire for the angels was one of His tactics for controlling them. It baffled them, those beautiful creatures, and so they sought more eagerly to court His favors —"

"Not sexual favors," Madame reiterated.

"I stated that earlier, Madame. There was no sex in Heaven. For God it was enough to know — and He did — that they all desired Him — and they did."

But there was desire, and longing, much longing in Heaven, a longing the angels did not fully understand. They felt it when they saw God so grandly handsome on His throne, especially when He wound His rainbow-colored scarf gracefully about His wrist and raised His hand from His lap. The angels felt longing, too, and much more immediately, among each other, toward each other, feelings especially aroused when, accidentally — and soon they began to pretend to stumble — their perfect nude bodies rubbed against others'. At such times, pretending to regain their footing, they reached out, touched more firmly, extending the charade of trying to regain their equilibrium, and wondered at the sparks of — What? They didn't know.

"I'm sorry, Lady, but how can *you* possibly —?"

"— know all that?" I had now surrendered to having to repeat certain answers about matters interviewers might continue to question insistently. "The same reason as before. Adam told me. That, Madame — that there was no sex in Heaven — is the reason he and I were at first confused and had to explore to locate the source of our yearning. And we did, so lovingly —" The memory of our bodies in Eden lit a glorious warmth in my heart.

"Ah, yes." Madame's mood mellowed. She beamed her most gracious smile at my facility in meeting her queries. "Still, you might reconsider describing —"

I thanked her for her confidence, but assured her I would describe everyone and everything as they were.

Other angels — even some who had not joined in the flight — moved closer to Lucifer as he addressed God. "We've flown beyond, far beyond these stars —" His voice grew in excitement. Cassandra stood by, her hand — two fingers — poised on her chin. She listened carefully, and watched.

God laughed. He knew that what Lucifer had said was true. He had Himself on occasion peered beyond familiar stars and seen other heavens, other, even brighter stars. He was apprehensive of the unknown power that might lie — and might be seized — within the unperturbed darkness out of which He had thrust Himself. So He claimed the world He had shaped and commanded was the universe.

Locating her knowing smile, God addressed Cassandra, "Darling Cassandra, isn't it enough that I created what you thought your imagination conjured, the grass and the flowers? *That* was amusing." He courted laughter from the other angels. "Now, My very dear, you've extended your imagination, with commendable power, I agree, to the point of having convinced Lucifer and" — He waved His hand in an arc to include all the questioning angels — "of something false, that Our Heaven has no limits, that it extends — impossibly! — beyond Ourself — that you flew beyond it, whereas all you did was spin within Our gorgeous orbit."

Cassandra raised her long neck to the sky, where the birds had disappeared this morning.

"Surely you do know," God addressed all the rapt angels in a stern voice, "that beyond Me there is nothing." One of His hands rose, then fell on the armrest of His throne. His stare captured Cassandra so powerfully that she felt her body pulled forward.

And then she heard a loud slamming sound.

Why didn't the other angels react to it?

They continued to listen as God's lips proceeded to spew effusive tributes to the wonders of His own Heaven.

Had only she heard the violent sound? How was that possible? It had been so loud, so distinct.

God's gaze remained on her, hers on Him, locked — even while He smiled for the other angels.

Now she heard a series of metallic sounds that resonated, so discordant, so deafening that she had to resist placing her hands on her ears to shut them out.

Still the other angels did not react, not even to the terrifying scraping and clanging that followed — and not, now, to a persistent, harsh, grinding sound. She knew! Distant chains were being tightly secured, rasping, grating.

She heard a horrifying clang.

God had created gates about Heaven and had locked them!

If they were ever to fly again through the vast universe they had discovered, they would have to crash through the powerful new gates — but could they? Cassandra's mind raced urgently while she continued to smile at God. There might be . . . war in Heaven!

What a strange new word that was — "war." It had occurred along with a flash of convoluted images — reflections from God's resplendent throne? — no, the images were now smeared over with deep, ominous red.

Cassandra looked about anxiously.

Heaven was unfettered!

Had she imagined it all? No gates? She searched for a deepened shadow such enormous gates would etch into the night, no matter how carefully hidden. She saw nothing but Heaven's fields.

Baffled, she locked her gaze to God's again. And — just beyond her penetrating gaze — she saw — she thought she saw — she perceived — a creature, not an angel. In a field — No, in a garden of glorious flowers — and he was alone, terribly alone, and sad, as he stared down at an empty bed of orchids.

God blinked, and a whorl of colors in Cassandra's mind wiped away the man alone in the garden.

"But, come!" God sounded jubilant again as He addressed the congregated angels. "I've just decided. I shall have a special entertainment for all of you. Tomorrow!" His darkening gaze bored into Cassandra, then into Lucifer beside her.

That night, Cassandra joined her brother, where he stood gazing longingly into the sky they had penetrated in their flight.

Sensing that she was troubled by developments — and so was he — Lucifer asserted with desperation: "I want to fly to distant stars again, this very moment!" He spread out his arms to the sky, anxiously, agitated. "Come with me, Cassandra." Nothing ominous could possibly be occurring on a day during which they had discovered a sense of — There was no word.

"Freedom," his sister said aloud. "Let's give that name to the exhilaration we felt today."

"Freedom." Lucifer tasted the delicious word, smiled, and prepared to soar again.

Cassandra reached for his outstretched hands and held them, restraining him. "There are other matters to attend to now." She tried not to sound as deeply concerned as she was.

"You sense betrayal." Of course, he had known that was the source of her worry. God's warning look at them had worried him, too.

"Yes." She frowned. How could she tell him that she had heard the gates of Heaven closing when clearly there were none? So she spoke aloud only the thought that had asserted itself, so quickly, so firmly that it was as if it had sprung out of God's mind and she had grasped it: "God intends to assure that we never again soar beyond His boundaries."

"We'll thwart Him, whatever it takes," Lucifer said. "You'll think of a way, won't you, my love? — and I'll help you, however it is!" His voice grew desperate. Forcing joy, he grasped her tiny waist in his hands, and he whirled her around. The filmy cloak she wore slipped from her breasts, small but brash and perfectly rounded, their nipples like two succulent pink berries, a spectacle he always cherished. Slowly, he released her. Her lithe body was tense with concern.

She said softly: "You loved Him, you loved God."

"Before He lied to us —" He gazed into the space through which they had spiraled.

Other angels who had joined in the flight, and still more who had now heard of it and longed to experience it themselves, assembled in the darkened field with the brother and his sister. Gabriel had told them that Lucifer and Cassandra "looked sad." Lucifer nodded toward them. In a silent promise, he raised his hands, up, out toward the limitless night of stars and moon.

Cassandra watched, with sadness and exultation, as the other angels answered her brother's message, imitating his motions in preparation of triumphant flight.

In the moonlight, blades of wild grass quivered silver. Across the field and in bold silhouette, the Angel Michael faced the Angel Lucifer.

When the other angels disbanded — and Michael had abandoned his post — Cassandra closed her eyes. The image of Michael remained! — but not as he she had seen him tonight. The image had changed: Michael standing beside God's throne, his hand poised on his sheath, which gleamed in the sun.

Tomorrow's destiny, she thought wearily. She opened her eyes, and the thought returned, with excitement: Tomorrow's destiny! And since it is tomorrow's, then it can be thwarted. Thwart fate! The words of immense challenge tasted as sweet, as delectable as the word she had invented earlier. She wanted to speak out the bold and thrilling words of certain triumph to her brother. But she must deduce carefully what had begun to stir in her, she must grasp it all exactly, what she had never before had need to explore fully.

Her racing thoughts fascinated her: The fields of grass, the daffodils, the wild flowers — I saw them because He was *preparing* to create them! I perceived His *intentions* — that's what displeased Him. Then why had He gone ahead and allowed the image to materialize? Of course! Because His plan was already too close to its goal. And the beautiful creature whose presence she thought she had sensed, alone in a garden, when she had locked her gaze to God's today? He was included in His vagrant thoughts — and that's why the image had faded into unshaped colors.

"The gates of Heaven are *not* closed, not even built," she said aloud in amazement. It was so clear now: The sounds she had heard had not yet happened. They were the sounds of God's intentions, shaping. The power of perceiving, which God had given her for simple entertainments, and which she had sharpened on her own, had located His plan *on its way to becoming*. She faced her brother, in growing wonder. "Fate can be stopped as long as it's still only on its intended course!"

"We'll stop it!" Lucifer accepted, without question, trusting his sister even when he didn't quite understand her intricate ways.

Cassandra shuddered, drew her cloak higher on her neck. More of God's intentions had already shaped. Her earlier perception of Michael had extended: He had pulled his sword from its sheath. No, no, he had merely clasped it more tightly. "There may not be time enough to change it all."

"There *must* be!" Lucifer demanded. He held her close to him, to join their determination.

Cassandra's look turned graver. This very moment God was pacing in His chambers, planning more of His terrifying entertainment,

223

deciding what exactly to execute — She heard the footfalls of His sandals. There was much more He intended than the shutting of the gates.

His sister's hand was cold, and yet the air was warm! Was there a vagrant chill within the night? Lucifer wondered.

Cassandra winced. Another piece of destiny had fallen into place. "He'll ask us, during His 'entertainment,' what it is we most desire," she announced.

"And grant it, or taunt us with the possibility?" Lucifer longed for the answer he no longer expected.

"That's all I can perceive now." Cassandra gazed ahead and saw the fields of Heaven bathed in the moon's spilling light. "God has fallen asleep. He's stopped plotting for now." She closed her eyes in relief, feeling so weary that she sat on the field surrounded by poppies. She took one, looked at it, dreamily wondering whether at this very moment it might alter its color and she would be able to detect that subtle change even in the night. Still holding the poppy — it had not changed its hue — she inclined her head, and then allowed her body to rest. She lay down. She dozed, only to wake startled at the prospect before them.

"Lady, let's pause here," Madame Bernice said, that afternoon at tea. "We agreed to discuss this, in its place, the tricky matter of changing fate. This is the time."

"I'm prepared to rehearse the matter with you *even more* thoroughly, Madame." I was pointed in my words.

"Oh, *I* understand all of it, but interviewers —" She shook her head at their potential denseness. Pressing her bejeweled fingers on her forehead in order to concentrate fully — I saw a new ruby — she said: "Cassandra was capable of foreseeing —"

"Perceiving."

"— deducing the very moment fate began to roll along —" She stopped.

Our tea setting was trembling, the whole château quivered for eternal seconds, even the lawn shifted, trees and flowers tossing about.

"I believe we're experiencing an" — Madame clutched the armrests of her high-backed chair — "a temblor."

I held on tightly to the table. Had the veranda tilted? If so, Ermenegildo was trying to hold it in place by clamping his feathers forcefully down on the steps. The table moved an inch or two. The vase containing Madame's favorite flower of that day, a proud triumvirate of hyacinths, fell over, spilling the blooms among the dainty cups and saucers, which tinkled nervously as they shook and shook and shook. The pastry plate rattled to the edge of the table and fell with a clang.

Then it was over.

Madame was so unsettled by the sudden shaking that she was mopping her brow with her bare hands. Although I, too — I readily confess — was just as unnerved, I was happy that the rattling had unsettled me more subtly. Ermenegildo had recovered with amazing aplomb, busying himself by gathering up the fallen pastries with his beak.

"It's over, isn't it?" Madame breathed in relief. "A brief one?"

Now the previous moments seemed to have surrendered to yet another rattling, but one that came from the road, the harsh grating of carriage wheels.

Madame reached for her opera glasses and scanned the direction Ermenegildo's alerted stare was indicating with his beak, the road that connects our châteaus. Trees had grown so lush that Madame could locate nothing of significance, I could tell by her frustrated persistence in readjusting the range of the glasses. If the sound of wheels had not scraped so harshly on the road, the carriage — it was definitely a carriage — might have passed undetected after the previous disrupting moments.

When I would return, soon now, to my château, what would I find on the gate? Another subtle threat? Another installment of the mendacious novel, with what new hidden horrors and warnings in its distortions? The "Final Installment"? Fulfilling the terrifying menace that ends the preceding one?

The sun shone harshly on me all at once! It blinded me! I turned away! The time for interviews is nearing! I breathed deeply, attempting to control a flood of dread.

"I think," Madame said — and I had been successful in concealing the moments of panic, "that what we heard was only the sounds of the wanderers from the City, their pitiful carts in which they wheel their possessions."

"I'm sure of it," I said, knowing she was trying only to convince me. She *had* noticed my anxiety.

Ermenegildo continued to direct his vision toward the road, his twisted feather — it seemed to me — angered.

The sound of the carriage faded, as if it had not occurred.

As quickly as it had assumed it, the sun lost its assaulting brightness. The mixture of soft shadows and filigrees of light was too gentle to contain any threat. Hyacinths were in full bloom in Madame's garden, donating a perfect alternation of colors: yellow, blue, fuchsia.

We continued — a grand feat — with our rehearsal as if there had been no interruptions, not the temblor, not the carriage. "Cassandra was able to foresee —"

"— perceive —"

"Cassandra was able to *detect* the very moment fate began to roll along" — Madame paused, to select each word precisely — "like a stone set into motion and aimed at a certain goal. What she was able to foresee — perceive, *perceive!* — was the *goal,* the *intended* goal!" Her voice rose in excitement. "But!" She raised one finger, on which I noticed a second new ruby. "But! Just as a stone set into motion moves along toward its *intended* goal, its *direction* might be shifted, diverted! — even stopped! And *that's* how you change destiny!"

At first I had been apprehensive of Madame's metaphor, but now I thought it marvelous. I congratulated her.

"Thank you," she said, and rewarded herself with her fifth crumb cake. "You may use the example at interviews, Lady — if you wish."

"Indeed I shall!" I was delighted to accept. "Cassandra herself could not have condensed the matter better."

"Oh?" Delight so overwhelmed Madame that she allowed herself a sixth pastry, a moon-shaped little thing sprinkled with cinnamon; it had escaped from the plate that had fallen over earlier. I could hardly hear the words she spoke next; she spoke them with a shyness I seldom notice in her — she tends to be quite forward, although always genteel. She said, "Do you suppose, Lady, that Cassandra . . . would have . . . approved . . . of me?"

"Oh, Madame." I was swept away by her touching question. "I knew her well through all my lives, and I can assure you: Cassandra would have *longed* for *your* approval."

Madame only smiled, but her smile was eloquent in its boundless joy. To celebrate her great pleasure, Ermenegildo swooshed his tail open for her, gathered it, then swooshed it out again, and yet again, in a display that brought a series of "thank you, thank you's" from Madame.

The day was dusking, but I wanted to continue with the events in Heaven — yes, and to keep in abeyance the discovery of anything that might have been left at my gates — something startling; the coach's scraping, echoing in my ears, had announced that. So I continued: "The next night —"

In Heaven, a band of young angels — beautiful youths, boys and girls, their bodies decked only in garlands of tiny orchids — but, Cassandra noticed, their eyes tilted with malice — announced:

"God's Special Entertainment shall commence!"

XXII

INSIDE MADAME'S CHÂTEAU, candles had been lit. Their glow created a golden fan where we sat on the veranda, Madame, Ermenegildo, and I.

"Madame, I shall continue. I'm not tired. I'm exhilarated to be able to speak all this at last."

"As well you might be, Lady! I approve our going on."

All the angels had assembled early in the amphitheater God had built before His throne. These gatherings were not rare. God would listen to a song, encourage a performance, a dance, a scene from a drama. He would then make some suggestions: "A more dramatic moment, a quiet pause to create a more impressive highlight. Perhaps a more resonant first line? Risk melodrama — *but!* — retain control." He Himself was well aware of drama. Before He appeared on His throne, there would occur a swirl of cumulus clouds, a flourish of invisible trumpets. The clouds would dissipate, and there He would be, sitting on His throne with His golden sandals and His rainbow-streaked scarf.

This much of what Cassandra had perceived last night had now occurred: Michael stood at the foot of the throne; he gripped the sheathed lance, firmly.

He was a strikingly handsome angel, but a certain sternness furrowed his brow. He was aware that he was among God's favorite angels, along with Lucifer; but at times Michael thought God preferred Lucifer above all the others — and that he, Michael, was second in God's hierarchy; Lucifer, after all, had been God's firstborn. Now that there was tension between Lucifer and God, Michael saw an opportunity to replace him, especially since God had, last night before going to sleep, encouraged him to stand beside Him today. Also, He had given him a new silver sheath "as a present for your loyalty to Me." All this might be intended to arouse Lucifer's jealousy, Michael considered, and to convey a warning of caution to the other angels. Still, he was thrilled by his placement so close to the power of God's throne.

As the flourish of trumpets faded and the mist before the throne cleared for God's appearance, Michael readjusted the sheath on his bare hip, to emphasize the gift God had presented him. The sheath caught a blade of golden sun, a stabbing warning.

"My children!" God welcomed, with extended hands.

Cassandra and Lucifer, and some of the other angels, always winced to be addressed as "children." Today the word assumed a threatening connotation.

"Because of what occurred yesterday," God continued, "Our beloved Lucifer's" — He leaned over conspiratorially to Michael, as if to allow him to hear a special tone, to pick up a nuance of added confidence and affection here and there, while His eyes remained nailed on Lucifer — "yes, and Our beloved Cassandra's, joyful imagining that he and she and others have discovered that more exists beyond Our Heaven" — with a spiral of gestures, He dismissed the idea — "yes, because of that, I have, as promised, devised a Special Entertainment, to bring us all much closer together *in the only Heaven that exists.*" He rested His hand — lightly — on His lap. "I invite My favorite angels — and all of you are favorites —" He inclined toward Michael, who smiled, a smile so grateful that it almost wiped away the furrow on his brow. "I invite you to tell Me what you long for most."

Just as Cassandra had perceived! Lucifer knew. But had God already planned further than what she had grasped — and might intercept?

Throughout the day, as a certain anxiety had seized Heaven about the coming "Special Entertainment," Cassandra had remained alone, walking along flower-strewn fields, pondering various strategies for several eventualities, pausing only to thrill to the deep blue of a gilia blossom, and to peer at a poppy in expectation — always — of witnessing the exact moment when it changed its tint. The smile on her face had remained, lovely, as if nothing were troubling her.

Now she stood against a marble column in the amphitheater and watched and listened carefully to God.

"And so, speak!" He commanded beneficently.

For a moment Michael felt brash enough, secure enough, to

consider repeating God's words. Instead, he clutched his sheathed sword more tightly.

Lucifer spoke out, "When we speak our wishes, shall they be granted?"

God's smile remained on His face. "Oh, but of course. Why else —?" He pretended to entreat Michael in His puzzlement.

Lucifer faced Cassandra quizzically. All would be won? This easily?

Cassandra shook her head slowly, no. To nurture the full spirit of his defiance — which her plan counted on — she had not told her brother what she had plotted to foil the shutting of Heaven's gates, now that she was certain of that much of God's design. Her plan relied on this: When He had plotted that yesterday, and in His own mind heard the reverberations that would occur, she had perceived them as part of His intention. Now she knew exactly what sounds would precede the imprisonment in Heaven. And when that began —

She glided gracefully toward the throne. Passing her puzzled brother, she whispered, "Nothing has been won. It's all still shaping, as He wants. Watch for my signal, keep our allies close to you, and be prepared!"

As the rebellious angels responded to Lucifer's invitation to stand near him — he still did not know, but trusted, what his sister intended — Cassandra moved closer to the throne, casually, as if only to hear better. Michael's eyes followed her. She smiled beguilingly at him, so beguilingly, enticingly, that he placed his sheathed blade between his legs, to conceal his —

Madame astonished me by tinkling her tiny teaspoon against her exquisite china, a signal she had used before but which continued to annoy me. "You said there was no sex in Heaven, Lady!"

"— placed his sheathed blade between his legs to conceal his threatening posture," I finished. "May I proceed?"

I suspected Madame blushed while she pretended to retrieve a napkin that had not fallen.

In Heaven, God encouraged, "Who shall begin?" It was difficult for Him to sound playful. When He tried, like now, it all seemed incongruous. Still, He went on, "Come, children, come! Let Me know what you long for most."

"Freedom!" Lucifer stepped forward and uttered the word Cassandra had invented yesterday. "To soar beyond all boundaries!" He added anxious words slowly: "And that we be allowed to love You, but not demanded to." He had looked down when his voice had tensed. Now, chin raised, he stared into God's eyes.

"Your wish is granted," God said to Lucifer. To emphasize the ease with which that would be done, He waved His hand in an arc, His palm open to the angels. "Is that all?"

Just like that? Lucifer was even more bewildered. So were the angels gathered about him. They looked at him, baffled, then at each other. Was it possible Cassandra's suspicions had been wrong, as conveyed to them by Lucifer? Had she misled them — and him? Lucifer shifted his stare to his sister. Why wasn't she coming over to share his triumph — theirs? Why were her eyes locked with God's?

Cassandra dared not look away from God. She must watch — and listen. When she heard the first sounds — scraping, discordant, metallic, harsh — she would know God's intentions had been set into motion toward their goal, and she would set her own scheme into action, announce, with evidence, what was about to occur. On her instant signal, Lucifer and the other determined angels would storm Heaven's forming bastions before they sealed; and barely gliding past the gates that God would surely rush into existence, they would soar, free, into the new realms they had discovered beyond Heaven's stars. All that would occur only by determining the precise moment to move. One second too soon, and God would shift His entrapment. One second too late, and she and all the other angels would be swept away into His plotted destiny.

Cassandra strained to hear the first warning scrape. Now?

No. Nothing.

In triumph at having secured his freedom and that of the other angels, Lucifer faced the angels gathering about him. He called out to his sister: "Cassandra! Look!" — and raised his arms in memory of their flight. She did not share his victory — why?

Cassandra did not shift her stare from God. Still no first signal of the forming of the gates. Was His plan changing, another chosen? She would have perceived that shift — and had not. Now she saw His lips forming silent words she deciphered: *Yes, dear Lucifer, My former favorite, I shall grant you your... What? Free —? Your odd word eludes me... Yes, I shall grant it to you, and in a most special place that I'll create for you, where you will rule... in Hell!*

No! Cassandra recoiled from God's thoughts.

— where you will rule in tortured exile — unless —

Wait! He was still only rehearsing His intentions! Cassandra's hope was resurrected. The closing of Heaven's gates was still foremost in His mind. This was judgment that would be possible only after that occurred. God added silent words:

—unless — yes, I will allow this — unless you deny that you soared beyond My realm, and convince the other angels they did not! — and assure by turning against her that Cassandra never again incites you to believe otherwise.

Cassandra smiled at Him, charmingly, yes, flirtatiously.

"Electra!" God avoided Cassandra's look and called to the angel approaching.

Electra was a young angel, aware of her body's beginning fullness; her nipples were already as solid as the tips of her small fingers, with which she often touched them. She was proud of the sensual arc of her slender hips, the perpetual blush on her cheeks, her amber eyes flecked with yellow. Often she found herself hoping — without actually identifying what she felt as hope — hoping for — At that point her wishes tangled into confusion and all that remained was a yearning that had found its definition when Lucifer had uttered the new word as the gift he asked for.

"And Orestes!" God welcomed the angel who joined Electra. He was her age, with a youthful awkwardness that he turned into unique beauty. He and Electra created a cherished sight as they roamed the plains of Heaven.

"I wish for . . . freedom . . ." Electra spoke the new word.
She turned to the awkwardly beautiful angel beside her, and he nodded in agreement:

"Freedom."

"From —?" God invited them to finish.

"From?" Electra couldn't answer. From something terrible? How could she say that when God was being so generous? Sensing her confusion, Orestes held her hand. Why fear?

"Granted, My children, My dear Electra, My dear Orestes." *You shall dance freely in a choreography of horror.* "Ah, Clytemnestra! Agamemnon!" God greeted the new petitioning angels. "I shall not even ask your petitions. I shall simply grant them!" *That you be bound forever to Electra and Orestes in their dance of terror!* God spread His hands out in an act of open beneficence as the proud angels bowed their heads in gratitude.

"Iphigenia, gentle, lovely Iphigenia. *I choose you to set into motion the perfect choreography of violence that I will design.*

God was conceiving yet another hell, different from the one He

232

was considering for Lucifer, Cassandra collected her new perceptions. This other hell would exist in a world not yet created. There, rebel angels would be reduced to — she searched for new words in this shaping vocabulary of connivance: — tragic pawns.

"Job?"

"You, too, of course, want your —" *That word! That word! What was it?*

"Freedom," the distinguished bearded angel said. "To love you, and be free."

I shall allow you the freedom to prove your love for Me.

"Lady," Madame interjected into the petitioning of the angels in Heaven, "Job was an angel —?"

"Yes," I answered, and continued:

"Lovely Penelope?" God acknowledged yet another angel.

"Freedom."

Your years of fidelity shall be disbelieved, and you shall be banished for adultery and infidelity; shall you call that freedom?

Adultery? Infidelity? As God's harsh vocabulary grew, Cassandra grasped its meanings, and the need to escape His Heaven became more urgent.

A radiantly beautiful angel had approached the throne of God. "Narcissus?" God welcomed him. "What is your wish?"

"A new beautiful flower in the fields of Heaven!" Narcissus' youthful request brought fond laughter from the other angels.

"Why, yes, and I shall even make it in your image, and name it after you," God said. "And I shall place it to overlook . . . a crystalline brook."

Narcissus was elated. Emboldened by God's reaction, he faced Him once more and deepened his voice: "And that we can fly as long and as far away as we want." He basked in the approval of applauding angels.

But — Cassandra noted this while still not removing her gaze from God — the approval was not being shared by other menacing factions of angels, who were gathering steadily about Michael, about God's throne.

Still, no rasp of metal —

"Tamar, you're more beautiful than ever," God received the exotic beauty, "and with you is — Of *course!* Absalom. You wish for freedom, too? Granted, granted!" *Roam together freely through a field of spilled blood.*

"Lady —"

233

"Madame?"

"Absalom —?"

"— and Tamar were angels, too."

"I see."

Cassandra felt an accumulating horror at God's distortion of the angels' wishes. In His urgency to punish further and as He exulted in various possibilities, was His mind keeping last night's intended destiny at bay — the gates about Heaven uncreated? Immediately after that thought had given her added hope, Cassandra felt a powerful sensation she couldn't identify, the perception of something — it was "something," that's all she knew — horrifying, and — a new word formed — evil.

She mustn't stray from present considerations, she warned herself. She secured her eyes more tightly to God's. She had learned to study the language of His gestures: She knew that when He decided — unswervingly decided whatever He decided — He would plant His hand, forcefully, on His groin, cupping it, so forcefully that she had often marveled that He did not wince in pain. That gesture — she took hasty inventory of all her past observations of Him — would always be accompanied by these words: "My will be *done!*" Until those words were finished — and His fist grasped his groin at *"done!"* — the stone of fate — and it was rolling — might be diverted.

Cassandra was baffled. Until He locked the gates, He could not execute His curses — His "will *done!*" Still no initial sound! Yet His hand was poised to announce His will . . . Act now? Risk that fate might stumble into place in moments of confusion?

"Ah, Ganymede! What could *you* possibly want?"

The young angel who had flown with the others the day before — and had attempted to touch the stars — smiled radiantly, now that God was granting all their wishes, the same one.

"Freedom!" Ganymede repeated the new word.

"What else but that would I grant you, dear Ganymede?" God shrugged His mighty shoulders. *You shall be free to serve the covetous King I will create, just for you, and he shall imprison your beauty.*

"Pretty, pretty Echo?"

"Freedom."

Oh, yes, yes, yes! This is inspired! I choose you, Echo, to love Narcissus!

"Fair Calamus," God greeted the proud angel. "And just behind you is —" He pretended not to recognize the other equally handsome youth approaching, but with more reticence.

"Carpus," Calamus introduced his constant companion. "I ask for freedom — and to love . . . whoever I love." He squared his young shoulders and beckoned the shy angel to stand next to him. Calamus sidled up to him shyly. No one could help notice that, embraced warmly by the fleece between his supple legs, Calamus's erection grew, and Carpus's surpassed it.

"Lady, you pointedly said there was —"

"Desire, Madame! There *was* desire, and there was longing!"

"Oh."

I shall pursue you through the ages with judgments and curses. God smiled beneficently.

"Ishtar!" *You shall bear children to be slaughtered.*

"Sisyphus!"

The bold angel thrust a strand of his long hair from his sculpted face. "Freedom!"

When the weight I'll place on your shoulders lessens — oh, just slightly so you'll recognize it as your "freedom" — you'll still feel a burden heavier than any rock!

"Hecate?" God instantly recognized the astonishing dark-haired angel. *Hounds shall accompany you in your search through the freedom of darkness.*

"Orpheus! Oh, and Eurydice!" *You shall lose each other in . . . Hell.*

"Isis! How beautiful you look." *Your love shall weave a chain of vengeance with —*

"Osiris! Granted. Your wish is granted!"

"Prometheus?" *Oh, I shall test your longing for your freedom!*

"Ah, and Our dark-complected beauty, Our beloved Taba."

The Angel Taba was glorious, with skin that glowed like darkened gold. With a proud lift of her chin, she announced her wish: "Freedom."

You'll wail your despair in dark jungles that you shall wander freely from night to night . . .

"The Xtabay!" Madame Bernice breathed, clearly awed to learn, in her garden, that the wailing woman was not only a woman my essence had inhabited during her corporeal life — a woman soon to be redeemed — but that she had once been a stunning angel with an olive complexion.

235

"I should have known, of course," Madame exulted. "Oh, Lady, was *La Malinche* —"

"— an angel? Yes, Madame, and every bit as beautiful then, with her dark-brown skin and almond eyes."

"Of course! Of course!"

God continued His excited greetings from his throne: "Cadmus!" "Sappho!" "Arion!" "All My very dears!" "And you, Oedipus, tell Me! What do *you* long for?" "Ravishing Jocasta, what can you possibly desire, My dear? . . . Ah, welcome, welcome, Laius!"

And so it went, more curses prepared for all the angels who had flown with her and Lucifer, a grotesque conversion of wishes into punishment for disobedience — and there was even more! Cassandra's vision blurred with horror but not before she had perceived a world of pain, and —

It was all *intended* punishment. Cassandra forced her concentration to return to what was actually occurring now, here, before her. Heaven was not yet a prison! And yet —

God's hand floated over His groin — and remained there, ready to fall with enraged finality.

But the sounds that must precede the closing of Heaven's gates had not occurred!

"My will be —"

Certainly He was not going to issue His command before the angels were imprisoned. Cassandra felt destiny rushing past her, heard its urgent whisperings and curses as it advanced toward its goal. But how? She must revise her plan — act before God uttered His decisive word.

She thrust herself before His throne, and fate twisted and turned, diverted from its course, then waited, bewildered, while God had to pause to discover what Cassandra would do now.

"Our *darling* Cassandra!"

She hated His calling her *darling*. Each time He did, she cringed.

"My lovely dear, you want another special gift, My special, special darling?" God tried not to edge His words with sarcasm.

"Yes!"

"Then speak it, My dear, though some would say the one gift We've already granted you may have been —" He sought Michael's approval. More menacing angels had joined about him and the throne. "— might have been . . . excessive?" He turned the word into a question and glanced it off Michael.

Michael could not bring himself to nod. He was bedazzled by Cassandra, who looked — oh, why this thought now? — more beautiful than ever. Her large eyes were fierce with . . . Passion, Michael gave his own feeling a name that would also describe what he saw in Cassandra's eyes, yes, fierce passion.

"I have another wish, yes," Cassandra spoke.

"And that, darling, is —?" God controlled His voice.

"That You tell the truth of what You're doing now."

Michael took a step toward her. It wasn't exactly clear to him why. To protest her effrontery of God? Or . . . just to be nearer to her? He ran his hand very slowly down his sleek sword. Cassandra fascinated him, not only because of her lithe beauty but because of her power, a power belied by her seeming fragility. No other angel rivaled her subtle might in Heaven. Michael thought she sometimes intimidated God. No, he chastised himself, when, beside him, God's body tensed. There was more he felt toward Cassandra, Michael knew. Often he daydreamed about her, envied Lucifer's closeness to her — and longed for the occasional mischievous breeze that would sculpt her cloak — so elegant — about her body so that he could see the outline of . . . everything! — yes, and especially the place that intrigued him most, the lightly shaded aperture between her legs. He had been so deep in his reveries that only now was he aware that all the angels had gasped at Cassandra's words, and that Lucifer had rushed to be with her as she confronted God.

Lucifer had believed his sister immediately when she had intimated, so clearly, that God was lying. The angel stood beside his sister, close, their bodies touching, to add his strength to whatever she might say now.

"The truth?" God dismissed the matter with the simplest wave of His hand, which floated away from the decisive gesture on His groin.

That's what Cassandra had intended! "The truth of Your intentions in Your entertainment —" She needed more time to adapt to, to explore, the unexpected.

"To grant all My children the freedom they've asked for, darling," God spoke with deliberate easy logic. "What else?"

"To distort it into doom," Cassandra said, "and thereby punish us for claiming there's anything beyond."

Lucifer noticed nervously that the other angels who had joined in the flight, who had presented their petitions, were whispering in agitation among themselves. Should they trust Cassandra? Oh, she was strange. Was *she* betraying them? What did she want? God had granted all their wishes. Was she bartering with Him for a higher place in Heaven, only for herself?

Cassandra whirled around, in one motion sweeping her cloak about her body so that it covered her entirely.

But the effect was to make her appear entirely exposed. Michael clung to that image. He squinted his eyes to intensify the impression.

"Our Father" — Cassandra always forced those words as she addressed the angels — "is planning —" Still only planning, still only planning, still intention, not fate, not yet the shaping of the gates! "— is planning a terrible destiny for us all, a hell" — she uttered the terrifying word aloud for the first time — "no, various hells He will create" — *intends* to create! — "and within those hells, He will, yes, grant us our wishes, twisted into punishments." She must keep His plan in check with her challenge — force all His attention to deal with her.

In a fierce voice, she announced the curses God had conceived for each of the petitioning angels. Their whispers rose in shock, then indignation — now rage.

About God's throne more threatening angels joined Michael. Gabriel moved toward them, then stopped, looked at Lucifer and Cassandra — and waited.

Lucifer said to his sister, "It's true?"

Cassandra nodded, "That's His intention, yes. Fate is very near its course." Her tactic would hold for only seconds more.

"But not there yet!" Lucifer grasped. He stood swiftly at the very foot of God's throne, before this God he had once loved. "We flew into the darkness out of which You emerged. Beyond that, there's a universe. I'll trade Your Heaven for what we felt — freedom! — beyond Your narrow boundaries."

God's body tensed with power on His throne. His rainbow-colored scarf drifted from His shoulders to His sandaled feet. "I forbid you!"

Lucifer had extended the seconds of possibility! Cassandra welcomed that turn. God's rage had diverted His attention further.

Lucifer stretched his arms up, wide, in front of God. Before he had completed his pantomime of flying, his hands clenched into fists, and he shouted:

"I defy You, God!"

There was a gasp in Heaven. Michael pointed his lance at Lucifer.

"My will be *done!*" God's hand fell on His groin. "I declare War in Heaven!"

As bands of uncommitted angels rushed to join Lucifer and Cassandra, and others joined Michael — and all in Michael's faction were suddenly armed — Cassandra closed her eyes. The gates were still not closed! The defiant angels could still escape. Had God been pushed to rashness?

She could not ponder that long. Before her, Lucifer and the rebellious angels confronted Michael and his army of sudden warriors. It was past them, the warriors, that the defiant angels must make their way to the edge of Heaven, from where they had first flown.

How was it possible that Heaven's gates were still not even poised to close?

Cassandra heard Lucifer shout to the angels who stood with them the words she had just uttered to him:

"Storm Heaven *now!*"

XXIII

"MADAME, I CANNOT GO ON." I was staring into the darkening sky, where that terrifying war had been fought so long ago, so present in my memories.

"I understand. But, Lady, I must know now or I won't sleep. Were Cassandra's perceptions wrong? — that God intended to lock Heaven?" Madame's voice rang with indignation that there could exist such a possibility. "Surely she didn't act rashly when she decided that the rebellious angels must storm Heaven then."

"Cassandra was *not* wrong, Madame, and she moved when she felt she must." That was all my sudden weariness could grant her. Further explication would come in detail, but not tonight.

The knowledge that Cassandra had not been wrong had satisfied Madame, for now. "I *never* doubted she was right."

Dusky evening had darkened into purple the flowers on the vines of bougainvillea draping the veranda. In the diminished light, surrendered lavender blossoms from jacaranda trees transformed the lacy veil of petals on the ground into a tattered shroud. Only the new orchid lilies thrived in this decreasing light, their near-oppressive perfume as powerful as that of rancid gardenias abandoned after an aborted wedding. I noticed all this as Ermenegildo escorted me to the road. I'm certain that he would have accompanied me all the way to my château, except that I assured him, and Madame Bernice, that I would be safe — we were all remembering the carriage that had sped past us earlier. Along the road, I glanced back to see Ermenegildo, verifying my safety. Behind him, Madame strained on her veranda to follow me as far as her vision allowed in this ambiguous light. I took her caring gaze with me as a blessing.

As I walked along the road, I heard anxious palm fronds struggling in a rising wind. I drew my cowl higher on my shoulders. I cannot become accustomed to the fact that a warm afternoon, like today's, may be invaded by as powerful a chill as tonight's, and that a cool afternoon may be swept away by heated winds. I slowed my steps. Would the coach still be at my gates? Caught in the invasion of recollections about the War in Heaven — I realized only now — neither Madame nor I, nor Ermenegildo, who would have signaled, had heard it rumbling back. It might have done so stealthily, to disorient us.

The carriage was not there. My relief was only momentary. My lantern revealed a wrapped package left attached to the grillwork of my gate. Rising wind whirled leaves about it, containing it in a vortex.

My hands — acting beyond my fear — reached for the package and unwrapped it: *"The True and Just Account of the Abominable Seduction into Holy Matrimony in the Grand Cathedral and of the Murder of the Most Royal Count by the Whore:* The Final Installment."

The Final Installment!

Those last words had been scrawled — not yet printed! — in bold black bleeding letters, as if intended in themselves to convey a sense of . . .

Still-forming menace.

Tired as I am — but aware that there is so much to go through and that time is narrowing — I shall share with you now in my quarters what Madame and I rehearsed today during our long, long tea . . .

There.

I've gone with you through all the matters we explored, up to Lucifer's echoing of Cassandra's exhortation to storm Heaven.

And it's all blasphemous!

I should pretend I didn't hear your accusation, even within the quietude of my chambers. But I shall answer you with all the force of my voice: *I* have been blasphemed against, blamed for all the world's sorrows! I am now at last about to present *my* case.

I note your abrupt silence.

I know it's only temporary. I anticipate that you — yes, you who thrust that accusation at me so loudly! — are merely waiting. When you spring, I shall be ready to answer you even more forcefully.

As forcefully as I shall answer the guaranteed libels in the "Final Installment," which I abandoned on the marble table with the earlier entries. It shall remain there for now. I reach instead for the "Third Installment," which I have not read entirely — except for its noxious ending "promise" that my eyes fall on. Madame says it's important that we attend, in sequence, to the evolving assertions in the "Account," since it's presenting its evil case carefully.

Is that the installment that describes the Renegade Nun?

Yes! But I have no guarantee that she appears again.

Although the "Final Installment" continues to command my attention with its imperative first page — my eyes return to it and pull away — I shall resume reading from the "Third Installment," as far as my endurance for vilification allows. I skip gladly the pages to which I've already exposed myself. I find the place where, an earlier night, my violated heart demanded that I stop, that I not even turn the page, and I read:

> Exhausted but undaunted by this *True Account* that he is honor-bound to record, the Writer now divulges that, throughout this pilgrimage of righteous exposure, he has been carrying an added weight of outrage: *knowledge of a most harrowing act in the Whore's contaminated past, an act so heinous —*

I turn the page, slowly.

> — that the Whore falsified it to arouse the Noble Count's compassion and to bind him closer to her with pity, adding that to all the other unholy coercions she and the Reverend Pimp exposed him to. Or (shall further exploration uncover?) did she *withhold* the monstrous act entirely from him, not daring to risk provoking a more deserving compassion that would incite him to recoil in horror from the said abhorrence, and from her? And what was that abhorrence? This: the violent death of her children within her profane past.

They dare.

> Being quick in considerations of morality, the Reader is surely pondering: Children fathered by whom? Did she know? Was it by the Reverend Pimp? How would such a man react to the blessing of Fatherhood? How indeed!

They dare. I shall not even pause, shall not even hold my breath. I shall persevere undaunted.

242

The Writer (stunned anew by the prospect of the atrocity involved) cannot bear to proceed into such a quagmire now, knowing that the cleansed of heart will understand his reticence and extend a benediction to him. Again he moves away from that information for now, to give the Reader and himself time to prepare for what is to come.

Again, imputations, only imputations left to fester viciously. I push on, to the relative mercy of — perhaps! — lesser outrages.

Because it has been some pages since the Reader was last made aware, by this faithful *True Account,* of the repellent conduct of the Whore and her Reverend Pimp, the Writer has thought it wise to chronicle more steps in this saga of debauchery intended to bring the righteous Count to his knees — both in situations the Writer blushes to remember, as well as at the altar of the Grand Cathedral.

The dissolute pair — the Whore and the Reverend Pimp — continued to force the gentle Count to indulge in "games" which (the Reader surely knows by now) were repugnant to the Count, who potently resisted them. (The Writer reminds that he returns to and dwells at length upon the harrowing concupiscence involved, *only* because it prepares the stunned Reader for greater transgressions to follow.)

In one such outrage designed further to undermine the Count's judicious morality and his loyalty to his class, the Whore and the Pimp set out to enact this scenario.

Shall I race ahead? No. It isn't easy to surrender to this abhorrent document too soon; it must be done slowly, step by ugly step:

The Whore pretended she was a Great Lady involved in a secret assignation in a rural inn with her Philanderer-Lover. Here, the Writer shares the Reader's indignant protestation: A woman of true nobility would *never* agree to an assignation in a rural inn. At this point in this journey to unmask depravity, the Reader does not have to be informed who would be inveigled into playing the sated Philanderer-Lover. The Noble Count.

In this charade, a Page would deliver a rose to the Lady-Whore's quarters. The rose was accompanied by a note explaining that the Philanderer-Lover would be late "because of unavoidable consultations with the King." "Take this rose," the spurious note read, "in my stead until I join you." The fraudulent note went on to suggest that the Lady-Whore employ the rose "imaginatively" to enhance the enticements and scents of her opulent body (that is how the writer of the *note* saw it).

The Lady-Whore was languishing in her bath (according to the script she and the Reverend Pimp had devised) when the hired Page, hearing no response to his gentle but not unmanly knocking, entered the Lady-Whore's chamber, just as was intended.

The role of the Page was performed by a young, sweetly naïve Lad from the country — told only that he was being hired to deliver a rose to "a lady." The Lad's unruly curls occasionally toppled to the edge of his enormous chocolaty eyes full of youthful dreams, eyes whose color was deepened by his fair skin, although, clearly, the sun had lingered on it with warm kisses. His uniform as Page was quite snug, and so revealed the sturdy firm buttocks that only good Christian labor can sculpt so round.

The Writer of this *True Account* dwells on the Lad-Page's description only because what occurs subsequently will be rendered all the more nefarious if the Reader retains the fact of the Lad-Page's youthfully delectable virginity and imagines the series of boyish blushes all this provoked.

Any doubt that the Pope is involved in the production of these pages evaporates.

Attempting to deliver the rose from the Philanderer-Lover in this repugnant charade, and still obtaining no response to his knocking, the Lad-Page wandered into the only source of sounds in the quarters, the Lady-Whore's bath, just as had been intended. (How his face must have flushed as he looked away from the extravagant spectacle of the Lady-Whore naked in her bath, foamy bubbles playing hide-and-seek with her flesh, especially where they nestled between her breasts — and, most especially, between her thighs, since she had crooked one leg slightly over the other, just so, so that a tint of hair at her parting peeked, just so, out of the bubbly water, even more when she moved, causing the soapy bubbles to burst, and then re-form, just so, delighting in their warm nest, just exactly so.

Alix's contribution.

Before the Lad-Page's astonished chocolaty eyes, the Lady-Whore emerged brazenly out of her bath (how other than brazenly!

244

the Reader rightly gasps), her skin smooth and glowing from the milk in which she had bathed. (Even the Chronicler of this *True Account* will not allow his imagination to abide what else it might have been that she bathed in.) Her hair was loose, not fully wet, so that it spiraled at the edges, falling onto her arrogant shoulders. As the Lad-Page turned away in horror, the Lady-Whore proceeded to rub her body lightly with an emollient, thus accentuating her lascivious sensuality and turning the nipples of her most insolent breasts into tiny pearls.

More of Alix's deliriums infiltrate the pages.

Trapped in the bewilderment of this shocking moment, the Lad-Page bravely attempted to perform the only function for which he believed he had been hired: He held out the rose for the Lady-Whore to take. Instead of taking the rose, she took *advantage* of the Lad-Page's position at the moment, in order to cause the rose to make contact with the place she had all along intended for this "accidental" touch, the often-violated parting between her lavish legs!

At that moment, the Count as sated Philanderer-Lover entered the room to see what the Reader knows was the Lad-Page's hand trembling (and not, as the gross of mind would have it, tickling what the Lady-Whore had presented to him like a banquet — her furry triangle, just a puff).

The Philanderer-Lover concealed himself, in this vile scenario, to allow these salacious encounters to proceed. The Reader, of course, knows that the Count was actually reeling in horror from it all.

"Cut the stem from the rose with your teeth, Page!" the Lady-Whore ordered the Lad-Page.

He did what he must.

"Now moisten the petals of the rose with your tongue," the Lady-Whore growled at the Lad-Page as the sated Philanderer-Lover watched, hungrily, although in actuality the Count had become frozen at a sight that his honorable mind could not yet grasp.

"Now place the rose, only with your mouth, between my luscious lips." (She did not mean her mouth.)

"But I'm a virgin, your Ladyship, a lad newly arrived from the country," the Lad-Page protested.

"So much the better," the Lady-Whore's lustful voice declaimed.

245

No amount of pleading could have saved the Lad from this outrage. The Reader can only imagine with what despair he placed the rose where he had been ordered to, so shamed that he attempted to hide his blushing face there for long moments.

"Remove your clothes at once!" the licentious Lady-Whore commanded.

The Lad-Page hesitated, but again he did what he must do. Who knew what menace lurked in these despoiled quarters? He peeled off his tight uniform — with some difficulty past his sturdy buttocks, especially the roundest part, mid-back.

(The good of mind can well imagine that while this depravity was proceeding, the Lad must have been uttering silent prayers, prayers rehearsed during lazy evenings in the country when, having tended to his Christian chores and inspired by the innocence of youthful angels romping in celestial orbs as depicted on church walls by the Masters, he had removed his clothes and lain on his stomach, pressing and rubbing, rubbing and pressing his young body against the grass, pressing and rubbing with a vigor possessed only by the young, all to accentuate his closeness to God's bountiful nature.)

Ensnared by the Lady-Whore, the Lad-Page attempted to cover his parts that the Creator did not intend to be viewed by other than the goodly wife he deserved, and, then, viewed only in the modesty of night in a connubial bed — but certainly not by the Lady-Whore. The bunched shirt he pressed to himself, though ample, was not enough to conceal his parts entirely.

"Now with your member, and only your member, replace the rose between my legs," the Lady-Whore, riding crests of lust, directed the Lad-Page.

The Count, trapped in this unscrupulous scenario, now attempted to save the Lad from this wretched initiation in the only way his sincere mind could grasp. "I'll show you how it's done, lad!" he shouted at the terrified Lad-Page (meaning he would show the youth the only way possible to salvage his vibrant virginity). Believing that both he and the Lady-Whore were now under assault from a crazed intruder, the Lad-Page bravely attempted to push the Philanderer-Lover away.

(The Writer pauses to gain his courage to continue.)

In the ensuing commotion, the Lad-Page and the Philanderer-Count grappled, rolling on the floor, both struggling in a confusion of noble intentions, a situation, however, that allowed the cunning Whore, practiced as she was, to seize ample advantage and thus

246

guarantee yet another penetration of her by the Count — whose frantic, scandalized blood had rushed to every limb and organ of his body — while the confused Lad-Page courageously continued to attempt to thrust himself between the two (remember his glorious innocence, which must have rushed him back to the memory of past insouciant moments of pressing and rubbing, rubbing and pressing against nature's bounty in the country).

Burning with indignation at usurped morality, the Writer here leaves to the imagination of the Reader what followed, while providing only necessary guidance: There was a melee of glistening flesh, sweating flesh — young flesh, woman's flesh, man's flesh — flesh, flesh, throbbing, thrusting, twisting, amid groans and explosions and — and — and —

Having dutifully conveyed what occurred, the Writer now sets down his pen and, wearied, rests before continuing in his travail of exposing even worse abominable corruptions.

I remember, with tears, the incident these pages have distorted. Yes, and you will note what unrelenting scrutiny the Count and I must have been constantly under by one or another of the writers of these pages — or their spies. How else to account for the fact that they possess the barest outline of the truth, which they distort? Here, they have twisted the cherished events of an evening when my beloved Count du Muir and I had taken quarters in an inn by the ocean.

We were lying naked in bed enjoying a gentle sea breeze and an occasional sprinkle of water from a high-cresting wave. We had just made love. Our love and passion were constant. Every few minutes, my beloved would lean over me idly and embrace, with his lips, softly, each of my nipples. It was during such a pleasurable moment that he whispered to me that a young man was peeking at us from our balcony. I was alarmed, but my beloved said there was no reason. He had seen the young man — he worked at the inn — a handsome young man of perhaps seventeen.

"He's overwhelmed by the spectacle of your body."

"By *our* bodies," I quickly amended.

"So we must teach him," the Count proposed, "let him know we're aware of him, that desire isn't shameful, to be hidden." Then he held my arms behind my back, and his tongue moved slowly down my body — and, stopping, he looked toward the balcony and spoke softly to the boy: "You can come in, don't be ashamed" — and then he raised himself and entered me once, again . . .

247

The young man moved into the room, his hands between his thighs as he delighted in this unexpected spectacle, a favor he reciprocated by undressing himself and displaying his own beauty. He gasped and came, just as my beloved Count and I did also. Then he thanked us, shyly.

"He'll make a beautiful young woman very happy tonight," my beloved said.

"Or a handsome young man just as happy," I amended, and we made love again . . . That was all. A moment of gentle sensuality, shared, the way we shared everything. *Even the enduring pain of past sorrows.*

I read on:

> Now having extorted the agreement by the Holiest of Popes to perform over the nuptials of the Count to the accursed Whore in the Grand Cathedral, she and her Pimp devised further their sinister plot. Once the nuptial ring was on her finger, there would occur an enormous disturbance in the Cathedral, created by shots fired at random by one of their minions. The ensuing moments of pandemonium would allow the wily Whore to shoot her husband of only a few seconds.

It was Alix who fired! — coaxed by the wicked Irena! My weary heart protests each time I encounter that repeated accusation, which strikes as if for the first time.

> The fiendish deed would then be blamed on those who truly loved the Noble Count *(those who have information about the Whore's past that even a whore would want to keep secret — from everyone).*

I kept nothing secret from my beloved. Nothing. *Nothing.*

> Thus they intended to dispose of all legitimate claimants to the wealth of the great dynasty usurped by their tactics. Everything would have occurred as they connived had it not been for the fact that the Count's ever-astute Sister grasped (with her always agile mind, the Reader truthfully compliments) what was occurring, and shouted out (ringingly, over the sounds of prepared confusion) her rightful accusation of the murderous Whore: "The Whore murdered my Brother!" — thus assuring that the vile creature would

248

be seen with the murderous gun. Even so, the Whore — having prepared for every eventuality — managed to escape *(where God, and perhaps others before Him, will finally locate her).*

The Reader will not be surprised to learn that, although confronted by such monumental evil, the saintly Holy Prelate blessed the horrendous woman as she ran away, trailed by her sullied marriage veil.

A blessing? — "Damn the wily whore!"? Run away? Never! I left the Cathedral, to live for both of us, as my beloved Count du Muir made me promise.

If at the time of my flight from the Grand Cathedral I had already had the good fortune to have met Madame Bernice, I would have been reminded of what Cassandra said to me long ago in Troy: "The unexpected is always to be expected." That is what allowed the Count to prepare for the trap in the Cathedral. Cassandra often added, "There is always a Trojan horse," referring to the folly of trust. I'll give her credit when I enter that into my *Pensées*.

I race through the few pages left in this "Third Installment," through more distortions of the love and passion that bound me and the Count. I read again its last words, words my eyes stumbled on an earlier time:

> In the following and Final Installment of this *True Account,* the Writer will fulfill his promise to reveal the most heinous of the Whore's despicable acts — the slaughter of her children.

I thrust those contaminated pages away. But I remain standing over the table where the "Final Installment" rests. I reach for it, I hold it, I open it. I turn the pages of this further vilification of my life with the Count, attempts to turn love into greed, passion into reckless lust, sorrow into abomination.

. . . found dead . . .

I back up and read again in terror the shocking words my eyes fall upon.

> The Writer, ever diligent in his goal of exposing villainy, here brings the Reader into recent events, as the chain of evil linked by the Whore extends. In a bizarre turn that would be out of place

other than in this *True Account* of the horrendous life of the vile Whore — she who befouled all she touched — the Count's Twin Brother, the Fair Brother of the two, was found dead in his Mother's bedroom, killed by a single gunshot —

Alix is dead!

— clearly fired by (the Writer will wait to allow the Reader to prepare for the approaching enormity) none other than his Mother, the dissolute Contessa.

That gentle loving lady, who so tenderly sought me out and befriended me in her coach? That gentle lady whose words of blessing gave me courage when I fled from the Cathedral? *She* fired the deadly blast? Oh, not she! Whatever is claimed in this vicious rendering, I shall know that the Contessa did *not* kill her son, malicious though he was.

Lest the Reader of this odyssey of debauch attribute perverted intentions to the Fair Twin of the late Noble Count, the Writer hastens to advise that the Son was in his Mother's bedroom *only* to hear more from her own lips about a sweet incident he had just learned of concerning the abundant tulips in their garden.

The tulips!

The Writer here records accurately the recent events that have added two more deaths to the murder in the Grand Cathedral —

Two? Alix, and —?

According to the most truthful *Account to the Authorities,* duly filed with appropriate Officials by the Fair Twin's benevolent Sister, this is what occurred "on the night of terrifying deaths":

Irena is alive, of course.

It began when the devoted Daughter and Sister went to receive a blessing from the Holy Pontiff (who gave it with added grace to the good and highly enlightened woman) before she set out that evening on one of her frequent rounds of charity among the worthy poor (not all the poor are worthy — and some not even

Christians). Having finished her saintly ministrations early, the upright Daughter impulsively decided to extend her benefaction to an old Nun who had years ago been retained by her Father as a helper to the Contessa and whom the virtuous Pontiff had earlier recalled with fondness.

The renegade nun! Oh, not that sweet soul.

"Seeking a sweet, mellow remembrance," the magnanimous Daughter of the Contessa reports in her *Account to the Authorities,* "I questioned the gentle Nun about my mother's youth, hoping to glean a portrait of her early years, as loyal children are wont to do. Perhaps for reasons attributable to the confusions inherent in her advanced age, the sweet Nun declined to share such memories, whereupon I tried gently to persuade her —"

Shaking her, demanding, threatening!

"— until, somewhat shyly, she confessed some details of intimate moments she had cherished for years concerning my devoted mother. To my horror, the poor Sister of God was soon after seized by a heart attack."

Frightened to death by Irena's threats after she extorted from the loyal nun the truth of the Gypsy. Or *did* she manage to extort it? Did the brave nun die with the Contessa's secret? — leaving Irena still with her suspicions, only her suspicions.

Accepting (as all souls who Trust the Mightiest of Mighty must) the Wisdom that had chosen to send the Nun to whatever place He would choose to assign to her, the Daughter reported the sad death to religious authorities, to notify further to necessary Officials. The Daughter (known for her charity as well as for her formidable intellect) returned to find her brother, the Fair Twin, the Brother of the Count, sitting in the garden of their mansion (where he often sat, pondering the state of goodness).

Joining him in those serene moments, his Sister informed him of the dear Nun's tender memories of their Mother, especially of one that had occurred in the very garden where they now sat. So moved was the Fair Twin that he gathered some of the profuse tulips that surrounded them, and he studied them lovingly in his hands. The moment shared by the departed Nun was so precious to

251

the Fair Twin that the considerate Daughter thought best to with-hold from her Brother the fact of the lovable Nun's departure to her just reward.

In the excitement generated by the borrowed — and not com-plete enough — memory of his Mother as a young woman, the Fair Twin could not restrain himself from going to her bedroom to extend his joy of discovery and beg for more exquisite details. The Contessa had retired early, resigned to her usual troubled sleep. Seeing Mother and Son facing each other (and longing for a Master Painter who might record this serene scene), the loving Daughter left them to their moments of filial devotion and moved on to rest in her bedroom (to recover from all her good deeds and prepare for more). Because in his urgency to extend these poignant moments the Fair Twin had left open the door of their Mother's bedroom, the most generous and bright Daughter could not help but hear her Brother's discussion with their Mother about the Nun's dulcet memory.

Irena, spying, lurking, always conniving!

In her most careful *Report to the Authorities,* and all consis-tent with her astonishing retentiveness (another aspect of her amazing intelligence), the devoted Sister and Daughter declares what she saw: "In a glimpse — since of course I did not linger at the door — I saw my Brother extending to my Mother a loving bouquet of the tulips he had gathered earlier —"

It was *not* a bouquet!

Although the upright Sister sought again to honor the privacy of this loving encounter between Mother and Son by moving away, she could not help but overhear words that baffled her but that, in her astonishingly astute fashion, she was able to retain, verbatim, and set down in her *Report to the Authorities.* No Writer could convey with more exactitude and eloquence than this fine Sister the dour events that even now flowed out of the Whore's past villainies, and so the Writer will here allow the Sister's ringing voice in her *Report to the Authorities* to relate what followed:

"My Brother held the bouquet of tulips toward our devoted Mother and said, so tenderly, 'Tell me *everything* about what happened in the tulip garden.'

" 'Go to hell,' my beloved Mother retorted, illogically."

252

I place these pages down, carefully, slowly, to control my rage, and to cleanse my hands for a moment before I can touch their poison again. I see it all clearly, buried in this maze of lies: Goaded by new — and still measured — information given to her cunningly — how else? — by the Pope, for nefarious reasons of his own — why else? — Irena sought out the trustworthy nun. Whether she was able to coerce the loyal nun into revealing the truth about the tulip garden before frightening her to death — or even strangling her — or whether she finally decided to divulge what she had long wanted to believe, Irena goaded Alix to question the Contessa about the interlude in the tulip garden, hinting that he, like his brother, was the son of a gypsy! Alix then confronted the proud Contessa, and —

I read on:

The Sister's unflaggingly accurate *Report to the Authorities* continues:

"My brother — with loving consideration — despite my Mother's odd reaction — had gone on to suggest that cherished moments that might have occurred among the luxuriant tulips would become even more treasured only as memories if the gardener were allowed to 'weed out the bulbs.' Since the disturbed often act in ways beyond the scope of understanding by the undisturbed, it is necessary, in order to give a Truthful Account of these events, as I am bound to do in my *Report to the Authorities,* however much it pains me, to state that my beloved Mother, the Contessa, had long ceased to be a stable woman. She raised her voice obnoxiously, accusing my Brother, the Fair Twin, of . . . I'm sorry that I did not hear the exact accusation because, at that moment, there was a clap of thunder, ushering in a storm and drowning out the altercation."

The unassailable *Report to the Authorities* made by the most reliable Sister continues:

"Hearing a sound that could be made only by a body toppling to the floor, I had to abandon my respect for privacy, and I rushed into the room.

"I saw my sainted Brother lying on the floor. Thinking he had fainted in the face of my obdurate Mother's illogical resistance to the tulips' being pruned, I knelt to minister to him. I saw blood on his chest, which had been pierced by a gunshot, its sound muffled by the clap of thunder. My dearly adored Brother, like his Twin Brother before him, was dead. I turned to the Contessa — my cherished Mother — and saw her attempting to hide a gun.

" 'Who put this in my hands? I don't know where this came from, I don't know where this came from!' she kept repeating, while trying to discard the evidence of what had occurred: My beloved Mother had shot my esteemed and noble Brother, the Fair Twin. And why? Impossible as it seems to those of sound mind, she did so simply because he had presented her with a bouquet of the flowers that he thought should be trimmed away into memory, flowers that were — I grasp for some kind of logic — apparently her favorites."

Irena shot Alix and planted the gun in the Contessa's hand, just as she planted Alix's in mine in the Grand Cathedral. What cruel cunning!

Confronted, benignly, by her caring Daughter, the outrageous Contessa insisted (with an enormous continuing lack of logic that the Reader will easily detect) that at one point the Fair Twin "insanely threatened to choke me with the tulips. After that, I know only that I saw him fall."
The Writer of this sad *True Account* pauses to ponder the enormous capacity of sinners to lie, the extremes to which they resort to cover up their foul allegations.

My sorrow wrestles with rage as I read on:

The Writer will again allow into his *True Account* the exact words of the honorable Sister as she reported these wanton acts in her *Report to the Authorities:*
"In a burst of obvious regret, the Contessa, my treasured Mother, begged me to go with her to the Grand Cathedral."

Ha!

"I had almost to carry her, she was so weak with the burden of her sins."

Irena pushed her along as the dear Contessa fought her!

"(My cherished Mother wanted to go to the Grand Cathedral finally to make peace with her turbulent life, and to do so before no less than the Holiest of Living Men, the Pope.)"

The *only* reason the Contessa *I* knew would want to go there would be to confront the Pope for all his appalling intrigues and manipulations, knowing he was the catalyst for these new developments.

While wishing that the very page on which these words are written might be able to mourn these terrible events, the Writer notes somberly that the truthfulness of the brilliant Sister's *Account to the Authorities* (is there even one Reader who would question it?) is confirmed (confirmation is not needed, the Reader rightfully asserts) by none other than the Pillar of Truth, the Pope Himself, who witnessed these dour events.

In the Grand Cathedral, he was praying late in his chambers when he heard an altercation in his Most Holy Turf and rushed there to see the honorable Sister trying to wrest a gun from her notorious Mother. Despite her devoted Daughter's attempts to keep her from this act of self-destruction for her evils, the Contessa shot herself with the same gun she had used on her own son, the Fair Twin, whom she now joined in death, if not in their destinations *beyond* death.

The Contessa is dead!
No, no, please no! Please!
Yet, even as my sorrow protests, I know it's true. *Irena* murdered the Contessa before the Pope so that nothing will be questioned! All, all plotted by the two.

I clasp the pages in my hand. There's more, but I cannot abide it. I rush out of my quarters. I'm oblivious to the night — no, it is almost dawn and I have not slept. Lurking presences scamper into the verdure of the countryside. I reach Madame's château. I knock, I knock! She comes to the door with Ermenegildo, and holds out a candle to identify me. I shout out:

"Madame! They murdered Alix and the Contessa!"

Madame quickly calmed me — as lovingly, as caringly, as a devoted nurse — yes, she ministered to me, so lovingly and so caringly that, before I knew it, the terrible night had passed, dawn broke, morning came, and we had resumed our more civilized roles: having tea on the lawn of her château.

XXIV

I FELT SO RESTED as I sat with Madame Bernice, who was about to pour our tea, that I wondered whether, in the onrush of events revealed in the "Account" that pursues me with its fury, I had had only the impression that my reactions happened in uninterrupted sequence. It was possible I had considered running at night to Madame's, but slept wearily instead while I imagined her gentle ministrations to calm my justifiable anxieties, and then, this early afternoon, had strolled over to her château, where we now sat on her veranda discussing the latest entries in the avenging "Account." Yes, that was how it happened.

"They're in collusion — for now — those two, the Pope and Irena." Madame shook her head at the wickedness of it all. "The events themselves have the ring of truth — there's no other reason for these deaths to be recorded," she agreed with me. "Only the motives have been altered — grossly. After consulting with the Pope, Irena killed her brother and the dear Contessa — may she rest in peace in Heaven with her beloved gypsy."

I gasped with renewed sorrow at the knowledge of that gentle creature's passing. From that past night, I could see her, vividly, in her carriage, her lace *mantilla* shading her perfect features. I joined Madame in moments of silence that honored her courage and just defiance — and her love of the fertile gypsy.

"And Irena probably killed the gentle nun —" Madame continued to muse.

"— after getting from her the information she wanted?" I needed to believe that the devoted nun had not divulged her secret even when confronted by Irena's powerful threats.

"The lovely renegade nun divulged *nothing*," Madame said with a jut of her jaw.

I was delighted! "But how do you —?"

She explained it: "If the loyal nun had revealed the Contessa's secret, that would be included in this installment. The matter of the tulips remains deliberately cloudy. That means Irena still doesn't know *exactly* what occurred." Now she reached out briskly toward the contaminated pages, to read what would follow.

"No more, not yet," I beseeched. We would eventually have to deal with whatever further horrors the "Final Installment" contained, including the outrage promised in the last page of the "Third Install-ment." Madame, I knew, had not yet read that part. I gauge carefully each day where she leaves off.

She accepted my suggestion with a long silence that confused me into wondering whether she *had* read ahead to the terrifying "prom-ise" at the end of the "Third Installment." "Now, Lady, please con-tinue with the truth about the War in Heaven."

My full strength restored — I'm sure I slept last night and strolled over earlier today — I resumed where I had left off, Cassandra's bewilderment that she had not heard the sounds assuring that the gates of Heaven were shaping, about to lock — and her deciding then to act:

She heard Lucifer shout to the angels who stood with them the words she had just uttered to him:

"Storm Heaven now!"

Lucifer and his band of angels had rushed up a hill, for full vantage of their destination: the edge of Heaven. On another hill, Michael had gathered his squads. The two beautiful angels faced each other, their glistening nudity illumined by Heaven's startled sun.

"Join us, Michael! You know we're right!" Lucifer shouted.

For moments Michael considered becoming one of the rebels, soaring with them, next to Cassandra. He paused to consider. Now, he would certainly replace Lucifer in God's hierarchy. And afterwards — his mind raced — who knew? *He* might — guided by Cassandra, whom he would ask for as a victor's prize — explore beyond the reaches of Heaven and into the territory Lucifer claimed existed and God denied. Then he, Michael, might inherit the whole universe!

God's presence swooped within a turbulent dark wind, whirling around Michael, whispering intimations of great tortures, of a new hell, and in the pit of that wind, which funneled inward, God allowed Michael to glimpse the bottom of the hell He was then conceiving, all its tortures — and Michael closed his eyes. "No!" he rejected Lucifer's invitation — and charged across the plains with his armed legions.

And there was War in Heaven!

The fierce warrior Michael and his cohorts, with arms prepared at God's instruction the night before, surged against the unprepared insurgents. With courage and equal ferocity, Lucifer and his legions fought back, unarmed, hordes of angels grappling on the plains.

Heaven waited in suspense.

This was the tactic Cassandra had hastily conveyed to Lucifer after her exhortation that war be declared: By their determination to win their freedom, they would gain more and more of the hostile angels to their side while fighting their way to the edge of Heaven, the gates not formed, still unlocked, that intention having been pushed away — this is all Cassandra could determine — by the immediate urgency forced upon God to cope with the sudden insurgents. From the edge of Heaven, the growing squadrons of dissident angels would take wing, beyond God's reach, into the space they had discovered, limitless, ruled only by the stars.

Now God unleashed all the horrors that had occupied His mind when Lucifer declared his defiance. And hail and fire mingled with blood. And the grass was scorched. And a great mountain was cast into the sea. And the sea became blood. And a burning star fell. And the sun was smitten. And the moon turned into blood. And stars fell burning and scorching. And —

"Lady, that's giving me a slight headache. Must we go through all those horrors in detail?" Madame Bernice interjected. "We know that's God's version recorded by John the Divine — it does have the undeniable ring of God's harsh thunder, doesn't it? Shall we just skip over it and get back to the truth?"

Ermenegildo sighed in relief when I gladly accepted Madame's suggestion.

In Heaven, and from His throne, God watched in fascination as His angels continued to grapple on the plains. The War of course would be won. Last night, late, He had instructed Michael to wake Him seconds after He fell asleep. Tired as she was, Cassandra — her honed powers of perception still astonished Him! — would seize that opportunity, herself, to doze, briefly but deeply — as she had. In those moments — oh, His own cunning thrilled Him and He laughed aloud in triumph now — He had created the gates of Heaven, and locked them, knowing that Cassandra would be anticipating the sounds she had heard when He had conceived the intention. He had to admit to a bad moment when she had, herself, wakened so soon after the interlude of dozing, just after He had winced at the vaguest suggestion of a lingering echo.

"He connived to entice a wearied Cassandra into a moment's respite —" Madame Bernice shook her head at the immensity of God's duplicity.

The insurgents did not know that, and so they continued to struggle, inching toward the edge of Heaven — and the locked gates they did not anticipate, which God had blurred with clouds.

On the plains of Heaven and from atop another hill, Cassandra watched the brutal War of angels. She knew God was allowing the angels to advance toward the edge of Heaven. Why?

Michael saw Cassandra pondering.

Breaking away from his troops, he approached her, slowly. Where she stood, the furious War — its raging fires — had not yet destroyed a patch of wild grass sprinkled with . . . white and yellow poppies! — like butterflies courting her, Michael thought, and stopped, to cherish the spectacle of her. He saw her bend, as if carefully selecting a particular poppy. Michael held his breath. As she stood up with the poppy she had chosen, Cassandra's delicate cloak parted at her breasts. Michael sighed.

Cassandra turned. "Michael —"

She was smiling! Even now that vague, beautiful smile floated over her face. "Cassandra —" It was the first word he had ever dared speak to her, though not the first time he had sighed her name over and over to himself.

"Are you here to arrest me?" she asked him.

For a moment he did consider enchaining her, to destroy the disturbing feelings whirling within him. The wistful smile conquered even his confusions. He wanted to do something special for her, to help her, to stop the War that would defeat her! The thought astonished him, but not as much as his sudden words:

"You must tell Lucifer the War cannot be won. God has locked Heaven's gates."

Immediately Cassandra knew: Oh, yes, He trapped me into dozing. So fate had shaped, and the War was lost. God was now extending His punishment, allowing a charade of possibility. She looked down and saw her beloved brother, determined, his body shining with the sweat of battle. She said easily, "Then we must surrender." She peered at the poppy in her hand, the one she had picked from among the others because she had determined, from having studied them so often, that this one might soon change color, and she would at last see its thrilling shift while she held it.

"Yes. That will disappoint Him, because He'll have to end the War, and He didn't intend that, not yet." Michael wished he were speaking other words to her, words that would announce his feelings, his — What word did God often use — so facilely — to express what He required of them — a word he, Michael, had never fully understood? He understood it now. He was longing for words that would announce his . . . love . . . for her.

"If we surrender now" — Cassandra immediately prepared for yet another ambush on fate, which was that very second rushing — "we'll baffle Him, and we'll have more time to anticipate — and intercept! — His new strategies of punishment." Her eyes brightened with resurrected hope.

Michael nodded. He could speak no more words before this extravagant figure.

Cassandra looked at the poppy in her hand, smiled in delight at what she saw, touched it to her lips, and held it out to Michael.

He took it. Was he imagining this? Had it changed color after her lips had touched it? No, he had not imagined it. The flower *had* changed color, deepening from yellow into pink, and now — was it possible? — into almost red, faintly red, the color of her lips. And — he did not want to think this, but he was aware of a flush of exquisite warmth — did it match the blush he felt on his cheeks? However God might retaliate for what he had done, he would not regret these precious moments. It would be worth it all, to be able to do this: He brought the poppy to his lips.

Cassandra was already rushing down the hill to tell her brother that they must instantly announce their surrender. It would be difficult, but she would convince him with the new information and what she was already planning. With more time, they might be able to stop the widening sweep of His punishment.

She addressed Lucifer: "It was too late to stop *this* part of destiny." She motioned toward where the giant gates loomed, locked with chains, all blending artfully into the backdrop of sky, whose beauty — after all it was His sky — God had been careful not to compromise.

Later, he would feel the pain of futility, be consumed by rage at the deceptions. Now Lucifer seized his sister's words to dredge hope: "Too late to stop *this* part?"

"Yes, there will be more." That's all she perceived at this moment.

Lucifer appeared before God, Cassandra by his side.

"You surrender?" God questioned in surprise from His throne. He had not counted on this, not yet. The War had not gone on long enough. He had prepared more, much more, a longer struggle before the dissident angels discovered it had all been for nothing. He let his rainbow-colored scarf drop to His feet, with that airy gesture reluctantly accepting their surrender.

For days there was silence in Heaven, days during which the smoke of dying fires and the dust of turbulence began to settle on the plains.

With her brother, on the unburnt hill she had located — there was a chill in Heaven, and she wore a veily cape that whirled about her — Cassandra breathed deeply until, beyond the stench of smoke, she detected an exact breeze, a breeze that connected her to —

God, pondering, staring down from His throne. He cupped His excited groin. "My will be *done!* Let there be light, and darkness, *much* darkness . . . and a garden, and a new creature, a man —"

"The real war has started," Cassandra told her brother as she followed God's gaze downward from the heights of Heaven.

"Beyond Heaven?"

"Into a Garden named Eden." Cassandra understood: During the War, while all their efforts had been aimed at the futility He had encouraged — their reaching the edge of Heaven, which He had locked — He had set other courses into motion, perfecting His plans; that is what she had sensed during the War, in a whorl of unformed colors. Readied, and with His declaration just pronounced, His plan had fallen into place.

Cassandra almost reeled! Her perceptions were invaded by new images, flashing, occurring almost simultaneously: The creature — a man! — whom she had discerned earlier alone gazing sadly at an empty bed of orchids now stood gazing with love at another creature — a woman! — and — How strange. God was suddenly enraged. Cassandra felt the heat of His anger, waves radiating across the calmed fields of Heaven . . . Now the man and the woman had . . . fused? . . . in the most extravagantly wonderful way near a flower so glorious it did not need the decoration of leaves. But there had appeared a contorted tree coated with lush berries, which the man was tasting from the woman's lips — and in the horizon, not yet seen by them, a storm was gathering fiercely —

"Tell me what you have discerned!" Lucifer demanded.

"The first steps in God's cruelest punishments." The distortion of the wishes He had invited in His cynical "Special Entertainment" —

she withheld that from her brother, because that had not yet begun. She gazed toward where God sat on His throne, her stare intersecting His. And now she perceived . . . What? A shadow . . . a cross atop a barren mount? The naked bloodied body of a man on it! Impossible! — he was not nailed to that brutal cross!

"It's a vast design He's plotting," Cassandra allowed excitement at the prospect of altering *this* course. "It ranges over time."

"And you have learned more of His tactics, knowledge we may use now." Lucifer understood.

"The two beautiful creatures in the Garden are in danger," Cassandra said.

"Oh, Lady, I, of course, remember that from your earlier account, and every single detail of the events that follow from that point, but Ermenegildo might need some reorientation —"

Disbelieving her audacity, Ermenegildo cocked his head at her, and — I believe — frowned.

"— although he, too, has a most retentive memory," she attempted, to placate him. He continued to eye her curiously even after I had begun:

After our lovemaking, the eating of the luscious berries, the exile from Eden, the Garden destroyed, the glorious blossom that grew only there plucked away, the snow that fell, the bleeding between my legs and my Adam soothing it — after all that, when Lucifer and Cassandra had led us away from God's fury and east of Eden, farther east, to the end of the world, the edge of a precipice lapped by the waves of a churning ocean —

Cassandra stared ahead and reared back.

"What did you see, sister?"

"The lineage of Adam and Eve."

Not understanding what I thought I understood — remember, he had not heard God's curse on me — Adam was elated, confounded that neither Cassandra nor Lucifer, nor I — although I tried to disguise my fear — shared his joy.

"Can that course be stopped?" Lucifer had inferred the horror his sister had perceived.

Cassandra gazed down into the precipice. "It's still only intention."

Adam advanced, to peer down. I kissed his eyes shut.

"Then they have to know what He intends," Lucifer urged his sister.

Taking my hand in one of hers, Adam's in the other, she led us to the very edge of the craggy cliff. Her vision, her perception, coursed from her hands into ours, flowing into our minds, our eyes, and we saw and heard and felt —

Torrents of pain and endless moans of grief, hunger, a million variations on cruelty, still more pain and hope crushed, and violence, horror, and more horror, mounting horror, and —

Cassandra let go of our hands, and the atrocities disappeared.

"It's what God intends for you and all who follow," Lucifer said, watching it all reflected in his sister's eyes.

Cassandra said softly: "It begins with you and extends to all your children, including a crucified man tortured beyond endurance, a man God intends to call His son, but he will be *your* son. They shall *all* be your children, cursed."

"*That* is His intention for the lineage of Adam and Eve?" Adam pronounced in disbelief. Then his hand rose in a fist. "We'll defy God!" he said.

In Cassandra's startled look, I saw that he had assumed the same stance that Lucifer had when he had challenged God. Was she marveling at how alike they were, the first man and the first angel? But Lucifer had not succeeded.

Cassandra continued to smile, although the edge of her lips quivered as she spoke: "There's only one way."

Adam clasped my hand. "How, Cassandra?"

"By ending it before it begins." She touched my eyes and then her own with my tears, sharing them. "There's hope, if we can find it in this: He has already planned a special punishment, just for you. He'll call it 'death.' "

We understood the new word immediately, my Adam and I, understood, as if Cassandra's touch had imbued us with her own powers of perception, that the only way to stop this curse on our children was to invite, before He unleashed it, what He had already devised for us.

"Death won't end our love," Adam asserted.

"Never that," I said.

"Never," Cassandra agreed.

"Only I shall go," I said to Adam, "and you, alive, shall retain our love." I inched toward the precipice.

He pulled me back: "No! From the beginning, we've shared everything. Your pain is mine, your sorrow is mine, your life is mine."

No further words were needed to decide.

We looked down. Gnarled rocks protruded from the agitated sea.

Holding each other, my beloved and I walked to the very edge of the cliff. By leaping into annihilating darkness, we would seal our love and separate our offspring from God's terrible intent.

Cassandra shook her head and laughed softly. "All this suffering as punishment . . . for eating the tasty berries!"

"Lady! I believe we should avoid sarcasm at this point," Madame Bernice said testily.

"If there was sarcasm, I did not put it there. Cassandra did," I reminded Madame, "and I believe her tone was more ironic than sarcastic. There's quite a difference."

"Please proceed."

Cassandra's eyes grazed the horizon. Then we all saw it, a mountain suddenly lavished with daffodils and marigolds and mariposa lilies, white sage, azaleas, heather, fields of green grass, trees laden with blossoms and fruit, gilias — and a proliferation of poppies — and cascades of tumbling bougainvillea under a sky so blue, wafted by fragrances so sweet —

"God can be lavish." Cassandra smiled at the spectacle.

"He's trying to tempt you again into proceeding with His design," Lucifer addressed me and my beloved. "We have to hurry before it's unstoppable." He reached for his sister's hand.

"You'll end your own existence, too?" I asked.

"Yes!" Lucifer asserted.

"We'll try," Cassandra said. "It might be our particular hell that we must simply" — she shrugged — "continue . . ." With her brother she walked gracefully to the end of the cliff, where it toppled onto the rocks and hungry sea.

My beloved Adam and I kissed, remembering the first kiss, cherishing the last. Our lips still open on each other's, our arms pressing our bodies together, we flung ourselves over the cliff.

We spun like stars as we fell, still embracing, whirling down, down, down, tossing, plunging faster, faster —

— and then a current of fierce dark wind captured us, lifting us, tossing us violently about, releasing us, and —

I woke on a clearing of rocks, my beloved beside me. Cassandra and Lucifer stood a distance away. I held my beloved's hand, to raise him with me as waves of dark water swept over us. My Adam didn't move. His beautiful body remained sprawled on the rocks.

As I screamed with a desolation I knew would never end —would continue howling into time — I wrenched with pain and felt a stirring in my womb, and knew that only my Adam was dead and I was alive with the flesh God had cursed.

How could silence be so loud? — the silence that captured Madame Bernice's garden and devoured the squawking of a hawk I saw descend toward us and then veer away. I covered my ears, and still I heard the protesting scratching of distant palm fronds, the shrill sounds of birds trapped in a thicket of branches. Then all sounds ended as slowly as the distant howl of a wolf.

Through that cacophony of silence, I heard, distinctly, Madame's sorrowing words, and then everything in the garden resumed its natural sounds.

"I understand your tears, dear Lady." Madame was holding my hands, warming them as I conveyed the despair that had seized me the moment when I realized that I had survived and only my beloved was dead. "Go ahead and cry. Cry in sorrow and anger and protest. Yes, go on, Lady, I'll hold you. They're tears of loss and anger. And of regret that, again, fate wasn't foiled!"

I cried. Huddled in her arms, I cried, and cried more, sobs of endless mourning.

"Cassandra has taught us how fate *can* be foiled, by ambushing its course at the *exact* time, in the *exact* way. She is with us, Lady, guiding us." Madame thrust her chin up.

The trembling of my body eased. I dredged at the hope Madame's words had intended to arouse. "You believe that, Madame? Do you? — although it wasn't possible, in Heaven, nor beyond Eden?"

"That was *then*, Lady, and this is *now!*" Madame leaned back regally in her chair, so regally that Ermenegildo bowed as if greeting a newly crowned queen. "We shall undo it *all* at interviews," she said firmly, and she snapped her fingers at destiny.

265

XXV

"BUT WE HAVE NO TIME TO WASTE — Cassandra has taught us that emphatically, and so we must return instantly to Patmos," Madame demanded.

That afternoon's tea setting — I had not even had a moment to comment on its elegant but simple design — remained on the table almost intact, that's how intensely we had roamed through Heaven and beyond Eden.

Madame continued: "In Patmos, *that's* where the mystery we're pursuing begins to unravel, that's where St. John the Divine claimed the word itself was written on your forehead. To determine what that mystery is, we must find the exact connection between Patmos, and Heaven and Eden. So, now, Lady, roam back. Think! Remember! Bring the fragments together. Put it all in order. Remember *exactly* what happened and how it happened in Babylon and Patmos."

I did.

The journey to Patmos began the moment I first saw John the Divine preaching to a throng on a street in Rome, during his sojourn there from Ephesus. He had come to confront the Emperor.

I stared fascinated at the evangelist, a man of stark, terrifying beauty — his hips barely covered by a swath of haircloth, which succeeded in suggesting what it was meant to conceal. His arms were decorated with drawings, a serpent coiled about flowers, a dagger entangled in vines, a skull out of whose hollow eyes protruded a dove, decorations so carefully drawn that it was as if each detail had been refined by a dyed needle, a series of tiny punctures, one so fresh that what I thought at first was the eye of a snake was a drop of John's

266

blood, like a red bead coursing down his white skin. I followed its trail down his arm, and then looked up at him.

His eyes sliced toward me, cutting so deeply that I heard only an echo of the words he had just spoken, his damnation of "all the evils of the earth — this *Babylon*." Had he singled me out? Did he know that I was surviving the only way I knew, in the shadows of alleys, stealing?

"God will soon expose a startling mystery. As His servants to record His exact words, He has chosen me and one other —" His steady look pierced me. "An angel and Our Lord shall bring His message to me."

In an alley that night, a merchant I had not been quick enough to rob flung me against a wall and raised my skirt — I was usually expert at enticing and eluding. His hands would have delved between my legs, but I wrenched free. He tossed a coin back at me as he walked away.

"She's worth more." I heard a deepened voice. It was John the Divine's. He had intercepted the merchant.

"I only raised her skirt," the man protested.

"Just that is worth much more."

Alerted by John's harsh voice, which contained strange laughter, the merchant tried to run. John pulled at something attached to the underside of his waistband — a knife! With it, he circled the man, backed off, approached in a taunting dance that he seemed determined to prolong even after the man emptied his purse for him. Laughing, John took the spilled money. He came to me and wordlessly gave me half of what he had extorted.

"Why did you do that for me?" I asked, not daring to face him, longing for exact words of caring.

"Because God has assigned a special role to you." He turned his back to me and walked away. I followed him along the cruel streets, just as he knew I would.

"A role . . . assigned to you." Madame pressed one hand firmly to her temples, storing John's curious words. "An *assigned* role." She directed those words at Ermenegildo, who had earlier cocked his ear as if he had not quite heard.

"Do you love me?" I dared to ask John as we sat that night on the steps of a crumbling building in the ghetto of the dispossessed of the City. I longed for the answer I would have given him. He was sharing his food with me. As he ate, he wrote words on a worn tablet he carried with him. Love poems? I allowed myself to wonder. Was the one he had just entered . . . about me?

He smiled, a smile that seemed abandoned on a face etched with anger and sorrow. With his hand he wiped the paint I used on my face to entice men I would then rob and elude. "You're beautiful, and so young, so unsullied despite everything, who wouldn't love you?" I felt warm and safe at the side of this holy man. I longed to rest my head on his wide shoulders, but I dared not.

Was it possible, was this the same man? That very night he sold my body on the streets, and I was taken on the ground while he watched. Afterwards, his strong decorated arms pinioned my hands, his feet clamped my ankles, spreading my legs, and as if I were only a target for his anger, he pierced me — once, fiercely, discarding my virginity as if it had been trash.

Swiftly, I rubbed my ankles, my pained hands, readying to run away from his cruelty. He burrowed his head on my breasts and he . . . wept, forlorn cries of pain. With his lips he soothed my ankles and my hands.

Oh, remember that in Babylon — and by then I, too, thought of the City as that — I was only a girl, a girl of fifteen years. I had never known a mother, never known a father. I knew only the streets. Remember that, when you ask why I loved this man, why I stayed with him, why I worshiped him. Because he had said, or I thought he had said, that he loved me.

Daily he returned to the streets to preach. Now to his curses he added blunt judgment on the House of the Emperor for "the gross fornications of a dynasty of lust."

Nightly he sold my body under the arches of the City, vaunting my sexual assets, holding my breasts up in his hands — "Look at their shape, perfect, the firmness of her nipples, just ripened!" — running his hands down my thighs — "Look at her flawless flesh, so smooth, ah, the touch of it" — raising my skirt, allowing a glimpse of my flesh — "the sweetest nectar for your delectation" — lauding each part of my body as he increased the price for it.

Always, afterwards, he would penetrate me, roaring his strange laughter. And always, still later, he would hold my face, kiss it, tenderly, over and over. "I'm preparing you for a special role chosen for you," he reminded me.

"Again, a role —" Madame mulled John's words. "A special role. A part to be played."

"His baffling words exactly."

"All according to God's careful instructions," Madame seemed to speak her thoughts aloud.

His preaching, his pandering — John kept them separate until one night on a shabby street as merchants milled about choosing among bodies for hire; he announced loudly, his resonating words startling the solemn nightly ritual of the hunt:

"I need witnesses to the word of God, to His choice!"

Alerted to something extraordinary, a shadowy crowd gathered about us. John invited them: "For a price, you may watch this performance with" — he paused, selecting each word — "the chosen woman of Babylon."

After he had collected all the coins for the "witnessing," he led the men into deeper shadows in a corridor that receded from the alley. At the top of a step — to enhance a sense of performance, or sacrifice — he stripped my body and his. With the swath of haircloth, bunched, he covered the parting between my legs so that, shivering on the cold stones, my body appeared for moments even more naked than if it had been entirely exposed.

In one violent motion, he pulled the cloth.

He took me over and over — while I fought and the others watched and goaded and pushed themselves higher up into the crumbling corridor. When it had ended, John stood over me while I covered myself with my shawl. His decorated arms thrust up. He shouted:

"Behold this woman is on a special mission for the Lord! I have taken her where we *all* are, where *you* are, where we all belong, in the filth, the mire, the garbage, the spillage of a violated paradise! And it shall all be written."

In Madame Bernice's garden a puff of white butterflies seemed suspended, trembling. " '. . . the spillage of a violated paradise,' " Madame repeated.

Increasingly, John the Divine was tortured, in his mind, his heart. Those times, he sought out the numbing white powder available on the streets, powder he used and sold. When he extended it to me, I only pretended to take it. Holding the arm that bled from the still-fresh decorations, he spoke as if dazed. "It makes it bearable, takes me to another world, sometimes violent, but never more hideous than this one." His weary eyes would glance in disgust at the street.

During another of his increasing invitations to sexual "witnessings" with me on this street of bodies and powders for sale, a group of five eager burly men pushed through the listening crowd.

"We've heard about your spectacular performances," one spoke

269

for all, "and we'd like to see for ourselves." Gladly paying twice the price so that others would not crowd them out, they watched hungrily, exposing themselves eagerly. All came openly, spilling themselves on the dirt. Erasing their semen with their feet, and restoring their clothes, they revealed themselves as the Emperor's soldiers and arrested John the Divine — "the hypocritical preacher of lust," the decree by the Emperor read.

For frantic days I huddled alone in the ruins and waited for John to return. I wept myself into troubled sleep. I learned he had been imprisoned in a cell where, daily, crowds would come to mock and ridicule him, those who had heard him preach, those who had bought his numbing powders, those he had solicited for my body in alleys and hallways. I saw him — through a small window in his barred cell. He looked more beautiful, stranger than ever, as proud as ever. He smiled at me, and I loved and pitied him.

In Madame's garden, I stopped my account of that painful encounter with St. John in prison when I heard her preemptive cough. She was leaning her inclined head on her fist. That sometimes indicates she's about to introduce a contentious view. She did.

"I was just thinking, Lady. We must be careful that we don't make St. John too . . . pitiful. I believe that the word 'proud' serves no purpose in your description there. It's just, Lady, that I think we must be careful not to turn *him* too . . . hmmm . . . sympathetic."

"Madame!" I halted her words. "Must we go through this again? I am committed to the truth. He did look proud."

"I just don't think we should risk deflecting the thrust of our discoveries," she said.

"Are you aware, Madame, that at times you tend to be . . . intransigent?" I had considered calling her impossible.

"I am *not*." She folded her arms across her bosom, then quickly uncrossed them.

Beyond my wishes, I had been touched by sorrow for John — and by the memory of what I had thought was my love for him. "John was once a dreamer, a poet, Madame. Reality assaulted him. I believe he yearned for peace, but he couldn't find it in the horror he saw about him, and joined." His eyes always seized the most brutal sight. I would see tears he tried to disguise. Once, as we waited in a darkened street for a man he had solicited for me, he said, "If I could wipe out all existence, and restore the purity of nothingness, I would."

270

Madame had been studying her rings as if they yielded more clarity than John's actions. I was certain she was trying to determine what might pull me away from the pain that the memory of John always aroused. She looked up, allowing a sly glance: "Of course, I suppose we mustn't think only bad about a man bold enough to tell us that God sent an angel to command him to eat his own book," she evoked that familiar passage in John's Book of Revelation. "Now isn't that one of the oddest of God's odd commands? What to make of it? — asking an author to eat his own book?"

I laughed gratefully at her attempt to pull me away from my darkening mood.

"That was very good, wasn't it? — my remark." Madame rarely congratulates herself, but this time she even turned for more congratulation from Ermenegildo, who — I thought — smiled his approval. "Nevertheless, Lady —"

"However I may pity him now and then, nothing wipes away John's cruelty," I said.

"That's all that I required to be kept in mind," Madame said.

Soon, John returned to me. The Emperor — no longer amused by putting him on display for the thinning crowds to heckle — had ordered him into immediate exile.

We journeyed the long road to Patmos. The leering soldiers who had watched us and then arrested us led us out. John said to me, "Today, your mission, and mine, will be clarified. God has promised it. The Mystery will be solved."

"You must be certain of his exact words, Lady!" Madame Bernice exhorted urgently. She had been listening so attentively that for long moments she had not even sipped her tea. "Did he say, 'The Mystery will be *solved*'? Or — which is much more likely, everything considered — 'the Mystery will be *announced*'?"

"I'm sure now that he said, 'The Mystery will be *announced*,' not 'solved.' "

"Of course, of course, dear Lady, I knew it, yes, of course . . . You're equally sure he said that your mission *and his* would be clarified? 'Clarified' does seem logical."

"Entirely certain, Madame."

On the cliff on Patmos, we lay naked on my shawl of ocher and indigo as I held a shimmering goblet of wine I did not drink from. That was when John stared at the ebony stone I had found in the City and had sewn onto my headband. And that was when he stood and waited as if to receive a command from the edge of the sky, which was setting in a burnished blaze while shadows lengthened into a tangled noose about us; and then the day turned dark with black clouds out of which bolted distant streaks of lightning, so distant that I could hardly hear their muffled thunder.

John stared into that vortex of darkness, stared longer, stared, turned his face away as if in aversion, and then again faced forward, in acceptance.

"Don't look, John," I begged him, fearing the darkness into which he was staring. Did I hear whispers? Exacerbated, excited, cruel.

"It is time," John said. That was when, touching the pendant on my forehead, he whispered one word:

"Mystery."

"What mystery, John?"

"The most profound," he whispered, "the Mystery of the Whore! *Whore!*" he shouted at me.

My essence —

"You forced me to become that! Why?" I stood up, gathering my shawl to cover myself from his accusing gaze, to pull away from his extending riddle aimed at me:

"Whore, arrayed in purple and scarlet, decked with gold and precious stones, a golden cup in your hand full of the abominations of your fornications!"

My essence began —

He tore the shawl away from me, pulled me down to face him as he knelt before me. "Remain exposed, like me," he said. "Let God utter the final judgment He has chosen me to record on you . . . *woman!*"

My essence began to stir —

He threw himself on me, straddling me, looking back briefly at the summoning horizon, charred black, and he pushed himself into me, adding words to his curse with each brutal thrust:

"Mother of Whores and of all abominations of the earth!"

My essence rushed back in time to the first garden, embarking on its journey from there forward to vindicate all fallen women unjustly blamed for great catastrophes from the very beginning —

When it was over, John touched his lips, as if his own words had baffled him, as if his further words baffled him even more: " 'Her sins have reached unto Heaven, and the Lord hath remembered her iniquities.' . . . That is what God has ordered me to write," he whispered, as if attempting to explain his cruelty.

" 'Let God utter the final judgment He's chosen me to record on you . . . woman.' " Madame echoed John's words, softly. " 'Her sins have reached unto Heaven, and the Lord hath remembered her iniquities.' " Madame stared away, far, far beyond her garden. "We have located the Mystery of Patmos," she said.

Can time reverse itself and return to its origins, can it sweep forward to search what became in order to locate what was, what happened, what did not occur even while it occurred and is occurring but can't ever happen unless it does? — and can it move toward the end of time while hurtling back unmoving into a garden — *where a flower grew, so beautiful it did not need the decoration of leaves and was destroyed?* — and can time whirl back into another garden where mystery —?

"The pieces are in place." Madame held both my hands in hers to share what I was sure would be the pain of revelation. She proceeded, gently: "Just as God tantalized the angels when He announced an 'Entertainment' to design His curses on them, so He announced a mystery to St. John when He chose him, a mad poet, a driven preacher, to be the author of His last book of Testament, a book to be called — oh, how appropriate! — *Revelation*. God's new 'Entertainment' in Patmos, dear Lady, was a piece of especially cunning theater, wasn't it? In it, you, a nameless girl of the streets of what John called Babylon — and he did so to connect you to all the past and present outrages he would accuse you of — you, that girl, were converted into a stand-in for God's true target."

I remembered the turbulent darkness stirring beyond the cliff of Patmos, and — Was it possible? Yes. I remembered it now, a presence, the same restless presence that had lurked, nightly, in the crevices of the sordid alleys of John's Babylon.

"John recruited you to be the substitute for the one whom God wanted to judge most brutally," Madame explained to me what I was already deciphering. "And why was it necessary that that judgment be recorded in that very last book of Testament? To add the emphasis of finality to His judgment."

Sensing the enormity of these moments, Ermenegildo had plucked a perfect white rose that had leaned over the veranda. He presented it to Madame to place in my hands. She did, unclasping my clenched fingers, gently, and then continued:

273

"The 'Mystery' St. John read on your forehead, Lady, and did not understand, was the mystery of your role in Patmos, and that was to evoke *another* woman to be damned forever." Madame's hands trembled. She leaned back, as if preparing to confront an implacable force. Her words lashed out: "Who really was God branding Mother of Whores, who did He consider the Mother of Abominations?"

"Eve," I answered.

XXVI

"WE'VE DETERMINED WHY God commanded St. John to speak his deadly words in Patmos," Madame bent down to explain excitedly to Ermenegildo after profound moments that acknowledged our enormous discovery. "He was reasserting His judgment on Eve!"

Ermenegildo thrust his head back angrily at the magnitude of God's connivance, although I was sure he did that for emphasis, since he had been listening raptly. Now he strolled over to me and pointed to the beautiful white rose I still held in my hand, reminding me of his contribution to its presentation.

Madame did not wait to thrive on the victory of our discovery: "There's more to investigate. I sense that we're very close to locating the *true* reason why God hounded Eve so fiercely from the very beginning, and we must —"

Not now.

The revelation of the true indictment of Babylon was enough for today. Ermenegildo thought so, too. He sighed.

"We shall do all that tomorrow," Madame allowed.

I never welcome my departure from Madame. I know she's equally reticent to separate from me. So we try to avoid usual words of parting, sustained by the fact that our parting will be brief, until the next afternoon. Of course, we're aware that at any moment events may push us to begin interviews.

Still, today's long tea — although we had hardly touched the pastries, a fact Madame sought now to rectify by reaching for two — no, three, one for Ermenegildo — yes, today's long tea and enormous discovery had added wistfulness to this brief parting, imbuing everything with sorrow, as I lit the candle in my lantern, having already adjusted my cowl. To bring them with me for rehearsals in my quarters, I raised the vase securing the pages of the "Account" we had not had time to delve further into, but must, soon.

A wind that seemed to have originated right between my hands plucked at the pages of the "Final Installment," which had lain on top, and it whirled them about and off the table. I grabbed at them urgently — and so did Madame, while I hastily clamped the others with the vase. Ermenegildo secured with his tail those that had spilled onto the lawn. The strange wind was carrying away one page, which tumbled, was abandoned, lifted, aloft again, borne farther.

Our straining eyes followed its course as the gust pushed it against the darkness of tangled bushes and overgrown oleanders that bordered and enclosed the lawn of the château down the road, the château of the new tenant. The desultory wind continued to shove the sheet as if to bury it within the bushes. The sheet disappeared.

"Perhaps that page is from those we've already read," Madame Bernice consoled.

"Perhaps."

As we restored the recovered pages to their numbered sequence, I tried to avoid reading any of their lies, but my eyes could not help but fall on phrases I should have by now become used to, but had not, its gross indictments:

". . . the vileness of everything she touched . . ." ". . . no degeneracy beyond the capacity of the Whore, even performing blasphemous charades in a house of dissolute lewdness . . ."

"The missing page is the very last one of the 'Final Installment.' " Madame announced what I had anticipated. She had hardly finished speaking those words when Ermenegildo sped away toward the darkened bushes in search of it.

"He'll find it, I have no doubt," Madame said staunchly. She held her opera glasses fixed steadily ahead. "He's pushed past the oleanders." Her voice was edged with alarm.

We waited in tense silence, tenser silence, longer silence.

Then with a speed I could not have imagined her capable of, Madame ran along the lawn, across its wide field. I ran after her, to the edge of her grounds, to the clutch of oleanders that were of an unnaturally dark red color.

"Ermenegildo, Ermenegildo!" Madame called out into them. She clawed at the underbrush of vines and bushes that tangled at the edge of the lawn of the new tenant's château. "Ermenegildo!" Dried twigs grappled with her, scratching at her hands, her face; a streak of blood appeared on her forehead.

I pulled her gently but firmly away. "You mustn't hurt yourself, please, Madame. I'm sure he'll be back immediately." I ministered to her bleeding forehead with my cowl.

"I know he'll be back immediately!" Then Madame's frown surrendered to a wide, knowing smile. "Oh, I know his ways, that Ermenegildo. He has a sense of drama, you know, and he's playful. I'm sure he found the missing page, and — Oh, how well I know him! You know where he is, Lady?"

"Oh, where, Madame?"

"Waiting for you at your château, to present you gallantly with the missing page, that's where!"

Claiming she was certain of that "beyond any doubt, no doubt whatever," she marched back toward her château, dabbing absently at her scratched forehead, repeating, "I'm sure of it, there's no doubt in my mind, none whatever, he'll be at your gates, I'm sure of it. Nevertheless, I shall wait outside on the veranda until he returns so I can congratulate him for his commitment to our cause — which, of course, is his, too."

As she moved along, I stood and watched this dear soul whom I have loved from the first moment she appeared in my life, this dearest soul I've grown to love even more, watched her as she trudged up to her "mansion." I realized then how weary she's grown in the years of her life. There was a slight stoop to her walk, an ample awkwardness that I didn't want to see. I realized how very little I know about this gentle, fervent, formidable, beloved soul. Why, I have never even asked how many years she's graced the world; after all, I've roamed through centuries but do not show it. Oh, I realized then how completely Madame Bernice has managed to keep her life a puzzle for interpretation.

I caught up with her and walked her back to her veranda. Night had once again found us at tea. There was no moon. Only the candle of my lantern cast any light. Even within darkened shadows, the new oppressive lilies glowed, exuding their dizzying perfume.

"Now go, please go, Lady, quickly," Madame begged me, "so you can continue your rehearsals in your quarters — and hasten Ermenegildo's return once he presents you with the missing page he's surely found and taken there."

I made my way along the darkened landscape, slowly, extending time, convincing myself that Madame was right — after all, she *is* a mystic — and that Ermenegildo would be at the gates of my château, with the missing last page.

I could not help but notice that the wandering souls from the City were beginning now to form small camps in the countryside, "ghost towns," Madame recently called them. That description seemed apt, towns populated by ghosts. Madame has informed me that after a recent temblor in the City, these dissolute souls occupied crumbling ruins of shattered buildings until the authorities routed them away with horses, and boarded up the dark crevices the destitute had claimed as their own. That may account for the increasing number of the wretched souls in the Country, although the practice of routing them has been occurring here, too.

I walked along. I saw that flames pocked the landscape. Some of the lost are no longer attempting to hide the fires that keep them warm at night. Madame believes this restiveness may soon erupt into open rebellion. "Why, new indignities are constantly added to their burden! — how much longer can they carry it?" she mused when we heard the distant but now distinct rattle of carts laden with the ragged possessions the poor souls cling to as they migrate, like an army of tattered skeletons, from makeshift shelter to shelter, often only an improvised shack of boards, increasingly only gathered debris.

And I, Eve, am blamed for it all! — for all the misery!

As I neared my château, I could no longer restrain my doubts: What if Ermenegildo wasn't there? Impossible. Madame was sure. But what if he wasn't and there was something else at the gate, a further "message" left beyond the "Final Installment" of the vile "Account"? I lingered along the road. I leaned for moments against a tree, staring up into the darkness. I was aware — in a stilled moment, as if it and I had been lifted from the earth itself — of the vastly indifferent sky that God had disturbed with his violent self-creation.

Hearing a rustle, I peered into the darkness. Nothing but the silhouettes of trees. They moved! Oh, more wanderers retreating into darkness, to resume —

What?

Their existence.

The stomping of horses' hooves! Was the carriage back? No. I heard shouts of protest as the desperate people were rounded up. I pushed forward into the clenched darkness to add my own protest to this injustice.

Stop! Stop!

I heard hooves approaching, rushing. Oh, I knew what would occur: One of the mounted officials from the City, the one in charge of this raid into the burgeoning camps of the indigent, would stop me. He would raise his lantern to my face.

"What is a lady of quality doing out this late?"

"I stayed late at Madame Bernice's —"

"She's the woman down the way, oh, yes."

"A countess, she lives in the château next to mine." I tried to add levity to this terrifying moment of confrontation: "She calls it a mansion."

"If I were you, Lady, I would get out of here." The voice was edged with intense warning.

The beating of hooves moving away from me muffled the shouts of the vagrants being gathered within shadows.

If I were you I would get out of here!

Was that what it had seemed? A warning, unwarranted, that a woman of my station and alone might be in danger? Or was a profounder heeding intended? Against interviews! Night pulled the event into its darkness, snuffing it out.

I walked on, still in measured paces, but faster.

Ermenegildo was not at my gate! Perhaps he was being playful — hiding? I moved the light of my lantern about. Something — Oh, what?

Attached securely to one of the bars of my gate was . . . oh, no, please, no —

— the twisted feather from Ermenegildo's comb!

Rush back to Madame's? Oh, surely Ermenegildo was back with *her* and breathless from his adventure, during which, perhaps, someone tried to capture him. Intending to hold him for ransom, in exchange for the canceling of interviews? Did Ermenegildo snatch the last page of the "Final Installment" of the salacious novel just as someone attempted to grasp him, but managed only to pluck out his lovely twisted feather, left now for me here as a warning of greater harm? Time enough to consider all that, with Madame. If Ermenegildo were not back with her, certainly she would have come here looking for him. Surely —

I must return to her.

Surely —

I must —

Surely —

I grew so weary that I huddled in the darkness against my gate, feeling my body sinking to the ground, the candle in my lantern dying . . .

The sun was out, a day that augured wonders, a summer day that had summoned everything to thrive, flowers, trees, grass. I had fallen asleep outside my gates. I had even dreamt. Yes, the recurring dream about that strange woman I don't recognize. I hear her scream. The dream is seizing me again even though I'm awake. I see the forlorn woman trembling. I'm awake and resting outside the gates of my château, and I still hear her scream!

A breeze soothed the perspiration from my brow. What was I holding in my hand? Oh, a feather . . . It all flooded back: Last night. The ambush of wind. The scattered pages, the last one lost — And Ermenegildo!

"Ermenegildo!" I screamed.

"No need to fret, Lady. He's back," Madame Bernice told me as I walked up the lawn for our afternoon tea.

There he was, his spread tail greeting me as he stood on the top stair of the veranda, on a carpet of myriad colors woven by the petals of blossoms that yesterday's wind had scattered. I thought it best for now to hide the twisted feather in my hand.

Madame was already seated, our tea impeccably set on the table and ready to be served. On a silver platter — a superb creation engraved with tiny silver roses — today's pastries, the daintiest yet — dabs of meringue and fluffs of sugar — awaited our delectation as we would continue to rehearse for interviews that will expose fictions long called truths. "Show her," Madame coaxed Ermenegildo.

Gathering his spectacular fan of colors, he revealed that under it, placed carefully, was the missing page the wind had plucked away from us last night.

I did not reach for it.

"Oh, he had quite a time of it, retrieving it, fighting the wind and all those bushes — I believe they're called tumbleweeds. And, Lady" — she whispered this to me, in confidence — "he lost . . . that one certain feather, probably tangled in the dried brush."

Oh, no, it had been plucked out and left on my gate. I still withheld the information, especially since Ermenegildo seemed not to mind the absence of his unique feather.

"The last page, Madame, it contains —?"

"Lady, I wouldn't dream of reading it without your permission." Madame's manners are beyond reproach. She served my tea, took a tiny dainty, and waited for me to pick up the retrieved page.

I placed it under the other pages that I brought with me every day to explore when necessary. I located all the installments on the table, securing them under Madame's usual vase containing her favorite blossom of the day, today — I did not tell her they disturbed me — a stem of blood-red gladiola.

Madame understood my decisive gesture with the installments. "We shall leave our exploration of the 'Account' for later, when you're ready. Now, Lady, on to Calvary!" She whisked her napkin on her lap and with aplomb popped a meringue fluff into her mouth. Perhaps it was Ermenegildo's return that had put her into such vigorous spirits, even as she dictated our tragic course of discovery for this afternoon: "Let's gather your memories as carefully as you did yesterday when we went so effectively back to Patmos. I'm sure we'll be as successful in discovering Magdalene's role in the vindication of blamed women — and we must explore more about the Blessed Mother's function in our journey, the beautiful blue lady, as you've so sweetly called her — and I suggest you resume with her in that same gentle, sweet spirit —"

My hand reached out and touched one of the deep red flowers in the vase. I pulled away from it. I looked at my fingers, almost expecting — surely I did not truly expect it — that the flower would have tinted it scarlet. I said firmly to Madame: "I shall now rehearse the rest of my life as Medea."

"Lady —"

"The time has come." Before she could protest, I resumed from an earlier afternoon: "After the death of King Pelias —"

"— which that woman coaxed his two daughters into performing, inciting them to hack their own father to death —" Madame's accusations shortened her breath. Apparently her resistance had not been entirely overcome that earlier afternoon. She folded her arms so tightly against her chest that she pinched herself and let out a cry. Ermenegildo rushed to her. But — this is how distraught she had become — she shooed him absently away, a fact Ermenegildo did not appreciate. He pecked at her hand several times, and moved away. "But what else would one expect from a woman who would destroy her own —?"

"— children, yes," I finished for her. "Now you shall hear it all."

XXVII

WE CAME TO CORINTH, Jason and I, and our love and passion — they were one — grew. The beautiful barbarian of Colchis and the handsome Greek prince! Everywhere, even in that City, where a plain face, a plain shape, were exceptions, where glorious bodies displayed themselves in exposed abandon on the shore — even in that City, Jason and I were stared at, marveled at. Just as I had done in my country, I wore no more than a translucent garment, a sheath for my body, my breasts all but bared, only strips of gold looped around, framing them — "brown and smooth as velvet," Jason proclaimed, his breath warming them. I decorated my arms and legs with bright, jangling things, bracelets, links, charms, which, by contrast, converted the brown of my flesh into a deeper hue of amber and proclaimed the approach of my presence.

As he matured, Jason's body grew more muscular. He needed and wore no adornment. A tan leather band slung over his shoulder crossed his chest to his waist and then wound about the brief white tunic he wore over sandals, whose straps coiled about his legs almost to his thighs. Other men of his status soon began to abandon their togas, in spring, trying — and never succeeding — to imitate his splendid display.

Although at times only our passion seemed to matter to him, at startling moments, even during our lovemaking, I would locate in his eyes the glint of the ambition that had linked him to me; and that would add to our desire. But now the ambition had no goal. We were allowed in Corinth, but we had no connection to the throne, had not been invited to Creon's palace.

I had learned from the women of Colchis how to determine certain matters in ways that others considered sorcery. With special roots and herbs I gathered from the Grecian hills and deserts, I discovered what I suspected, and longed for, that inside my womb two children were forming; one would be fair like Jason, the other would be dark like me. Both would be powerful and beautiful, and loved.

"The sons of Jason and Medea!" Jason lifted me in his strong arms. He kissed me where he had entered me, where our children had begun, kissed me so long there that the moisture of his tongue penetrated the flimsy cloth and joined, warm, with mine. "I will love our sons," he said, "but not as much as I love you, my savage princess."

"Love them just as much," I said. "They will be you and I multiplied."

"Then I *shall* love them as much — but not like this —" He buried his mouth in the opening of my womb. "You see, I've already begun to be a good father!"

When I was not with Jason — when for long hours he was at the shore to direct the building of his fleet of ships — I remained alone. This was not my country, where I had been a princess. The women envied my dark beauty, and, I knew, feared me. All I had done with Jason to assure our love was whispered about and interpreted as "sorcery." More and more, with increasing apprehension, I considered the future of our children in this foreign land.

In the market, I saw Creusa, Creon's daughter, his only child, a dainty young woman, quite pretty in a delicate way. She had a reputation for shunning those who attempted to court her, a reputation for being somewhat prudish; in this land of sensual display, she wore clothes intended to conceal, though unsuccessfully, her full breasts, especially startling because of her small stature. Today, the drapes of a carriage hauled by four sturdy men awaited her return nearby. Two soldiers guarded it. Surely behind its drawn drapes Creon himself watched.

Before his gaze, I would make friends with her, strengthen ties to the ruler of the country that must accept our children. I removed one of my gold bracelets to give to her as a gift.

Before I could present it, she reared back in horror from me. "You're the barbarian!" she blurted. "You're the savage woman who killed King Pelias and has bewitched Jason."

I tried to control my rage, to protest her accusations, but I had already said: "Yes! I'm the barbarian" — and I had already reached out toward her, turning my hands into tiger's claws. In a moment I would rip the top of her loose tunic, expose her breasts, shout my laughter at her, "Now *you* can be a barbarian, and allow yourself to be desired." I compelled my hands to withdraw, my mouth to utter no word. Anything else would ensure my reputation as a savage. I forced myself to hold out the bracelet to her, letting the sun emphasize its golden beauty. "For you, Creusa."

"Don't touch me with your sorcerer's charm. It's filthy with wild blood," she screamed. She brushed her arms as if even my proximity might sully them. "If it were up to me, you would be banished!" Then she rushed away.

Banished . . . no! The children of Jason and Medea would not be sentenced to roam from island to island, royal beggars pleading for shelter.

I would curb even hints of my rage, for the sake of my children, perhaps now by greeting King Creon. I walked toward the carriage. Its drapes parted. Creon, a handsome man —

"Lady, even he — a man one knows to be your enemy — even *he* you're willing to describe as handsome?" Madame interjected.

Was she commending my honest impartiality in my commitment to truth? I might have countered that she was not entirely correct. I had described Herod as horrendous as he was. Yes, and I had not spared the gaudy Pope, especially awful when he had exchanged his opulent robes for the garments of a matron with a partridge feather in her hat.

"And I suppose eventually we'll see Creon nude?"

"Yes, and yes. He was very handsome, and we shall see him nude."

Creon, a handsome man, leaned out of the carriage. On his bare chest a mat of dark hairs gleamed.

"Medea."

By the way he pronounced may name — his breath halted — I knew he desired me.

On the eve of a full moon, I walked into the desert, to plan under the clear eyes of Heaven how to secure the welfare of our children. Evoke the ancient spirits of my land for guidance? Use my knowledge of herbs and roots, the manipulating of fears and longings? For our children? No, that was risky. Those who dared not move against me as the princess who was Jason's wife would move against someone branded a witch — and against the vulnerable children of a witch.

In the isolated desert, I felt my stomach wrench, as if my children were asserting their own demand not to live as orphans in a foreign land. I lay on the cool earth for seconds. Then, gathering my strength, I stood. Under a gray moon, I raised my hand in a fist and swore:

"The Gods are my witnesses, my children shall never want, no matter what I have to do!"

That evening I told Jason: "Creusa is dangerous."

"Creusa? Dangerous?" He roared with derision. "That prissy little dove? What can a dove do to a glorious hawk like you?" He turned his hands into talons.

"She may be pretending to be a dove. Creon loves her, and that gives her power." I told Jason about my encounter with her in the market, her rejection of my bracelet, about Creon's clear desire of me.

His eyes on me, unblinking, Jason considered that. "Creon desires you?"

"Yes. Powerfully."

He remained thoughtful. Then he smiled. "Of course he would desire you. What man wouldn't, my beautiful wife?" How deeply he trusted my loyalty to him, as I trusted his to me. He discarded the matter with laughter. "Don't be concerned about any threat they pose. Leave it to me to defuse any hostility. I'll do it all now. You've done so much, for me —"

"— for us. And now for our children."

"Yes!"

A few days later Jason was exuberant: "We're invited to the palace. I managed it!"

"How?" I was proud of him. Always before, it had been I who maneuvered.

"I have powers, too, my barbarian sorceress." He laughed, and explained: "It was simple. The workers on the docks talk. I let them know — as if it were a secret, though — about our knowledge of the rulers Creon must deal with. It's come back to me that he would welcome my — our — counsel."

This is how it would be. We would become close to the rulers, while always gaining our own power. "Creusa is conservative, I shall match her at the court, wear garments that will cover me —" That would keep Creon's desire in check.

Jason frowned. "My barbarian princess? — abdicating to that prissy prude? You shall appear dressed only in your beauty, and new golden adornments I'll have made for you by that fellow, that Daedalus, who works at the docks. After you appear, no man in Creon's Court — including Creon! — will be able to make love to his wife, or his mistress, without evoking you! But only I shall have you."

"Only you," I repeated the promise overheard by the ocean on

285

which we first fled. "If I do appear at Court in defiance, it will arouse Creusa's anger —"

"— and Creon's desire. But that poses no threat to me, to us."

I would not go as Jason demanded. Creon, further incited by the wine he was known to cherish in the evening, would act rashly on his desire. Jason would react in outrage. Our cause would be ambushed.

Jason had turned sober: "I would rather not go than have you be other than you are."

"We can't risk turning this kingdom hostile to our children," I warned.

"Nothing will."

"Then *you* must go alone."

"Whatever," Jason dismissed the matter. "But now!" He pulled off everything I wore, and then he decorated my body with new adornments — he surprised me with them often, glittering gems and bracelets, long necklaces that he wound about my hips, strung beads that dipped between my legs.

I stood before him and spread my arms, like the hawk to which he had compared me.

Soon after, Jason announced: "I believe Creon is about to offer me a high post in his kingdom. I told you I would achieve this, my beloved queen, my beautiful barbarian."

And why should Creon not be impressed? We were, after all, prince and princess, though exiled. I loved Jason's arrogance, just as he loved mine.

"And," he read from a new invitation, "I'm being instructed to bring you to the palace, my barbarian queen."

Not yet. After Jason found full favor with the Court, I would go with him. By then Creon's respect for him as a powerful ally would keep desire in check. I would gain Creusa's trust, gradually teaching her to free her spirit. "What is the post, my prince?" I asked.

"Oh, something or other. You know about those things. Some territory to rule over." He smiled.

A territory for our *children* to rule over. Yes!

Throughout this time, I knew, Jason's ambition had been merely waiting, preparing for the exact opportunity. With my encouragement, it would be seized fully — at the exact time, he would reveal his tactic to me. Step by step we would then plot the triumph of our children. The strength of our mutual determination would assure victory.

"What will Creon want in return?" Everything must be considered.

"Our allegiance, which we'll give him — and gain his!" He added: "The point is to extend whatever Creon will offer me into a position of greater power —"

"— so powerful that our children will never have to fear."

"Exactly."

I loved the look of certainty on his face, a certainty to which I added my own. He appeared even more determined than when he had confronted my father in Colchis and demanded the Golden Fleece.

"Tell me exactly how we shall do that," I teased his secrecy. I didn't want to know, not yet. I delighted in the boyish pleasure it gave him to keep his plan to himself, for now, to surprise me with his own "powers," his own cunning. I bit his ear, softly, then harder. "Tell me."

"Shhh." He bent before me. His mouth searched my breasts for the pendant that rested there. He held it in his mouth: "Look! A golden jewel between two greater jewels, my queen," he said. "As your body fills with new life, you grow even more astonishing, my beloved."

I knew the trickery of the women in Colchis. Almost to the very day when they bore their children, they moved their bodies in expert dances that kept their lines solid, their sensual beauty intact.

That night, we drank — no longer did we have only to sip — the magical wine of Colchis. Ambition, determination, power — constantly stirred — poured into our mutual coming that night.

"Perhaps our children shall rule Corinth." Jason stood by the window, staring out at the City. A slash of blue dawn illuminated the lower part of his stripped body, his face remained in shadow.

"To accomplish that, *you* must rule first." I pressed my naked body behind his, wrapping my arms over his shoulders.

He faced me, his confident smile even wider. "Yes! That will be the goal."

"Which I will encourage with all my force when you ask for it, my beloved." I touched my stomach, where our children were forming. Something even more powerful bound us now, our love for each other and our allegiance to our children, our determination for their triumph.

He was gone often until evening, gaining the loyalty of those men who worked with him on his ships, considering everything, I knew proudly, that would aid our goal. My love for him, and for the children we would soon have, made almost bearable my longing for him during the hours we were apart.

One evening, a Greek evening, the blaze of the sun a fiery streak at the edge of the sky, I sat on the floor, humming the songs of my country. A shadow touched me. I looked up to see a tall figure wearing a cape with a hood — to disguise his identity as he had made his way through the City, I knew, because I now recognized him from the powerful frame of his body. Creon.

I rose, intending at first to greet him into our home. I stopped so abruptly that my metallic decorations clanged as if in warning.

He flung the cape from his shoulders. Already aroused, the handsome King stood naked before me. A smile twisted on his face. He advanced toward me.

"You haven't come to me, and so I've come to you, Medea."

He reached out. With one powerful hand, he grabbed the top of my garment and ripped it away in a single movement.

I reached behind me, locating the stem of a lit torch. I grasped it and held it firmly before me. "I'll burn you, Creon," I warned. "I'll scorch your flesh!"

He smiled. "You'd really use it?"

"Yes!"

He took another quick step, to the right. I followed his movement with the torch, holding it closer to him, backing it away, holding it still closer, the reflections of my bracelets needling his eyes.

His voice was a growl of lust. "Will you teach *me* to be a barbarian?"

My hand — not I — my hand lowered the torch. The words he had spoken belonged only to Jason. I felt a wailing desolation, not yet defined. My strength returned with this memory: One night, some men of Corinth had lurked near our windows when Jason and I made love. Surely they had heard him utter those words and had bruited them to the King.

My hand grew strong again. I slashed the torch several times before Creon's face. He turned away, dodging, advancing — laughing hoarsely.

"Burn me with your savage fire, Medea!" he taunted.

"I swear I will!" I jabbed the torch toward him, like a spear aimed between his legs.

"Oh, but you already burn me there." He circled me, weaving about me. I matched his movements, swirling the torch before him in wide circles, smaller ones, then a slash, another, closer. The flame of

288

the torch was diminishing. I pointed the torch at him, inches before his face so he would feel the heat. He turned away. In that movement, the flame was swept away. He wrenched my hands behind me, wresting me to my knees. I tore at his legs, bit at his arms. I fell back on the floor. He threw himself on me, grasping my breasts.

Never would I allow him to enter me where the children of Jason and Medea stirred at this very moment. Never would I allow his filthy seed to touch them. Never would I allow him to invade the place that only Jason's love and passion might touch . . . I twisted away from under him with all my strength, twisted myself over him, slipping down quickly along his body with my mouth. My lips encircled his arousal. His violent movements relented, just as I had counted on. He thrust his head back with a moan. My teeth clenched down. He screamed, and came, but not in me, not in any part of me! His desire spilled on the floor.

I pulled back, a slight tint of his blood on my lips. "You wanted a barbarian!" I stood up.

He touched his groin, where my teeth had scratched the skin. "Ah!" He greeted in surprise the hint of violence that had incited him to come.

I spat the blood-tinted spittle. I had not only meant to make him spill outside of me. I had meant also to threaten real blood.

"Your cunning worked, Medea. Only for now. I'll have you as I want you, when I want you."

I shook my head, swearing, no.

"Oh, then, let's see. Perhaps I'll exile you into the desert, where eventually not even your full breasts will be able to nourish your children."

How did he know I was pregnant with two children? I would not let him see my sudden fear. I arranged the bracelets and necklaces on my body. I said, "No, you shall not, Creon, not as long as I and Jason —"

"Jason?" he laughed. "He knows I'm here, Medea."

I felt each word like the stab of a knife. I retained my smile, I did not swerve in my defiant stance before this man. I remembered Jason's eyes when I gave him the Golden Fleece; remembered his eyes when I made it possible for him to conquer the wild bulls in my country, to conquer the armed warriors; remembered his eyes when I avenged his father's death with that of Pelias. I remembered his eyes each time we made love. What I had seen in them throughout — but recognized only now in my accumulated memories — was his unquestioning expectation, and acceptance — always — of his own triumph, triumph as his right. Now, before Creon, I heard myself wailing, silently, the howl of a wolf.

Creon continued colder words. "You'll need someone to protect you, Medea. So why not the King of Corinth? I shall keep you" — his feet pushed away some of the trinkets that had fallen from my bracelets during the furious encounter — "I shall keep you supplied with the precious gems that cannot rival your body."

All those nights away, Jason had been at Creon's Court, preparing for his own ambitions.

And he had offered me to him!

"I shall see that the children of Jason will be brought forth by the best — and most loyal — midwife." His look grew even more brutal. "We have arranged it, Jason and I. As soon as you give birth, your children will be taken immediately from you and delivered to Creusa, who shall from then on be the mother of Jason's children. News of her 'pregnancy' has already been spread about the City. She has gone into a period of necessary seclusion." He stood only inches from me so that I felt the impact of his words. "Find pleasure in this, Medea. I shall be generous to the children of Jason . . . and his wife, Creusa." He waited, allowing his words to stir more pain as I grasped their full meaning.

Creusa was barren, my children would be given to her — sold! "Creusa? Jason's wife . . ." I tasted the vile words, masticated them.

"Yes, his wife. They've been married, quietly, of course, while matters proceed. Oh, he's told me about your own fraudulent 'marriage' under the gaze of Hecate, not under the laws of civilized Gods."

How quickly I accepted cruelty! I had learned it from masters. Love and hatred — easily now — wrestled in me and formed a new emotion greater than both, one without name, one that would rule my life from this moment forward.

He extended his curses: "If anything happens to me or to my daughter, or to Jason, before all this is effected, Medea, instructions have been left to destroy your children."

I opened my arms, presenting myself to this King. "Even a barbarian knows when to surrender."

"I accept your surrender, and I shall retain the memory of this brief encounter between us to augment desire with anticipation of our next times. Now I shall return to celebrate with my daughter the approaching birth of her children."

He reached for his cape, preparing to leave.

"Wait!"

He turned.

"Let me join in your celebration with your daughter, Creon. Allow me to be a part of the toast you and she shall drink to the extension of your dynasty, and Jason's." How quickly I had abandoned hope, how quickly I had to substitute justice. I located the wine I had brought from my country.

"Oh?" He smiled. "*You* drink from it, Medea," he tested.

"Oh, but I shall!" I tilted the decanter, filled a goblet. And I drank all that I had poured, silently toasting my country with its wine that must be sipped, only sipped at first, preparing the body gradually for more of its enticing powers, power so vast that, without gradual initiation, it would scorch like fire, and —

Assured, Creon took the bottle from me, sniffed with curious delicacy at it. "Yes, it is sweet indeed . . . I accept this gift to, finally, a dynasty of Creon — and silently I shall also toast you, my willing slave, Medea." His lips twisted. "My . . . whore —"

My essence —

"Which is all you have been to Jason, a whore," he extended his judgment.

My essence stirred — "Yes, toast that, too, Creon. I shall be there with you in spirit."

Covered again with his cape, Creon left, a shadow as he had entered.

I stood at the window facing the palace. I waited. I waited long, longer, waited for what I knew I would soon hear.

It came!

A howl of pain rushed to me across the streets of Corinth from Creon's palace as my barbarian wine raged like melted fire through every vein of his body.

"I told you I would scorch you, Creon!" said my new voice.

I waited. There would be more! Another scream, this one Creusa's. Yes! It came ripping through her father's wail as the wine with which she had toasted *my* children wound its fierce way into her heart and burned and killed.

I hurried to blend special herbs and roots I had gathered during my excursions into the desert at night. I mixed the chosen ingredients with water in a goblet. I placed the goblet in the center of the room. Then I decorated my naked body only with the new golden bracelets and anklets that Jason had ordered made for me for my appearance at the palace. I rubbed a light sweet unguent on my body, so that it glowed golden, too. I stood in the last shaft of sunlight slashing the room.

And I waited for Jason.

"They're dead! Scorched with your wine!" he gasped.

"Our wine, Jason, the wine I taught you to drink like a barbarian. *Our* wine killed them. They didn't know they were toasting your betrayal of me and *my* children!"

"Our children, whom I sought to protect by making them —"

"Hers?"

"It was necessary!" His proud face broken, he stumbled toward me.

"Stand there!" I commanded. He froze.

Now, responding to Creon's prepared instructions, his guards would be advancing. If my children were to die, they would die with love, not hatred.

I held the goblet filled with the fresh mixture. I swallowed. The liquid coursed down my throat, past my heart, down, into my womb. For moments it soothed my children with its warmth — and then it mixed with their blood and flowed out.

Before Jason, I stood on a flowering pool of darkening blood, mine, our unborn children.

"*Medea!*" But he could not move.

I felt unendurable pain. I had to dredge more strength to remain standing before him.

"Medea —" This time he staggered.

Did I hear regret in his utterance of my name? Darkness coiled about me. "The Black Sea heard you make me promise to remain a barbarian, for you, that's how you loved me, you said."

I thrust away the darkness that narrowed in a circle about me. My bare feet felt the fading warmth of the spilled blood of my children as it turned cold, dark. I held my braceleted arms out to Jason.

"Love me now, Jason, keep your promise, love the barbarian now."

He staggered toward me, fell at my feet, on the blackened blood. Before darkness and pain smothered me, I laughed, but all I could hear was an endless wail of despair, mine and Jason's conjoined.

XXVIII

"LADY, LADY! I didn't know. Who could have guessed the truth? Only you, who experienced it. And you were blamed!"

"And I was blamed."

"I understand why your essence persevered, even against me, to redeem her. And we *shall* redeem her. I understand so much. Please, Lady, stop pounding on your stomach. Please stop! It can't hurt anymore! It's over. Take your tea, please, Lady."

Madame's words brought me back to her garden, away from the blood in Corinth, away from the blood in —

I heard the forlorn screaming of a woman!

Echoes from the past?

No. The scream was piercing through the quiet of Madame's garden. From one of the destitute wanderers? No, the scream was much too close. But why was Madame not reacting? Oh, she was — by simply lowering her head sadly. I had been wrong, the scream was *not* close — it came from afar, yes, from one of the derelicts wandering the countryside displaced. No, it came — I shouted, to drown the scream, which had become a wail that swept the garden: "I feel the mounting horror of it all!"

"Of course, Lady, oh, of course. The death of children always arouses despair —"

"That, yes, *that!* — and more — horror, terror, unending sorrow — *and, oh, Madame, the unceasing cruelty of every moment of existence!*"

"Lady!" Madame placed a firm arm about my shoulders. "You *must* remember that we're about to shed the burden of unjust blame. Feel triumph in that."

I sipped the tea she was holding to my lips. Ermenegildo rested his head on my lap, to add his reassurance to Madame's. That, and Madame's words of confidence, assuaged the pain — some of the pain — that had ambushed my body.

And the forlorn wail I had heard died.

To show that I was in control, I took the cup of tea Madame was holding toward me. I touched Ermenegildo's head in acknowledgment of his concern. My eyes swept over Madame's beautiful garden, inviting the spectacle of it to bring further surcease, and it did, lulling me. Warmth returned to my body — only now that I had stopped did I realize I had been shivering. I closed my eyes.

When I opened them again, the slant of the sun was lower, shadows had lengthened, and the afternoon was fading.

"Oh, Lady, where did you get —?"

When Madame spoke in surprise, I discovered that, during the extended interlude when I had closed my eyes, I had released, onto the table, Ermenegildo's unique feather left last night as a vague but terrifying warning on my gate.

"A further message left last night," I whispered my answer to her.

But Ermenegildo must have heard me; his head shot up. Gliding my hand over it, I attempted to conceal the feather — I wasn't entirely sure Ermenegildo wanted to see it again.

"Did someone try to harm you when you recovered the missing sheet?" Madame Bernice asked him; she could not keep apprehension out of her voice.

Ermenegildo nodded.

"Who!"

Ermenegildo pointed with his beak toward —

The château down the road!

Madame Bernice stroked and soothed him — unnecessarily, since he seemed in total control. "Tell me exactly how!"

He scurried along, his feet racing —

"Someone chased you —?"

Yes.

He tossed about — being attentive to position himself even then to good advantage.

"— and tried to capture you?"

Yes.

"— but you escaped?"

Of course!

"How?"

He pecked and pecked and pecked.

"You defended yourself with your beak!"

He held his head back proudly. *Yes!*

"Why didn't you let me know, last night?"

He nestled his body against hers.

Madame explained to me: "He didn't want to worry me." She touched his comb. "But your twisted feather —"

He bristled.

"I mean," Madame adjusted quickly, "your singularly beautiful feather — it was plucked out?"

What?

I raised my hand on the table, revealing the feather to him.

Ermenegildo looked at it in surprise: How did you get it?

"It was left on my gate, last night," I told him.

"Was it a man who tried to capture you?" Madame continued questioning him.

Yes and no.

"A man and a woman?" She understood.

Yes.

Madame crumbled the largest pastry on the plate — and then added another — and served them both to Ermenegildo. He raised his head even higher.

"They'll go to all lengths to try to frighten us into canceling interviews," Madame evaluated like a seasoned general. "This rash act is evidence. Since we won't be scared away and they'll know it soon enough, we must assume they'll release every tactic now to ambush interviews. I may not have time enough to prepare a formal presentation — amenities may have to be relinquished. So we must be ready to reveal your truths at any moment! We have little time to idle." She adjusted a blossom within the vase on the table; today she had chosen to grace it with upright lilies of the valley. "We must go immediately to Calvary."

The sorrow of the procession we must soon take through my memories saturated Madame's garden. Mist had crept in. The sun paled into a blur of gray clouds like smeared tears.

I took Madame back to the crucial encounter when Judas demanded that Mary tell Jesus the truth of his birth. Mary — coldly, Judas claimed later, but I said it was with quiet dignity — upheld that she *had* done so, that her son, like her, had been "purely conceived."

"The Angel Gabriel announced that to me." Mary had spoken the words as if they were not remarkable.

Jesus' attacks on the corrupt priests and aristocrats of the land grew as fierce as we had long ago planned, but he denounced the commanding sects as "sinners," not exploiters, and he did so "in the name of God," not of justice. To the destitute, he extended the promise of an eternal reward, in Heaven.

"Look at them, Magdalene. They used to chant defiance, now they bow and pray — and accept. Justice should be demanded here, now. Just as he used to demand it — as *we* used to demand it," Judas remembered quietly.

That night, when we had pitched a tent in the desert, as we often did, for a night, two, Judas challenged Jesus: "The people suffer enough! It's here, now, that their lives need relief."

"What price should be put on attaining Paradise?"

"More of your riddles, just riddles," Judas said.

It was true. Increasingly, Jesus spoke in riddles — and seemed, only seemed, to answer whenever he was questioned. Was it possible that he himself was not yet entirely certain of the reason for his journey?

Madame Bernice startled me by tinkling, although softly, on the side of her tea cup for attention, apparently having tried otherwise to summon it unsuccessfully, so immersed had I become in my life as Magdalene. "Let's pause a moment, Lady. The possibility that Jesus himself, at least at this point, was not entirely sure of his true purpose may prove vastly important in our deductions."

"I had the feeling, Madame, that for all the firmness of his declarations, his mission was evolving —"

"Hmmm. We have to consider that." Madame's jeweled hands remained on her forehead, storing significant evidence.

As growing numbers responded to Jesus' messianic presence, Judas and I began to locate among the crowds quiet, attentive presences. Spies? That meant that Jesus was arousing serious suspicions among the rulers — what was this once-radical really plotting?

"He's in danger," Judas announced.

We would approach Mary again, Judas and I, with that blunt assertion of danger. We went to her home, where Jesus still dwelled when he was not with us or preaching outside the City. In the courtyard, we encountered Joseph. He was just standing there, looking forlorn.

"He fades more every day," I whispered to Judas.

Judas agreed sadly, "One day he'll be gone and no one will notice."

Near Mary, who was weaving, Jesus sat on the floor carving out a rose from a piece of wood left there by Joseph. He smiled a warm greeting at us.

Judas was bold: "If you continue to allow the rumors that you're the Messiah, you'll give the rulers reason to arrest you for blasphemy. They're already watching you," he told Jesus in a voice intended to extend his warning to Mary. "Your promises of Heaven are making your followers meek, they won't have the spirit to rebel if you're arrested now . . . Years ago, we planned —"

I knew he had been about not only to remind him of our fervid plots, but to evoke the intimacy among us when we had planned them, the long conversations we had had — so long ago, it seemed — about justice, revolution. In my memories, growing distant, those interludes had occurred always on warm nights while palm trees held benign witness under bright stars.

Jesus held out to Mary the carving in his hands. She took it. "Lovely." She sniffed it, as if its form itself would scent it with perfume.

Judas's hand rose over Jesus' head, yearning, I knew, to stroke it, as he had done before in the many moments of controlled intimacy, those moments that attempted to calm desire. He withdrew his hand when Jesus did not look at him. Judas turned to Mary, and blurted desperately: "Blasphemy is punished with —"

Would he speak the words that he had not been able to speak during our rehearsal of this encounter earlier?

"— blasphemy is punished with death by crucifixion."

My mind rejected the sudden image —

Mary said, "Dear Judas, you still don't understand. Jesus *is* the Messiah, the Son of God." Her lips hardly moved; those words now formed themselves.

She smiled, the beautiful enigmatic smile that would haunt me at Calvary. Is she saying he can't be harmed? I wondered, with fear. "Please, help us, Mary," I added to Judas's plea. "You're the only one who can convince him he's in danger" — I couldn't keep out of my voice a note of lament at our own inability to be able to persuade him — "and you love him —"

"— with all my heart," Mary asserted . . . "I've heard rumors about danger. So has he. So of course I shall exhort my son to shift his holy journey."

Her casual words startled us. I looked for doubt on Judas's face, but he was eager to believe.

Mary addressed her son: "They're beseeching me to tell you to shift your mission," she told him. "Do it, my beloved son."

"Please listen!" Judas demanded.

"My mother is she who shall do the will of God," Jesus seemed — only seemed — to chastise Mary. He had smiled at her, and his words had been so soft they evaporated in the blue light that bathed her from the window.

Mary faced us triumphantly. She had staged a charade for us, to dramatize Jesus' unswerving mission, his — and hers. "You see?" she said. "No one can stop what God has appointed."

At the door, I turned back to face Mary. "What guarantee do you have that Jesus will be saved from the rulers' anger?"

"God has given His word, through his messenger, the Angel Gabriel. Jesus will *not* be harmed. God has promised."

"She said those exact words, Lady?" Madame Bernice asked me. " 'God has promised.' "

"Those exact words, yes, Madame."

Across the land, we followed Jesus like shadows as he continued his sermons. At times, over Jesus' words, Judas would utter his confused love and pain: "He's a kind man, a caring man, a man committed to justice — and he does love us. But he's a *man* nonetheless." As Judas grew more despondent, he became more stunning in his appearance as if, now that his desire — and Jesus' — threatened to remain unfulfilled, it must find another manifestation, and found it in sensual, angered beauty.

"Lady, do I infer correctly that by then all overtly sexual manifestations among the three of you had ceased?" Madame strained for casualness.

"Then, yes."

"Good." She abandoned trying to sound casual. She was relieved.

"But later, Madame —"

"Might you" — I would say she added this almost peevishly, except that Madame is not peevish — "remind yourself that during this rehearsal we must concentrate on deducing why exactly it was that your essence so emphatically chose to live as Magdalene, who is not a woman blamed?"

"I shall, and we shall."

Jesus stormed the Holy Temple, enraged by the greed of rich merchants. Judas rushed into the fray to help him overthrow tables, booths laden with cheap but expensive wares. I cherished the spectacle of the two together again. They laughed as furious merchants ran out, clutching what they could of their spoils.

Then, suddenly somber, Jesus stood on the steps of the Temple and warned the scurrying merchants: "Never again violate the sanctity of My Father's Temple."

"Who are you to chastise us?" one merchant demanded. He had stopped, with others, to gather his gaudy wares, which had tumbled.

"I am the Messiah," Jesus answered.

The deadliest of words had been spoken. In public, to the enemy. Judas closed his eyes and bowed his head.

That nothing happened in the days that followed — no stronger intimation of danger — only intensified the sense that it was stalking us, growing.

Now, one by one, a small band of intense, serious men enthralled by his stunning force, gathered about Jesus for "instruction." Soon they followed with us from place to place. For all their imposing presences, these striking, handsome men, who soon called themselves "disciples," were restless wanderers seeking an alliance that might bring meaning to what till then had been their desultory lives.

They envied the special place Judas and I occupied with Jesus, a specialness they inferred because Jesus never addressed it. They were startled by my presence, a woman among them, but Jesus made it clear that he would permit no objection. With a steady glare, Judas would underscore even a silent questioning of my position. Deriding their solemnity, Judas accepted them with no sense of rivalry or threat.

That was not true of them. An impetuous burly young man from the country, Peter was particularly resentful of us. Judas claimed he was "humble to the point of arrogance." For all his proclamations about "serving you, Lord, serving only you," Peter at times seemed to want to compete even with Jesus. A sudden burst of summer rain had created a pool in a dip in a jagged street we traveled over. While the rest of us, even Jesus, avoided it by walking carefully around it, Peter attempted to glide on it, lost his balance, and toppled face down.

In a mocking voice, Judas told him, "The point is to *walk* on water, not to muddy yourself."

Peter was quite proud of his manly presence. All eyes and cocked eyebrows, he would flirt silently with me, as if he thought he must. Once I saw him surreptitiously dip his finger into a bowl of olives and dab the hair on his chest with oil, to highlight it.

Soon, he and Judas only mumbled greetings.

299

Of this band of men, I preferred young John, finding him poignant. An orphan like me and Judas, he had haunted the shoreline, thrusting his own name at the ocean to hear its echo come back at him, pretending he was being summoned by a distant, loving presence. He would stare with adoration at Mary, not daring to speak to her. When Mary smiled at him — and no one in the world smiled more radiantly —

"Be sure to emphasize that, Lady," Madame Bernice approved my accolade.

— young John would hide his face because he had flushed with delight.

James, a haughty fisherman, was so proud of his imposing height that he would locate himself next to another James, the shortest of the disciples. For all his impressive stature, James was fussy, constantly rearranging the table setting when we gathered, on special occasions, to have supper on a grand table Joseph had long ago carved and that Jesus and Judas had carried to a room we had claimed as our own, a room that had remained among the ruins of a once-grand dwelling near the Mount of Olives.

Another fisherman, Andrew, often reminded everyone that it was *he* who had "discovered" Jesus. Judas and I would share smiles. Andrew had been at the baptism by the River Jordan — avoiding, himself, being baptized — and he had later heard John the Baptist's words celebrating the youthful Jesus.

The others in the group remained vague figures to me. At times I confused even their names and wished that I had had only a portion of Jesus' ability to remember everything about them, where they came from, how they had lived. That, of course, made them adore him even more.

As we continued to wander about the villages, Judas and I preferred to remain a few feet apart from these men. We cherished the knowledge that among the three of us there was a special bond the others would never share.

On a night when there was no need for a moon because the stars were so bright they created shadows, we gathered outside a tent in the desert. Only three of the new disciples remained. The others had returned to their families — only Peter was married, to a plain woman he avoided — to inform them that they would soon leave them to travel with Jesus.

I had gone to fetch a platter of dates inside the tent — dates I had candied especially for Jesus, knowing he loved their honeyed glaze. As

I was arranging the platter, it fell. Judas responded to the clanging sound and hurried to help me. Hearing subdued voices, we waited tensely inside.

Peter had said to Jesus, "I was the first chosen of your disciples, Lord."

John said, "But I'm the most beloved?" His intended statement swerved into a question. He had spoken with much more hope — and the arrogance of his youth — than with certainty.

Jesus said, "Judas is first, and he is beloved."

Peter demanded: "And the whore? Magdalene?"

I restrained Judas. I needed to hear what Jesus would answer.

"You must never call her that. She's a righteous woman, purged of her sins, and she, too, is beloved . . . And here they are, with delicious sweet dates, dear Magdalene and Judas," he greeted us.

I did not like that Jesus had chosen to defend me as "purged." I did not consider the way I had lived sinful. It had allowed me to survive. The fact that, with Jesus and Judas, I no longer had to sell my body did not indict what I had done. When the others had left that night, Judas asked Jesus what I would have: "What sins of Magdalene's did you claim are cleansed?"

"Whatever they want to believe," Jesus answered.

"Why so many damned riddles and vague parables?" Judas refused his evasion.

"Because whoever hears them will turn them into what he needs or wants to hear." Jesus reached for a date.

"And why do you keep our love secret from those bastards?"

"Lady, the language?" Madame Bernice had halted her teacup on its way to her lips.

"Madame, Judas could be a rough man. He had been raised on the streets, which do not teach one to be prudish." The last word had slipped out. So I continued quickly.

Jesus removed from his tongue a piece of date, as if he had found it bitter. He answered Judas, "You heard me assert our love."

"You didn't tell them about our *real* love."

"Nothing must be allowed to intrude on their loyalties to my —" Jesus stopped, finished: "— to our mission."

"*Your* mission," Judas corrected. "It's not what we intended. What *is* your mission now?" He had begun his questioning with sarcasm but had ended it with urgency.

"To redeem the sins of mankind, to restore man to a state of grace under God."

301

Judas stared at him as if at a new presence.

But the earlier one would return during cherished times. As we made our way along a twisted street with the disciples, we came upon a group of people deriding a pretty, highly decorated young woman, with spangles, her colored hair intricately curled, her lips so red they glowed even under a thin veil she held partially over her face. Cornered against a wall, she cringed in terror from advancing hecklers. Increasingly incensed, a few, then more, reached for stones. They stood with armed fists raised over the trapped girl. Reminded of the assaults I had endured, I ran to her, to cover her body with mine.

I saw then that the pretty young woman was a young man in the gaudy attire of a woman. As I knelt, sheltering him, Jesus reached down, clasping the boy's hands in his, holding them, warming them. Judas stood with us, adding his own defiance of the crowd.

One of the men recognized Jesus and breathlessly informed the others of his miraculous identity. They knelt before him, but they still clung to the menacing stones — hidden behind them. Jesus raised the painted young man by the shoulders. The boy was trembling, his beautiful dark eyes captive within the heavy outline of paint on his eyelashes.

"But, Lord, he's a —" one man began his accusation.

"When you harm anyone who's vulnerable to your hatred, you harm me, you hate me," Jesus stopped the man's words, and wiped away the boy's tears, which streaked his cheeks with melted colors.

The hecklers retreated.

The painted boy disappeared along the streets.

For the rest of this day, Jesus, Judas, and I walked together, ahead of the disciples, who discussed the matter in subdued tones. I noticed that John, the young disciple, had assumed a new spring to his gait.

An impoverished old woman threw herself at Jesus' feet and begged to anoint him with precious oils. We had paused under an arch of the City, needing respite from the sun's blaze. "I know you're the Lord!" she said. "Let me honor you."

Judas exhorted the woman, "Sell the oil, it's expensive, you can buy food with it, share it." He turned to Jesus for the acquiescence he counted on.

"She has to be allowed to do what she must," he startled us, and allowed the kingly anointing.

"He's two men, the one we knew, and the one that Mary has convinced him he is." Judas gave our apprehension words.

As we journeyed from dusty village to village, now drawing

larger and larger crowds, Jesus no longer hesitated before pronouncing his emboldened proclamation:

"I am from God, I am the Light of the World."

Judas and I walked away from the cries decreeing him the Messiah. Judas asked darkly, "Is it too late, Magdalene, to bring him back to us?"

"No!" I refused, just as he had counted on my doing in order to resurrect his determination.

That night, we all rested by an oasis in the desert, the water a dark jewel surrounded by tarnished gold. A sliver of a moon soothed the heat with its cool presence. Jesus announced, "It's time. I have to return to Jerusalem to conquer and to rule. My Father is waiting. His will shall be done, His Kingdom will come." He spoke the enigmatic words —

"— with certainty!" Judas marveled later, when we waited by a fountain in a village while Jesus preached.

"Yes, with complete certainty." I pretended to be rubbing away dust from my face, to disguise the fact that I had suddenly needed to cover my eyes because, when I had heard Jesus' strangely confident voice, I thought I had seen, detected, perceived —

"— fate, shaping," Madame Bernice finished for me.

"Yes."

"Lady, I believe — and we must be careful to keep this to ourselves so we won't dissipate our discoveries — yes, I do believe that a bit of Cassandra's essence was linked to yours, in Magdalene."

"If so, it was only to allow me to *perceive*," I qualified, and was about to remind Madame that I am not a mystic.

"Exactly what I meant." She defused any need for adjustment. An amethyst on one finger of the hand clasped to her temple was like a teardrop tinted blue. "I begin to see —"

Frenzy preceded Jesus now, carried him aloft. When he entered to preach in Jerusalem, a multitude — alerted by the disciples — led him on their shoulders into the sacred city. They climbed tall palm trees and tore down branches to spread like a carpet before him. Others held the fronds over him, to create a passageway through which he walked. "Praise to the Lord!" they shouted. Judas pointed, and I followed his gaze. From their rich towers, the rulers of the City watched.

"They'll be moving against him soon —" Terror scarred Judas's voice. "Very soon." Abruptly, he stared ahead toward the gates of the City.

I saw what he had seen. I didn't know then why I felt a chill under the sun's heat. More mobs were invading the streets. They had at first appeared together, men, women, even children, but they quickly dispersed among the crowds about Jesus. They did not seem to belong with the others; they were too vibrant, too exuberant, almost as if they had just entered the City from the desert.

"Who are they? The others don't seem to recognize them," Judas asked my own question. "They may be professional instigators." Alarm rendered his voice hoarse. "Sent by whom? Hired by whom? Why?" he wondered aloud. "Maybe the rulers aren't sure how much loyalty Jesus has aroused among the people, how strong it may be, and they want to assure —"

I tried to dismiss my own apprehension — and tried to coax Judas out of his. The people who were just now surrounding Jesus, melding with the others who had greeted him with hosannas and palm leaves, were dressed like the people of the City — but their clothes were — seemed — *were* — newer, as if only made to look used, even ragged. Several of those now joining the mobs squinted at the sun. Not used to this brightness? Were they from a darker country?

The next moment I was certain of this: They were only people from neighboring villages, drawn by the spreading fame of Jesus, and the day was so starkly bright — the sun rested on a golden dome — that even I had to shelter my eyes to keep from squinting. I heard the new joiners — and there were hundreds more — greeting Jesus exactly as the others had:

"Praise to the Lord!"

Looking at Jesus that evening as he drank a glass of wine and ate from a loaf of bread I had baked especially for him — next to dates, he loved sweet raisins, and I had sprinkled them abundantly into the flour — I knew this: He was not afraid of the dangerous currents threatening him. He truly believed, like Mary, that nothing could ensnare him. I told Judas that later when we were alone.

"No, no." Judas's answer was feverish, as if his fervency would will this to be so: "I've figured it out. He'll pursue this dangerous road only to a point. Then he'll deny being the Son of God and, before the gathered multitudes, pronounce himself the leader of a revolution that we'll join. He's attempting to confound our enemies until then, that's all." His weary look told me he had not convinced himself.

"Or perhaps" — I moved slowly — "it's true" — I became even more cautious — "that God *will* save him from any harm." There were now moments when I wasn't sure whether I was coming to believe that, or only wanted to believe it; moments when, as I listened to a phrase or a word in his sermon, I would see him radiant with belief.

"If you believe that, you'll encourage his doom!" He turned angrily away from me.

I didn't want to believe that. It would not happen!

Judas had whirled around to face me. I had never seen his face more intense, more passionate, more determined, more beautiful. "There's only one way to break this trance he's in."

I knew instantly what he meant.

"I believe he knows it, too; and if so, he won't want to be alone with us."

And he hadn't been, not for very long, assuring that there were others present with us.

"I'll go to him and tell him that you're ill in our tent, that you're asking for him," Judas said urgently.

"I won't lie," I refused.

"It's a lie that may save him." Judas held me by the shoulders. He added in a whisper: "It's the only way."

I agreed to the ruse.

Jesus stood at the entrance to the tent we had erected on the side of a hill, a hill like the one near the River Jordan where we had first met. The heat of the afternoon, beginning to cool at evening, had formed rivulets of perspiration that etched the striations of his body. His beauty caused me to gasp. Judas stood to greet him.

"Magdalene isn't ill," he said quickly. "I lied because we must be with you."

Jesus turned — and left. Judas stared ahead, disbelieving. Then on the side of the tent we saw a shadow. We walked outside.

Jesus waited.

Judas embraced him tightly, urgently, at the same moment that with his other arm, he drew my body firmly against theirs. Judas pressed his lips to mine — desire finally exploding — and then he turned to share the hungry kiss with Jesus, to make it ours. Jesus turned his face away, but he did not pull back from the joined embrace. Again, Judas's mouth searched Jesus' lips. Jesus uttered a soft moan of resistance, then acceptance, as he received and returned the urgent kiss.

305

So swiftly that it was as if the moisture of the day had undressed us, we were naked in a tight embrace that contained the longing of years. Our hands explored, as we had yearned so long. Jesus' and Judas's lips met on mine.

Then slowly — releasing time, which had stopped to capture these treasured moments — I eased my body away, allowing their lips and bodies to connect without mine.

I gathered my clothes and moved away.

"Magdalene?" Jesus called, and Judas echoed my name. "Stay with us."

I thrilled to hear that exhortation, but I did not turn back. I was surrendering my own desire. This passion must play itself out only between them, these moments must exist only for them, moments determined from the beginning. I knew they both loved me, wanted me. But a singular love had to bind their destinies now or they would be bound by death on Calvary.

I walked to the slope of a nearby hill, where jonquils sprouted everywhere and joshua blossoms held up their clusters like white torches. I sat down. I did not dress. I wanted to share their nudity, even if distantly. I knew I had to witness the truth of what would now occur between these two men I loved. I watched them, in awe of their naked beauty, the intensity of their desire, their lips united fiercely, their limbs interlocked.

"Lady, I'm not sure we should dwell further on any lovemaking." Madame tried to make her admonition seem one that any reasonable person would agree to without objection, but her voice quavered, her breathing rising nervously.

"Oh, but we *must* dwell there, Madame — and I shall." My words could not have been firmer. I wanted, with my exact memories, to celebrate that cherished time.

In the shifting light of a benign evening — a sprinkle of stars had appeared where the edge of the sky was preparing dusk — their bodies on the ground glistened golden with the moisture of perspiration and desire as one movement glided into another, as if their bodies were involved in a beautiful dance of sensuality.

I leaned toward them.

A sudden breeze coaxed the leaves of palm trees to thrust a shadow on the sand. Under the enthralled gaze of the loitering sun, the shifting bodies pressing against each other became one. That united body moaned softly, thrust, and spilled.

Judas lay back, and held one arm out for Jesus to rest his head on. It had worked! The deadly journey would not occur!

Jesus dressed. Without looking back, he walked away, disappearing into waves of desert heat.

Judas's arm remained outstretched, embracing nothing.

XXIX

EVERYTHING PROCEEDED as if the interlude in the desert at dusk had not occurred. In his sermons, Jesus spoke harshly about "Heaven's judgment on sinners."

When Judas questioned him — with a dark look and a tilt of his head — Jesus would answer only, "My Father decrees judgment."

"On our love?"

I wished that Judas could have withdrawn his words. I dreaded what Jesus might answer now. I should not have been afraid.

"I shall never judge our love wrong," Jesus said.

Judas sighed. My heart rejoiced, for me, yes, but far, far more for Judas . . . and for Jesus.

"Then why —?" Judas did not finish; Jesus had already said:

"But nothing must compromise my Father's business." He had moved on to join the disciples nearby. Peter's hostile stare remained on Judas.

"Lady," Madame interrupted emphatically, "this is a point I'm sure will come up at interviews, perhaps even belligerently. I think it wise to deal with it forthrightly." She fingered her necklace of marquise emeralds as if it were a simple rosary; Madame does not believe that jewelry should intimidate. "You make it clear that Jesus had *not* become a moralist . . . about . . . about . . . about such matters as you described during the incident at dusk."

"I did indeed make that clear, Madame. Jesus *never* became a moralist." She was right, however, that the point must be emphasized. I did not even attempt to restrain the passion I knew would flow into my sharp denunciation: "Others — twisted preachers, ministers, cardinals, rabbis, and especially popes — including, yes, the Pope who now conspires against me from the Grand Cathedral — it was they who distorted Jesus' teachings into props for their own fears, inadequacies, envies — and especially into the shape of their own cruelties. Although Jesus' means of achieving his goal shifted, he remained committed, in his heart — and Judas and I never questioned this — to *true* morality and —" I forgot her phrase.

"— social justice," she supplied.

"— yes, for all the dispossessed."

Madame sighed. "Oh, I'm relieved to have this cleared, because people are so peculiar about" — she coughed — "such things — and do prepare yourself, Lady. Mild as you may believe you made it, your description of what occurred at dusk between Jesus and Judas as you watched — resplendently naked —" She awarded me the last two words graciously, although her voice did rise precariously high. "— will not be greeted easily."

"If my description was 'mild,' Madame" — I did not like the ring of her word — "it was so only because I viewed that beautiful interlude from the distance."

"Precisely."

Had she forgotten that she herself had often expressed more than a modicum of resistance in the area of "such things"? My look of surprise may have helped her to recollect just that. With a smile determined to be subtle, she said, "I've warned you, Lady, that, now and then, I might be forced to stand in as a cynical interviewer. Perhaps in the area in question — the matter we've been discussing — I succeeded so well that you may have thought that I was speaking for myself." She studied her cup of tea intently — or she was simply hiding her face because surely she had every reason to blush at such a declaration.

She must have perceived that I knew that because she did this:

She held her head up, a motion that could not help but lift her bosom proudly, and said, "Whatever! I can tell you *now* that I am not — repeat, am not — a prude." She emphasized her conviction by treating herself to an especially large almond tart that she had been courting all afternoon but had so far managed to avoid. She did not even notice that Ermenegildo was stretching his neck, having himself been courting the very same tart.

A waft of the stale, opulent perfume from the new flowers, whose shape distorted those in Eden, pushed me away from the present, and back to Jerusalem.

It was now clear — Judas reported this to me after wandering

about the City to gather all such possible information — that Jesus'
transformation from rebellious reformer to God's messenger was be-
wildering and frightening to the rulers of the State. His claim that he
was the Messiah — other roaming preachers claimed that and were
laughed at — did not threaten them so much as the power that might
be seized by someone who was *believed* by the populace to be the
Messiah. Although his promise now was of a vague kingdom as
reward for suffering — and subservience among the people would
only strengthen the rulers' power — hadn't this same man not long
ago been a radical? Was his new "vision" a ploy to gain more power as
a perceived Messiah and then shift his message and use his vast
authority to stir the growing numbers of his followers to rebel? If he
was to be checked, it must be while loyalty to him was still only
shaping.

On a day when the sun blazed fiery orange in the City and yellow
waves of heat radiated from the desert, Judas told me urgently, "The
talk on the streets is that he'll be arrested. Tonight. Jesus knows that."

I didn't believe him, didn't want to believe him. So my heart sank
when, immediately after, Jesus called us and his disciples to join
him — "for a very special supper" — in the abandoned room we had
made our own near the Mount of Olives.

We sat at the long table Joseph had carved. That was all that was
left of him, I thought.

Jesus spoke in solemn riddles:

"This is my body." He passed pieces of bread to the disciples
seated with him.

"This is my blood." He poured red wine.

The disciples welcomed participating in these mysterious rituals
and ceremonies as added confirmation of their closeness to Jesus.
Whether they understood his riddles or not, they joined unques-
tioningly, devoutly. I myself attributed these rites to Jesus' glorious
sense of drama. Most often, Judas would agree with me, while adding
with a smile, "But sometimes — don't you agree? — it veers on melodrama."

Tonight Judas was not accepting.

He rose angrily from the table and grasped Jesus roughly by the
shoulders, pushing the robe off his torso so that he clasped bare flesh.
"*This* is your body," he said. "And if you're crucified, your blood will
be real. Not *this*." He had struck the table so hard that a glass of wine
had overturned and spilled, deep red.

Peter challenged Judas: "How can you doubt our Lord?" He

rushed to Jesus' side, to cover him with the robe that had fallen off his shoulders.

Judas answered heatedly, "What's said between me and Jesus is not for you to question. Or even listen to." Peter reached out to grab Judas. Judas thrust his hand away. The two scuffled. I marveled at Judas's agile strength. Jesus restrained them.

We ate silently — tensely aware of the sounds of a dry desert wind that had begun to gather at sunset. I rose from the table, as if only to reach for a bread basket, but actually to do this: I touched Judas, trying to calm his anger and fear.

"Tonight I'll pray in the Garden of Gethsemane," Jesus said.

At any other time, I would have been impressed by the stroke of drama in his choice of that garden for evening prayers on this night of heated desert winds. It was an ominous garden of interlocking shadows created by olive trees and the jagged ruins of a temple. But this night was tense with real danger. Soundless distant lightning sliced like a glinting knife into the dark sky.

Judas and I joined Jesus when he stood ready to make his way to the garden. When they realized that we would go with him, Peter, James — the tall one — and John decided to follow.

We reached the garden. The hot fitful wind gnarled the branches of trees into coves of darkness. Then it subsided, leaving only the scraping of falling palm fronds to fade into a waiting stillness.

Jesus knelt, his elbows on a craggy stone, his hands pressed solemnly before his lips. No breeze sighed now for moments. The moonless night draped heat over us.

He wants us all to remember all this exactly as it's occurring! I was certain.

Uncommonly deep into the night, Jesus knelt and prayed. No, this was not his usual mysterious drama. Something enormous was being prepared for.

Does he know exactly what? That question occurred powerfully now.

Peter, James, and John fell asleep.

Only Judas and I kept our vigil with him, as the night — impossible — grew darker, hotter. Even the few stars that had dotted the sky earlier melted into the blackening sky.

When Jesus rose, Judas blocked his path. "They're planning your arrest, you know it, and you're directing it. It's gone far enough. I won't allow it to proceed. We'll make our way out by the back of the garden, and then —" The sound of his raised voice violated the sudden

311

hot, but frozen, quiet of the garden — the leaves of surrounding trees stirred, but without making any sound; they just moved as the wind waited to spring again.

Jesus faced Judas, faced me, all dark shadows. Although he whispered, we recognized the voice we had cherished during intimate moments: "Beloved Judas, beloved Magdalene, trust me. Trust God. It will proceed only as far as He intends, no more."

"And how far will that be? To Calvary, to Golgotha? The place where even stones form skulls, where everything reeks of death? Does God intend *that*?" Judas challenged.

"I won't be harmed," Jesus said. "God promised me that. You were with me; we were together; remember, Judas, Magdalene? Remember?"

"I remember when we ate the mushrooms," Judas asserted, "when we *all* saw visions, heard voices — hallucinations!"

Jesus said firmly, "He asserted what I hadn't believed before from my mother — what she already knew — that He had chosen me to carry out his mission —"

"Oh, don't you see? Mary prepared you to be convinced. Then you were — under the spell of the mushrooms — but none of it was real, just your imagination, guided —" Judas challenged.

"My journey has been dictated by God —" It seemed to pain him to have to explain words that might separate us. "— and that mission is to purge mankind's sins, from the beginning, to allow salvation at last. There is no substitute for salvation."

Judas turned away. "Riddles, riddles."

Jesus spoke his words with even graver care. "What better time to spread the word of His power than when He'll thwart all the harm they'll attempt on me?"

What guarantee? I longed to ask. I had experienced too many betrayals on the streets to allow unquestioned hope.

He answered my unasked question: "No harm shall fall on me. God won't betray me — and he won't betray my mother."

His lone shadow flowed into the darkness as he moved down ancient crumbling steps. With renewed force, gathering even more heat from the desert plains, wind swept across the garden.

I detected the powerful, almost overwhelming perfume of flowers, a heavy redolence — it was not a scent — I had never before noticed. I looked around. There were no blossoms in this Garden of Gethsemane. From within the remains of the fallen temple, a bird flew out. The rustle of its wings scratched at the wind. Cawing — or did it scream? — the bird disappeared, a slice of blackness, darker than the sky.

"Jesus *is* certain God will save him before anyone can harm him," Judas said in awe as he continued to stare after Jesus. He was only now allowing himself to face that Jesus believed, truly believed, that he was the Messiah. Judas seemed to be about to shout his protest of impending danger — he looked up, challenging the sky — but all that came from his throat was a sigh.

We hurried to catch up with Jesus as he walked down the stone path toward the edge of the garden. We passed Peter, James, John, who woke, startled, aware only then that they had fallen asleep.

"I closed my eyes only briefly, Lord," Peter asserted.

The light of distant torches advanced, streaks of fire in the wind.

Judas grasped Jesus, turning him around. "Run away!"

Jesus did not move.

As if the power of his passion would convince him, Judas kissed Jesus roughly on the lips.

He would respond, I prayed. Then, this spell would break, and we would run away, Jesus and Judas and I, and we —

Peter stepped forward in bewildered threat at what he had seen, the kiss.

Jesus faced ahead, waiting. Judas withdrew, surrendering in horror to what was happening: Soldiers — and some of the rulers and a smattering of priests with them, half-hidden, intermingling — surrounded us.

And behind them all, as if materializing out of the darkness, strange bands of men, women — old, young — were approaching. I could hear their voices — no, only angered, wordless sounds.

Peter whispered urgently to James and John: "Judas betrayed our Lord, with a kiss. Whatever else happens tonight, remember that." Only I overheard those terrible words, but there was no time now to deny them. Events were crashing about us —

"But, Lady, there would come a time when you would tell the truth," Madame gladdened me by saying firmly.

"Yes, Madame. Yes!"

One of the priests derided Jesus: "Are you the son of God?"

"Deny it!" Judas begged.

Hope sputtered again. Jesus would disclaim what they wanted him to say; he would not allow the easy charge of blasphemy.

313

He remained silent, serene.

"You'll answer that to the high priest Annas," one of the rulers sneered.

The soldiers advanced to bind Jesus.

Jesus held out his hands to them, without fear. He glanced up as if in assertion of a sacred covenant.

As they marched Jesus away under disintegrating arches choked by coils of dark vines in the garden, Judas said urgently to me, "The rulers want him dead now — but only Pontius Pilate can pronounce the sentence." Even within the increasing blackness of this night, pain and fear darkened Judas's face as if a heavy shadow had been flung by the wind only on him. He rushed his words: "Pilate loves his wife, go to her, Magdalene, persuade her, do whatever you must, we need more time to —" He could not find definite words. "We need more time! I have to stay with him."

Already, Judas was wending his way into the crowd of shadowy men and women who had just joined in the arrest — their voices only a steady drone of menacing sounds.

How was it possible that night was extending so long?

Disguised as a servant, I made my way toward the chambers of Pilate's wife. I heard moans, sighs. I waited, pretending to be sorting flowers in a vase, an arrangement of white orchids that seemed to have been sprinkled with golden pollen. I pretended to be peering at them when I heard Pilate emerging out of the chamber. He was adjusting his toga. He called back, grumbling, "I'm sorry, dear, they're bringing someone over. So early, too," he seemed to lament to himself.

At any other time I would have noticed that he was a handsome man.

I moved into the chamber he had just left. His wife was lying naked on the bed, a beautiful woman. One full, milky breast was partially concealed by her long hair, which parted exactly to reveal its nipple. She uncurled her smooth legs, and I could not help but notice in surprise that the light patch between her thighs glistened with what looked like the golden pollen on the white orchids I had seen outside in a vase. One of the flowers rested nearby, abandoned, on the marble floor. The woman started when she saw me — and then quickly recognized me.

"You're the woman who follows that man they claim is holy."

I simply nodded.

"I remember even more now, some time back," the woman said.

"I was in my carriage. A crowd was about to stone you. The man they call Jesus interceded."

"Yes, but we staged it all, to teach those vile men a lesson."

Pilate's wife stood up, unashamed in her nudity, exhibiting it. A sprinkle of golden pollen fell to her bare feet.

"You staged it?" she asked.

"Staged," I reiterated. Had I begun with a misstep?

"How delicious!" she laughed.

I wanted to embrace her with relief. "Now I'm here to beg with you for his life."

"He's in danger?"

"They're bringing him before your husband." I rushed my words. "They say he's committed blasphemy, that he claims to be the Messiah."

"How silly." She sat before a mirror and dabbed at her face, cleansing it.

"Yes, but it can lead to crucifixion, unless —"

Pilate's wife turned to face me. She stood up. Sequins of glistening pollen from the white orchid fell as she walked slowly toward me. She stood close to me. She drew my dress from my breasts. "Beautiful," she said. "My dear, I do believe there is nothing in the world more beautiful than the beautiful breasts of a beautiful woman. Men are so wise to notice that." She touched the dab of hair between her legs, then touched one of my breasts with the same finger; a dot of golden pollen remained there.

She moved away, to the window, surveying this foreign city. "We come from Rome, Pontius and I, we don't understand all this furor about messiahs and —" She threw up her hands.

"He's not the Messiah." I wanted to convince her to help me. "He's just a man, a good man, a very good man. When they bring him to your husband, for sentencing —"

She had listened intently. "No, I don't understand anything about these dangerous politics and intrigues; I don't care to. But, my dear, I do understand a woman in love. You do love this man, don't you?"

"With all my heart."

"Then I shall help you. Tell me how." She folded her hands over her breasts, raising them delightedly.

"Convince your husband —"

"Easy enough — when he's in bed with me." She smiled. She picked up the abandoned orchid from the floor and inspected it. All its golden pollen was gone. She smiled at a fresh memory. "But when he dons his official robes —" She became serious. "How can I intercede, my dear?"

I had examined every possibility as I had hurried here through dark streets. "It's known that Pilate is superstitious."

She laughed. "Oh, he would hate it if he knew that that's been discovered. He denies it, but it's true." She kissed the orchid, and held it to her cheek.

"Tell him that in a dream —"

"Create a dream for me, my dear. Go on. I welcome some intrigue."

"Tell him that in a dream you perceived a warning that this man must not die."

She shrugged. "Done. I shall write him a note, and" — she laughed a throaty laughter — "I shall sprinkle it with ... orchid pollen!"

I reached for her hand, to kiss it in gratitude. She clasped mine, brought it to her own lips and held it to her mouth, moistening it with her tongue, which rose slowly along my arm. "Do you have time to —?" She looked up at me and nodded toward the rumpled bed.

I shook my head.

"Ah, well, perhaps another time, my dear, we shall ... dream ... together?" She released my hand slowly, and I ran out, hearing the curiously muffled murmurs of the mob following Jesus, who was being led through back alleys to the old priest named Annas.

Night remained. Tangles of weeds gathered from the desert by the wind tumbled desultorily along the strangely empty streets.

I found Judas among the strange crowd. He was no longer attempting to hide his presence — nor did I, but no one seemed to notice us. We entered the courtyard of Annas. Tall torches, one on each side — the only light — flanked the priest where he stood on a balcony. A very short man wearing elevated sandals in an unsuccessful effort to disguise his lack of stature, he peered at Jesus for ominous moments.

In the barren courtyard, dying bushes revealed a failed recent attempt to create a garden. Weeds, with tiny dots of grayish flowers, had been shoved by roaming whirlwinds against the edges of the gates. The tall gates that had opened to bring Jesus in had remained parted. An invitation to the crowd that had appeared at the garden?

Staring at the sinister, anxious people rushing in — allowed, expected? — I recognized them, these men and women who had appeared immediately after the arrest in Gethsemane; they were the same that Judas and I had seen infiltrating the festive throngs when Jesus entered Jerusalem days earlier.

Judas, too, recognized them: "They were brought here to demand a brutal sentence," he said with certainty.

"Pilate's wife will stop it all." I was certain the beautiful woman glittering with the golden pollen of white orchids would keep her word. The dab of gold dust she had placed on my left breast — was it still there? — yes — had asserted her promise.

But where *were* the people who had truly rejoiced for Jesus that earlier Sunday? Not the people in Annas's courtyard now. Did it seem so only to me that this night and its long darkness were supporting a conspiracy of secrecy? Would there be time enough to rouse, from whatever slumber enveloped them, those who had greeted Jesus joyously into the City? Time enough to spread word of his arrest? Would Jesus' real followers be ready to storm these gates in protest?

Judas winced at the harsh sound of scraping locks, as if he had been trapped within it. I looked behind me. The tall gates into the courtyard had been bolted. Armed soldiers guarded the portals. No one else would enter.

"Lady, who do you suppose sent the people who were let into the courtyard of the corrupt priest?" Madame Bernice interjected. Ermenegildo leaned his head to one side, then the other, wondering the same.

"The rulers — Whoever stood to gain the most from the unfolding horror, whoever —" I stopped. My own words resounded.

Whoever stood to gain the most from the unfolding horror!

I inhaled. For centuries my essence must have pondered the question.

I thought I was about to answer it, but before I could, Madame had clamped her hands to her temples and stored the matter firmly for future important consideration.

XXX

WE HAD EXTENDED OUR EXPLORATIONS deep into the night. We realized that when we sipped our tea and found it cold. The pastries were stale. We discovered that when Ermenegildo emphatically rejected one. The night was warm, almost hot, as if some of the dark heat from Calvary had seeped into Madame's garden — heat in which, I noticed without calling Madame's attention to it, the strangely distorted lilies by the veranda thrived, their petals fully open. We sat in the glow of candles that spilled from inside the château. Late as it was, I must continue:

Those who had hailed Jesus would not be allowed into Annas's courtyard. But when the shut gates opened again and it was daylight and the word had spread, they would surge in protest — I clung to hope, hope I tried to share with Judas by holding his hand in mine.

The fat priest Annas leaned his fleshy elbows on the railing of his balcony, attempting to raise his body so he might be able to peer down at Jesus. One elbow slipped. Doubly angered, Annas shouted at Jesus:

"Are you the Messiah? Are you!"

Silent, Jesus stood in stunning dignity before his grotesque tormentor.

The fat priest screeched like a petulant child: "I demand you tell me, Jesus! Are you?"

The crowd added heckling sounds to their muffled curses, which the resurgent wind multiplied, and over it all there emerged only one clear word, still only whispered, slowly:

"Blasphemer."

Jesus did not wince.

I understood — unequivocally and with startling clarity — what was occurring. Jesus was awaiting the moment when God would free him. That would be now while he stood before this marionette of a man.

But — I noticed this and winced — Jesus had made a slight movement to loosen the knots clenching his wrists behind him. When he couldn't, he frowned in surprise, as if realizing only now that he was truly bound. I saw Judas twist his own hands behind him, as if to share the pain of his beloved's restraints.

The priest screamed: "I can't tolerate this false prophet anymore. Take him to Caiaphas!"

"To Caiaphas!" Several voices out of the mob demanded. Others, contorted with hatred, crouched, hissed, repeated the terrifying whisper into the dusty howling wind:

"Blasphemer."

Armed centurions surrounded Jesus. Anticipating a riot when the people woke from the spell of this eternal night? A helmeted soldier tied a long heavy rope to Jesus' wrists, to lead him out of the courtyard in humiliation.

Jesus was not humbled. He knew that God would not allow this to move much further. It would all end triumphantly, and soon. Jesus' resolute smile told us that as he located us and nodded, without fear.

Outside the courtyard, Judas and I wedged forward. A group from the crowd encircled Jesus —

"— hiding him!" Judas shouted over the howling desert wind. "They don't want the people to know what's happening. Why is the night lasting so long? Why is the City so still?"

Yes, it had all grown increasingly still. I was aware only of the sound of the wind assaulting palm trees, shoving dry fronds against the walls of the City.

We followed as the soldiers led Jesus along hidden back streets, a circuitous route that avoided the center of the City. Clusters of weeds scraped into vacant alleys.

The Court of Caiaphas was in the largest hall of a building of arches and austere vestibules. The hall was sheltered from the wind but not from its heat nor its howling.

A tall, thin, powerful man of stern features — his eyes seemed to have been scorched into their sockets — the high priest sat in his courtroom flanked by the rulers of the City — other priests, aristocrats, rich merchants. I recognized among them the merchant who had questioned Jesus in the Temple. He leaned toward the high priest and said: "His grasping for power must end this night!"

When Jesus heard those words, a look of bewilderment flickered on his face. This night? — when events were racing? His brow smoothed, thrusting concern away. He raised his head before the gathered men, his faith in God's promise intact.

Behind us, the deadly mob surged in. Here, too, the portals locked.

"You are facing, Jesus" — Caiaphas paused between each word, adding gravity — "the Supreme Court of the Land."

A growing film of perspiration on his face — that was all that indicated the ominous words might have touched Jesus. Was there a slight toss of his head? In disbelief? No, it was a manifestation of his defiance, the certainty that the violent currents swirling about him would be thrust away no matter how close they came to him. His serenity assured that. A miraculous coolness that seemed to have sought him out within the hot room evaporated the moisture on his body.

Rising, Caiaphas walked toward Jesus, step by slow step. He stopped abruptly. "Are you the Christ!" he hurled his words.

Judas's lips moved in a silent exhortation to Jesus: Deny what they need you to claim!

Jesus did not wince, did not look down in fear, did not retreat as the high priest approached closer.

"Do you deny being the Messiah?" Caiaphas's voice had become almost gentle. "We know you have claimed to be. Why deny it? If you are His son, God will surely protect you. Are you the Messiah?"

No! Judas shouted soundlessly. Say no!

Jesus stared ahead, up.

Swiftly, Caiaphas circled Jesus, moved away, advanced within inches of him, moved back again, resumed his stalking, stopped abruptly and confronted him again: "Are you afraid your God will forsake you? Betray you?" Caiaphas's words were a kind, sweet whisper. "Don't you trust God?"

Jesus nodded.

After *this*, God will intercede! I longed for Jesus.

"Your silence contradicts you." Caiaphas began to turn away from Jesus. Then he whirled about and shouted: "Are you the Messiah, Jesus!"

Jesus opened his mouth, to speak.

The perspiration on Judas's hand as he clenched mine was cold, colder than mine.

With raised, mocking eyebrows, his head cocked, Caiaphas faced the stern judges and rulers. "Clearly, this man distrusts his own God."

"I am the Messiah," Jesus said. "My Father shall protect me against you."

Judas turned his head to one side, rejecting what was now in motion.

"We have heard blasphemy," the high priest announced calmly to the rulers and priests leaning back in relief at the table.

A man out of the mob rushed at Jesus and spat on him: "Blasphemer!"

Judas pushed forward to shelter Jesus. Bodies thrust him back roughly.

Jesus tilted his face, to discard the spittle. Had he understood this damning occurrence? He had not flinched. His eyes sought me and Judas. I saw in his look — this cut into me like a shard — a spark of . . . panic. No, no, not that; only a flicker of uncertainty — not even that. It was gone now, whatever I thought I had seen in his beautiful eyes.

The mob swooped on Jesus, tearing at his clothes. As he was tossed about, I saw — yes, it *was* there, the beginning of bewilderment on Jesus' face. Perhaps fear. Perhaps — *No, it was not fear!*

Judas struggled against the wall of bodies that separated us from Jesus. Caiaphas's terrifying words stopped him:

"What shall be the punishment?" the high priest asked the mob. "Crucify him!"

Stripped to tatters, Jesus looked down at his sides, where his freed hands would have been, looked down in puzzlement. He pulled at his restraints, as if with little force he might free himself. His body wrenched as the rope dug into his wrists. His mouth opened — to utter a cry? His lips closed firmly. When he aimed his gaze at Heaven, all doubt had disappeared.

"Take him to Pontius Pilate!" the high priest demanded. "And assure the sentence is death."

"No!" Judas shouted. "No!" I echoed. Our protest was drowned by the mob's chanted taunts:

"Death to the blasphemer! Death to the powerless king!"

Outside, we struggled to keep within sight of Jesus. Surging bodies about him had grown in number, more bands of the same shadowy men and women that had appeared at the arrest, that had followed its course.

And still not yet dawn! I searched the edges of the sky for the beginning of light. Nothing but darkness.

Only when I saw Peter lingering outside with John and the tall James did I realize I had not wondered where the disciples had gone after the arrest. Had they fled? Jesus was led past them. I saw tears in Peter's eyes, and John's. James covered his mouth.

"Do you know that man?" a soldier barked at them, and pointed to Jesus.

"No!" Peter denied. James and John remained silent, their heads lowered.

Judas pushed forward. "*I* know him! *I* love him!"

"I, too, know him," I said. "I, too, love him!"

Our words were swept away by the rising curses of the mob.

Although spittle dripped down his bound body covered with shreds that the wind flailed about him, Jesus was unbowed. A few more steps, only a few more, and it would all end in his vindication. He would be freed by God. I knew it was that certainty that supported him.

Between the columns of his stately Roman home, Pontius Pilate waited outside on the steps of his portico. The wind abated briefly, dust hovered in thick clouds.

The moment I saw Pilate, I was sure that Jesus would not die. Pilate was looking on with bemusement, only bemusement, at the crunching crowd before him. They had formed an arc, like a curved wall, enclosing the scene unfolding.

Jesus was thrust forward to face Pilate.

"From all I know, this man has done nothing," Pilate said easily, moving to end it all, perhaps to return to his wife.

"Magdalene, Magdalene" — Judas allowed joy into his words — "it won't happen, he won't die. *We* won't die."

"This man — this Jesus — he's not only blasphemed," one of the rulers at the head of the crowd shouted to arouse Pilate's anger, "he's denounced us. Your emperor and Rome are next — and you!"

Pilate laughed. He asked Jesus, in a kind voice, "Are you really claiming to be the Son of God?"

"It's they who say that," Jesus answered.

Had his voice wavered? Was the certainty that had sustained him beginning to crumble? Those considerations didn't matter now. Pilate would release him.

The mob chanted their accusation at Jesus: "He's a blasphemer!"

322

Pilate looked about him as if perplexed by this excess. He said aloud to himself, "Will dawn never come?" He addressed the mob: "Let this man go." His eyes raked the crowd. He located me. He smiled. "Besides, I had a very strange dream —"

The priests led the crowd forward, narrowing the circle that enclosed Jesus as he faced Pilate.

Jesus' body remained unbent. But he seemed . . . startled, and . . . No, no, not afraid . . . But . . .

"Does he look to you as if he's hurting, Magdalene?" Judas begged me for the answer he needed.

"No, he's strong, remember that, Judas; he's strong."

"If I could shield his body with mine, I would," Judas said, "so that *he* would not hurt. I would die for him —"

"He won't die!" I asserted.

"No, he won't die," Judas said.

The priests and rulers had bunched before Pilate. "You insult us!" "The law demands sentencing." "He'll threaten Rome next." "And you."

Pilate stared at them with contempt. "Very well," he said calmly. "It's the time during which the custom allows one convicted man to be freed. There's only one other, Barabbas, a brutal rapist, a murderer who has sworn to rape and kill and torture again. Your wives and daughters will be in danger — Now! Who shall be freed?" His smile was confident, attempting to shame the mob.

"You'll have to keep your word," a priest hissed at Pilate.

"I shall — if you will give me yours" — Pilate added more confidence to his words — "to leave me in peace once the choice is made."

The priest faced the crowd: "Who shall be freed?"

"Barabbas!"

"No!" I screamed. No, it was Judas who had screamed.

As the crowd shifted in exultation, we both saw it clearly, the look of astonishment on Jesus' face. Perspiration flowed down his body; the shreds of his clothes, suddenly wet, were pasted to his flesh. His eyes darted everywhere, as if to locate evidence that this was not still proceeding.

"Crucify him!" A priest ascended the steps to face Pilate.

Pilate looked angered, trapped. "I shall not sentence an innocent man!" He turned to ask a hovering servant for a basin of water. He washed his hands. "If you do this, you'll spill innocent blood. It shall not be on my hands — only on yours. I give you another opportunity to choose!"

323

It would work! They would cringe from this abomination.

Jesus looked up at the black sky. The wind was rising with a shriek.

Out of the mob came a firm, harsh voice, which coaxed: "Let his blood be on us and on our children."

The others repeated the evil prayer: "Yes, let his blood be on us and on our children."

Jesus closed his eyes. His body rocked as hands plucked at the shreds of his clothes. Judas hurled his own body forward, to reach him. But Jesus was already being led away to the place of skulls and death, to Golgotha.

"Let his blood be on us and on our children," Madame Bernice repeated the words the savage mob had chanted. She spoke them quietly, hushed. I was enveloped by the heavy perfume of the grotesque orchids that had invaded the garden overnight.

Madame resumed in a controlled but angered voice: "Those gathered for the condemnation were brought there to assure that it would all proceed." She sighed, shaking her head at the horror.

"They were sent by God, Madame." I announced the verdict I had earlier withheld.

"Why would He want this brutality to proceed?" Madame's voice brought immediate urgency to the events of centuries past. "Oh, Lady, Lady, I understand your weeping, but even through your tears, dear Lady, you must go on now. We're again within the core of the Mystery we explored to Patmos."

I choked my sobs. Ancient pain had resurged. Time — centuries — had not been able to alleviate it, the pain I had carried without surcease through all my life, through all my lives. The blame! All would be vindicated soon! I clung to that certainty.

Pushing against the raging wind and the searing dust, Judas and I followed along the road out of the City.

Still night!

"I have to be with him, to help him!" Judas cried. But each time he advanced, soldiers thrust him back. As the road turned to dirt and ascended toward the barren mountain of Calvary, waves of shifting dust and the mob encircling him blocked Jesus from our vision.

Then Mary was there. She reached urgently for my hand as I marched on. "Is it true, Magdalene?" she gasped.

John, the young disciple, had rushed weeping to tell her what was occurring and had accompanied her here. Then he fled.

Mary's words affirmed what I now knew entirely: She, too, had been certain it would not proceed into pain and torture. "They've sentenced him to —" I couldn't finish.

Pain etched her face. She wrapped her blue shawl about herself, holding it tightly against the wind's insistent grasp. She raised her head. "God shall save him!"

The procession wound into our full view at a twist in the road. Wind had whipped the dust away. Men with torches lighted the ascent. Mary gasped. She saw her son bound, stripped; and — I realized this only now — he was being forced to carry a heavy wooden cross, his own, to Calvary. His strong body staggered under it, his muscles straining to keep him erect.

Madame Bernice's sigh echoed from the present into my thoughts of Golgotha. "The vile cruelty of it," she said. "To torture a human being like that." She made a silent sign of the cross. Within her château candles lighted earlier were fading.

Following Madame's reverential gesture, I made a sign of the cross of my own, but I withheld the words that revered "the Father." I said, "In the name of the Son, and of the Holy Ghost," and, realizing with a jolt that this sign of remembrance did not honor Mary, I added: "And in the name of the Blessed Mother."

"Oh, yes, she!" Madame crossed herself again, altering her words into mine: "And in the name of the Blessed Mother."

With a strength belied by her fragile body, Mary pushed at the mob surrounding Jesus. Or — was it possible? — even they cringed before her awesome presence.

"My son!" she screamed, embracing him.

Jesus turned. "Mother —"

Mary struggled to support the cross. "I'll help you, my beloved son."

"No, Mother —"

"It is *our* burden." Even when she fell to her knees, she reached up with her hands to lessen the weight on her son's shoulders.

A soldier eased her away — gently, yes, responding to her wondrous presence. Mary said: "God will intercede!" She had intended to say that to her son in reassurance, I knew, but at the last moment she had flung the words at Heaven.

I did not realize until I saw him with us now that Judas and I had been separated during his attempts to reach Jesus.

Mary held his hands.

"Blessed Mother," he said. He kissed her fingers, and I loved him even more for his reverence to Mary.

325

She touched him. "You're trembling. Why? Don't be afraid." Her own voice trembled. *"Jesus will be saved."*

"Yes." Judas's single word was no more than a breath. He walked away. I reached my hand out to him. "Judas, wait —" He did not turn back. I followed him with my eyes as he moved farther away from us. When veils of dust parted, I saw him standing by the tree he had once pointed out to me, where he and Jesus had sat, alone, for treasured moments. Now dark wind obscured him.

Within spirals of dust, a man and a woman crouched with a crown of thorns toward Jesus. They pushed it onto his forehead, while others laughed and a band of young men and women scratched at his flesh like predatory birds. A centurion placed a mockery of a scepter in his hand. Jesus looked at it, startled. No longer able to reject this relentless reality? Or was it possible that he still hoped?

Grief swept over Mary's face. Drops of Jesus' blood had marked the ground where we stood. She bent to blot them with her blue shawl. She stifled a sob with firm words: "God *will* save him, Magdalene." She held my hand tightly, ice on ice. I realized then how vulnerable she had always been, and how profound their love was, hers and Jesus', love that had allowed the blind trust that had shaped the deadly procession to this mountain.

Dawn was beginning! It had finally managed to push away the terrifying night, yes; and the wind, which abated, was now clearing the sky, cleansing it of dust.

I looked back, toward the City. Now — this terrible violence exposed — the people would protest this secret sentence, would rush into the streets. But I saw squads of soldiers preparing to keep them away, gathering in a rim about the mountain, assuring that only the violent crowd that had appeared from the beginning, in Gethsemane, would rule to the very end.

We were on Calvary, on Golgotha. Nothing grew there, nothing had ever grown there. Gnarled rocks were scarred into the shapes of skulls, eyes hollow and black.

Soldiers yanked the cross away from Jesus and placed it on the craggy ground. Jesus' body collapsed. He tried to lift himself, failed. He looked . . . terrified. No, disbelieving — no, understanding — no, not yet understanding — Terrified.

"Save him!" Mary screamed into the sky. "End it now!"

I prayed — yes, prayed — that Mary and Jesus would be vindicated, even as I saw his body trembling. His perspiration moistened the seared earth. He attempted to raise his head. He gasped with pain.

And still, God was silent!

Then with astonishing strength, Jesus stood.

The soldiers reeled back from his power. One extended a cup of wine with myrrh: "It'll lessen the pain."

Jesus thrust it away with his fist.

Even those who had come into the City to assure this atrocity pulled back from him, grew silent, spellbound. The magnificently uncaring sky — I saw that the night had abandoned one single star within dawn — even that uncaring sky, through which the rebellious angels had once soared beyond God's wishes, even it allowed three glorious shafts of intersecting light to spill on Calvary.

Within that astonishing light — which extended to create an azure halo about Mary — Jesus stood triumphant.

Nothing moved, not even time.

Tearing his gaze away — and even that moment seemed to resist — a priest broke the spell. "Proceed!" he ordered.

Soldiers grabbed Jesus and laid him on the prone cross. Beyond, I saw Judas thrust a rope over the heaviest branch of the tree where he stood. I heard the pounding of nails. They were being hammered into Jesus' hands, his feet. Judas, naked like Jesus, stood on a stone and allowed the noose he had shaped to fall over his neck.

Judas, my beloved.

Jesus, my beloved!

I saw the cross raised with Jesus' body nailed to it. Under it, the soil was drenched with blood.

Mary screamed back at me, "Magdalene! It is not happening. God promised!" When had she managed to break through the barricade of guards? She stood before her son.

The strength Jesus had regained earlier had grown. Even nailed to the cross, he was powerful and beautiful. The end of hope had resurrected all his strength, now that he no longer expected he would be saved from this unraveling torture — oh, how keenly I *felt* that realization with him. He stared enraged and defiant up at Heaven and he said:

"Your terrible will is done!"

Mary's pain darkened into rage. She stood, rigid, and screamed at Heaven: "It was *all* betrayal and lies and deception!"

Jesus looked down at her, with love.

Judas stepped away from the stone. The rope tautened about his neck.

The naked bodies of Jesus and Judas turned toward each other and died.

I closed my eyes. I imagined them as they had been that first day by the River Jordan. Then I saw them again as I had watched them together at dusk while I sat on the slope of a hill covered with jonquils and joshua trees.

I heard Mary's words: "It was all planned to deceive, from the beginning." Her head rose wearily. Then, just as her son had done, she gained strength in those tortured moments. She stood proudly, encased in a glaze of azure light the sky allowed to bathe her and her son. That, I knew, was how I would finally remember her.

The wind, kept in abeyance by the rising sun, resurged, swept terrifying clouds across the sky.

In me, an ancient memory stirred . . . of another storm, of a beautiful garden destroyed . . .

I saw blood under me. I was bleeding . . . between my legs . . . where God had struck me painfully beyond Eden.

Within whorls of the storm that again controlled the sky, I heard whispered words I would remember only centuries later in the garden of Madame Bernice, words aimed at me — no, not at me, at someone else I had become for those moments, on that most cruel day on Calvary:

"All this because of your sin, the first disobedience of My will, the original sin — yours! You are to blame, Eve! For all of it! From the beginning of time! You, Mother of Mankind! You, Mother of All Abominations! You, *whore!*"

XXXI

"THE ANSWER TO THE QUESTION we've long pondered has fallen into our hands like a ripe plum," Madame Bernice declared. "Your essence chose Magdalene so she would witness — and so finally tell — the truth of Calvary, the horror God designed to add unspeakable blame to Eve — to you, dear Lady. Whose testament more reliable than Magdalene's? — herself called 'whore' though not blamed — and I don't know how *she* escaped *that*." She directed her last words at Ermenegildo, who shook his head in added puzzlement. "What more evidence do we need of God's intended connections to form a chain of blame than His own renewed denunciation of Eve?" Madame's words barely contained their rage as she repeated the accusation still ringing from Calvary: " 'All this because of your sin . . . You're to blame, Eve! . . . You, Mother of Mankind! You, Mother of All Abominations! You —' " She stopped.

I supplied the last word: "— *whore!*"

I now grasped fully the dizzying moments on Calvary when I heard the whispering Voice that branded me *whore,* and I was Magdalene and Eve, and my rebelling essence soared back to the lost garden, forward to Babylon and Patmos, and it surged ahead on its journey to establish the continuity of guiltless blame to be finally exposed and redeemed at interviews.

Light from candles within Madame's château flickered, about to die, surrendering even vague shadows to encroaching darkness. Very few stars glinted on the black horizon. Even distant fires of the wanderers had been snuffed for the night. Madame reached absently for a stale pastry. She withdrew her hand and sighed with the weight of our discoveries.

But this long, long tea would not end yet. We must continue, as if to honor with our own endurance the eternally long journey along the skull-shaped rocks of Golgotha.

"Oh, the *gall* of it!" Madame pounded the table with her bejeweled fist. "He allowed the 'son' He so grandly claimed to love — and who was really *your* son, Lady, yours and Adam's — allowed him to be cursed, tortured, crucified —"

"— and sent the strange night people to assure it all on that hot windy night," I said what I must have known that very night.

"— and yet what did He claim! That all the brutality was necessary to save mankind because of *your* 'original sin'! That's what He intended with the Crucifixion all right — and *damned* be all the innocent others who would be destroyed through the ages by His pursuit of Eve! Imagine, Lady! He would have gotten away with it — and has for very long — if your essence had not been there in Magdalene to witness the truth you'll soon reveal."

I calmed my sorrow by remembering the moment of glory when even the uninvolved sky acknowledged Jesus' triumphant courage after false hope had died; remembered the dazzling shafts of intersecting rays of light that had graced him at their point of intersection and extended an aura to create a blue halo about Mary. Had a ray of that light touched Judas, too?

"Oh, *I* knew all along that the Holy Mother would be revealed as an unjustly used woman herself," Madame affirmed. She whispered to Ermenegildo at her side: "I had a few uncomfortable moments about that along the way, though." She said wistfully, "The beautiful blue lady . . . quite possibly a frightened, vulnerable young woman, a victim of barbaric times — and He cunningly chose *her,* and sent a lying angel to —"

I remembered Cassandra's description of Gabriel's gentle, sad eyes when he realized the rebellious angels would never again soar beyond the restricted boundaries of Heaven. "God lied to the Angel Gabriel, Madame," I said with certainty.

"Of course!" Madame understood. "In that way the trusting angel would be convincing when he assured the Holy Mother that she was 'pure,' a declaration she was eager to grasp, especially since it was accompanied by the heady promise that her son was chosen as Savior." She added with deep sorrow in a quiet voice: "When the gentle blue lady referred to you as a prostitute and you felt separated from her — that was part of God's plan, Lady. You understand that now, don't you?"

330

I did, and I loved Mary more than ever.

"By convincing Mary that she herself had been immaculately conceived," Madame extended her careful phrasing, "she would become the only woman untouched by Eve's 'original sin,' the only woman who was not Eve's daughter. Lady, it's so clear. He intended to sever allegiances, separate the Holy Mother from all blamed women. Why? In order to make her an unwitting ally in His conspiracy aimed at adding —"

"— judgment on Eve," I finished.

The garden mourned and turned so dark that not even silhouettes survived.

"But he didn't succeed in separating you, Lady!" Madame said triumphantly. "The Holy Mother saw the deception at the last, and you and she were there, together, close."

"Yes!" I welcomed the rediscovered conciliation between myself and the Blessed Mother.

The solemnity that had befallen the garden lifted. A gentle breeze whispered among the flowers. Weariness was a pool in which I only managed to swim. I leaned back and closed my eyes.

"Yes, rest, Lady. Yours has been a long journey." Madame's voice was so quiet I thought she was speaking in my dreams.

I dreamt —

I dreamt that the woman who screams in my recurring dreams finally spoke. She said:

Redeem me!

I echoed her words aloud: "Redeem me." Oh, I was still dreaming. It was she, that forlorn creature in my dreams, who had repeated her own exhortation, silently. I only thought I had spoken her words. I realized that now, when I was truly awake, facing Madame on her veranda.

"Did you speak, Lady?"

Then I *had* spoken the words aloud. "I thought that I was dreaming; that *she* had spoken in my dreams."

"The unknown forlorn woman?"

"Yes."

"Lady —"

"Madame?"

"Is there . . . just perhaps, *only* perhaps . . . one more life we didn't rehearse? Another blamed woman, oh, so very unfairly blamed."

"No, no!"

"Not one more life pleading to be redeemed? Not one more?"

"Oh, she — the forlorn woman? She exists only in my dreams."

"Ah! Still, in redeeming the others, shall *she* be redeemed?"

"I believe that, then, yes, her screams will end in peace at last." I closed my eyes, to test my words. "I believe I hear them . . . fading."

"Because *she* is not to blame."

"No, she is not to blame."

"I suppose that the mysteries of great events are much more easily solved than the secrets of a single violated heart."

"Madame, you whispered —"

"I was musing to myself, Lady, wondering whether we should leave in ambiguity what the heart can't solve."

"Yes."

"I understand, dear Lady. Yes, I understand, and I would say you're entirely ready for whatever interviewers may ask."

So puzzling, when things are not what they seem. Now that I was surely awake, I thought my dream had extended until now, that I had dreamt, earlier, that I had wakened, but had awakened only now — and into a greater lucidity within the subdued light: The dim gleam of candles veiled Madame in such a way that she glowed within the darkness, a luminescent silhouette.

I saw, in that mist of bluish light, another face: that of a pretty young woman with a wry smile, and — a candle glimmered, creating a delicate further radiance as it prepared to fade entirely — I saw that she was draped in an elegant cape, azure! It was the same impression, somewhat, but now even clearer — yes, that dusky perception contained its own sharp clarity — that I had had, on that very first day when I met Madame, when she had watched me from the slight incline that spills from her château as I sat weeping on an elaborate bench at the periphery of her lawn! I smiled at this new impression, this new yet not unfamiliar presence, and she smiled back.

And when she did, it was again the beloved, handsome visage of Madame Bernice, the woman I have come to trust and love. Still, the earlier impression lingered like a hidden presence. "Madame, are you Cassandra?" The words lost their strangeness the moment I spoke them.

"Grown a few pounds heavier through the centuries?" She laughed.

"Madame, I know so little about you except —"

"— that I'm your neighbor, living in the mansion down the road from yours," she said.

"Yes." I remembered this with gratitude: "That day when I was so full of despair —"

"— I appeared," she said simply.

Waiting for me? I longed to ask. Waiting for centuries and nurturing my essence? Determined to thwart the extension of the design of unjust blame? — unsuccessful until now, very soon, when, during interviews, the truth will finally be told. "Who are you *really*, Madame? *Are* you Cassandra?"

Ermenegildo cocked his head at her.

"Ah!" Madame made an undecided movement — she touched her chin, with one finger, and — what significance should I attach to this? — it was only that one finger that did not have a jewel on it. "Why, Lady, of course —" Her smile spread, capturing the only radiance left from the last of the waning candles. She leaned closer to me. "Why, Lady, of course! Of course, you know who I really am. I'm your *friend,* what else?" She spoke so softly I heard a breeze over her words. "And," she added, "I'm your fellow conspirator —"

Ermenegildo raised his head proudly.

"— I *and* Ermenegildo are your fellow conspirators in uncovering buried truths," she revised, and touched my hand.

The moment possessed such a unique wistfulness that I had to restrain tears.

Now the weariness we had managed to stave off had finally conquered us. That weariness and the approach of dawn accounted for all the strange hallucinated moments of impression, I was now certain. I saw Ermenegildo trying to disguise the fact that he had nodded in a doze; he jerked himself back into stiff alertness, only to nod off again for an instant or two. Gathering him against her, Madame ended our longest tea: "We must leave the rest for tomorrow."

With that, I made my way back to my château.

Dawn tinted the horizon. The wandering figures hidden by the night were locating sheltering shadows.

I reared back!

One of the wanderers was rushing at me. He halted only inches before me. Behind him, others gathered — three, four — a woman, a child? Others! More! Ten — They all faced me, their shabby carts cluttered with ragged possessions. All were in tatters, their faces gaunt with hunger and grief and pleading. And anger! Yes, defiant anger, seething — I easily detected that, defiance.

I said aloud to them: "I am not to blame."

And they moved away into the twilight, their carts rattling behind them.

In my chambers now, I yearn for sleep, but time narrows, and so I shall rehearse with you today's revelations. They are already yesterday's . . .

There.

I have managed to tell you all that we discovered —

And it's blasphemous!

What!

Bringing God in like that! And Jesus! And Judas! Turning everything impure, unholy — and even — even —

Your repeated accusation resounds in my quarters. I hear you, yes, you, the same who tries so eagerly to enlist others. I note their silence. They shall hear my rebuttal when you terminate your sputtering reproach.

— and even introducing sexuality where there wasn't any, couldn't have been any, mustn't be any!

Must!

Not!

Be!

Any!

Your extended stutter speaks for itself. I thank those of you who still await my answer, and I shall give it now: I have told the truth. I was there. What is impure here, cruel — unholy? Answer that by answering this: What was the greatest barbarity at Calvary? The slow torture and betrayal of Jesus! And who was finally blamed? Eve — for introducing sin into the world! And ponder this: What was the charge brought against Jesus to assure his murder?

The charge was blasphemy.

I accept your silence.

I wander to my journal and enter an earlier thought into my *Pensées:* "So puzzling, when things are not what they seem!" I add this: "The world is all sadness, and death is the universal painkiller."

I reach for the gun I keep near me always, in case of danger. I study it. It's as if I'm seeing it for the first time, this odd iron cylinder out of which a bullet may be sent hurtling by the touch of a finger — my finger — on this slightly curved protrusion, this trigger, which I feel. My finger warms its initial coldness as it slides on the smooth surface. I hold the weapon to my ear, to discover whether I can hear . . . its sounds. It's dormant now, this object that can erupt in one second.

In one second.

One second.

I replace the gun on the table.

Night came and went!

Soon I shall be on my way to Madame's château to continue our quest through my centuries-long odyssey, about to end.

I wait. I wait. How slowly "soon" arrives!

Before I left for tea with Madame Bernice, I entered that into my *Pensées:* "How slowly 'soon' arrives!"

A few minutes earlier than usual, I was walking up the marble steps to Madame's veranda.

She was eager to resume — and so apparently was Ermenegildo, who had strolled down the road early to greet me. Madame quickly poured our tea, the most savory brew yet. She had dressed resplendently for today's revelations. Her full skirt, silk, had a sheen that turned gray into silver. She wore a new pendant, a pearl touched with purple, and a gold tiara flecked with gems I could not yet identify. Noticing that I was admiring her appearance, she waited before beginning.

"Madame! You look ravishing!"

"Thank you, Lady."

If I did not know her better, I would be tempted to say she primped. She smoothed the folds of her skirt to display even more silver highlights. Ermenegildo carefully straightened a fold that had eluded her. Now Madame took a piece of shortbread and dabbed it with bramble jelly, a delicacy she had presented with no introduction other than a hugely satisfied smile, which waited for my comment.

"Delicious," I complimented.

"Yes, isn't it? Now! We must move on. First we must deal with the last entry in that vile 'Account.' " She reached for the pages I had already placed at the center of the table, under the vase, which today hosted a cluster of red-dabbed white carnations. Madame's fingers prepared to leaf through the pages. "May I?"

"Yes." But I wasn't sure I wanted to learn how this "Final Installment" ended.

Madame's eyes raked each page. "The usual malicious accusations." As she neared the last page, she read intently, until the end.

She held out those sheets for me to read. I did. Then she showed the pages to Ermenegildo. He looked up at me, to gauge my reaction.

Madame and I spoke, words, just words.

I said to Madame —

Madame said —

Oh, the matter was too numbing to discuss further.

I pushed the pages of the "Account" away. I would consider their meaning later.

Madame set the vase firmly on the pages, indicating she would honor my decision to discuss them no further than we had. Then, like a grand detective with a bejeweled tiara, she announced: "Now on to God's motivations. Why really did God despise Eve?"

Ermenegildo was particularly attentive, even ignoring a magnificent blue butterfly that was floating about us.

"And He did despise Eve — you," Madame extended, "from the very first moment you sprang —"

"— to life — out of Adam's longing . . . And I stood on a bed of orchids, near the flower so glorious it did not need the decoration of leaves." I spoke that warming memory.

"Out of Adam's longing you sprang," Madame echoed my words slowly. She leaned over and repeated them to Ermenegildo: "Out of Adam's longing —"

Did Ermenegildo peck her dazzling earring gently, or did he whisper into her ear?

Madame sat up. "That's it! Oh, Lady, how could it have evaded us?" She was wildly excited. "God intended no such longing in Adam. It came from the spurt of life that had spun into the Garden in the very beginning and on which Adam woke. When Adam located the yearning in his heart — and it was a longing for completion, Lady —"

"— God thought the yearning was in his rib —" I fully trusted that Madame's recapitulation was leading to a startling revelation.

"— and He plucked it out, to *end* Adam's longing. Lady, Lady, Lady!" Madame's jubilant words tumbled out exultantly: "God's wrath at you was aroused because *He* had not counted on you." She surged on: "His wrath increased when He tantalized you with the forbidden berries He connived to use to separate you from Adam. When you ate them — oh, Lady, Lady — it was *you*, Lady — you, Eve! — *who first expressed free will!*"

I was yanked powerfully — almost violently — by a sudden perception of something known but not known, something always there and visible but seen only now, revealed now, something found beyond the known, the unknown finally known.

Madame added proudly: "And *that* was the 'abomination' He could not forgive, the assertion of free will. So He called it the original sin, the sin He loudly claimed brought about the fall of all mankind because you ate the forbidden berries."

Ermenegildo shook his head in renewed amazement at such mysterious ways.

"Now God was sure that Adam would not risk being accursed — that he would separate himself from you. God even offered him a servile creature to replace you, but —" Madame waited for me to finish.

I did, victoriously: "But my beloved Adam chose me!"

"— and so he asserted both his love and *his* own free will!"

Oh, I longed to share again with him the delectable berries that Adam's tongue had tasted in my mouth.

"God *never* granted *any*one free will — not the angels, not Adam, and certainly not you," Madame extended her discoveries.

"Yet He claimed that *He* donated it."

"*After* the fact. What else could He do?"

Why in this heady moment on the veranda showered by brilliant sunlight were my eyes drawn to the powerful odd new lilies along the ledges of the garden, those flowers that evoked, yet distorted with their rancid beauty, the special leafless ones in Eden? I turned away from their overwhelming scent. My aversion seemed to cause the drench of perfume to evaporate. Of course, it was only a warm breeze easing past palm fronds that had smothered the aggressive scent.

Madame's voice was hushed: "Ah, but, Lady — for all the horrors we'll soon expose — think of this and assert it during interviews: Adam, your beloved, chose *you* and your defiance instead of accepting God's offer of paradise and a servile creature. Dear Lady, what a miraculous love, yours and his. A love story never before acknowledged."

I whisper to my memories: Adam, my beloved, soon, at interviews, the whole world shall know our great love story, and that we are always together, Adam and Eve, Eve and Adam.

Ermenegildo's gaze alerted us to the direction of agitated sounds.

Madame fixed her opera glasses on the château of the new tenant. "There's hectic activity. More people about the mansion. Lady, I believe they know we've neared our goal. So we must hurry preparations for formal interviews."

"I will be ready, Madame," I said with certainty.

"Are you *sure*? You really want to proceed with this?" Her eyes were on me, steadfast; I might even say, relentless.

No, I did not mind her startling words. "Madame," I said, "throughout all our teas, from the moment we met and you explained my essence to me, I've grown strong, as strong as my memories, as strong as my determination to speak at last . . . Oh, yes, Madame, I'm *sure* I shall be ready when interviews begin."

Madame seemed to speak to herself, quietly: "And you shall convince everyone — because — because — because —"

Madame seldom hesitates to speak her mind. Why now? "Because, Madame?"

"Because you have convinced *me*."

"*What!*"

"I finally do believe you. You've convinced me that you *are* telling the truth."

How could I give words to my disorientation? I found only these: "You weren't sure?" Should I feel victorious or despondent? I stood up, ready to run away, to —

She held my hand, easing me back down.

"Oh, Madame, Madame, again you were being an interviewer. Weren't you? Weren't you?" I wasn't begging. I laughed away this distressing moment. "I see, of course. I understand! Even now, you're preparing me for interviews, aren't you, Madame? Aren't you? You were playing *converted* interviewer!"

"Converted, yes — the most resistant one." Madame retained her serious tone: "I have no doubt now that you're the bearer of the essence of all women unjustly blamed for great catastrophes — and that you *will* redeem them."

How well she played her roles! How solemn she looked in her "confession," as if, yes, as if truly I had only now convinced her of my truth. I acknowledged all that with a smile, just a smile.

I must not linger, I must return immediately to my château, to rehearse the very last details. Madame agreed. I grasped the installments of the vilifying "Account" and hurried along the road.

I approached my gates cautiously. A leaf there . . . ? Just a leaf. Nothing else? I looked around. No, nothing! Was *that* a further message?

When I rushed into my quarters, I realized how short today's tea had been; sun spattered into my quarters. I shall not miss my lavish surroundings when I surrender my wealth to the poor. I shall always carry beauty with me.

I enter this hurriedly into my *Pensées:* "The power to convert the drab and the ugly into beauty, to transform the ordinary into the extraordinary — only magicians, dreamers, and the insane possess it."

I shall rush to rehearse with you what occurred just minutes earlier before I left Madame's garden, before the urgent activity at the château of the new tenant intruded.

Read us what you so carefully avoided telling about earlier, what's contained in the last pages of the "Final Installment."

Oh, but I shall!

And so the noble Count du Muir is dead, murdered at the very altar of the Grand Cathedral by the vile Whore, who fled into hiding *but shall be located* (as sure as God is powerful). Now the upright Twin Brother of the Count du Muir is murdered, too, by his very Mother, the Contessa. The Renegade Nun has been hastened to her reward (if any). And the dissolute Contessa is dead, by her own hand. All silenced in this giant trap set by the Whore.

Still, there is hope that out of all this depravity, now that the Whore's villainy has been exposed in these pages *(but not fully, there is more that the Writer promised to reveal but veered away from at the last, overwhelmed by horror; abominations that evolving circumstances may yet expose).* As sure as God is powerful, the Whore shall not be rewarded in any way, including by an unjust inheritance.

Surely the Count's beneficent Sister is clearly the only rightful heir to both the spiritual and actual wealth accrued by this great dynasty. Surely — *there is no doubt of this, none whatever* — the honorable Sister shall turn for divine guidance to the Mighty Lord's representative on earth, the Holiest of Prelates, the Pope. Upon her death, which all good people pray will be long, long, long delayed (but who can predict life's sudden ambushes?), her inherited beneficence shall shower the Holy Defender of the Grand Cathedral.

"Irena's next," Madame had interjected when we reached that point. "The Pope has been pulling all the strings from the beginning, allowing her to think she's in control. But she's cunning, and may yet get him first."

Now the Writer as recorder of these nefarious deeds tires exceedingly, having dutifully and honorably produced this *True Account* of baseness. Having done so, he ends like this:

What punishment befits the vile Whore who set into motion

all this corruption by attempting to change the course of Destiny on its intended righteous path? Only God shall determine that punishment, and He will. And if the Whore should dare attempt to claim —

The "Account" ends there. Abruptly. Unfinished —?

It was then that I pushed the contaminated sheets away and Madame honored my intention.

Jagged pieces of the sun flash into my quarters.

Reflections from Madame's château! I look outside. When did dusk fall?

I see Madame at her window. I read her signal for urgent attention. I adjust the panes of my window, preparing to respond — I shall augment reflections with a mirror. I signal her that we are in touch.

She begins to spell words:

L —*!*
E —*!*
A —*!*
V —*!*
E —*!*
LEAVE!

Another word begins:

M —*! I* —*?*
S —*!*
I —*!*
O —*!*
N —*!*

LEAVE MISSION? — in her urgency she missed a letter. Abandon our mission? Abandon interviews?

Never! I flash anxiously that she must repeat the second word. She does.

M —*!*

A —*!* . . . Not an "I" — I missed the downward slope. No, that belongs to another letter. No, it begins another —

N —*!*
S —*!*
I —*!*
O —*!*
N —*!*

LEAVE MANSION!

Letters follow rapidly:

340

N —!
O —!
W —!
LEAVE MANSION NOW!
Reflections stop!
Did Madame have to run out?
Shall I rush out?

Furtive motions outside the gates of my château stop me. Figures rushing onto my grounds? I must retreat from sight. I hide quickly beside the drapes.

I must consider everything. When I left, Madame was preparing to arrange formal interviews, to give my presentation the needed order we have discussed. This signal might be a ruse to bring me out of my château before those preparations are completed. Has Madame detected an attempt to throw interviews into disruption? Has our code been discovered by hostile elements? — the message not from Madame Bernice at all?

We never devised a sign that would convey that it was truly we who were communicating! Surely there's a way to verify — Surely — Mansion!

The message is unquestionably from Madame Bernice. No one else calls a château a mansion.

Who is that figure rushing across my lawn? It's Madame! No — I can't be sure from here, and I must remain hidden until I know what is occurring.

An altercation at the entrance to my château!
Doors closing forcefully!
Footsteps!
Closer now!

A scuffle at my door? No. A branch just brushed my window. I shall rehearse — I cannot think — I cannot think — More footsteps! It's only the servants, having heard me pacing in my chambers.

A familiar voice — Madame's? Yes. But another's, so familiar! Another woman . . . And a man's voice, too, heard where, when —? Other voices! The servants —?

I am not to blame!

I must remain calm. I shall assure that like this: I shall remember the victorious moment that occurred just before Madame and I parted earlier and she said:

"Our case is made: God is guilty, Eve is not to blame."

We were standing on the veranda. Beside her, Ermenegildo shared our triumph, his head thrust back exactly like Madame's. I noticed that a new feather, with a slight twist, was growing on his comb.

A struggle outside my quarters, someone pushing against the door!

This thought assaults me: After Madame announced our victory earlier, I gasped out a question she must have been asking herself because she, too, had become somber:

"Madame, who will protect us from God, now that we're about to begin interviews that find Him guilty? What will He attempt?"

What will He attempt? What will He attempt? In my quarters, that question persists with even greater urgency as the altercation outside my door grows, and —

XXXII

"Lady!"

"Madame!"

"Lady, let me in and lock the door behind me. Too late. They're in. Give me the key!"

"Madame, who is this woman who pushed her way into my quarters — and this man with her — and those others making so much noise outside? Lock the door!"

"I have!"

"Madame, have interviews begun?"

"They may have to, very soon."

"Without formal preparations —?"

"Our intentions were discovered before I could make arrangements. I tried to signal you."

"You were asking me to leave —"

"To gain more time for our presentation."

"No final rehearsal?"

"Only what we can squeeze in now."

"The terrible Inquisitor, the spy — Outside?"

"Yes, among the interviewers. They followed these two."

"Why are this woman and man studying me like that? . . . How dare you push past Madame Bernice and invade my quarters? Who are you?"

"You know who I am, I'm your sister in —"

"— my sister-in-law — Irena!"

"— your *sister*, in*censed* by all the scandal and —"

"Madame, Irena's pretending to be my sister. Why? To assert some familial power over me?"

"We'll soon find out why, Lady. Let her spill her venom."

"Call me whatever you want, sister, deny we're your family, you've done it before. Just stop this madness, if only for the sake of our father — and you'd better know I'm here on his behalf. He agreed I'm the best to set things right with you."

"What a clever ploy, Lady. How cunning, to send a woman to collaborate against us."

"You, sir, behind those terrifying glasses that magnify your eyes, who are you? The new tenant down the road?"

"I am the senior representative of the most prominent and proud dynasty that you . . . uh, miss . . . uh, Mrs. . . . uh, Lady . . . ma'am . . . have been defaming — especially, with unmitigated malice, the Father. I'm here to advise you that we're aware of the slanders you've been uttering. We know that you intend to add unspeakable imputations."

"Threats to keep me silent! You hear, Madame?"

"I do indeed, Lady."

"In other words, sister, he's here to *order* you to stop the gross distortions concocted by you and this soothsayer, this Madam —"

"*Madame* Bernice. Her name is pronounced in the grand style. She's a unique mystic, in the tradition of Cassandra. She may even be —"

"Whoever she is, this . . . Cassandra . . . has been interfering with our reaching you, dear sister."

"Sister-in-*law!* I refuse any other connection, Irena, and the one I assert is one I would reject, if I could, but you're the sister of my beloved Count."

"*Half*-sister, Lady, remember the tulips — shhh. That's information they wanted to draw out of you in that 'Account.' "

"What is that man writing down, Madame?"

"Every lie you utter, ma'am. For the record."

"I shall speak only the truth, sir. I am the es —"

"Don't start yet, Lady. We need to adjust to this sudden development."

"Madame, I've seen this man before —"

"Keep this to yourself, Lady; he might be the Pope, assuming another identity."

"You, behind your glasses. I *do* recognize you from another time. But you were wearing —"

"— a gray dress and a hat with a partridge feather, Lady? — as he did when he was spying on you from a window?"

344

"I have never worn a dress in my life. I have not even considered it."

"Look sir! . . . Aha, I caught him, Lady. Did you see him look down as if to locate reflections of pink little buttocks?"

"I looked down in *shame* at your foul suggestions."

"He may not be the Pope, Lady, but he certainly has knowledge of the unique predilections of *someone* close to him, a *very close* representative."

"I shall ignore your reckless insults, ladies."

"If this man is not the Pope, Madame, might he be —?"

"Yes, Lady, very possibly."

"Stop trying to divert us from our purpose, Bernice . . . Sister, we're here to squelch your lies about our great family, lies that have only one purpose — to shift the blame for everything from you to Father. You know who's to blame for all the horrors in our family. *You* are, sister, for *all* of it —"

"You hear that, Madame? Blame!"

"Only too clearly, Lady."

"Let's get to the point. Can it be possible, sister, that what we've been hearing is true, that you, my dear sister, are actually claiming to be —"

"Creature, know this — the Lady *is* all she claims. I explained it to her."

"I'm sure you did, Bernice . . . Sister, did you ever ask yourself why this woman is so involved with your life?"

"Because, like me, Madame's committed to the truth. And to righting the injustice of centuries."

"And because, creature, I *understood* her immediately."

"You never questioned, sister, why she's *really* preparing you for . . . interviews? . . . When did you start plotting all this, Bernice? — when you read those salacious stories about her? . . . Sister, listen! This woman is exploiting you. She'll benefit from all the notoriety."

"Oh, Lady, even beyond your vivid descriptions of this creature's evil, she surpasses everything! — attempting to wedge between you and me, our special friendship —"

"No one could do that, Madame! . . . Irena, know this: Madame and I are allies in truth. You'll never separate us. She's been kind to me, cared for me, given me courage to continue, helped me through the time of terrible dreams —"

"— which were not dreams but memories, true memories. Keep that in mind, Lady."

"Not only did we go through hell to find you, sister, but on top of it all, we have to face this soothsayer —"

"I am a unique mystic, *and* a countess."

"— a crazy, fat old woman with a cloudy past, Bernice."

"Irena, how dare you accuse Madame —"

"Lady, whatever else the creature intends, this much is clear — she wants to unsettle you. Ignore all they say."

"No, she will *not* ignore us, *Meh*-dam. Please, sir, tell them what we intend —"

"I shall. If your rash accusations, continue, ma'am . . . uh, Lady — ah-*choo!* — *ahchoo!* Did you know . . . uh, Madam . . . uh, Madame . . . that that bird of yours shook his feathers at me when I passed him, and I'm allergic?"

"He knew you were allergic, sir — to truth!"

"I'll talk to my sister while you recover from your allergy, sir . . . Do you have any idea how painful it is, to discover you here in this — this — terrifying place?"

"The Count's château? My château? A terrifying place?"

"She's giving herself airs, Lady, implying *hers* is so much grander. Insecure people do that. They've envied my mansion."

"Mansion!"

"Is yours grander, creature? I doubt it."

"You really pick them, don't you, sister? A tawdry fortune-teller with an odd bird —"

"An odd bird? My Ermenegildo? Creature, utter one more word about Ermenegildo, and I shall —"

"Don't come closer, Bernice."

"I won't because I don't want to contaminate myself. But one more word of slander against my beautiful Ermenegildo, and —"

"Uh, ma'am . . . uh, Lady, aren't you afraid of those derelicts roaming everywhere outside?"

"Restive wanderers, sir, displaced by the turmoil in the cities. Why should they harm me? They're kind enough to accept me as an exile. Like them. Despite my background of wealth."

"I'm glad to hear you admit at least that, sister — and now here you are in this . . . this . . . place. No wonder we couldn't find you. You led us on a mad hunt through every ugly street and alley. We even had to hire someone to locate you —"

"I was aware of at least one spy in the corridor, another in —"

"Dear sister, you've ignored our communications. Even from Father, bless him, who prefers to let people write for him . . . I wish

346

they'd stop that clamoring outside. Those so-called interviewers have been hounding our whole family constantly, dredging up all those rumors. We've denied everything, of course. Haven't *you* had enough of their dirt, sister? — those hateful printed installments that mock our family?"

"Are you going to pretend it wasn't you who dictated the vicious 'Account,' Irena? — you *and* the Pope, and Alix until you were through with *him*. Madame and I saw through your attempt to corrupt my loyalties, my love —"

"— and to frighten and threaten you, Lady — remember that — taunting you into correcting their smears — and so give information that the creature wanted for her own purposes."

"Surely you don't mean to link us to those vile stories, Bernice."

"Oh, Lady, Lady, she's just confirmed what I've often suspected. The writer they hired to record their lies — and did — interjected his *own* discoveries and conclusions here and there, beyond their intentions, information *we* can use; and that's why they're denying it all now."

"I won't sully myself by answering, Bernice."

"Sully yourself, Irena? You — the woman who coaxed Alix to kill his twin brother, my beloved — your brother."

"*Half*-brother, Lady. Remember the tulips. Shhh."

"You, Irena? — the woman who then murdered your co-conspirator and blamed your mother, then killed *her*, the noble Contessa, dragging her to the Cathedral so the Pope would lie for you? Oh, believe me, I shall tell of the dear Contessa's devotion to the passionate gypsy and of your long revenge."

"Sister, is nothing beyond you?"

"As the senior representative of the great family you well know of, including this noble and brilliant woman with me and especially the Patriarch of the great dynasty that you, ma'am, have so grossly maligned and which you belong to no matter how fervently you choose to deny it, I must inform you that unless you refrain from the course you've embarked upon, we are prepared to take the matter to the highest authorities, *for the very strongest action.* Now! I am in a position to propose conditions, Lady — ma'am: First, a period of medi —"

"— tation? I have been in meditation, in seclusion, except for afternoon teas with Madame. I have avoided contact with even my most loyal servants, who shall inherit my wealth, along with all the destitute wanderers."

"Underline *that* in your notes, sir! . . . Dear sister, your so-called egalitarian leanings, especially your maddening talk about leaving your inheritance to derelicts — whatever you think *that* inheritance will be — doubly upsets Father. You know how proud he is of his prominent conservatism — which I share —"

"Collaborator! The creature's a gross collaborator!"

"Are you crazy, too, Bernice?"

"Creature, how dare you call sanity madness and truth lies?"

"Sister, how can you expose us to this circus? How can you do this to Father, who loves us all?"

"Ha!"

"Isn't your father already dead, creature? — according to that 'Account' you commissioned — the parts that didn't run away from you — he died. Was that just another attempt to invite complacency against more villainy?"

"Father is not dead. My sister knows that better than anyone else. Even when people think he's dead, there he is, crafty as ever —"

"*Cruel* as ever, Irena!"

"Oh, Lady, look, the creature's about to try something *most* drastic — she wants us to believe she can cry."

"I'm crying, yes, because I'm wondering what brought you to this . . . my sister . . . you with all your education. Your father — and he is your father however much you may deny him — gave you everything —"

"Not my life! Not my freedom!"

"He was strict because he loved you so much —"

"— that he tortured everyone? Is that next, Irena?"

"You've always wanted to destroy the family name, sister — and this woman's been encouraging you for her own purposes."

"How quickly the creature's tears stopped!"

"From the very beginning, sister, you caused Father enormous grief with your disobedience, your rebellious willfulness, running away when you were only fifteen —"

"I was *banished* for wanting to live!"

"— by denying you were his daughter? Taking up with that lunatic rebel and his strange sister, who taunted our father — and only God knows how involved they were with each other — who claimed they could fly —"

"They did fly, beyond the boundaries of Heaven!"

"Lady, tell that only during interviews."

"— and they introduced you to that man — that . . . dreamer, the

348

man you claimed brought you to life out of the narcotic haze your sad existence had become, sister — that dreamer longing for some impossible paradise, to the point that you talked each other into suicide, to seal your love, you said — and he died and you survived, and it was all your fault!"

"We were *driven* to the edge — by despair and banishment and blame and threats that would have extended even to our children!"

"Not yet, Lady! We have to know exactly what the creature is up to."

"— and then you were taken over by that drugged pimp, sister, that sacrilegious preacher, that so-called reverend, the madman who sold your body in alleys."

"He *was* mad — *and* brutal, Irena, mad with the pain of existence!"

"You, dear sister, a member of one of the great families — he sold you on the streets and then pushed you into that notorious House of Fantasy or Dreams, or whatever it is they're claiming. You do know they're calling you a whore —"

"They have called me that for centuries."

"— and when that wealthy man who claimed to be an aristocrat took you out of the filth that he himself knew so well, then brought you into his own corrupted life —"

"You'd sully even him, Irena? Your own brother, my beloved Count?"

"— and when he even agreed to marry you, he was murdered by your pimp, all because of *you* —"

"Murdered by *Alix,* coerced by *you,* Irena!

"Are you hallucinating again, sister — taking drugs?"

"Hallucinating? No! No!"

"Calm yourself, Lady. She's trying to change the truths we've discovered back into the lies they uphold, convince you you're not who you know you are."

"So you're prepared, dear sister? Ready to tell the truth?"

"What is truth? What is a lie?"

"Gather all your strength, Lady. It's coming. I see the malice on her face. Remember she's an expert at distortion."

"You're ready — are you, sister? — to speak it all publicly, about the drugs, whoring, suicide, murder, and about —"

"It's coming, Lady, it's coming."

" *— and about the slaughter of your own children? — the twins you would have had.*"

349

"Madame!"

"Are you ready to tell it all, sister, that you drowned them in your own blood and then claimed you did it because your pimp denied they were his and was arranging to *sell* them as soon as they were born?"

"Madame!"

"You're sure, sister, that you can face those jackals outside, answer *all* the questions you know they'll ask? Can you answer? Can you? Can you, sister! *Can you!*"

"Madame!"

"Listen to *me*, dear Lady. Can you? Tell *me*. *Will* you be able to face all the questions they'll ask about *all* your lives, excluding none? Not one? Not a single one? Lady? Lady . . . ? Lady —"

"*Yes!* Because you've prepared me, and I've become strong, and sure."

"Then you *are* ready, Lady . . . Now let's see if *they* are."

"What are you up to, Bernice?"

"It's our turn, creatures. You've been lying in wait, resorting to spies, doing everything to stop the Lady from speaking her truths. But she resisted your every ploy —"

"You and I, Madame; *we* resisted."

"*We* resisted all your schemes. So you decided to risk everything by unmasking yourselves, rushing here, sure you could stop the interviews. Well, you've trapped yourselves *in* them."

"Trapped, Bernice? Oh, sir, did you hear her?"

"I did, yes, I did."

"Trapped, creatures, yes, because I'm going to make sure that *you're* asked questions you've long left unanswered, about sordid secrets in your family for generations — and there are so many concealed with lies. Are *you* ready to speak at last about real deceptions and depravity, about countless brutalities and excesses the Lady will expose, the extremes your father went to, to assume power — even to the point of torturing his own son and his son's mother —"

"— and his son's beloved friend, remember that, Madame! — ostracized and cursed, maligned unjustly. Unjustly! *Unjustly All* were betrayed, mother, son, his beloved friend!"

"Are you ready to talk about all *that,* creature — what your beloved father *really* did to his first son?"

"How can you know about that, Bernice? Those infamous rumors —"

"Everyone knows *about* it, creature, but not the truth."

"You'd go so far as to bring that up in your distorted scrutiny? Our dear oldest brother's death, that awful way —"

"— the most barbaric way, creature."

"— in the hands of that mob, because of all those radical ideas he and that strange friend of his were spewing, running around with those ruffians. Father tried to save him, but it was too late, the mob —"

"— aroused by *your* father, creature!"

"Naturally Father would want to keep quiet what happened to them. Naturally he'd want to avoid any misunderstanding —"

"Enough! As senior representative of the great family involved here, I want to assure you, Lady, that the record of that noble dynasty will remain unsullied. Whatever stern means are required, we will assure that all is reported as *we* say, as we have said all along."

"No, sir — no, creature. *We* shall foil the ending you were counting on, leaving it blank in your 'Account,' so certain you would succeed in silencing the Lady. *We* shall write our own ending!"

"We'll change destiny at last, Madame! Cassandra taught us how!"

"Ambush fate before it reaches its intended goal! Ah, yes, Cassandra taught us that indeed, Lady. We'll shift the course of blame by turning it all back on *them,* let *them* face the interviewers at last."

"Bernice —!"

"Terrified, creature? Didn't count on this when you burst in — so sure you could assault the Lady's truths during her most vulnerable moments when interviews are about to begin? — claiming to be her sister to confuse her by shifting identities — your father's, your family's, even your own — all to make her doubt who *she* is — and to add even more blame to her, make her responsible for *your* father's *real* transgressions. Well, it's all going to turn around — on *you.* You didn't realize how strong the Lady has become."

"Move away from that door, Bernice. You intend to go out and stir those horrible people — don't you? — so they'll be even more eager to hear her lies."

"— her *truths, your* lies, creature."

"She's gone. Bernice locked us in! Open! . . . the! . . . door! . . . I'll listen! . . . She's telling them to ask us —! Now she's saying that *we're* —! And *now,* she's accusing Father of —"

"Madame, you're back!"

"Yes! The interviewers have agreed to certain ground rules. It will be rough at times, Lady, very, very rough, but I've assured that you'll have allies. And think of this — *you're* prepared and the creatures aren't! They're caught in their own scheme, what they most dread, interrogation about all their lies. Your weapon is the truth, Lady."

"I am committed to the truth. And I am not to blame."

"Can you believe this, sir? My sister is about to claim that Father is to blame, that *she* is not to blame! Can you believe it?"

"I have believed it from the beginning."

"Don't open that door, Bernice! . . . Sir, stop her! If all this gets out, it will kill Father."

"Why, Lady, look how grim the collaborator is. And look at 'the senior representative of the family.' He's even put aside his notes . . . Close your eyes for a moment, Lady. There. Banish him and her into the shadows where they belong, where they have always existed — where they're trying to hide now from all the questions they've never wanted asked . . . There — they're banished. Open your eyes, Lady, and everything will be splendid! Yes. Now stand up proudly. That's how they must see you first. A little to the right. A little more. There, that's the best light. Oh, Lady, you look more beautiful than ever. Resplendent!"

"Madame, outside the window! Ermenegildo is on most sumptuous display — spinning about on the marble stand on your veranda. Now he's looking up at us, and —"

"— sending you his blessing."

"Your garden, Madame, it's never been more beautiful. Those strange, distorted flowers that grew overnight near your veranda — they're gone. Look! In their place, Madame, *new* flowers, like the ones that bloomed only in —"

"The doors are open, Lady . . . Come in, ladies and gentlemen . . . Lady, they're all here to listen to your unassailable truths."

"Madame —"

"Lady —"

"Give me your hand so I may start . . . Thank you."

"Ladies and gentlemen! Interviewers! Inquisitors — including representatives of the terrible Enquirer we've known all along to be pursuing us: In the beautiful Lady you see before you is the essence of all unjustly blamed women, women unjustly blamed for great catastrophes and labeled . . . whores. Our Lady has lived all those lives, which have been buried under centuries of lies. You'll hear the truth for the first time. You'll learn why and by whom the Lady has been pursued, from the beginning to now — you may even detect lurking shadows in this very room . . . Now, ladies and gentlemen, you shall learn the Lady is not to blame, and you will learn who is. Tell your story, Lady, so that we may know the truth at last."

"Madame —"

"Lady?"

"I'm af —"

"— a *freed* woman at last, freed from all blame and armed with the truth as only you know it. Commence, please, Lady, with your great love story."

"Shall I begin in the beginning?"

"Yes."

"There was a flower that bloomed only in Eden, a flower so glorious it did not need the decoration of leaves. When he saw me for the first time, as I lay within the verdure of Eden, my Adam plucked a blossom from the leafless stem. He knelt, and with its petals grazed my body.

"I sprang to life on a bed of orchids!"